## Praise for Mark Aber

'*Golden Serpent* is the most accomplished spy-thriller we've seen locally, a discerning read, full of action and a kind of knowing wit.'

The Australian

'Abernethy conjures echoes of Fleming, Ludlum, Clancy and the Jack Reacher novels of Lee Child.'

Weekend Australian

'Abernethy has once again hit the mark. Gripping.'

Herald Sun

'Fast-paced and action-packed, *Second Strike* is one of the better post-9/11 thrillers.'

The Age

'This is a rip-roaring tale of espionage, terrorism and counter-intelligence.'

Sunday Tasmanian

'Abernethy's first novel follows the Tom Clancy model, but with an irreverent, distinctly Australian twist . . . Abernethy writes of a world where Maori mercenaries meet hi-tech shipping and the most inventive ways of killing people . . . For those who like thrillers, this is satisfying fare.'

Sunday Age

'I have had the pleasure in recent years of discovering several Aussie authors – Matthew Reilly, James Phelan and David Rollins – capable of taking on the world's best in the "techno-thriller" stakes. Now add Mark Abernethy to the list.'

Sunshine Coast Daily

Mark Abernethy is a former newspaper reporter and magazine editor whose first novel, *Golden Serpent*, was published in 2007. Its sequel *Second Strike* was published in 2008 and *Double Back* in 2009. Mark lives in New South Wales. Read more at:

www.alanmcqueen.com.au

# COUNTER ATTACK

## MARK ABERNETHY

ARENA
ALLEN&UNWIN

First published in 2011

Arena Books, an imprint of
Allen & Unwin
83 Alexander Street
Crows Nest NSW 2065
Australia
Phone:    (61 2) 8425 0100
Fax:      (61 2) 9906 2218
Email:    info@allenandunwin.com
Web:      www.allenandunwin.com

Cataloguing-in-Publication details are available
from the National Library of Australia
www.trove.nla.gov.au

ISBN 978 1 74175 939 6

Typeset in Joanna MT 12.5/15.5 pt by Midland Typesetters, Australia
Printed and bound in Australia by Griffin Press

10 9 8 7 6 5 4 3 2 1

For Natasha,
Georgette and Luke

# CHAPTER 1

There were three of them in the fifteenth-floor suite of the Hotel Pan Pacific, waiting for the radio to confirm the quarry was on its way. Alan McQueen stood at the large windows of the suite, looking over the oily waters of Singapore's Marina Bay.

Draining his coffee, Mac thought about the plan. His job was to trap a Chinese spy and persuade him to work for the Australian Secret Intelligence Service. If Mac was successful, the doubled spy would be reporting to the Firm while pretending to take his orders from Beijing.

Looking into his empty cup, Mac pondered the eternal question of why hotel crockery was so small.

'Any real mugs back there, Matty?' he asked Matt Johnson, his comms man.

'That's the biggest I could find,' said Johnson, an operative in his early thirties who sat at a laptop computer beneath a street map of Singapore. Mac saw his younger self in Matt, an athletic field guy who was probably starting to wonder if being good at tails and infiltrations was a clever career move in Aussie intel.

'Might have to use one of those tumblers,' said Mac, seeing the rows of glasses in the kitchenette.

'Bring out the inner-city tosser in you, eh, Macca?' said Johnson, smirking behind the mic in front of his mouth.

A raw snort came from the sofa on the other side of the room, where Raymond Hu's face had set in the serious rictus of sleep.

'Ray!' said Mac, raising his voice at the native of Yangzhou. 'Wake up, sunshine!'

Hu's lips vibrated in a rattling snore.

Johnson threw a peanut. 'Ray.'

The first nut missed but a second landed on the sleeping man's left eyelid.

'Wah?' said Hu, sitting up.

'It's four o'clock, old boy,' said Mac. 'Ready for your close-up?'

Groaning, Hu pushed himself off the sofa and walked stiff-legged to the bathroom.

'Fricking Sing'pore,' said Hu, his thick Chinese accent echoing out of the bathroom as he relieved himself. 'What point in a free world if I can't have a smoke?'


Dressed in his four-thousand-dollar suit and Spanish shoes, Hu slipped out to attend the five o'clock meet-and-greet function of the Asia-Pacific Naval Contractors Convention. Hu could blend into a bar or a cocktail party and be gathering information before anyone had even noticed that he'd joined the conversation. The plan hinged on the grumpy financier and Mac trusted him to perform.

The radio speakers crackled to life on Johnson's desk as the door shut behind Hu. It was the voice of Cam Bailey, an Aussie SIS operator who had started his career at naval intelligence.

Mac listened as Bailey and his Changi Airport-based team got visual identification of the target – code-named Kava – and followed him from the T2 taxi rank. One of Mac's agents was in a cab behind Kava's while Bailey and a driver brought up the rear in another cab, ensuring there was no Chinese counter-surveillance.

Mac raised the field-glasses on the windowsill to his eyes and idly checked Raffles Boulevard. He was looking for tradie vans with no tradies, men on park benches reading upside-down newspapers and 'tourists' walking about aimlessly pretending to look at maps. Singapore was a modern republic but it was in South-East Asia, which meant it was crawling with Chinese spies.

'We're on,' said Johnson, fiddling with the laptop that showed him the location of the agents' cell phones.

'We're on when Kava is sitting in a puddle of his own piss, begging me to make him a double agent,' murmured Mac, eyeing two SingTel workers on the street who didn't seem to be working.

Kava was a Brisbane-based scientist, Dr Xiang Lao, who worked for the defence contractors Raytheon Australia. His main responsibility was making sure the electronic networks in the Royal Australian Navy's SEA 4000 Air Warfare Destroyer program would issue the commands they were supposed to, even when under attack. SEA 4000 AWD was Australia's new destroyer-based defence against anti-shipping missiles, the most likely of which were China's old but reliable Silkworms and their recently upgraded ballistic series, the Dong Fengs.

Sitting back on the sofa, Mac picked up the file: Lao had come to Australia as a sixteen-year-old prodigy to study avionics engineering at the University of New South Wales; he completed his doctorate at RMIT and then landed a plum job at Raytheon in Brisbane. Several weeks later, Raytheon won the contract to supply the Navy's SEA 4000 upgrades.

A photograph of Lao had surfaced ten months later, taken by a police narcotics squad watching the Colmslie Beach Reserve on the Brisbane River.

Queensland Police supplied the surveillance file to the Australian Federal Police, who claimed no interest in Dr Lao. But the biggest bounce from Lao's photo had come from the Defence Security Authority, the internal vetting and security office under the Defence Intelligence Organisation. The DSA had issued Lao a 'Top Secret' clearance to work at Raytheon, but had flagged him because he applied for clearance only a few weeks after his first ten years' residency in Australia had elapsed. To receive any of the higher security clearances in government or at defence contractors, applicants had to have lived in Australia for at least a decade, and DSA had him flagged as a 'watch'. Now he was hanging around in Brisbane parks being photographed by the police.

By the time Mac had been pulled into a taskforce of ASIO, AFP, ASIS and DIO, a team of operatives had been watching Lao walk every Monday lunchtime to a park bench at Colmslie Reserve, eat his lunch, and then carefully put his garbage in the bin. It was Lao's drop box and it was traced back to a person who cleared it, and then back to Lao's controller, a mortgage broker in Logan City named Donny Koh.

Mac was supposed to be sitting in on the taskforce, as passive eyes and ears for Aussie SIS. Almost forty, he was semi-retired from the Firm and was sent up to Brisbane because he lived on the Gold Coast and sending him was easier than taking a staffer from a desk.

As the drops were intercepted, it became apparent Dr Lao was an enthusiastic seller of Australian naval secrets. There was pressure from Canberra to pounce and put on a show trial – a sort of return to glory for Aussie intelligence after the apparently bungled Dr Haneef case.

Mac had made the mistake of suggesting another way forwards: let the traitor run, see what advantage Australia might gain from it. Dr Lao seemed to be a good fit as a double agent – he was selling naval secrets direct to Chinese military intelligence, he had a young family and Aussie intel had identified his controller.

Someone high up in the bureausphere – perhaps even in the Department of Prime Minister and Cabinet – had read the minutes of that taskforce meeting and Mac had felt the tap on his shoulder.

So Mac was back: back in South-East Asia, back in SIS and back in a world of gut-churning worry.

'They're five minutes away,' said Johnson, breaking into Mac's thoughts. 'You want Yellow team alerted?'

Nodding, Mac reached for the room's phone and dialled reception. He'd sent Hu in clean in case the Chinese had any of their fancy electronic eavesdropping devices at the convention.

'Could you page Mr Chan – Johnny Chan – please?' he said into the phone. 'I think he's in the bar.'

Walking to the big windows with the phone in one hand and the handset in the other, Mac looked down on what had been 'turn six' at the F1 Grand Prix two weeks earlier. The traffic seemed normal on Raffles Boulevard and it was late enough that the cops were starting to clear parked traffic – surveillance cars would either be moved on or would stand out to a trained observer. Nothing looked amiss, which didn't mean it wasn't.

'Ray,' said Mac as his agent came on the line. 'Kava's two minutes away – blue cab, white roof.'

'Okay,' said Hu.

'The place clean?' said Mac, adrenaline surging.

'It a naval contractor convention, McQueen,' said Hu. 'It all spook.'

'You've got backup, Ray,' said Mac. 'Let's get Kava tucked away asap, okay? No dancing with this bloke.'

'Okay. See you when I see you.'

Putting the phone down, Mac pondered the 'ifs' of the operation: if Dr Lao had worked out that Aussie intelligence were running the drops at the rubbish bin in Brisbane; if Ray Hu had not been accepted in his masquerade as Lao's controller; if the mortgage broker had made an unscheduled and unexpected phone call or email to Dr Lao, and discovered he was in Singapore, not Brisbane.

Mac's ruse relied on inexperienced Lao being manipulated into bringing naval secrets to his fake controller in Singapore. All of which had to happen between Monday drops and without the Chinese getting wind of it. The idea was to bring Lao out of his comfort zone in Brisbane, to elevate his importance and to have him physically more involved in espionage; to get him alone in a room and thinking he was speaking to his man from Beijing. Then record the whole thing and close the trap: *We got you on tape selling Australian Navy secrets to the Chinese, Dr Lao. The Chinese don't want you going through an Australian court system, spilling everything to the newspapers, and you don't want to worry about your family, so why not just keep business as usual with Beijing but have a little chat with us a couple of times a week? How would that be for you?*

It was blackmail but it usually worked. If Mac's team got it wrong, and they were being followed themselves, it would be a painful lesson in the interrogation techniques of the MSS – China's CIA.

'Will this work?' said Johnson.

'Like a dream, squire,' said Mac, raising the field-glasses and checking out the telecom van parked on Raffles. 'Like a fucking dream.'

# CHAPTER 2

Three short knocks sounded on the suite's door and Isla Dunford moved into the room. She'd just left her post at the hotel's entry as Bailey had followed Kava into the lobby and assumed the surveillance.

'Looking good,' she said, pulling up a chair beside Johnson and peering at the laptop screen. 'Kava's in the hubcap.'

Among Aussie intel types, a meeting at the hubcap meant the Pan Pac's lobby lounge, which had a huge round mezzanine ceiling floating above it.

'We okay?' said Mac. 'You followed?'

'We're sweet,' said Dunford, grimacing slightly as she pulled her Colt handgun from the holster at the small of her back and placed it on Johnson's desk.

Isla Dunford was just starting her career with SIS and the fact she was actively in the field owed a lot to Mac championing her over the policy that women didn't work on gigs involving firearms. Mac had noticed her at a field-craft module he'd given in Canberra two years earlier. Dunford was a smart, calm, good-looking woman and he'd fought for her not only because she spoke Cantonese, but because female officers broke up the male pattern and made it harder for counter-surveillance.

The chaps in Canberra had a sense of humour, and the first operation Mac had scored after his return from retirement featured Isla Dunford on the surveillance team. Now, seeing the bright-eyed youngster place her gun on the desk, the responsibility of his position came into focus. Mac could no longer just do the gig and go victory-drinking with the troops. When you ran the operation, the most important part was bringing everyone home with their fingernails intact.

All of Mac's team in the lobby of the hotel were now stripped of radio gear. It wasn't an ideal situation and it made Mac nervous to be off the air, but the Chinese comms-intercepts were so good that even the Americans and Israelis couldn't rely on encryptions and scrambles when they knew the MSS was about. The next-door suite they'd wired for sound had no radio transmissions – it was wired directly into their own suite.

'How's the set-up in 1502?' said Mac.

'Good,' said Johnson.

'Check it again,' said Mac, grabbing the field-glasses and having another look at the SingTel van on Raffles. It hadn't been moved by the cops and the tradesmen were standing at a junction box, the door flapping open.

The suite's door shut behind Dunford as Mac focused on one of the SingTel guys: his red overalls looked clean.

A voice crackled out of the speakers on the desk – Dunford speaking in Cantonese from 1502, next door.

'What's she saying?' said Mac.

'Here I am in the lounge, here I am in the bedroom, that loo needs a clean, and . . .'

'Well?'

'She's saying, "When this is over, Macca shouts the beers."'

'Cheeky bugger,' said Mac, lifting the field-glasses back to his eyes.


Once Lao was in room 1502 with Ray Hu, the meeting proceeded as expected, every word being downloaded onto the laptop's hard drive. Johnson adjusted the speaker volume and translated as Ray Hu coaxed the Raytheon documents from Dr Lao's attaché case and then kept the traitor talking about progress on the SEA 4000 upgrades: the key scientists, the names of the managers, the main difficulties and the testing that had taken place.

As the talk got more technical, Mac asked Dunford to grab the glasses and keep an eye on the SingTel van, tell him if there was any change.

Lao opened up about the AESA-defeat project at Raytheon which was going to form a major plank of SEA 4000. Lao explained that he was trying to get assigned to AESA-defeat but security was being run by the US Defense Intelligence Agency and the project was above his clearance.

Mac pricked up his ears at the mention of AESA, a high-tech radar that could take millions of snapshots around the plane it was mounted on, in such short bursts that it was almost impossible for detectors on the ground to pick up the radar emissions – one of the main ways that defence systems detected enemy aircraft.

An AESA-type system was probably the only hope the Chinese had to make their ballistic anti-ship missile – the DF 21 – operate properly. The DF 21 was being developed to fly between one and a half and two and a half thousand kilometres from China's coast as a deterrent against US Navy carrier strike groups. A ballistic missile was a rocket that flew out of the atmosphere and on its downward trajectory took its warhead at great speeds onto the target below. To be accurate against a moving target such as a ship, it needed an AESA system onboard to steer it as it re-entered the atmosphere at speeds approaching mach 10. An onboard AESA system was about the only way that ballistic missiles could be controlled by terminal guidance – that is, the missile could be made to fly into its target rather than simply being aimed accurately at take-off or tweaked in its mid-course trajectory.

Raytheon was the AESA pioneer for the American military and it stood to reason that the same company would be working on a weapon that defeated AESA. So Mac wasn't surprised that the Pentagon's spooks were overseeing who did and did not work on the project.

Ray Hu's interest had been aroused too. 'You got your name down to work for Raytheon in the United States on AESA-defeat?'

Mac listened as Dr Lao stumbled. 'What's he saying?'

'He's saying, "No, you got it wrong – I don't have to go to the US. I've been waiting to tell someone this",' said Matt, concentrating. 'He's giggling, proud of himself. Says he's got good stuff.'

'Yeah?' said Mac.

'Yeah, wait,' said Matt, holding his hand up as the Cantonese bubbled out of the speakers. 'He's saying that he found out two days ago that an AESA-defeat prototype system is being brought to Queensland for beta testing – Raytheon and US Department of Defense are going to test it in the Aussie desert. Totally top secret: USEO.'

'Shit!' said Mac. When a project was stamped 'US Eyes Only', the problem became political.

'It gets better,' said Johnson.

'Tell me,' said Mac, his dream of doubling Dr Lao all but gone. There was no way they could put a Chinese spy with that sort of information back into circulation in the hope that he wouldn't blab to his Beijing masters. It wasn't worth the risk – not to Australian military security and certainly not to the US–Australian alliance.

'Ray's asked him how come the Australian outback. Why not Alaska, New Mexico?'

'And?' said Mac as the sound of laughter roared out of the speakers.

'He says, "Nah – America full of Chinese spies."'

'Funny guy,' said Mac, grabbing his handgun from under the sofa cushion.

Matt held up his hand. 'He's saying, "Aussie intel is only interested in beer and girls – we can be using the beta telemetry even before the Pentagon sees it."'

'Yeah, yeah,' said Mac, checking his Heckler & Koch P9s for load and safety. 'I'll let ASIO know they have a fan club. Matt, get on the phone, tell Doug at the embassy to fast-track an extradition order for Xiang Lao. Make sure he gets the address and date of birth correct, okay?'

Johnson reached for the phone.

'Isla, we need an AFP agent here now.'

'We going to arrest him?' said Dunford.

'We need to formally arrest Lao for terrorism financing and conspiracy, and then we'll trigger the transnational crime MOU with Singers,' said Mac, trying to stay one step ahead of the game. 'Don't use Doug for that one – go straight to Tommy in legal. The Memorandum of Understanding needs to be cited and acknowledged by Singapore Police within twelve hours of the arrest, so shake a leg.'

'Sure, boss,' said Isla, standing and holstering her handgun.

'This is now about containment,' said Mac, moving towards the door as he shoved the Heckler into his waistband. 'I don't want that little weasel telling his secrets to some Chinese consular lawyer. If we do our job, the tests go ahead in the desert without any Chinese nosey-pokes.'

Looking back as he opened the suite's door, Mac saw Dunford looking down through the window. 'Everything okay?'

'Yeah, the SingTel van's gone. One less thing, huh?'

Mac stepped into the corridor of the fifteenth floor, approached 1502 and slowed, readying to go through that door and shut down Kava.

As he paused, he sensed movement from his right and then someone grabbed him by the hair. Knocked off balance, Mac tried to turn but his head was smashed hard against the hotel wall. Bouncing off the wallpaper, stunned, he was kicked hard in the solar plexus – so hard he doubled over. The hand grabbed his hair again and pushed him upright into the hessian-covered wall and a suppressed handgun was jammed into the back of his mouth.

Unblinking eyes stared out of a black ski-mask as a second man disarmed him and took the door card from his hand. The silencer drove further into the back of Mac's throat, choking him and pinning him to the wall, making his eyes water. Lifting his knee reflexively, Mac thought about lashing out but his captor cocked the action on the 9mm handgun and pushed harder.

Mac watched in mute horror as the second shooter pushed the door card into 1502 and entered with the elongated handgun held down his thigh. Half a second later there were four popping sounds that Mac recognised as suppressed small-arms fire. Then the shooter was back in the corridor, walking up to Mac as he shoved a handful of casings into his left pocket.

Thinking he was about to be executed, Mac started his prayers as he panted for breath. But the second shooter didn't level his gun – he raised it quickly and brought it down hard above Mac's left ear.

Mac's last thought before he blacked out was: *Red overalls – red SingTel overalls.*

# CHAPTER 3

The Qantas 747's engines changed tone as the plane banked for the final approach to Brisbane. It was a little after 6.40 am and to Mac's left the Pacific Ocean wore a pink and purple halo, waiting for the sun to peek over the edge and turn up the heat.

He'd spent the last twelve hours reliving the scene in the hallway of the Pan Pac and berating himself. He'd seen the SingTel van on Raffles Boulevard, he'd noticed something wrong about one of the technicians, and he hadn't acted. The old Mac would have gone into counter-measures, regardless of how unnecessary it seemed to those around him. But he'd let it slide and the price to pay was Ray Hu slumped in a hotel chair with bullet holes in the forehead and heart. Ray, who'd taught him the intricacies of banking and funds transfers in Asia; Ray, who knew exactly which corporate tax scams were being pulled by which accountants and bankers; flat-footed, desk-jockey Ray, who'd once held a gun to a bunch of thugs who'd cornered Mac in an apartment in Pandang – the chubby banker had stood tough even when he was shitting himself.

Catching his own eye in the reflection of the window, Mac turned away. His return to the Firm had been as a manager in Operations, a step up from his previous career as a field agent embedded in companies that operated across South-East Asia. As a vice-president of sales for Southern Scholastic Books, or as an executive with Gondwanda Consulting, Mac had been under constant stress, knowing that at any moment the Indonesians or Chinese might discover his real identity and whack him. But in that role he hadn't been responsible for others. Now he was running operations and managing teams, and his first assignment had ended in a double murder.

The ice he held in a plastic bag against his left eye socket was melting and the second round of Nurofens he'd gulped down an hour earlier wasn't doing much for the vein that throbbed against his cheekbone or the egg that was still growing above his left ear. Mac had never had a headache quite as bad as waking up in a hot tent with a rum hangover, but this was running a close second.

'Can I take that, Mr Davis?' asked the hostie, and Mac handed over the ice bag, which he'd wrapped in a business-class face cloth. He wasn't just embarrassed about the shiner; people with concussion weren't supposed to fly long distances, and he hadn't wanted a bright-eyed hostie trying to throw the medical rule book at him. He'd have plenty of that waiting for him at home when Jen lectured him about how a father of two young daughters shouldn't be playing dice with aneurisms.

Emerging from the customs hall with his black wheelie bag, he spotted a small 'Davis' sign above the crowd and headed for the casually dressed man who held it aloft.

'Mr Davis!' said the man. 'Welcome back, sir – the name's Kendall, the car's this way.'

Mac let himself into the back seat of the white Holden Statesman standing at the apron.

Waiting in the back seat was Greg Tobin, the Firm's immaculately groomed director of operations for Asia-Pacific. 'Macca! Been in the wars, old man?'

'Something like that, Greg,' said Mac, shaking Tobin's strong, soft hand. 'How are things?'

Greg Tobin was only a year or two older than Mac but he'd succeeded the former director of operations, Tony Davidson, in the year he turned forty – an unprecedented elevation to run what was Australia's most important espionage territory. Mac remembered Tobin from the University of Queensland, where he was studying

13

law and dabbling in conservative politics. Even then there'd been something of the born-to-rule about the tall, athletic form of Greg Tobin. He was the sort of person who compelled smarter people to listen to him, then do as he said, and he did it with a combination of charm and authority. Even on the greasy pole of Canberra, Tobin had a reputation for never losing his temper.

Making their way across Gateway Bridge as the sun rose, Mac made small talk while his mind scrambled to understand why such a senior person had waited outside Brisbane International for him. It had to be bad – Operation Kava was a disaster and Mac had been running it.

'So, Greg,' he said, after they'd discussed why the Brisbane Broncos had missed out on a berth in the rugby league grand final, 'you giving me a lift to Broadie?'

'Afraid not, old stick,' said Tobin, leaning in to indicate most-favoured status. 'That Colmslie taskforce is reconvening.'

'Great,' said Mac, grabbing the handle above his door, wishing he'd slapped on some Old Spice. Taskforce Colmslie was the interagency group that had authorised Operation Kava and Mac dreaded having to face them – it would start as a debrief but inevitably would disintegrate into an exercise in blame-shifting between agencies.

'When?' said Mac.

'Tapes start rolling at eleven, right, Kendall?'

Kendall kept his eyes on the Gateway traffic. 'Correct.'

The Qantas flight from Singapore had taken off the previous night and Mac hadn't slept. He'd had no respite since regaining consciousness in the operations suite at the Pan Pac and ordering the escape and evade phase of the operation, where the players scattered. Mac's team all had their own rat-runs, right down to cars rented in certain identities and hotels ready to book into. Mac's run had been the 9.25 flight out of Changi as Richard Davis, sales executive at Southern Scholastic Books; he could have taken earlier flights via Cairns or Darwin, but the basic rule in the spy game was that when travelling under an assumed identity, you took the direct flight when you could. You removed as many variables as possible – you rigged the game.

Tobin fixed him with a look of concern. 'You must be shattered, Macca.'

'Rolled up wet, put away dry,' said Mac, as the car veered left off the freeway, swung right and headed west into Fortitude Valley. They drove in silence for eight minutes, before Mac recognised the area – west Valley, up against the Victoria Golf Course.

'We'll make it brief, I promise,' said Tobin with a caring smile.

'We?' said Mac, wondering if Tobin had invited himself into the taskforce.

'Just an informal chinwag, eh, Macca? Before we throw you back to the wolves?'

Kendall steered the car into the driveway of a three-and-a-half-star hotel.

'You don't mind if Kendall has the Davis collateral?'

'No, Greg,' said Mac, resenting it but staying professional. Handing over his Richard Davis phone, wallet and passport, Mac pulled out his chinos pockets to show they were empty then held open his sports jacket for inspection.

'Perhaps let Kendall have the jacket?'

'Ray was a friend of mine, Greg,' said Mac, struggling out of the dark blue blazer. 'You think I'm happy about this?'

'Of course not, old man,' said Tobin, passing the collateral forwards to Kendall. 'That's why I need some horse's-mouth before you get cornered by ASIO and Defence.'

'Okay, Greg,' said Mac, fuming.

'That's yours,' said Tobin, passing over a cardboard-wrapped room card. 'There's a change of clothes in your room – but let's not use the phone just yet, right, Macca?'

'Sure,' said Mac, opening the door and getting out.

'Meeting at eight-fifteen in room 403?' said Tobin. 'You might like a quick shower. There's a good sport.'


Recounting the order of events at the Pan Pac, Mac noticed Tobin's restlessness a few minutes into the debrief.

'You didn't enter 1502?' said Tobin, reaching for the teapot and pouring.

'No,' said Mac. 'When Lao started gasbagging about Raytheon's AESA-defeat testing coming to Queensland, I decided to shut him down.'

'Not –' started Tobin.

'No, no,' said Mac, annoyed that his colleagues had characterised him as violent. 'I was going to relieve Ray and let Lao know that the meet had been a set-up.'

'Tell him he'd been caught out,' said Tobin, 'and have the AFP arrest him?'

'Exactly,' said Mac. 'It was too risky to double him. This was the first time he'd blabbed about the AESA-defeat testing being carried out in Queensland and I decided to wrap him up with an extradition –'

'Rather than let him talk to the Chinese?'

'Yes,' said Mac. 'If we could get him on the terrorism charges, we could lock him away for a while. Remember, this Lao guy is an Aussie citizen and the Chinese embassy would have no excuse to go visit him.'

'So you didn't see Lao and Hu executed?' said Tobin.

'No. I saw the shooter open the door of 1502 and fire four suppressed rounds into the suite. I'm pretty sure it was a nine-mil – the one in my mouth was a SIG.'

'The shooters?' said Tobin, sipping the tea.

'Brown eyes, SingTel overalls, ski masks – about my height and build. Perhaps shorter.'

'No voice?'

'None,' said Mac, putting himself back in that corridor, feeling the suppressor jammed against the back of his throat. 'They were totally pro.'

'Hence, this,' said Tobin, tapping a piece of notepad paper covered in ballpoint scrawls. 'Federal Police liaison with Singapore Police got the initial crime scene report from the Pan Pac. It's a double murder; victims are two men, Sino-Asian appearance. One they're calling Chan and the other Lao. There were four shots – nine-mil soft-noses. No casings.'

'Figures,' said Mac. 'The shooter came out with the casings and put them in his pocket.'

'The deceased had single shots to the forehead and heart.'

'It all fits,' said Mac. You had to be highly trained to walk into a room, make four shots like that and still have the ticker to pick up your casings.

Tobin enmeshed his fingers. 'The local detectives won't hush this up.'

'I think the Firm's clean, if that's what you're asking,' said Mac.

Tobin's real job was to be able to tell the deputy DG that there were no comebacks to the Firm, so the deputy DG could assure the DG that Aussie SIS couldn't be implicated, meaning any annoying interview requests from China or Singapore could be dismissed at the political level as well as the departmental. There was only one rule in spying: don't get caught. And Mac was confident the E and E had worked.

'Okay,' said Tobin to Kendall, and his typing stopped – redundant given that when opening an ASIS debrief template, the MS Word document recorded audio.

'How should I handle the taskforce?' said Mac, aware that interagency manoeuvring was a key aspect of the debrief.

'Tell them everything. I'll talk with the deputy, recommend we hand this back to Defence. We'll never hear the end of it if the Firm's to blame for bungling those tests.'

Mac nodded. The Australian Defence Force relied heavily on being the respected junior partner in a very one-sided military alliance with the Americans. The entire culture of the ADF's intelligence apparatus was to never give the Yanks an excuse to roll their eyes and mutter about 'leaky Australians'.

Kendall shut down the laptop as Tobin slipped his hand onto Mac's forearm and walked him to the door.

'One thing,' said Tobin, lowering his voice as they eased into the hallway. 'I suppose you've had time to wonder . . . why those two . . .'

'And not me?' said Mac.

'Well, yes.'

'Maybe the shooters didn't know who I was,' said Mac.

'Or maybe,' said Tobin, 'they did.'

# CHAPTER 4

The draft final report of Taskforce Colmslie was brief and vague – so brief that Mac had read most of it before the taskforce chair, Alexander Beech, had finished handing out the copies and taken his seat at the head of the table.

'Okay, we're all busy,' said Beech, a Defence Intelligence Organisation operative who was universally known as Sandy. 'Let's get this signed off and go to lunch.'

The draft mentioned Dr Lao and Ray Hu. It covered Lao's knowledge of Raytheon's AESA-defeat testing in Queensland and concluded that Lao's Australian controllers had not been alerted to the top-secret project.

'I suggest relevant DGs, commissioners and chiefs will be told as follows,' said Beech, resting his thick forearms on the table as he read his draft. 'We discovered a Chinese spy working on the SEA 4000 AWD program at Raytheon Australia; we intercepted his drops and identified his controller – a mortgage broker working in Logan City; we used a Singapore asset – Ray Hu – to masquerade as Lao's controller and lure him to Singapore; Lao travelled with a Raytheon document that we fabricated; we planned to use this journey as a sting in which Lao would be caught red-handed and persuaded to work for Australia while not alerting the Chinese. What is known as a double agent.'

'Sounds fair,' said Grant Shannon, the AFP's representative on the taskforce.

'During the operation in Singapore,' said Beech, clearing his throat, 'Hu and Lao were murdered by two males. The operation withdrew from Singapore without being identified.'

Looking up from the draft, Sandy Beech eyeballed Mac. 'This last sentence is crucial − can we claim, one hundred and ten per cent, that Lao waited until he was in that hotel room before mentioning the AESA-defeat testing?'

The taskforce members looked at Mac.

'We were intercepting Lao's drops, right, Mike?' said Mac, looking at ASIO's representative, Mike Donnell.

'Sure, Mac,' shrugged Donnell.

'We had an agent on the plane, watching Lao, from Brissie to Singapore,' said Mac, fatigue making his words echo in his head. 'And there was no contact. He was double-tailed to the Pan Pac where he was met in the lobby by Hu. He told Hu that he'd been saving his scoop on the testing for when they met. I think we're clean.'

Beech paused. 'You think?'

'We're okay,' said Mac.

'We don't want to be halfway through this testing and have the Yanks complaining that their telemetry is being sucked up,' said Beech. 'We can't afford a Marshalls.'

The Americans had tested a new naval rocket series in the Marshall Islands two years earlier, in a joint exercise with Japan's navy. One of the Japanese engineers was in the pay of the PLA, China's army, and vast amounts of performance telemetry had been siphoned from the Pentagon's hard drives before anyone could stop it. The Chinese liked to steal defence-testing telemetry because once they had the data they could accelerate their own programs without having to build and destroy prototypes, and they could plan their own counter-measures to what the Yanks were testing.

'I'm confident that Lao kept the AESA testing to himself until he spoke with Ray in Singers,' said Mac.

Dropping the draft on the table, Beech slapped his hand on it to signal the meeting over. 'Okay, then.'

'Actually, we're far from okay,' said Shannon, his thick ginger moustache failing to hide his sneer.

'What's up, Grant?' said Beech.

'With all due respect to the intelligence community,' said Shannon, jerking his thumb over his shoulder, 'we've got this prick Donny Koh down in Logan. Bloke's begging for a shake-up.'

'What did you have in mind?' said Beech, doing a perfect job of showing no enthusiasm.

'Get Koh in an interview room,' said Shannon, crossing his arms like he was strangling his security lanyard. 'Take his office apart, his house, the computers – you know, the whole bit.'

Silence fell and Mac could feel the old culture clash between cops and spies reappearing.

'I think that's outside our terms, Grant,' said Beech.

'Our terms?' said Shannon, sitting up. 'Fuck the terms. I'm talking about the law, mate. I'm talking about a list of charges longer than this table.'

'I think Mr Koh should be left out of this,' said Beech. 'He's probably worth more to us if he keeps operating.'

'Oh, that's great, Sandy,' said Shannon. 'We played that game already with Lao, remember? And now he's brown bread, along with Hu.'

'It's the way these things work,' said Mac, his heart not in it. 'If the benefits are worth the risks, we let it play out. Often we get it right.'

'Hey, Macca, I went along with the spooky fun and games,' said Shannon, pointing at Mac. 'I heard your plan and I went with it, right? But it went pear-shaped, mate. Now if you want a real benefit, think about a Chinese spy in a courtroom, being hammered with evidence and cross-examination for a week. We could still get something out of this debacle.'

'Perhaps,' said Beech. 'But the time's not now. If we get nothing, Koh is still there to be taken down later.'

'What if he does the Harold?' said Shannon. 'The bloke's a Chinese spy – it's not like he doesn't know how to disappear.'

'Mike?' said Beech, looking at the ASIO representative, who'd been ducking the argument.

'No one touches Koh,' said the officer, with middle-aged eyes that had seen it all. 'No one even looks at him funny.'

Beech turned to Shannon. 'You want a vote?'

'Fuck's sake,' said Shannon, throwing his pen on the table. 'You spooks are your own worst enemies, know that?'

They were just south of Beenleigh, on the freeway to the Gold Coast, when Sandy Beech broke out of the small talk.

'Shit, Macca – you see Mike's face when Shannon was talking about raiding Donny Koh?'

Mac laughed. 'Looked like he'd swallowed a spider.'

Come morning, the *Courier-Mail* would run the story of the two Australian-Chinese men murdered in a Singapore hotel, and ASIO was going to be listening to Donny Koh's phone calls, reading his email, bugging his offices and following him wherever he went. They'd even have a team on Donny's children, since the Chinese had been known to use their kids' school bags as drops. Beech would have military intelligence spooks inside Raytheon looking for anyone racing for the exits as the newspapers were unfolded. The idea of a bunch of cops stomping into Donny Koh's offices and tearing down the ceilings was anathema to the intelligence community; putting Koh in a courtroom and reading out the charges was simply a waste of good talent.

'By the way,' said Beech, 'sorry about Ray. You guys were friends, right?'

'Yep,' said Mac, looking out of the Ford Falcon's passenger window as the new suburbs flashed by. 'You could say that.'

Ray Hu was a Chinese-born orphan who had developed a passionate hatred for Communists. While completing his doctorate in economics at the Australian National University, Hu had approached ASIO to defect. Australia's domestic spy agency had declined the offer and fast-tracked his citizenship, but when Hu was looking to apply for a job at a Singapore fund manager a few years later, specialising in equity investments in defence-related technologies, Australia's SIS paid him a visit. Ray Hu was one of the smartest people Mac knew, and his wife Liesl got along particularly well with Jenny.

'Any theories?' said Beech. 'About the murders?'

'I have a lot of questions, but the theories aren't exactly piling up.'

'I start with the shooters and I come up with MSS or PLA,' said Beech.

'I start with the shooters, too,' said Mac. 'And I come up with questions: why are they outside the Pan Pac? Are they waiting for Lao to show up?'

'The Chinese knew Lao had been compromised by the Firm?'

'But they whack him rather than allow the meeting to go ahead?' said Mac, looking at Beech. 'Doesn't make sense, Sandy.'

'No, mate – they could have just stopped using Lao and Koh. Or they could have acted dumb and used the situation to misinform Aussie intelligence.'

Mac smiled. 'It's what we'd do.'

'It's what we'd do, sure, but just so we're clear: I won't be dropping this,' said Sandy, his tone changing. 'I don't want the word getting around that the Chinks can just whack one of our guys and walk away from that.'

Mac turned sideways and looked at the DIO man. Sandy Beech had served in the SAS before going back to the intelligence staff. During the peacekeeping phase of East Timor a political war between the intel staffers in the field and the DIO pointy-heads in Canberra had raged out of control. It had culminated in a clever-clogs in Canberra denying field access to the intelligence database when a team of intel staffers in East Timor needed it. The first inquiry into the scandal had been a cover-up, which led to a second inquiry. Sandy Beech had been elevated to DIO after that snafu, as a 'healing' exercise, but now he was signalling to Mac that he was still an SAS-trained field guy.

'Okay, Sandy,' said Mac, 'let's keep the file open – but, you know, Ray was my friend, okay?'

'It's okay, Macca,' said Beech, chuckling. 'You have the honours.'

Mac got out of Beech's car on Cavill Avenue in Surfers Paradise and walked a route south to the house, using a couple of zigzags and double-arounds to shake any nosey bastards. He'd always been careful, but the events of two years earlier, when a Pakistani hit man and a rogue MI6 agent had kidnapped Jenny and one of his daughters, had made him anxious about inadvertently leading the wrong people to his family home.

As he walked the five blocks to the Broadbeach house, Mac got himself into character. He didn't like lying to his wife, but she'd worked out most of the truth about Mac's life and he didn't want her knowing any more.

It was almost seven pm as he turned into the small front yard and pulled the mail from the letterbox, casing the street for eyes as he did so. He was exhausted, feeling guilty as hell about Ray, and he wondered if there was any way he could postpone the assessment he was due for the following morning. When employees of the Department of Foreign Affairs and Trade turned forty, they were required to undergo a detailed assessment.

Mac had never thought he would turn forty – hadn't prepared for it or talked to anyone about it. He'd upgraded his DFAT life insurance policy and he'd drafted his will after Jen had nagged him to do so. But he'd basically kept the Big Four-O to himself. There were a few regrets, he admitted to himself, as he dragged his wheelie suitcase up to the front porch, but his marriage and his two daughters – Sarah, with Jenny, and Rachel, with his old girlfriend, Diane – were his crowning achievements. With those three people at the centre of his life, Mac found it easy to shrug off the career angst that so many Commonwealth employees of his age were consumed by.

The key turned in the heavy German lock, and he pushed into the cool of the house. A horn sounded and something flew at his face. Ducking and crouching into a counter-attack, Mac heard a crowd roar, 'Surprise!' and then a tall brunette had him pinned to the wall.

'Happy birthday, hon,' said Jenny, and planted a wet kiss on Mac's mouth.

# CHAPTER 5

Feeling better after the second beer went down, and having managed to blow out forty candles in one breath, Mac put the girls to bed.

'I hope your skin feels better, Dad,' said Sarah in a serious tone as he tucked her in and gave her a goodnight kiss.

'I think it's his bones, Sassa,' said Rachel, fourteen months older than her three-year-old sister, and clearly confident that she had a lifetime more wisdom about facial injuries.

'Don't you girls worry about old Dad,' said Mac, winking as he switched off the light. 'I'm doing fine.'

Pausing outside as the girls yelled goodnight, he leaned his forehead on the bedroom door. Making himself breathe, Mac felt the spasms in his facial muscles that always came with fear and worry. The journey from the murder at the Pan Pac to his daughters in their sun frocks giving him their presents had been too short. He'd needed another day, perhaps a big bout of drinking or some lone surfing. When Jen's work got too close to her family, she lashed out, got angry, got in someone's face. But Mac internalised it, tried to swallow it down, where it festered and came back as facial twitches and nocturnal teeth-grinding.

'Okay, love?'

Looking to his right, Mac faced his mother, Pat McQueen. The party raged down the hall, his friend Anton Garvey shouting for Mac to rejoin the drinkers.

'I'm fine, Mum,' he said, cracking a smile.

'This doesn't look fine,' she said, grabbing him by the chin and poking at his injury. 'Been fighting?'

'Walked into a door,' said Mac, twisting out of her grip.

'That book company has a lot of doors,' said Pat.

'Yeah, well,' said Mac, heading off in search of a beer.


Mac shared a cab with Garvs to Brisbane airport to catch the 5.10 am Qantas flight to Canberra.

'Shit, mate,' said Garvs, his bull-like body awkward as he read the *Australian Financial Review* in the back of the cab. 'How're we gonna do on the assessment with three hours' sleep?'

'You too?' said Mac, as they slid over Southport Bridge in darkness.

'I'm forty just before Christmas, mate – they're still checking for cocaine and ecstasy.'

'As long as they don't breathalyse me,' said Mac, regretting that the party had finished with rum shots and dirty limericks.

Handing the *Fin* to Mac, Garvs shook out the *Courier-Mail* and scanned the front page. Good intelligence operators were supposed to read at least one newspaper a day, cover to cover.

'Shit,' said Garvs, as Mac started reading about the Chinese using intermediaries to buy into Australian iron-ore miners.

'What?' asked Mac.

'Oh, interest rates,' said Garvs, distracted.

'When they're low, you're supposed to borrow; when they're high, you're a fool for having borrowed so much,' said Mac. 'Prime Minister wrote a whole essay about it.'

'Yeah, mate,' said Garvs, slapping his leg with the paper and staring out the window as they got out of the suburbs and onto the freeway north.

Mac and Garvey had entered the Firm in the same intake and quickly become friends. They'd both gone to big St Joseph's boarding schools – Mac at Brisbane's Nudgee, and Garvs at Joey's in Sydney.

They'd played First XV and shared a sense of humour and a love of beer. But on entering ASIS Mac had been singled out to undergo training with the Royal Marines in the United Kingdom while Garvs had moved into Karl Berquist's office clique – Berquist was the director of assessments who'd recently taken John Gleeson's old position as deputy director-general.

As their careers advanced, Mac had moved further from the Firm's centres of power in Canberra and Jakarta, and found himself spending time alone in the field. Some of those deep-cover stints in South-East Asia had made Mac thin-skinned and cranky, prone to accusing his higher-ups of motives that they didn't always hold. At the same time, Garvs had moved seamlessly up the ASIS tree, always remaining loyal and sensible around the right people. Garvs was now the deputy to Jakarta station chief Martin Atkins, while Mac found himself with a roving commission – technically a 'manager', but in reality an officer assigned the tough gigs.

The friendship had shifted and Mac had felt the twinge of disloyalty on a couple of occasions. They could still drink a few beers and watch rugby league, but professionally they were at the point where Garvs would read about Ray Hu's murder and not say a word about it to Mac. Even when they were sitting together in a cab.


The box of Tic Tacs took the edge off his breath, but Mac was pretty sure the doctor was reading road maps when he shone the flashlight in his eyes. In a medical consulting room at HMAS Harman – the naval comms and intel base on the outskirts of Canberra – they worked through the list, from flexibility and chest sounds to the eye chart and a probing gloved finger.

'Any medical treatments since your last assessment?' said the doctor when he'd cleaned up and seated himself.

Mac's last full medical check-up had taken place ten years earlier at Larrakeyah Base in Darwin, shortly after his operation in East Timor.

'Yeah, just the usual. Bullet grazes, concussions, broken nose, cracked cheekbone, broken bone in my wrist – all declared,' said Mac.

Flipping through Mac's medical file, the doctor nodded amiably at the sheaf of emergency-room discharge sheets, medical-clinic slips and ship-doctor reports that Mac had collected during the past decade. There was even a medical report on US Department of Defense letterhead, which Mac assumed was from an afternoon in Denpasar many years ago.

'You've been in the field for most of your career, Alan – any other visits to a doctor? Any minor treatments you may have overlooked?'

'I went to the dentist in '04,' said Mac. 'Had all my amalgams removed.'

'Why?'

'I wanted white ones,' said Mac.

Mac had heard about an Israeli technology where they took a snapshot of a person's dental work which was locked into their databases. Having a dental map allowed intelligence services to track people from satellites, the unique spacing of metal in the mouth apparently creating a traceable electronic signature. Mac had decided a mouthful of non-metallic fillings might be better for him.

'Let's have a look,' said the doctor, pushing Mac's lower jaw down with his pen and peering in. 'Where was this done?'

'Singapore,' said Mac. 'At the time I didn't think about it as medical, but if we're including –'

'That's okay,' said the doctor. 'Nothing else? Treatment for substance abuse?'

'No, doc.'

'No men's clinic visits?'

'Shit,' said Mac, laughing. 'The finger in the bum was intimate enough, don't you think?'

'You're forty, Alan – if you're having problems with your ejaculations . . .'

Mac held up his hand. 'No problems with the plumbing, okay?'

'Good,' said the doctor, scribbling a note. 'And nothing else? No psychological services? No psychiatry or other forms of mental-health therapy? Prescriptions, perhaps? Sedatives, anti-anxieties, anti-psychotics?'

The memories flooded back: it was Sumatra 2002, he'd pursued a bunch of Pakistanis suspected of the Kuta bombings, and as the bombers had made their escape they'd kidnapped a young boy and shot his sister, left her for dead in the jungle. That incident had made him feel incompetent, useless and culpable. He had hidden those kids in the jungle when he knew the bombers were about, and they'd done what he'd asked. They were good kids and they were punished for it.

Mac's voice dropped. 'I saw a shrink for eight weeks in 2002.'

'Where?' said the doctor.

'Manila – Dr Lydia Weiss, a Canadian. I didn't declare it.'

'Why did you see her?'

Mac looked at the eye chart and the plastic skeleton for inspiration but found his gaze returning to the doctor's face. 'Some children were hurt during an operation – I felt I hadn't done enough to protect them.'

'You blamed yourself?'

'At a point where I could have covered their interests,' said Mac, thinking it through, 'I looked after my own interests. I couldn't really . . . well, I couldn't talk to anyone. You know, I started self-medicating and –'

'Alcohol?' said the doctor.

'Yep.'

'And once that became a problem, you saw Dr Weiss?'

'Yep,' said Mac. 'I used a false identity.'

'And you improved?'

'Yeah. It was good, actually.'

'Good for you – that all sounds healthy,' the doctor said, making a quick squiggle and shutting Mac's file.

Mac sensed a trick. 'That's it?'

'Sure,' said the doctor, emotionless. It was a joke in the armed forces that to be a naval ship's doctor, you were first checked to ensure you had no pulse. When everything went to crap on a ship, the doctor had to be as calm as a lizard sunning itself.

'Okay,' said Mac.

The doc gave him a sudden smile. 'You felt terrible about those children, which is a healthy reaction. And when you realised you were drowning those feelings in booze, you found a professional. I have no problem with that, Alan.'

'But I didn't declare it,' said Mac.

'You have now,' said the doctor with a wink as he stood. 'We clear?'

'Crystal,' said Mac.

# CHAPTER 6

Mac was halfway to Canberra in a navy car when the Nokia buzzed – a text from Rod Scott, Mac's original mentor in ASIS.

It said, *Nosebag fgc 1pm?*

Getting the driver to drop him in the suburb of Garran, Mac ambled three blocks to the entry gates of Federal Golf Club, sweating in the late spring heat and deafened by the roar of cicadas. Checking for surveillance as he walked to the clubhouse he scrolled through messages on his phone: several voicemails and two missed calls – numbers he didn't recognise. Dialling into voicemail, he heard Jenny reminding him to pick up a smoked ham from the German butcher, and then a second message from Jen, upset after reading the news about Ray Hu. Jenny didn't know Ray Hu and his wife Liesl as well as Mac did, but the four of them had enjoyed some big nights on the grog and Jenny adored Ray's sense of humour.

He tried to filter out the emotion as he walked through the sunshine. The assessment had turned out okay, if you took the hangover out of the equation. The full medical had been followed by a short psych interview and a session that used to be called 'the polygraph' but now included a voice-stress analyser – a lie detector that identified variations when interviewees were asked about drugs, child porn and undeclared holidays with their Chinese lover. There'd been a twenty-minute debrief, where an office guy from the Firm grabbed the file of an old operation in the Philippines and quickly quizzed Mac on the basics, looking for any discrepancies between the official record and Mac's recollections – the same debrief Mac had done with many operatives from the Firm.

Strolling past the practice tees, Mac watched a man in pressed golf shorts stare impassively as a woman swung, topped a ball, and then threatened to hit the ground with her club. The bloke reset a new ball without meeting her eyes, and Mac marvelled at how quickly a married man got himself trained.

Moving up the steps and into the dining room, he found Scotty sitting at the bar, reading the *Australian* and nursing a glass of beer.

'Man's not a camel,' said Mac as Scotty stood. 'There a beer round here for a bloke?'

'Shit, mate,' said Scotty, his round face ripped with a smile as he shook hands. 'Forty years old and still in shape – what's your secret?'

'Lots and lots of bullshitting,' said Mac, as Scotty motioned with two fingers to the barman.

'Yeah, well, how come I ended up looking like Buddha?' said Scotty, leading Mac out into the dining room.

Eating from the buffet and downing two beers, Mac relaxed as he looked out the big windows and saw players teeing off at one and holing out at eighteen – the low-scorers obvious by how quickly they reached for their cards.

They talked quietly, pulling up some of the memories from their first gig together in Iraq, at the finish of the first Gulf War.

'See those AWB blokes are finally coming up for court,' said Scotty, tapping his newspaper with his beer glass. 'Poor bastards.'

'Yeah – seems that Saddam was too pure to invade but too evil to do business with,' said Mac.

The Australian Wheat Board had secured some enormous supply contracts with Saddam's Iraq in the late 1990s, which included side contracts to pay for in-country freighting of the wheat using a Jordanian trucking company. The trucking charge was paid from a UN escrow account which released otherwise-embargoed Iraqi oil revenues to pay for essential and humanitarian services – of which distributing wheat to Iraqis was one. It was just that the Jordanian trucking company was an Iraqi front, a way for Saddam's regime to collect hard currency through the UN under false pretences. Now the AWB executives who paid the Iraqi trucking fee were turning up in court – a move that had surprised people in Mac's world, given how relentlessly Australia's diplomatic, trade and intelligence outfits had worked to ensure the success of Aussie wheat against that of Canada, the US and Russia.

His first live operation was a wheat gig: four in the morning, riffling through the files of the state-owned freight forwarders in Umm Qasr, flashlight between his teeth, looking for the paperwork on Iraq's wheat imports from Canada and the US. He was in a rush because the Canadian SIS operative who'd been masquerading as a journalist had been locked in an underground garage by Scotty. And at nine that morning the US and Australian naval clearance teams were going to declare the Umm Qasr port area 'open' and free of live ordnance and booby-traps. Mac had infiltrated the building at the Bulk Grain Terminal, found the files and got them out by secreting them in an Australian Navy air-compressor unit used for the clearance divers. When the port had been reopened and the Canadians had rushed in to secure the freight-landing records of several decades, they found the filing cabinets empty. While they gnashed their teeth and looked for a scapegoat, the files were en route to HMAS *Kanimbla*.

'Makes you wonder why we were getting all that intel on North American wheat when the blokes who could use it were just going to get shit-canned,' said Scotty.

'Yeah, well the Canadians got their payback,' sniggered Mac, referring to the fact that Canadian SIS had ensured that the Australian media was put on the trail of the AWB arrangements with Saddam.

Iraq seemed like a lifetime ago, right back at the start of it all. Mac had moved quickly from being a teenage rugby league player in Rockhampton to a rugby scholarship boy at Nudgee. He'd gone to the University of Queensland and then into the DFAT campus recruitment process. In those days, the Australian Secret Intelligence Service didn't advertise. It was a part of DFAT, sharing the stables with diplomats and trade commissioners, and the Firm didn't let you know you were being considered for the spy game until they thought you might have the stuff. Times had changed, but back in 1990 the Firm essentially recruited from four universities and a group of about thirty schools. Nudgee College and UQ were part of the matrix.

When Mac had realised what he was being offered, he'd had visions of dinner suits and glamorous women hanging around the baccarat tables. It was all he knew about the intelligence world. But after six weeks of the ASIS field-craft program, he'd been whipped away to do basic training with the UK's Royal Marines and follow-up with their Commandos program – a challenge he probably took too far when he completed the brutal swimmer–canoeist course in Brunei and qualified for selection in an SBS squad.

It had been a whirl, and one in which few medium-term consequences were spelled out to a young inductee: namely, that the intelligence assignments involving paramilitary elements were carried out by a very small band of officers, and that the true nature of this work would often not be known to colleagues. He'd gone into ASIS feeling educated and special, only to get ten years down the track and realise he was never going to gasbag at a whiteboard, or sit in meetings all day trying to put the blame on someone who wasn't in the room. Mac was isolated: he'd always be that Rockhampton footy player who did the dirty work.

'So, you're back?' Scotty asked, after an awkward pause.

'They pushed me up a grade and let me live in Queensland,' said Mac. 'Couldn't argue.'

'I'm going to be running you for a while, you okay with that?' said Scotty, levelling his gaze.

'Not like the Firm to give me a choice.'

'Not a choice – just courtesy.' Scotty held up two fingers to the waitress. 'You're old school, mate. Not many of us left.'

Scotty had been seconded into the Firm after a stint in the Australian Army's Intelligence Corps. He could inveigle himself under a corporate cover along with the best, but he also had big forearms and hands that could hurt.

Mac scanned the room for eyes and self-conscious newspaper-reading. 'So, what's the gig?'

'One of ours — from Trade — logging a lot of unaccompanied hours,' said Scotty, eyes lighting up as the next round of beers arrived. 'Long lunches, early departures, vague diary — that sort of thing.'

'Surveillance?'

'Nothing yet. I've had a look at the notes, and had a chat on the phone with the consulate.'

'Where?'

'Saigon,' said Scotty. 'We need to design an approach, get eyes on this guy, write an initial report.'

'And if something's cooking, get close?'

'That's why I like you, mate,' said Scotty, sipping on the beer. 'You're faster than a robber's dog.'

'Why me?' said Mac, watching the husband and wife from the practice fairway making their way onto the first tee. 'Joe's in Manila and Terry's in Honkers — they can't do this?'

'Greg wants an outside team.'

'Outside team? Thought I was back in?'

'Special Projects,' said Scotty, looking at his hands. 'Welcome aboard.'

'Even after Singers?'

'Sure,' said Scotty. 'I looked at the report — you did it by the book. Who's to know where Lao was leaking? I'm betting his wife.'

'You think?' said Mac.

Scotty shrugged. 'The wife might have been the real boss and she went straight to the MSS when she knew he was going to Singapore.'

'You couldn't have hooked Garvs for this?' said Mac, trying to figure out how Jen would react to him leaving again.

'Garvs?!' said Scotty with a smile. 'I remember that gig in Manila. I had to go in there and find the silly prick.'

'That wasn't his fault, was it?' said Mac, chuckling.

'Shit, mate — I found him in a bar in Angeles City, so pissed he couldn't work out why these ping-pong balls were flying round his fucking head!'

Beer spurted out of Mac's nose as he laughed. 'Shit, Scotty. You're a worry.'

'Yeah, well,' said Scotty, mischief in his eyes, 'I need an operation going down the toilet, I'll call Anton Garvey. But I want this done right.'

'Okay,' said Mac, recovering. 'Who's the target?'

Scotty and Mac looked out at the first tee, where the wife was readying herself with a three-wood.

'Jim Quirk,' said Scotty from the side of his mouth, as the woman swung like a cheap robot and topped her ball for a first shot of about seventeen inches.

Mac paused. 'Mate, I know Jim – you aware of that?'

'Yep, Macca,' said Scotty. 'Let's do this once and do it right.'

'Okay,' said Mac.

Down on the first tee, the woman stamped her foot as the husband teed her up with a new ball. Her second shot was a flier. As she got in the cart she was smiling again.

# CHAPTER 7

Grabbing a BRW and making for a corner armchair in Canberra airport's business lounge, Mac thought about Jim Quirk, a young trade secretary at the Aussie embassy in Manila when Mac had his first diplomatic placement as a second-secretary. They hadn't been enormously close, but they'd had a few laughs and Mac remembered Quirk had been a schoolboy star at cricket or footy, something like that. He could catch up on the details later; for now he wanted to get a good look at who had followed him up the ramp. Holding the magazine in front of his chest, he eased back and watched a fortyish Anglo male with dark hair saunter into the lounge, a black computer bag over his shoulder. The man poured a mug of coffee and walked directly towards Mac, a smile on his face.

'G'day, mate,' said Dave Urquhart, an old school friend of Mac's who had been around the intelligence traps for years.

'Davo,' said Mac, standing and shaking hands. 'It's Alan.'

'Of course,' said Urquhart, observing the etiquette that you let a spy who might be using a cover tell you the name he was using.

Mac's mind spun as he looked around for a backup man or a partner. Was this an approach? They made small talk, but Mac was nervous – the woman sitting on the other side of the coffee table was within earshot.

Dave Urquhart had been at Nudgee College with Mac but then he'd gone to the University of Sydney to do law and economics and Mac hadn't reconnected with him until he'd started turning up in briefings. Mac knew that Urquhart had started at the Firm, but as his career took off he was used as a political liaison guy, between ASIS and the Prime Minister's office for a start, and then later between the Office of National Assessments and the government. There'd recently been a new oversight office established called the National Intelligence Coordination Committee, with a new national intelligence adviser appointed to assist the Prime Minister. Mac had heard that Urquhart was working for that adviser while apparently still trying to stay close with ASIS.

'So, where are you off to, Davo?' said Mac, searching his old mate's eyes.

'Darwin,' said Urquhart, looking upwards to his left; a lie.

'Nice up there right now,' said Mac.

The woman opposite them closed her laptop, put it in her carry case and left.

'One of yours?' said Mac, nodding after the woman as she left the business lounge.

'Shit, Macca,' said Urquhart.

'Well?' said Mac.

'How did you know that?'

'She only typed when we weren't talking,' he said. 'Gotta learn to listen over your own key strokes.'

'Okay,' said Urquhart.

'And she dressed professional, but with secretary make-up.'

Urquhart sighed. 'All right, all right.'

Mac was enjoying himself. 'She one of those ASIO idiots?'

'You've made your point,' said Urquhart, turning and looking him in the eye.

'So make yours,' said Mac, checking his watch.

Urquhart sipped his coffee. 'We had a look at the Colmslie report. Bad business.'

'I wasn't thrilled,' said Mac.

'Sad about Ray, huh?' said Urquhart.

'He knew the risks,' Mac replied. 'Listen, who do you work for now?'

'The government, mate,' said Urquhart, in a tone Mac didn't like.

'Government?'

'Executive arm. So I guess there're some questions in your mind, right?'

'About Colmslie?' said Mac, annoyed that his old friend had turned the tables, made him chase the subject.

'Yeah – everything's going gangbusters and then, *boom*, the trail goes cold.'

'The trail goes cold?' said Mac. 'Shit, mate, you've been watching too much TV.'

'Come on, Macca – I *know* you.'

Mac sneered. 'Oh really? So tell me what I'm thinking.'

'You're wondering if you can hit me and get away with it.'

'Ha!' said Mac.

'Look, you put together an operation that was supposed to turn a Chinese spy, and then right at the point you get him in the hotel room and talking, he's assassinated. A little too convenient, right?'

Mac controlled himself. 'What do you mean by that?'

'It's obvious, isn't it?'

'Enlighten me,' said Mac, amazed that the slippery machinations a sixteen-year-old had used at boarding school had been honed into the weaponry of a first-class political shit.

'Okay,' said Urquhart. 'It was a joint taskforce, but Operation Kava was the Firm's gig, right?'

'So?'

'It was a closed shop – no one else knew the plan, the venue, the timing . . .' He tailed off, numbering them on his fingers.

'Of course it was closed,' said Mac. 'What was I going to do? Take an ad in the *Straits Times*?'

'So you're okay with how it happened?'

'No, I'm the opposite of okay – what are you getting at?'

Urquhart leaned towards Mac, his eyes goldfish-like. 'If there're any rotten apples in the barrel, then the political will exists to move on that right now, understand?'

'The political will?' said Mac, deflated. He was tired, he was hungover, he was forty, and his head still ached from being pistol-whipped. Now someone from the Prime Minister's office was asking him to work against Aussie SIS. The Firm wasn't perfect, but the day Mac honestly felt endangered by a colleague, he'd leave. Until then, he'd keep the family fights in-house and he'd hold the line, like everyone who worked around him.

'Of course, you know none of this reflects on you, right, Macca?' said Urquhart, like a man who lied because he could. 'There'll be no blow-back on your career; in fact, it might work the other way.'

The departure board clicked up two notches and the top bars started flashing, one of them the five pm flight to Brisbane.

'My career blew back a long time ago, mate,' said Mac, standing and looking down on a person he'd once protected in the Nudgee dorms. 'But I've learned to live with my anguish.'

'Think about it,' said Urquhart, holding out a card.

'What's this?'

'My numbers,' said Urquhart. 'In case you want to talk.'

'You wanna talk?' said Mac, as he turned to leave. 'Get a one-three-hundred number.'


The house at Broadbeach was empty when Mac let himself in. A note on the kitchen bench from Jen said she'd taken the girls for dinner at Hungry Jack's with Frank and Pat – she'd drop Rachel home to her mother afterwards.

Stowing his case in the bedroom, Mac kicked off his shoes, grabbed a beer and clicked on the TV. Making his usual rounds, he shut the curtains from the side of the windows, checked every room in the house, ran his fingers around the TV screen to see if it had been pried open and then checked the wall-mounted phone socket and the phone itself. Finally, Mac picked up the handset and listened for the dial tone. The tone beeped back at him, signifying voicemail. Dialling in, he listened. He deleted the message and went to the second. He deleted the second message and hung up.

An ABC current affairs show blared on television. Mac hit the mute button and thought about what he was going to do about Dave

Urquhart and his ridiculous approach. As much as he loved telling Dave to go screw himself, there was only so long an intelligence officer could defy the Prime Minister's office.

He also had to act on the two messages. His heart beating in his temples, he grabbed his Nokia and made a secure call to ASIS head office in Canberra. Giving his code name of Albion, he was challenged for the week's security code, and he gave the one that told the woman at the other end he was safe.

'Field services, thanks,' said Mac, and waited while he was transferred.

'Henry, here. How can I help you, Albion?'

'Henry, I need an immediate residential phone number reassignment,' said Mac, sipping at his beer as he watched a TV reporter pointing down from a helicopter at Queensland's bushfires.

'Certainly, sir,' said Henry.

They both waited until Telstra's government and consular system shut down Mac's old number and reissued a new one. As Henry read out the new home number, a key rattled in the door. Jenny pushed through, Sarah on her hip.

'Hey, darling,' said Mac, going over to them and giving Jen a kiss as she handed him their daughter.

'Do the honours, Macca?'

'Sure,' said Mac, walking his sleepy daughter through to her bedroom.

When he'd put her to bed and shut the door, Mac padded back to the sofa where Jen was curled up under a blanket, the TV switched off.

'So, I guess you weren't really in Perth, right?' she said, her eyes boring into him.

'This week?' said Mac.

'Don't do this, Macca,' said Jen, pushing dark hair out of her face. 'You were with Ray. You were in Singapore.'

'Would it make a difference?'

One of the benefits of having a wife in the federal police was that the Firm's vetting job had been made easy when he married her, but it was still difficult being a spy with a nosey cop in the middle of his life.

'Don't do the weasel words with me, mister,' she said, raising her voice. 'I can get a ton of that shit all day, in any interview room.'

'Ray was a top bloke, and I'm very sad about this,' said Mac, holding out his arm and letting Jen snuggle into his chest.

'He was such a nice man. And what about Liesl? I should call her.'

'Perhaps not,' said Mac, alarm bells ringing. 'She's a very private person.'

'I guess you're right,' said Jen, pushing her athletic, shapely body into Mac. 'Might give it a couple of days.'

Mac stroked her hair and wondered what he was going to do. The two voicemails he'd deleted were addressed to Jenny Toohey; calls from Liesl Hu, asking Jen to become personally involved in her husband's shooting.

But that wasn't the worst of it. What made him change the phone number were Liesl's final words, gasped out through her tears: 'I think the Australian government is involved.'

# CHAPTER 8

Packing his suitcase, Mac tried to focus only on the job ahead and the corporate cover he had worn for most of his working life. He had a routine for packing his wheelie bag and readying himself for the Richard Davis collateral that would be waiting at Brisbane International Airport.

'Think we'll be okay with Sarah,' said Jenny, sitting on the bed with a towel wrapped around her chest, tied off in her cleavage. It was just past eight am but she'd already done her laps at Southport pool and would be starting work at the federal police building in Robina at ten o'clock.

'Yeah?' said Mac, distracted.

'I'm sharing a nanny with Sian,' said Jenny. 'She's flexible. Basically, I call her when I need the help.'

Mac felt excluded. 'Oh, when *you* need it?'

'Yes, when I need it, Macca,' she said. 'Like this week. I don't see you juggling when Sarah needs to be minded.'

'Yeah, well . . .' said Mac, taking his own Brut 33 deodorant from the toilet bag and replacing it with Richard Davis's Old Spice. The SPF 30 sunscreen actually contained a gel that would turn his hair dark brown, and the tube of men's face scrub was the Schwarzkopf N10 blonding agent that would take his hair back to its natural colour when required.

'I mean, you only told me about this Auckland trip on Friday,' said Jenny. 'And you say you're going for two weeks, but that's not set in stone.'

'I'm sorry,' said Mac, reluctant to snap out of his focused state. 'I told you as soon as I knew.'

It was a marriage where both of them trod carefully around the subject of their work. Jenny didn't like to feel guilty or distracted in her job any more than Mac did in his. It was made more difficult by the fact that when the juggling had to be done, it was Jen hitting the phones and calling in favours. Mac knew that, but there wasn't a lot he could do about it.

'You can make it up to me,' said Jen.

'Sure,' said Mac, preoccupied with getting his boat shoes into exactly the placement he liked. He travelled only with cabin luggage to minimise officials touching his belongings.

'I mean, you know,' said Jen, lying back on the bed, the towel falling off her hips. 'Sarah's watching the Wiggles, and . . .'

Mac's wife had been a high school swimming star and an Australian Universities rep in basketball. She worried that her stomach was loose and her bum was sagging after having Sarah, but Mac reckoned that she looked better in a tank top and a pair of Levis than most women looked in hundreds of dollars worth of lingerie.

'The Wiggles, eh?' said Mac, moving to her.

Putting her hand into his thin blond hair, she gave him the smile and Mac bent down to her, smelling the apple-scented shampoo that she used to get the chlorine out of her hair.

Kissing her, Mac let his hand slide up under Jenny's towel, feeling the muscles and curves. Jen hooked a thumb over the band of Mac's undies, but then suddenly pulled away.

'Door,' she said, pushing his chest.

Leaning into the hallway, Mac heard a famous song from the kids' TV show, and a thumping sound that indicated Sarah was trying to dance to it.

Shutting the door quietly, Mac crossed the floor to the bed, where Jen had shoved the suitcase to the floor.

'Thank God for the Wiggles,' she said, grabbing him by the thigh.

'Choo choo, chugga chugga,' said Mac, and Jen giggled as she pulled him onto her.


The Airtrain between the Gold Coast and Brisbane airport was crowded with backpackers and retirees. Summer was starting to kick in for real and the hiss of the air-conditioning in the carriage was almost louder than the rattle of the tracks as they headed north.

Sitting at the back, Mac read the *Financial Review* and avoided eye contact. Something was niggling him about the Pan Pac shootings, and he couldn't quite get it straight. The approach from Urquhart in Canberra had been a shock. Taskforces were put together to secure outcomes that were jointly agreed; even Grant Shannon from the AFP would not dispute the consensus. So why was Urquhart flitting about, looking for a traitor in ASIS?

The scenery flashed past, made dark by the heavily tinted windows. Also annoying him were the phone calls from Liesl Hu – the tone of fear that rose above her grief. Mac didn't feel good about his lack of contact, but it wasn't in a spy's DNA to soothe wives when the aim was to get out of Dodge before the crocodile clips got warmed up.

Mac was worried about how much Liesl actually knew – or had guessed – about Operation Kava. Ray Hu's cover in Singapore was genuine: he was a fund manager who took equity positions in small defence-oriented technology companies, even if many of his leads came from Aussie intelligence. He was the real thing and he was the embodiment of the espionage cliché of hiding in plain sight. He'd been written about in the *Far Eastern Economic Review* and was a regular in the Asian *Wall Street Journal*'s tips for hot investments in the new year. He was even on a Singapore government think tank for identifying future niche industries and getting universities to support them. But aside from this public profile, Ray was a stickler for secrecy and his double life with ASIS was walled off, even from his wife.

So why, wondered Mac as the train pulled into the international airport station, did Liesl get on the phone to Jenny and allege Australian government involvement in her husband's murder?

He wasn't comfortable about Liesl being a loose end, even if he did like her and owed it to Ray to look after her. Emotional, grief-stricken women making phone calls about Australian complicity in double murders in a foreign country was bad enough; when they were on the right track, it could be disastrous.

As he stepped onto the platform, Mac turned for the bridge to the international terminal and breathed deeply as he walked. He had to establish if Liesl's and Urquhart's stories overlapped. And to do that, he would have to talk to Liesl Hu.

Waiting for his courier, Mac sat at a coffee shop on the upstairs deck of the terminal, eating a filled croissant. His seat gave him a view to the lower airside level of the large, naturally lit terminal, while also allowing him to see anyone approaching on the upper level.

At 12.15, the heavyset yet quick-walking gait of Rod Scott came into sight. He bought two Crown Lagers at the counter and moved to the table.

'Cutting it fine,' said Mac, whose Qantas flight left at 1.40. 'And why're you here? Bit below your pay grade, isn't it?'

Sipping his beer, Scotty put his folded *Courier-Mail* on the table and Mac pulled it towards him and let a plain envelope slide out of it and onto his lap. Removing the Richard Davis passport, he placed it on the table with his ticket in the name of Davis.

'I thought we should chat,' said Scotty, removing his sunglasses and rubbing his right eye with the heel of his hand.

'Okay,' said Mac, not wanting the beer.

'Mate, what was Urquhart after?' Scotty looked around discreetly.

'Shit, Scotty. You had someone on me?'

'No, mate – just a routine check of the tapes in the business lounge.'

'Bullshit,' said Mac, catching Scotty's guilty smirk. 'Urquhart tried to co-opt me – reckons what happened in Singers was due to a rotten apple in the Firm.'

'Really?' said Scotty, brow furrowed. 'Urquhart came out and *said* this?'

'Sure,' said Mac.

'And you said?'

'I told him to get fucked.'

Scotty looked confused. 'And that was it?'

'He gave me a card, in case I wanted to talk.'

'Really?' said Scotty, relaxing.

'He wouldn't tell me who he worked for,' said Mac. 'Just that it was the executive arm.'

'Got the card?'

'No, mate – I'm clean, remember? But I can tell you the stamp on it was a federal coat of arms.'

'Okay, leave it with me,' said Scotty. 'And if he contacts you again, bring him along and let's see what he's on about.'

'I'll let him talk,' said Mac. 'But I'm not snitching on my own people.'

'Oh, by the way, Macca,' said Scotty, chugging at the beer, 'the name is Operation Dragon, the contact protocol is standard, and your team is in place.'

'Team?' said Mac.

'One asset. Local.'

'What about Bailey?' said Mac, who'd wanted the former navy spook.

'Bailey's heading up to Thailand for an APEC junket.'

'So who's up?' said Mac, tasting the beer.

'Name's Tranh. English is passable. Has his own little IT consulting business in Saigon. He hires himself out to visiting reporters and film crews as a driving contractor.'

'Good cover.'

'Yep,' said Scotty. 'He's also nicely connected with some of the old ARVN networks and the black markets. He can get stuff, make things happen.'

Mac looked around the concourse as a person with a Chinese name was paged. 'Local, eh?'

'Not that kind of local,' said Scotty, clocking Mac's face.

'In Saigon,' said Mac, 'they're all that kind of local.'

# CHAPTER 9

Booking the express checkout option at Changi's Crowne Plaza, Mac asked for a steak and chips to be sent up before taking the elevator to his fifth-floor room overlooking the drop-off aprons of T3.

After a quick shower, he changed into fresh clothes and ate most of the steak before walking into the humid evening air. The cabbie looked at him once too often, so Mac asked him to take a left exit off Pan Island where he stopped outside a large shopping mall. Paying the fare, he walked through the concourse of the shopping area and out the side exit, where he hailed another cab and asked to go to Holland Park, but this time via the East Coast Parkway.

The humidity of pre-monsoon South-East Asia created a smell of dirt and leaves as they hooked north out of the traffic and gradually got into the quieter and leafier streets. Asking to be dropped beside a pay phone, Mac alighted and stood in the booth, pretending to talk but watching the almost-dark streets for silhouettes in parked cars or headlights being switched off.

Venturing out, he walked for eight minutes, passing Singaporeans as they took their evening walks, eventually stopping outside a plain white home. It was set back from the road, guarded by a stand of bamboo and a few palm trees. Walking past Liesl's BMW and Ray's Toyota, Mac chuckled at the different cultures of Hong Kong and

Singapore: if Ray had lived in Honkers, he'd have worn garish gold watches and driven a Bentley. In Singers, he drove a Camry and owned a house that looked almost modest from the street.

Walking softly across the paving stones, he stepped up onto the porch and rang the bell, shifting to the side of the door as he did so. Standing still, Mac rehearsed what he was going to say to Liesl, but nothing cute and insincere came to mind. He was going to wing it, look into her eyes and decide on the fastest way to the answers. If that meant getting on the turps and talking about Ray all night, he'd do it. If he had to scare her, take her immediately to the worst case, he'd do that too.

Looking through the glass side-panel beside the wooden door, Mac squinted to see if there was movement, and then pressed the doorbell again. Glancing back, he walked to Liesl's blue BMW, put his hand on the bonnet. Cold. The Toyota too.

Walking around the side of the house, he winced as the security lights came on, revealing a double camera which looked either way down the alley. A thick, deadlocked gate blocked his passage and he grabbed the top of it, pulling himself up until he could see over. Through the kitchen window of the house next door a maid washed pots and pans while a couple of young kids in pyjamas chased each other around.

Easing over the gate to the other side, Mac caught his breath from the exertion and became aware of a new sound. Someone crying? Moving slowly down the side alley, he wished he was armed. Poking his head around the corner to a poolside area where he had cooked many barbecues and finished a few beers, Mac saw the source of the crying. The black cocker spaniel stopped his whining and stared at Mac, posing a challenge.

'Woody!' said Mac under his breath and the animal came to life in a squeal of joy and greeting. He released the slobbering dog from his leash and the beast sprinted down the side of the pool and darted under a tree to relieve himself.

Opening the patio ranch sliders, Mac peered into the dark house. 'Hello!' he said, the silence ringing in his head. 'Liesl? You home?'

Easing into the living area, Mac listened and sniffed the air for alien aftershave or stale cigarette smoke – something to tweak him. But the front part of the house seemed empty.

As he moved across the expensive carpet, the Chagall and a Basquiat glimmered out of darkness along one wall and the huge Whiteley hung over the Santa Fe fireplace. The massive Middle Ages chess board dominated an alcove like a challenge to anyone who entered this house; Ray was an excellent chess player and the chess set he called 'the Dominican' was one of his most cherished possessions.

In the kitchen, a stack of Straits Times lay on the bench, the top one opened to page five, where the ongoing murder investigation from the Pan Pac was being followed.

The place seemed untouched yet not like someone had gone on holiday. Woody came into the kitchen and Mac found a bag of chicken wings in the refrigerator, threw a few on the tiled floor and poured a bowl of water for the animal.

He wandered into the bedroom area of the house. Was she out with a friend? But left the back door unlocked? Had to leave suddenly? But tied up Woody without a water bowl?

In the master bedroom a dark green dress lay on the bed. Liesl had been getting ready to go out, but was surprised?

In the walk-in wardrobe, he noticed the full-length mirror at the end of the room was slightly off its hinges. Taking a closer look, he swung back the mirror and saw the large safe set into the concrete wall, door ajar. Using a pen, Mac pushed the door fully open and looked inside: a file box with the label Shares, another which said Bonds and three four-hundred-ounce gold ingots stamped with Tanaka Kikinzoku Kogyo. If Ray's spy collateral had been in the safe, it was now gone, as was the tape in the surveillance machine housed under the safe.

'Shit,' muttered Mac, crouching to look at the black machine that looked much like a stereo tuner but had a small screen embedded in it.

'Not enough for you?' came the voice, and Mac spun, throwing himself sideways, as the light came on.

'Easy, champ,' said the tall man, who carried a bunch of flowers and a bottle of wine. 'You'll blow a fuse.'

'Shit, Benny,' said Mac, slumping on the carpet, his chest heaving with adrenaline. 'You've got a timing problem, mate. Swear to God.'

The sounds of Benny Haskell barking orders into his mobile phone echoed around the large kitchen as Mac watched the head form on the beer in his glass. Benny had a team from his professional services firm working on Liesl's possible disappearance; Mac was holding off on informing ASIS.

'And when you speak with Max – and it has to be Max – you tell him this comes from me, right?' said Benny into his phone, pausing to suck on his smoke. 'And this is off the air, okay? We're all buddies here, we're not sending out the cavalry.'

Signing off, Benny poured a bottle of beer into his glass. Benny Haskell was at least twenty years older than Mac and a veteran of Aussie intelligence. A chartered accountant by profession, he'd worked in ASIS, held overseas posts as a trade commissioner, and had been one of the designers of the AUSTRAC system that tracked all banking transactions inside Australia and between Australia and the world. He now ran a firm in Singapore with a former legal executive from the Australian Taxation Office, facilitating banking options for people not officially residing on the island.

'Got a line into SID,' said Benny. The Security and Intelligence Division was Singapore's ASIS. 'We'll see what comes back, but are you sure you don't want the Firm to know about this?'

'For now,' said Mac, his mind spinning.

'Why? 'Cos you're not supposed to be here?'

'Maybe,' said Mac. 'I'd like to start with the security.'

'Like, there is none?' said Benny, shifting his ashtray closer.

'Yeah.'

'Well, there's no reason to put security on the wife of a random shooting victim.' Benny shrugged skinny shoulders under a red polo shirt. 'It was a hit on Lao, wasn't it? Ray was wrong time, wrong place?'

'Yeah,' said Mac. 'So what are you doing here?'

'We spoke yesterday, when I was up in KL. She was going to get the barbecue going – there was something she needed to discuss.'

'So you turn up with wine and flowers.'

'She hates a drink,' said Benny.

'And . . .'

'And I'm about to ring the bell when I see the front door's open – but no lights on. A bloke gets curious.'

'Fuck!' said Mac, not liking the bit about the door being open. 'There was someone in here?'

Benny ducked that. 'I'm here for dinner. What's your excuse?'

'Liesl called me – thought I'd drop in on the way.'

'To?'

'Colombo,' said Mac.

Benny lit another smoke. 'What did she say?'

'I don't know if it's relevant,' said Mac.

'If you're crawling around in your friend's safe, it's relevant,' said Benny.

Mac poured the remains of the beer into his glass. 'Well, it was two voicemails, and in the second she said there might be Aussie involvement in Ray's death.'

'Was there?' said Benny.

'Mate!' said Mac, in the long, drawn-out way that means *do you mind?*

'So, either Liesl has found some evidence that Ray was working with the Firm when he was hit . . .'

'Okay,' said Mac, following the logic.

'Or . . .' said Benny.

'Don't make me say that,' said Mac.

'Been known to happen. McLean, Philby, Burgess . . .'

'Fuck's sake, Benny.'

The mobile phone on the marble bench top rang. Standing, Benny took the call, lowering his voice as he turned away.

'Yeah, yeah, okay, mate – thanks,' said Benny. 'And you got that memo from Sally, about the earlier flight to Bangers?'

There was a pause while someone spoke.

'Yeah, mate, I know five's a little rude, but try to doze on the flight, okay?'

Folding the phone as he sat, Benny crushed his cigarette. 'ISD's involved,' he said, referring to Singapore's internal intelligence organisation. 'So the Singaporeans think there's a foreign government in this.'

'Jesus,' said Mac.

Benny looked into Mac's eyes. 'You telling me everything? I can't help Liesl unless we're a loop, okay, Macca?'

'Yeah, Benny.'

'Because it just occurred to me.'

'What?' said Mac.

'Liesl didn't know you were a spook – she thought you were a publishing executive doing deals with Ray's fund.'

'Yeah, well . . .' said Mac, thinking.

'So why was she calling you? What was a book salesman going to do for her?'

'It wasn't – look, Benny,' said Mac, but Benny caught something. He laughed. 'Oh, fuck!'

'What?' said Mac, face burning red.

'Don't tell me you intercepted a call that was supposed to go to a certain federal cop?' said Benny, slapping the bench top. 'A certain cop who lives in your house? Oh, brother! You're a brave man, mate.'

'Yeah, yeah,' said Mac.

'Or fucking stupid,' said Benny, his laughter bouncing around the house.

# CHAPTER 10

The lines of war-era concrete bunkers slid past the windows as the 777 taxied to the Tan Son Nhat international terminal. Passing quickly through customs and immigration, Mac wove through the swirling human traffic of Terminal 2 towards the huge glassed exit. During Mac's first visits to this city, the terminal was a converted hangar with an old Pan-American airstair bolted to the inside of the far wall, creating a stairway to the next level. Now it was a modern, open space, like a cross between Brisbane International and Toronto's Pearson.

Emerging into the sticky mayhem of Vietnam at 9.20 am, Mac dodged the private taxi drivers, van owners and cyclo riders that teemed on the aprons, keeping his wheelie bag close and his travel documents jammed tightly under his armpit. On his left, officials with handheld radios tried to organise a crush of humanity onto the correct buses, while a long taxi queue had formed on his right, with all of the anarchy that thrived in the world's most overregulated territory. Saigon was proof that the human heart beat harder than the fantasies of the totalitarians – even its Marxist–Leninist name, concocted to emphasise a Communist victory in the South, was never used by the people of this city.

'You need ride?' came the voice of a local. Looking straight ahead, Mac saw a Vietnamese man leaning against a silver Toyota van, smoking a cigarette.

'Maybe,' said Mac, stepping forwards. The man wore aviator sunnies, black trop shirt and grey cotton slacks, with sandals on his feet – the city's male uniform, from the mayor to a criminal on his first day out of prison.

'Are you looking for a blue-sky tour?' asked the man, cool as an ice cube and not moving from his position.

'I'm looking for a golden sunset,' said Mac, checking the apron for eyes as a bus sounded its horn.

Giving the bus driver a nasty smile, the man stood up, pulled the side door of the van back and gestured for Mac's bag. Putting it in the back himself, Mac closed the sliding door and got in the passenger side.

'I'm Tranh,' said the man as he put the van into drive and the bus sounded its horn again.

'Call me Richard,' said Mac, as they pulled away from the apron. 'Let's go to the Grand.'


The blue VinaPhone box on the floor was still sealed. Tearing it open, Mac pulled out the cheap Nokia and, slotting in the battery and SIM card, reached for Tranh's car-charger and plugged it in.

They dodged a cyclo rider who'd veered sideways. 'You got a number, Tranh?'

Without slowing, Tranh recited his number as he steered them past small shops, street stalls and motorcyclists. Old women swept the pavement and yelled at children while men sat on boxes in groups, small coffee cups resting on their knees.

Entering Tranh's number into the phone, Mac hit the green dial button. When Tranh's phone rang, Mac hung up.

'We're in business,' he said, looking at the low-hanging cloud and wondering when the monsoon was going to start. 'I'm assuming that phone is clean?'

'I bought it yesterday morning. Five recharge cards, in here,' said Tranh, indicating the console between them.

'Good,' said Mac, grabbing the cards and noticing that Tranh had that Vietnamese quality of looking young at first meeting; up close, Mac reckoned he was in his early thirties and educated. He combined a certain coolness with a willingness to please – qualities Mac liked in a local asset.

'Shall we start now?' said Tranh.

'Sure,' said Mac, eyeing a large water bottle between the front seats.

Tranh let a brief smile go. 'That's yours.'

'Keep the Uc hydrated, eh, Tranh?' said Mac, grinning. 'Maybe he'll last beyond lunch?'

'No,' said Tranh, serious. 'I'm not meaning that.'

Uc was the Vietnamese word for 'Australian' and Mac was always amused that the locals were embarrassed about using the term. Australians didn't particularly mind it, especially since the formal version was Uc dai loi, or Lucky Australia.

Mac swigged at the water. 'So, what have we got, mate?'

Putting a hand under his seat, Tranh pulled out a beige A4 envelope with a small metal press-down seal on the flap. Opening it, Mac slid out a slim file on James Quirk. The black and white eight-by-five looked like a DFAT file shot, back when the 1989 intake was brimming with confidence, having earned their degrees, passed their tests and gone through their induction courses. QUIRK, James Douglas was an open-faced, confident Anglo with a natural smile; darkish eyes, pale brown hair, fine features.

The second photo, also a black and white eight-by-five, showed a puffier James Quirk in a safari shirt and slacks, emerging into the sunlight of an Asian streetscape – Mac would have guessed South-East Asia or India. The small white sticker on the bottom of the photo identified it as Cholon – HCMC, Saigon's huge Chinatown, and the date was ten days ago.

Attached to the pics were two A4 pages: the first was a standard intelligence bromide of age, height, weight, marital status and the rest of the lines that make up a man's life.

Reading quickly, Mac saw a good CV. Quirk had captained Geelong Grammar's First XI and played Victorian schoolboys cricket – an all-rounder averaging forty-six for batting and eighteen for bowling.

He had an MA (economic history) from the University of Melbourne, was recruited at uni by ASIO, trained and received a grading. During his early ASIO stint he made the Victorian state cricket squad and was subsequently given a leave of absence to play county cricket for Sussex; came back and tried out for DFAT, passed the personal vetting no problems. Married Geraldine McHugh, a Treasury star who made director at thirty-nine. Quirk and McHugh had divorced less than a month ago – no kids.

The ASIO–AFP rider to the divorce – standard for anyone working in Australia's foreign missions – was 'third party/wife, no security concerns'. So poor old Jim had been lion-taming in Asia while some bloke warmed his bed.

The second page listed Quirk's job title – deputy trade commissioner – his address in Saigon and briefly summarised the limited surveillance that he'd recently been subjected to. The main problem with Jim Quirk – aside from the gaps in his diary – was an interagency report indicating a verbal connection between Quirk and Vincent Loh Han, a Chinese nightclub and hotel proprietor, who the briefing author had flagged as: *Head of the Loh Han Tong, one of the three crime families that run Cholon; possible connection PLA intelligence.*

Jim Quirk hadn't been seen with the wrong people, and hadn't been doing anything shady. Interagency reports – probably from AFP or Customs, via FBI or New Scotland Yard – had picked up Vincent Loh Han, through their informants, referring to Quirk in conversation or email. And if Loh Han was a wheeler-dealer in the booming Vietnam, he'd be dropping names like a socialite at the races.

Mac remembered Jim Quirk from Manila. He'd seemed smart and friendly and was entertaining with a couple of beers in him. It was obvious that DFAT thought the bloke was shady, but Mac had an open mind.

'So just us, right?' said Tranh, keeping the speed up through the hundreds of motorbikes on the roads.

'Yep, Tranh,' said Mac. 'No travelling circus.'

Mac was relieved that Scotty hadn't insisted on a bigger team of the type he'd used in Singapore. He preferred working in small teams for security reasons and because it didn't attract the attention of the local cops.

'Also, I have message from Paragon,' said Tranh.

'Yep?'

'He saying you have your fun at Singapore, now it time for Dragon.'

Mac laughed. 'Cheeky bastard.'

'What is that?'

'Nothing — bloke's taking the piss,' said Mac.

'Begging the pardon?' said Tranh.

'You know, pulling my leg,' said Mac, playing with his new phone. 'Anything else?'

'No,' said Tranh. 'But this would be normal?'

Mac drank some water. 'For what?'

'If Paragon pissed on your leg?'


Opening the double French doors of his suite at the Grand, Mac cased the building across the road before walking onto his Juliet balcony and looking over the Saigon River. The Grand was at the higher end of the mid-level hotels, not obvious like the American chains and not too far from the centre of the city. The hotel was on Dong Khoi Street, a busy cafe-lined avenue that ran from the river to Notre Dame Cathedral downtown.

When Mac had first rotated through Saigon in the early 1990s, the Grand was called the Hotel Dong Khoi — which translated as 'general insurrection'. In those days it featured toilets that you flushed by tipping a bucket of water into the bowl and showers that had no cubicle — the sprinkler head stuck straight out of the wall and the cold water splashed all over the black and white tiled floor. It had an ancient grille elevator that didn't work and a staircase that climbed to the fourth floor by wrapping around the elevator shaft. It also had an open-door policy towards Hanoi's spies and police — the Cong An — so that every time Mac left, he was logged by the desk manager and his bags were routinely searched when he was out.

Now the place had been upgraded but he demanded his usual room — a two-bedroom colonial suite in the old wing looking over the river.

Plugging his phone into the power jack, Mac took off his shoes and padded across the living area. Standing beside the doorframe of the main entry, he listened. Holding that position for two minutes, he heard the hallway creak and what he thought was a whisper. And then there was the sound of a fire door opening at the end of the hallway, and swinging shut.

Sitting back on the bed in the room nearest the river, Mac sipped at the water bottle. He'd barely slept the night before, wondering how to proceed with Liesl. Had she been abducted or just bolted? He would wait twenty-four hours and talk to Benny again. He needed time, and he didn't want to blow the whistle on Liesl – not if Urquhart was right and there was a traitor in Aussie intel.

Mac would have to trust Benny – a person he'd met in his induction year when the accountant was teaching the youngsters about how bad guys hid behind banking domiciles and front companies. Benny had then showed the inductees how they could use the same techniques when they were in the field.

Right now, Mac needed a nap. Then he was going to have some lunch and go to work. As he dozed off he thought about his first trip to Saigon and how the night manager – Mr Skin – slept on a stretcher inside the front doors of the Hotel Dong Khoi. One night Mac had staggered back to the hotel after a big go at Apocalypse Now bar and Mr Skin had answered the door. The first thing Mac had seen was a bare-chested bloke, built like a jockey and holding a billy club at shoulder height. Right at the point when Mac thought he was going to be clobbered, Mr Skin had stopped, smiled the big Vietnam welcome, and ushered him in.

That was the enigma of Vietnam: the friendliest violent place on earth.

# CHAPTER 11

Walking with the one-way traffic flow of Dong Khoi Street, Mac kept his pace to a relaxed tourist stroll. Wearing the Aussie traveller uniform of boardies and surf T-shirt, he could also be mistaken for an Aussie soldier on leave if the political police were being nosey.

The temperature had climbed over thirty-five degrees by Mac's estimation as he crossed Dong Khoi Street at the riverfront lights and walked into the Hotel Majestic. Maintaining his languid pace, he crossed through the vaulted foyer and into a cafe before spilling out onto the riverside boulevard on the other side of the building.

Walking to the tourist information pillar, he grabbed a visitor's map and positioned himself to see who or what would follow. Seven seconds later, two men on a Honda step-through accelerated around the corner with the rest of the traffic, the pillion passenger anxiously looking into the Majestic's wide windows. When he hit the driver on the shoulder to stop and started getting off the bike, Mac walked towards them, map in hand.

'Excuse me, fellers,' he said, coming alongside the motorbike's driver, a late-twenties Khmer wearing a Yankees cap and aviators. 'Looking for the ANZ bank – it's around here, right?'

The driver shrugged and pointed to the pillion passenger, who swaggered towards Mac, the minicam in his left palm disappearing into the pocket of his windbreaker.

'Xin chào,' said Mac with a smile and quick bow. 'I'm from Australia, looking for the ANZ. Name's Richard.'

The pillion guy waved away the hand Mac offered. 'You want bank – go down to round 'bout, then left,' he said carefully, like someone who didn't want to miss the 'ft' sound that so many Asians couldn't quite reach. 'Bank there, okay?'

'Thanks, champion,' said Mac, turning and crossing Dong Khoi Street again.


Casing the Black Stork tailor shop in a small side street off Dong Khoi, Mac took his time. It was a little after two pm when he entered the shop. Moving into the cool darkness, he walked towards the stooped old man behind the huge cutting desk but caught sight of Tranh peering through the fitting-room curtains.

Mac followed Tranh into the hall of mirrors of the fitting room.

'Get eyes?' said Mac, looking around the musty old space. 'On Apricot?'

'I did what you say,' said Tranh, keeping his shades on.

'Stayed back?'

'Yes, Mr Richard,' said Tranh. 'He left the consulate at eight past twelve, I followed him along Ton Duc and he got cyclo.'

'Return?'

'Yes, mister – he come back one-forty.'

'Same cyclo?

'No – he change.'

Mac wanted a local's view of Quirk. 'How's he looking?'

'He not so young no more,' said Tranh with a shrug. 'Maybe too much the coffee or the wine?'

'Okay, let's have a chat,' said Mac.

He followed Tranh up a flight of stairs and through an old door into a reminder of French-colonial Saigon. The twelve-foot ceilings and the slow fan created an eerie theatre for the tailor's dummies and old bolts of cloth. Pushing open large wooden French doors, Mac eased into the heat of the day beneath a veranda and glanced up and down the street.

'Show me the back,' said Mac, and they moved through the storage area and onto the rear patio where a table and chair were set up on the tiled slab, overlooked by several new skyscrapers.

'Good,' said Mac, walking back into the room. 'From now on, you don't come here, okay, Tranh?'

'Sure, boss.'

'We change the meet each day – we'll rotate four venues. But you don't come to this one, got it? This is the fallback meet.'

'Okay,' said Tranh.

Leaving the Black Stork, Mac eyed a white Toyota Camry he recognised from before he went into the tailor's. It was parked on the other side of the road. It wouldn't have been odd that it was still there, except this time it had two people sitting in it.

Raising his hand, he stopped the first cyclo rider and got on.

'Ben Thanh market, *cam on*,' said Mac, putting on his sunnies as he pulled the sunshade over his head. Mac liked cyclos for counter-surveillance because the cyclo rider sitting at the rear of the vehicle gave him an excuse to turn in his seat and talk, allowing him a view of the tail.

'Nice day for it,' said Mac with a smile. 'Rain held off.'

As they turned right and headed for Le Loi, Mac looked past the rider's legs and saw the white Camry pull out of its parking space and follow slowly.

Sitting back, he let the middle-aged rider work up a sweat as they pedalled along Le Loi and up to the sprawling market building with the clock tower.

At the rear of the market, Mac hopped out and made his way into the building as the white Camry stopped a hundred metres back. He had no idea who was in that car, but in South-East Asia a Camry pulling out five seconds after you left was usually the wrong kind of attention. Maintaining a brisk pace through the crowd, he navigated the tiny aisles, heading for one of the far corners where men's shirts hung thirty feet in the air. The noise was deafening – Ben Thanh was the biggest and most central market in Saigon, and it was so chaotic that he could barely hear himself think.

Pushing diagonally across the teeming space, Mac finally got to the men's section. Catching the eye of the bloke with the black money-belt and the thirty-foot pole with the hook on the end, Mac pulled out a small wad of US dollars.

'I need a red shirt, for dance club,' said Mac. 'Black pants – nice pants. A belt, black shoes, and . . .' He turned and searched across the sea of Vietnamese faces until he saw the hat store. 'A hat,' he said. 'Big white hat, okay?'

Eyeing the money, the trader handed his hook to a sidekick and started yelling orders at his people, pushing, jostling and cajoling. In Australia it would be called harassing an employee; in Saigon it was called service.

Mr Hook pushed forwards the young fellow who'd arrived back with a couple of red shirts and a selection of black pants. Taking the combo that made him look least like a pimp, Mac slipped into the makeshift changing room that sat between the racks of knock-off polo shirts and the shelves of counterfeit Billabong boardies.

Emerging, Mac let Mr Hook manhandle him, turning him around, pulling at the seams of the shirt, running his tape across Mac's shoulders and all the time yelling at his cohorts. One got on his knees and started fiddling with Mac's pants, but they didn't need fixing. Whoever Mr Hook was, he'd nailed Mac's fitting card with one look.

'You are like movie star, mister,' said Mr Hook, his smile glinting with gold. 'I give you best, sir, and you can be in movie. My guarantee for this.'

Another youngster arrived with three hats and two shoe boxes under his arm. Snatching them, Mr Hook snapped his fingers and a pair of black socks was placed in his hand. The first pair of shoes fitted well, and Mac took the hat that gave him a Miami trumpet-player look.

As Mr Hook looped a belt through his pants, Mac peered between the racks of the clothing section to see if he was still being followed.

'What's the damage?' said Mac from the side of his mouth.

'For you, sir, eighty dollar,' said Mr Hook.

'*Ma qua*,' said Mac, as a sidekick handed him a paper bag with his old clothes and shoes in it.

'What?' asked Mr Hook, his face confused. '*Ma qua?*'

Mr Hook started laughing and grabbing his employees, telling them what Mac had said, all of them doubling over. In Saigon, *ma qua* was old haggling slang that basically translated as 'too much'. If you had the guts to try *ma qua* on a market trader, and do the whole shrugging and eye-rolling song and dance, they'd reward you for it.

'Uc, okay,' said Mr Hook.

'Saigon, okay,' said Mac, giving him the thumbs-up.

'Okay, forty dollar,' said Mr Hook, smile suddenly gone.

Giving him fifty, Mac grabbed his bag and moved along the menswear aisle, trying to sense where the tail was now. Adjusting his sight line, he glimpsed a person in aviator shades moving down one of the main aisles towards him. The tail hadn't shifted his aviator sunnies since Mac had first met him on the back of the surveillance motorbike.

Moving in the opposite direction, towards the south exit, Mac tried to make time through the mass of haggling women without attracting attention and without breaking into a sprint. He was slightly claustro at the best of times, but the tide of locals in such a confined space was messing with his breathing.

Bursting into the heat of the early afternoon, he almost walked straight into the side of the white Camry.

Skirting the car's left headlight and keeping his head down, Mac averted his eyes as the person in the front seat turned to look at him. His heart thumping like a steam engine, Mac kept a steady course through the shadow of the market building as he prayed that his change of clothes had created a sufficient diversion and that no one was going to yell for him to stop. He'd have to make a decision about that: would he run, or stay and fake it out?

The choice was clear: he wouldn't be running – they already knew where he was staying and he had a gig to manage. That meant he'd be faking it if the cop in the car called him back. Under normal circumstances, Mac would talk a load of turkey for as long as it took. He was comfortable with his cover of Richard Davis from Southern Scholastic Books, and he'd keep it simple: he was on holiday between Singapore and Honkers, with three go-see appointments with officials in Saigon's education board and the

University of Medicine and Pharmacy in Cholon – appointments that the political police could see for themselves in his diary when they searched his room.

But as Mac walked around the rear of the market building and hailed a cyclo, he realised that things had just become more complex. The government seemed to have a team on him, never a good sign; and this wasn't going to be about confusing some dumb-arse cop. He knew that because the cop in that car wasn't a he – it was a she, and that was never good news for a man who lied for a living.

# CHAPTER 12

The phone rang just as Mac got under the shower. Capping the water, he walked into the living area of the suite and answered.

'You called?' came the snippy voice of Chester Delaney, the Aussie consul-general, whose offices were around the corner from the Grand.

'Nice to hear from you too, mate,' said Mac, water dripping off him in the sticky heat of late afternoon. 'Thought we could catch up for that beer.'

Delaney sighed. 'Where?'

'Majestic roof, seventeen hundred?'

'I think we can dispense with the army affectations, can't we?'

'Just testing, Chezza,' said Mac.

'And why the Majestic?' said Delaney. 'Can't you come up for a coffee?'

'I don't approach consular property when I'm in the field,' said Mac. 'Protects me, protects you.'

'Okay,' said the diplomat. 'Five it is.'

Throwing a towel on the parquet floor, Mac started with fifty push-ups, followed by a hundred crunches and then forty lunges with each leg, finishing with five minutes of basic ballet exercises.

Letting the warm shower water run off him, Mac decided on minimal involvement from the consul-general. It was courtesy for someone in Mac's position to touch base and announce to the chief what he was doing, but in embassies and consulates the community was more like a colony – people didn't always like a blow-in from Australia spying on one of their own. Instead, he was going to pump Delaney for background, and then have little to do with him. There was a building behind the Hotel Rex where the Australian government kept serviced offices, one of which featured the shingle *Southern Scholastic Books Pty Ltd*. It had secure computers and data connections, and a phone line that was virtually impossible to hack. That would be Mac's base in Saigon, and would double as a crib should the Grand prove too open to the Cong An. The Black Stork would be the fallback.

Drying off, Mac placed his new clothes in a paper bag and screwed it up before dressing in his chinos and polo shirt. The new clothes might trigger someone's memory, so they'd be in a dumpster before he ventured out.

Dialling a Singapore number, Mac walked onto the balcony, hoping that by talking outside the room he'd defeat the political police's listening devices. His bag had been expertly looked through and his diary and book sales catalogues had been read – just as he'd wanted. But you never really knew about bugs.

'Benny,' said Mac, as Haskell came on the line. 'How we looking?'

Benny didn't waste time. 'Can you talk?'

'Listening is better.'

'Okay, mate – it's good news and bad. She's fine.'

'But?'

'But she's left the house and fucked off.'

'Where to?' asked Mac.

'Our friends say she's jumped a plane to Melbourne.'

'Screw them,' said Mac, who'd tell a lie like that to rival spooks as a knee-jerk reaction. 'What do you think?'

'She's done the Harold,' said Benny. 'But if she's worried about Aussie intel then I agree. Why would she be flying to Melbourne?'

Mac rubbed his face.

'There's something we should talk about,' said Benny, 'and not over the phone.'

'What?' asked Mac.

'Our friends' involvement,' said Benny.

'What about it?' said Mac, thinking the ISD had circled back after Ray's death and kept an eye on Liesl.

Benny's voice lowered. 'You're assuming our friends became curious *after* a certain incident.'

'What?' said Mac.

'I can't stay on this line – I'll call later,' said Benny, and hung up.

Looking at the handset as if for an answer, Mac was astonished. Singapore's ISD had been watching Ray Hu? Had he been made as an Aussie SIS agent? That would explain why Liesl had been asked to open Ray's safe, been taken for a long ride, had the facts of life explained before being put on a plane. It was standard procedure for intelligence services when they were clearing up a spy network: give all associates the no-tears option before moving to interrogations and lengthy trials for espionage. If that was the scenario Benny had been talking about, then Liesl would have spilled her guts and taken the fast way out. But if she was really worried about Canberra, she would have stayed in South-East Asia.


'You're not going to get me drunk, you know, McQueen,' said Chester Delaney as the waiter deposited two more ice-cold Tigers on the table.

They were sitting on the rooftop of the Majestic as the sun set on the Saigon River, the lush green of Vietnam's former battlefields evident in the distance.

'Don't worry, Chezza,' said Mac. 'Just a couple of looseners.'

'Okay, but can we drop the Chezza? It's Chester, actually.'

Mac raised his glass. 'Okay, Chester.'

Slumping slightly, Delaney removed his wire-framed glasses and massaged his eyeballs, his long fingers reaching around his bony nose.

'I'm sorry, Alan,' he said, cleaning his glasses and replacing them over piercing grey eyes. 'I seem to get on the wrong foot with you, without ever intending to.'

'Wouldn't worry about it,' said Mac.

'I wanted to debrief, after Kuta,' Delaney said, referring to the night of the Bali bombings, when he had been flown down from Jakarta to run the DFAT response and Mac had been sent in to control the media output. 'I said some things that I regretted.'

'Like what? Jenny Toohey has a great arse?'

'No!' said Delaney, blushing. 'No, when you were running around trying to find – what was it? – Pakistani terrorists, when you were supposed to be running the media side for us. I needed you, Alan, and you'd palmed it off onto those kids.'

'Yeah, I did.'

'I was cranky with you but, as it turned out, you were probably chasing something far more important.'

'They weren't really kids, mate,' said Mac, remembering the young DFAT and AFP staffers who'd run the media operation under Mac's aegis. 'I thought they were up for it – that bird Julie was basically running the show when I got there.'

'You're probably right,' said Delaney, relaxing some more. 'She jumped a couple of grades pretty quickly after that. Made director, last I heard.'

'Let's talk about Jim,' said Mac.

'Let's.'

'Like, what's not in the brief?'

'Okay,' said Delaney, taking a swig of the beer. 'The absences from his desk, the rather loose diary, and something I didn't want to put in writing.'

'Okay.'

'The Saigon chamber of commerce put on a big mining expo ten days ago, in the convention centre.'

'Yes?' said Mac.

'And Jim wasn't there.'

'Not there? I thought he was the trade guy for us in Saigon?'

'So did we,' said Delaney. 'I covered for him but it was embarrassing. We had some big companies come up here and we like to have a few beers, do a barbie and invite other nationalities over – it's a big networking event, and Jim Quirk was AWOL.'

'You must have an idea,' said Mac, trying to work out what wasn't being said. 'I'm not exactly the soft option.'

Delaney laughed. 'No, you're not. That wasn't my call, but I've come to agree that we should keep it in-house, hence the Firm.'

'So, what's the theory?'

'Well, people have seen him in Cholon – Chinatown,' said Delaney. 'It's not damning but he's been looking terrible and there're fears about who he's hanging around with, I suppose.'

'Think he's spying?'

'I don't know,' said Delaney.

'Any top-secret access?'

'He's TS-PV,' said Delaney, meaning Jim Quirk had Australia's highest non-codeword security clearance, with a PV or personal vetting. 'But he's no longer seeing anything sensitive.'

'What's this about the divorce?' said Mac. 'He on the sauce?'

'Definitely,' nodded Delaney. 'He split with Geraldine recently and it went downhill from there.'

'The drinking followed the divorce, or the other way around?' said Mac, trying to set the scene.

'Can't remember,' said Delaney. 'I wouldn't want to get that part wrong. What I do know is that I've been waiting two weeks to get someone up here. We kept being told to let Jim run, that we'd have a team soon.'

'Is he stealing anything?' said Mac. 'I mean, illegal downloads or files tucked down his shirt?'

'Our dip-security guy's been keeping an eye on him – hasn't caught him doing anything.'

'Where does Quirk live?' said Mac, wondering if he should be having this chat with the first assistant secretary, diplomatic security – also known as the dip-sec.

'At An Puh,' said Delaney. An Puh was the expat compound across the river in District 2. 'The BP compound. He's got an apartment near the supermarket, I'm told.'

'He drives?'

'A red Corolla.'

'What time does he get in to work?'

'Eight-thirty.'

'Okay,' said Mac, slugging at the beer. 'But tell me – why am I up here? What happened to the resident in Hanoi?'

Delaney smiled. 'Can't use any of the Firm's people down here if they've been in Hanoi, Hong Kong, Shangers, Beijing or Seoul.'

'No?'

'No, Alan,' said Delaney. 'The Chinese know exactly who they are. If we used them on Jim, the Chinese would have an insight we don't particularly want to share.'

# CHAPTER 13

Emerging from the double doors of the Grand at 7.28 am, Mac turned sharp right and walked up Dong Khoi Street. The one-way traffic came towards him in the first trickles of what would be a deluge in half an hour; Mac was hoping to make any vehicle tails show themselves by having to turn against the traffic or make a box-loop to catch him at an intersection.

Before he could get to the next intersection, Mac crossed the street to the cover of trees on the other side, and ducked up the side street to a cafe where he ordered coffee and an omelette and watched for unwanted interest.

The coffee was dark and strong and he picked up a day-old *Jakarta Post* from a pile of newspapers by the cutlery and flipped it as he surveyed the street. The anchor story along the bottom of the *Post*'s front page carried the headline MISSILE TESTS PROVOCATIVE: CLINTON, and was followed by the regular Asian media obsession with the North Korean missile tests, predicting whether they would fly over Japan and their boosters fall in Japanese waters. While few countries in the western Pacific were friendly with North Korea, the region held its breath for the day Japan had an excuse to abandon its self-defence force and start rebuilding its military. Mac chuckled grimly as he read the US Secretary of State's careful words: they reflected the delicate situation America found itself in whenever it stood between the two Koreas, Japan and China. If diplomacy in the Middle East took place over a gunpowder factory, North Asian rapport was built on a thermonuclear trigger.

Across the road two youths tried to strap a large sofa onto the roof of a tiny Suzuki van as all around them people came out of doorways and started motorbikes or clipped their trousers before they got on bicycles. Pretty soon the flow of motorbikes, carts and vans would hit full force as the locals went in search of a living.

Even though he considered himself an experienced traveller, Mac was always confused by Saigon. How did Ho Chi Minh ever think he was going to make the people of the Mekong Delta adopt communism? Or even aggressive socialism? Like most Aussies of his generation, Mac had been raised on post-1975 Vietnam as a story of 'reunification' in the face of imperialist France and the United States. Yet most people living in the south of Vietnam saw 1975 as a Communist invasion and subsequent occupation.

Convinced he wasn't being tailed, Mac keyed the phone and gave Tranh the okay to pick him up.

Climbing into the silver van four minutes later, Mac kept looking through the back window until they'd turned right and accelerated for Le Loi.

'Where to, boss?' asked Tranh, who Mac noticed was now wearing a small silver crucifix.

'BP compound, An Puh,' said Mac, grabbing the water that Tranh had left for him on the floor. 'I think it's called APSC now.'

Crossing the Saigon Bridge heading north, they stuck with the flow of the traffic on Hanoi Highway for a few minutes and took a left turn into Tao Dhien Road, a quiet residential street that looked more like a suburb in Brisbane than Saigon.

On their right loomed a supermarket, indicating the beginning of the huge expat residential compound that extended to the river. Mac asked Tranh to keep driving as if going to the end of the street.

Doing a u-turn and pulling in at the kerbside a hundred metres short of the compound entrance gate, they stopped the van and rolled down the windows as the heat rose.

Tranh lit a cigarette. 'We going to follow?'

'Just establish his route,' said Mac, pulling field-glasses from the glove box and getting eyes on the gate. 'I want to get a feel for his day.'

At 8.08 am, a red Corolla stuck its nose out of the compound's gate and Mac lifted the glasses. It was Jim Quirk.

'Okay, Mr Tranh,' said Mac, 'let's see your field craft.'

Following Quirk at between three and ten car lengths, Tranh was an excellent tail, sometimes letting the Corolla get a long way ahead, and at other times pulling up near to it but in another lane. The best tailers broke the pattern that people like Mac looked for.

Crossing to the west side of Saigon Bridge, Quirk went into the massive roundabout and made a looping left turn onto Nguyen Huru and drove south past the water treatment plant, following the river. As they drew parallel with the shipyards on their left, Mac lost interest in Quirk and turned in his seat to see who was behind them.

'Shit,' said Mac. 'See that white Toyota?'

'Cong An,' said Tranh with a shrug. 'They found us after we crossed the bridge.'

Mac saw a coffee cart ahead, just past the Buddhist pagoda. 'Pull in here,' he said.

Watching the white Camry sail past, Mac lifted his field-glasses and focused on the registration plate. It was the same car that had followed him to the market.

Mac pointed. 'Okay, let's find Apricot again.'

They wound southwards, through the heavy traffic, but Mac and Tranh had to stop at the lights where Nguyen turned left into the riverside drive, and they lost the red Corolla.

'Okay,' said Mac, slugging on the water, 'let's do a box, come around to the Landmark building the wrong way.'

Tranh took a secondary street running parallel to Quirk. Then they turned and went with the traffic down Dong Khoi Street, hooked left and drove north up the riverside road towards the consulate.

'All okay, boss?' said Tranh as they drove clear of the Landmark.

'Depends what you mean by okay,' said Mac as they passed the white Camry, parked and waiting beyond the consulate. 'If we need the Cong An to help us follow Quirk, then we're great.'

* * *

Shortly before midday, James Quirk walked out of the consulate and headed for the bus stop. Keeping a good distance behind the Cong An, Mac and Tranh followed Quirk's bus into Cholon – the world's largest Chinatown. Situated about a ten-minute drive from Mac's hotel in downtown, Cholon had a reputation for harbouring some of the hardest criminals and canniest entrepreneurs in South-East Asia. Whether you wanted your husband murdered or to shift massive amounts of cash to another country, you could get it done in Cholon. Mac's overwhelming memory of Cholon was of a place with a million bookmakers. Fancy a bet on a cockfight in a storeroom, a bare-knuckle fight on a local gangster's rooftop, a girl fight in a warehouse, or a horse race at the Puh To track? Cholon was where you found the odds. Cholon was an exporter of its culture: after the arrival of the Communists in 1975, it was harder for the Cholon tongs – the crime families – to make a living, and the South Vietnamese diaspora included a lot of Cholon criminals. By the 1980s, the kidnap gangs of Hong Kong, the casinos of Macao and the cage fighting in Bangkok and Manila were all run and protected by the spitting patriarchs of Cholon – old men who lived humbly above shoe-repair shops and controlled rivers of cash around the South China Sea.

Jumping off at a bus stop, Quirk – in a light charcoal suit and no tie – hit the pavement and kept walking, scything through the milling locals, around a corner and into a side street.

'Quick,' said Mac, as the watcher Mac had met on the motorbike got out of the Camry and followed Quirk. 'Right here, and head him off at the pass.'

Accelerating down a parallel side street, Tranh slowed at the mangle of cyclos and motorbikes at the next intersection and turned left. As the streetscape opened up, Mac watched Quirk dart across the street and disappear into a club called Mekong Saloon. But it was the action around the club that Mac noticed. Frantically, Mac looked around him: one man sat at a bus stop bench; he folded his paper as Quirk entered the building, turned and walked away.

'Keep moving,' snapped Mac, his breath coming shallow and fast. 'Don't look around.'

Tranh sped north, down Hau Giang and out of Cholon.

'You get that third item Paragon would have mentioned?' said Mac, when they were almost back at the riverfront.

'Yes, Mr Richard.'

'Good. Show me.'

Parking in an alley north of the Landmark building, Tranh led Mac down to a series of small private jetties on the river.

'What happened back there?' said Tranh.

'I'm trying to work it out,' said Mac, thinking about the men around that nightclub: not Cong An and not Aussie intel.

At the end of the jetty, Tranh stopped at a powerboat with a large black outboard motor on the back. Climbing into the cockpit after Tranh, Mac watched him unlock the small hatchway to the space under the bow deck. Climbing down, Tranh grabbed a steel box off the small mattress and slid it across the cockpit. Picking up a stainless-steel Ruger handgun from the box, Mac weighed one of the two 9mm clips that came with it and then slipped it into the handgrip and slammed it home.

Mac looked around the small marina. 'No Hecklers, eh?' He usually used a Heckler & Koch P9s.

'No, boss – but Ruger is okay, right?'

'Ruger is great,' said Mac, stashing the handgun in its box.

Having established his regular meeting places with Tranh – a rotation of four cafes around Dong Khoi Street at nine each morning – Mac asked Tranh to time Quirk's return to the consulate. If his trips were regular, it made things easier and faster.

Walking along the riverside boulevard, Mac tried to recall everything about the man he'd seen waiting outside the Mekong Saloon. Euro in looks, but not in dress: 1980s sunnies, the Sansabelt trousers and the shoes just short of nerdy. As if someone had tried too hard to dress down, or had never lived with a woman.

And it wasn't just that man: Mac had seen another two, just the same, acting casual around the Mekong. They weren't cops and they weren't Asian.

Mac wandered into the shade of the Cyclo Cafe and slumped in a wicker armchair. He needed a cold beer, and then he needed to work out why another team was tailing Jim Quirk.

# CHAPTER 14

Finishing his Operation Dragon update on the codeword-secure computer at Southern Scholastic Books, Mac hit 'send' and watched the intranet system issue a log number and time/date/location stamp for the filed report. Then, having made a pot of coffee at the small kitchenette at the back of the first-floor office suite, he picked up the secure desktop phone and dialled.

'Scotty, it's Mac,' he said when the phone was picked up.

Intelligence officers sent reports in the Firm's format, not unlike the way newspaper stories had a certain structure. But if it wasn't going to endanger the operation, Mac also liaised directly with his case officer.

'Macca, how are we doing?'

'In place, made contact with Apricot today.'

'Route?'

'Into Cholon, to a nightclub that's open during the day.'

'The Mekong Saloon?'

'You know it?'

'It's a Loh Han property. You read the file, right, Macca? They've got places in Vung Tau, Nha Trang and around Saigon.'

'Yeah, yeah,' said Mac, distracted. 'I read it.'

'You all right? Drinking heaps of fluids?'

'Yeah, mate,' said Mac, pushing the coffee aside and reaching for the water bottle. 'Any further intel on Quirk?'

'No. We asked Chester and his security guy to hold off on the questions. Why, what's up?'

'I don't know,' said Mac, trying to form the thought. 'It was just . . . there was this guy outside the Saloon this arvo. I didn't like it.'

'Surveillance?'

'Probably, but I couldn't be certain.'

'Asian?'

'Euro,' said Mac. 'Mediterranean Euro.'

Scotty scoffed. 'That's it?'

'I didn't like the set-up.'

'You're hinky,' said Scotty.

'Don't start that paperback detective stuff,' said Mac.

'Got a pic?' said Scotty.

'I didn't want to use the camera,' said Mac. 'The Cong An's been hanging round the hotel and following me in the street.'

'Okay,' said Scotty, knowing that a camera full of surveillance photos had been the downfall of too many intelligence officers. 'I might send up this whiz-kid from Bangers.'

'Oh really?' said Mac, reluctant to have someone foisted on him. 'Who?'

'Lance Kendrick – one of the new guard.'

'Shit,' said Mac. Aussie intelligence had been finding it harder to recruit youngsters from university who hadn't used drugs, who didn't have tattoos and who didn't lie in interviews. ASIS was recruiting so many women because they didn't seem to lie as much as the young blokes, and 'new guard' was code for men who ten years earlier would never have made it past the second interview.

'Yeah, his thing is *technology*,' said Scotty, as though it was shameful. 'Knows about BlueBerries and Tweetering – all that shit.'

'Can he use a telephoto?'

'Yep.'

'Run a concealed video? Wire a car for sound? Won't get me light beer when he goes to the bar?'

'Yes, yes, yes, mate,' said Scotty. 'He does cyber counter-measures, and he's a whiz with getting data out of phones and making phantom chat sites or whatever they're called. He's done rotations with the NSA. He's one of these modern spooks, mate – gonna put us out of business.'

'I don't care how modern he is,' said Mac. 'Don't send me some spinner.'

'Thought you might like to hear some post-modern theories about how the Vatican is worse than Hitler's –'

'Watch it, mate,' said Mac.

'–Third Reich, or how the White House is the same as al-Qaeda.'

'I'll give him a first-hand demonstration of what al-Qaeda's internal security people do to defectors,' Mac said. 'And it's a little meaner than outing some diplomat's wife as CIA.'

Scotty turned serious. 'Look, he's an individual but he's smart and he's trained.'

'I don't care if he's one of a kind,' said Mac. 'If he's got a pierced tongue and he's taking ecstasy, then he'll come back to you in a diplomatic pouch, minus a few teeth. Got that, mate?'

Scotty laughed. 'Sure.'

'Deadset, Scotty,' said Mac, looking around him. 'Saigon is no place for a spy who wants to stand out.'

Locking up the offices, Mac skipped down the stairs and into the brightness of the street. Squinting, he reached for his sunnies and decided it was time to buy a couple of trop shirts before he started swimming in his polo.


The shop owner folded the green, black and sky-blue trop shirts on a large piece of brown paper, and then put Mac's polo shirt on top.

'That twenty dollar, mister,' said the man, giving Mac a wink as he sellotaped the brown paper parcel and slipped it into a plastic bag.

Handing over two US ten-dollar notes, Mac grabbed the bag and adjusted to the loose fit of the dark blue trop shirt he was wearing. With the pre-monsoon humidity he needed something that ventilated itself, although he usually avoided wearing them:

fifty years of CIA men charging around South-East Asia dressed like Ferdi Marcos had made many Asians think that a white man in a trop shirt was armed.

'I like that colour,' said a woman's voice, close enough that Mac jumped slightly.

Turning to his right, Mac came almost eye to eye with a tall Vietnamese woman, her long black hair pulled back in a ponytail.

'Guess the humidity makes our visitors dress local,' she said, an Aussie accent evident in her English. 'My dad always wore the ones with the silk-cotton blend this time of year.'

'Yeah,' said Mac, trying to make light. 'I think mine's a —'

The shop owner interrupted, running around the counter and grabbing Mac by the collar. 'See, it silk, it silk,' said the owner, nodding furiously at what Mac assumed was the tag of his shirt.

Tensing as he realised the owner was scared, Mac heard the woman rattle off a Vietnamese phrase that sounded something like, *It's okay, no trouble.*

'Wow,' said Mac, looking for her backup at the glass entry. 'Making sure I'm not overcharged, eh? This must be the tourist police?'

'No,' said the woman. 'Just the police.'

'Okay,' said Mac, keeping the smile on his face.

'Let's talk,' she said, and led Mac to the door of the shop, her black slacks swishing.

Mac thought about running out the back door and into the alley, making a dash for it. But he knew that if he went out that door there'd be more Cong An and perhaps a long stay in the basement of some shithole.

Pushing the colonial door back on its spring hinge, the woman pulled down her sunglasses and waited for Mac. Walking past her, his heart pounded up into his chest as he emerged onto Dong Du Street and looked around, feeling like a tin duck on a sideshow rail.

'Tea?' said the woman, perhaps enjoying Mac's discomfort.

'Well . . .' he said, making a show of looking at his watch.

At the kerbside the Cong An from the back of the motorbike sat in the passenger seat of a white Camry, chewing gum.

'Come on,' she said, flicking her head. 'Green tea with a dose of jasmine — it's the best cure for the heat.'

Mac followed her into a cafe. Casing the other customers and the rear exit as he sat, Mac assessed his chances of attacking the cop and using her as a shield so he could leave out the back. But he couldn't see a gun on her – the slacks and the simple white blouse didn't leave much room for a holster.

'Name's Richard,' he said calmly.

'I know,' she said. 'Richard Davis, books executive, from Brisbane.'

'Nice work,' said Mac. 'Have to beat that out of the night manager?'

'No,' she said seriously, before realising she'd missed the joke. 'I'm Captain Loan,' she said, pronouncing it low-arn.

'Captain?' said Mac, shaking the hand she'd offered. 'That's a pretty name.'

'Ha!' said Loan, her glacial demeanour cracking for a second. 'It's Chanthe – Chanthe Loan.'

'That's an Aussie accent,' said Mac, as the tea service was placed on the table by a stooped old woman. In Vietnam the women never seemed to stop working, even the old ones.

'Sure,' said Loan. 'Last two years of high school in Melbourne and then Monash for three years.'

'What did you study?'

'BA – philosophy major,' said Loan, pushing her sunnies up into her hair. Mac put her at thirty-four, thirty-five. 'Now some questions for you, Mr Richard.'

'Sure,' said Mac.

'How well do you know James Quirk?'

Mac liked her craft – she built the assumption into the question, so to answer was to verify the assumption.

'I don't,' said Mac, sipping the tea. 'I know of him.'

'How?'

'Years ago, when I was starting in the books business, he hosted an Aussie exporters bash up in Manila. I was at the barbecue and the piss-up.'

'You were in Manila?'

'Sure,' said Mac, warming to his back story. 'And we're in Indonesia, Malaysia, Singapore, Thailand, Cambodia and Vietnam.'

'I don't care about *we*, Mr Richard,' she said with a patient smile. 'It's you I'm interested in.'

'Okay.'

'This is your fourth visit to Vietnam?'

Mac shrugged. 'That many?'

'Sell many books?'

'Not enough, I'm afraid,' said Mac. 'There's only one buyer in Vietnam so there's not many ways into the market. You come runner-up in the beauty parade, there's no one else to dance with.'

The captain levelled a cold stare at him. Mac reckoned she was wondering whether his reply was an insult to communist governments or a fair depiction of doing business with them.

'What about Mrs Geraldine?' said Loan. 'His wife.'

'What?' said Mac, genuinely surprised. 'Quirk's wife?'

'Yes – Geraldine McHugh.'

'Never met her,' said Mac, trying to figure out what she was getting at. 'I don't know Jim Quirk either, except to say hi.'

'So you do know him?'

'Except to say Hi, remember me from that trade barbecue in Manila? I was the one who got pissed and knew all the moves to "Greased Lightning."'

She smiled quickly and recovered. 'Never met Mrs Geraldine?'

'Look, Captain Loan – I met Jim once, years ago. I've never met Geraldine. Can you tell me what this is about?' Mac tried to hold her gaze as she stared at him.

'I thought you'd tell *me* what this is about,' said Loan.

Standing, she downed the remaining tea and shook Mac's hand. 'Thank you, Mr Richard,' she said. 'I'll be in touch tomorrow.'

'Tomorrow?' said Mac, watching Loan move to the door. 'Why tomorrow?'

'That's when you tell me why a man who doesn't know Jim Quirk is waiting outside his house.'

As she walked away, Mac wondered if this woman was going to be a problem. His mind spinning, he became aware of the tea woman standing over him.

'One dollar, mister,' she said, jutting out her chin. 'You pay now.'

# CHAPTER 15

The streets got darker the further Mac's cyclo ventured into the sector of Saigon that sat between the huge boulevards of Ham Nghi and Nguyen Hue. Rounding a corner, Mac found himself in a street which was home to a market in the day, a place where hotel managers warned the tourists against going.

Paying the rider, Mac slipped out of the cyclo seat and clocked the washing lines that spanned the street three storeys up, the kids squatting at buckets of water on the footpath, having their evening bath, and the tiny restaurants and cafes that advertised themselves with a paper lantern hanging over the doorway. The whole place reeked of old cabbage and dry sewer drains.

Walking into a dimly lit hole in the wall called the Green Duck, Mac spotted Tranh against the wall and sat beside him.

'Eaten yet, Mr Richard?' said Tranh, who was sitting cross-legged on the chair, eating with chopsticks from a bowl.

'I'll have what you're having,' said Mac. 'And a beer.'

When Tranh yelled at the man in a singlet behind the counter, Mr Singlet had to stop yelling at his wife, who was also yelling. The duo stopped and stared at Mac, but within forty-five seconds Mac had a bowl of duck and noodles and an icy Tiger beer.

'Got the alternative vehicle?' said Mac, when Mr Singlet had gone back to the open kitchen and resumed the marital yelling contest.

Tranh finished his duck and wiped his chin. 'Out the front.'

'Good.' Mac didn't want to rely on a van the cops were interested in. 'But before we head off, let's get a few rules out of the way, okay?'

'Okay.'

'Actually, there's only one rule I want to talk about. We're a loop of two – we have a conversation, and it doesn't get reported to anyone else, okay?'

'Okay, Mr Richard,' said Tranh.

'So it's a choice, and I'm giving you the choice right now,' he said, pointing his chopsticks at Tranh. 'If you want to drop out of this gig, you can walk away now, tonight. You'll get paid, no hard feelings.'

Tranh gulped. 'Yes, Mr Richard.'

'So – you in or out?'

Tranh looked Mac in the eye. It was an intelligent and honest face. 'I'm with you, Mr Richard.'

'Okay, Tranh,' said Mac slowly. 'Then we are the loop, and that means no more talking to Captain Loan. Understand?'

Tranh's face dropped. 'I'm sorry, Mr Richard.'

'I don't care about sorry, mate,' said Mac, feeling for the bloke. 'When people leak it's always the innocents who get hurt. So you need to feed Captain Loan, keep her happy, but tell me first and we'll put some sugar in her coffee, okay?'

'Sugar?' said Tranh.

'Keep her sweet,' said Mac.

'How did –'

'She didn't give you up, so don't worry about that,' said Mac, smiling. 'I worked it out.'

'How?'

'She asked me about everyone in Saigon,' said Mac, 'except the bloke driving the Uc around in the van.'


The Mekong Saloon was lit up and buzzing as they made their first pass, Mac riding pillion on Tranh's motorbike. It wasn't how Mac enjoyed travelling but in Saigon it was fast and anonymous, and he liked that Tranh had a solid 400cc trail bike, not one of the flimsy step-throughs.

Circling back, they parked in a service alley and Mac pulled some money out of his pocket. 'Buy a magazine, get some food from a vendor,' said Mac, handing over some dong. 'Just stay in sight of the entrance, okay?'

Walking across the road, he remembered something. 'And stay off the phone – I don't care if your mum or girlfriend calls, keep the line free, okay?'

Nodding to the doorman – a squat Filipino – Mac slipped into the Saloon. It was a dark, loud pit, with a mix of the young crowd and expat businesspeople.

Moving to the busy but not crowded bar, Mac ordered a beer and looked across the auditorium, a space dressed up to look like an old French saloon. It was expensively fitted out, except that where the can-can dancers should have been were naked women of various stripes, squirming around shiny poles to a disco version of ZZ Top's 'Arrested for Driving While Blind'.

'Mot Tiger, cam on,' said Mac as the barman swaggered over and threw his vodka bottle in the air, catching it backhand. Dickhead Barman was a language spoken all over the world.

Paying with dong, Mac moved to a stand-up table near the far wall, checking for eyes. He may have been slightly ahead of himself by entering the club, but now that the Cong An was taking an interest in Quirk he wanted to push the operation along, stick his nose where it didn't belong before the fuzz scared everyone away.

'New wee, mister,' said the young girl with the bag of magazines and newspapers. 'Tine, new wee, new paper?'

Putting a day-old South China Morning Post on his table, she gave him the look and Mac sighed, pulled out some dong and gave it to her.

As the child walked away to harass a table of German tourists, Mac realised there was a mezzanine floor looking down on the main room. It looked quieter up there; if nothing else it would be a much better place from which to survey the club.

Mac stepped over the rope across the stairs and ascended into semi-darkness where the tables and chairs sat in an eerie silence compared to the noise down below. There was a disused bar, secured by a pull-down grille; there were two locked doors along the rear wall and a corridor at the end of the balcony section.

Moving to the balcony rail, Mac looked down on the pole dancers, but kept his head back.

His phone vibrated against his leg and he answered it immediately.

'Hey, mate,' he said to Tranh.

'I think Apricot's on his way,' said Tranh, breathless. 'A car just pulled up and they got out and walked into the club. I called as fast —'

'They?'

'Apricot and three others,' said Tranh.

'Locals?' said Mac, sticking his head over the balcony. Below him two Euros in trop shirts pushed through the club, a third bringing up the rear. Between them, and not looking happy, was Jim Quirk.

'Okay, mate,' said Mac, 'I see 'em. Keep the lines open and bring the bike to the front.'

Ringing off, he watched the leader — a burly, bald guy with a red shirt — unhitch the rope on the stairs and wave the rest of them through.

Pulling back into the shadows, Mac found a dark alcove and decided to observe. He didn't want to go back to Scotty and admit he'd blown the operation because he'd been blueing in a strip club in Chinatown. Besides, he wasn't armed, and the way those trop shirts were hanging he figured Quirk's friends were.

Spilling into the mezzanine area just ten metres away, the two thugs pushed Quirk against the wall and stood around him, hands on hips. Quirk, still in his suit, was a mess; it looked like he'd been crying.

Approaching the group, the man in the red shirt walked up and kneed Quirk in the balls, grabbing a handful of hair as the Australian bent double.

'We were just starting to make friends, eh, Jimbo?' said Red Shirt in an accent that may have been Turkish or Bulgarian. 'And now, you make me very angry.'

'I've done what you wanted,' said Jim, purple in the face.

'No, Jimbo,' said Red Shirt, as he nodded his head at a henchman. 'I don't care about the codes – the deal wasn't the codes, the deal was access.'

One of the henchmen peeled away from the group, unlocked a door and walked through, light spilling out.

'So, Jimbo,' continued Red Shirt. 'We're going back to the computer, and we'll start again, and then everyone's happy. Okay?'

As they moved towards the open door, Mac's heart pumped in his neck. He'd heard enough. Quirk was selling something – codes, access, whatever – to foreign nationals, and if he could extract the traitor from this mess, the Firm could take it from there, do the debriefs and the prosecutions. But right now he couldn't just stand by and let a bunch of Turks slap an Aussie consular official. It didn't work that way for Mac.

Red Shirt slapped at his trouser pocket and gabbled something in a foreign language to the henchman in the white trop shirt. Mac knew that language but couldn't place it. Not Turkish . . . perhaps Hungarian?

The henchie took off for the stairs and vaulted down them. Stealthing back to the balcony, Mac watched him stride out of the club. Forty seconds later, he was walking back into the Mekong Saloon, jiggling something in his hand and making straight for the mezzanine stairs.

Red Shirt had disappeared into the room with Quirk and the door had almost swung shut. Moving to the head of the stairs, Mac ducked down and waited for the footfalls to reach the top. As the white shirt rose above the banister wall, Mac powered off his right leg and threw a fast right-hand uppercut. He caught the thug on the right jaw rather than the point of the chin and the victim staggered backwards but not off his feet. Throwing a left elbow into the bloke's temple, Mac followed it with a straight right in his teeth which sent the man into the wall, spraying the white shirt with blood.

Using the wall for balance, the man stood straight and kicked Mac in the groin as he reached back for his handgun. Doubled over with the kick, Mac managed to keep the momentum going forwards and launched himself into a basic finger-strike to the eyes. As the man's hands came up to his face in a reflex action, Mac threw a hand hold under the bloke's chin and swept with his left leg, slamming the thug to the ground and smashing his head into the carpet.

Mac pushed the thug's jaw to one side and struck him hard with a carotid punch to the neck. Watching the man's eyelids flutter and his eyes roll back, Mac shoved his hand under the trop shirt and pulled out a matt-black SIG Sauer handgun.

Checking for load and safety, Mac dropped the clip into his hand and saw it wasn't full – four, maybe five rounds remaining. As he heaved for breath in the semi-darkness, the voice of Red Shirt echoed out into the mezzanine – Mac's victim was being called.

Moving along the wall, Mac tried to work his chest to control his breathing. He was nervous and sparking with adrenaline, and he made himself do what they used to tell them in the Royal Marines Commandos: if you couldn't control anything else in your environment, at least control your breathing.

Gulping as he got to the doorway, he took a deep diaphragm breath and eased around the corner, squinting slightly into the fluorescent light. Holding the gun cup-and-saucer, he pushed on the door and as it swung back he arced back and forth, waiting for the shot opportunity. But it wasn't a room. He was looking down a corridor, with a security door at the end.

'Shit!' he said, standing back a half pace and checking on the thug in the white shirt: still dazed.

Looking down the hallway again, Mac saw a potential trap. He saw bad odds, he saw zero element of surprise, he saw a situation that gave his wife the right to say, *You said no more field work!*

Mac's breathing had slowed to normal but his pulse thumped in his temples as he moved down the corridor as fast as he could without running. The gun's hatched grip swimming in his hand, he checked on the door – it was locked.

Tapping on it with the SIG, he mumbled a generically male series of monosyllables and stood back, holding the weapon against his thigh. Watching the handle move down until it clicked, Mac took two steps forwards and brought his foot up parallel to the ground in a hard kick, sending his hundred and five kilos into a small point above the lock.

Hearing the grunt of surprise as the steel door flew back and whacked into flesh, Mac thumped open the door with his left shoulder and burst into a small room, gun held in two hands. The thug lying on the floor was groggy and his forehead was split from the blow, but he had managed to pull a handgun from his waistband. Throwing himself to his side, Mac shot the thug in the face and then throat before rolling once and springing into a crouch as he looked around for Red Shirt.

Blood poured across the lino and Mac panted like an animal, tasting the gunpowder residue in his throat. Rising slowly, nightclub music pounding in the background, Mac realised there was a glass panel along the wall he had rolled into. Behind the glass was another room from which two men stared back at him: Jim Quirk, seated in front of a computer terminal, and Red Shirt, who placed a handgun against Quirk's head.

Red Shirt smiled, his tanned face crinkling with mirth, eyes black like a shark's. Mac moved to the door of the glass-sided room and kicked it open, keeping his weapon trained on Red Shirt.

'You're on private property, sir,' said the man, screwing his handgun into Quirk's head as he got a handful of the Aussie's hair.

'The only private property is the bloke sitting in front of you,' said Mac. 'Let him go and we all walk away.'

'Ah, another Aussie,' said the hostage-taker, manoeuvring himself behind Quirk, who was stiff with anxiety. 'But you've come far enough, my friend.'

The sound of the gun's hammer being cocked was obvious in the confined space but Mac kept his stolen gun trained on the man's forehead. 'I don't care what this is about, but it can end in two ways.'

'Two?' said the gunman, eyeing the computer screen, which had become very active, lines of numbers and letters seeming to spill down the page.

'In one, you live,' said Mac, aware that Quirk had now closed his eyes. 'In the other, I kill you.'

Red Shirt stayed cool. Reaching over Quirk's shoulder, he hit a button on the computer, which then seemed to die. His hand moved lower, to a series of ports, and as he tried to pull a chip from one of the holes, the memory card fell from his fingers and bounced on the floor.

Raising the gun in a threat at Mac, Red Shirt turned slightly and tapped a code into a keypad on the wall and pulled at another security door.

'Okay, Mr Aussie,' said the gunman in the red shirt. 'We do it the first way – we all walk away?'

'Let's see you,' said Mac, the SIG lined up perfectly between button-like eyes.

It happened in slow motion, like Mac was in a dream. The man in the red shirt pulled the door back, slipped a leg through it, and then simply lifted his gun and shot Jim Quirk in the right temple.

Leaping back as viscera flew, Mac recovered his shooter's stance but Red Shirt was out the door, the security bolts locking as it settled back into place.

'You'll keep, you bastard,' said Mac, grabbing the memory card and moving to the immovable security door as Jim Quirk's body collapsed on the floor. 'You'll bloody keep!'

# CHAPTER 16

Covering the hallway in what felt like three strides, Mac burst through the door into the mezzanine area.

The stunned thug was sitting up, resting back on his arms, and Mac kicked him in the jaw as he ran for the stairs, bounding down them into a sea of faces looking up, confused about the gunfire.

Mac crossed the club floor and ran headlong into the Filipino bouncer, who shouldered him into a wall in the entrance hall. Presenting the SIG, Mac shrugged: the doorman smiled and stood back. A girl waiting at the door rope started screaming as Mac emerged into the heat of the evening.

Tranh revved the bike directly beneath the marquee bulbs and Mac leapt onto the back, telling Tranh to circle behind the club.

Accelerating, they took the first left and motored through a darker side street, the motorbike seeming very loud among the smaller scooters and cyclos.

'There,' said Mac, pointing to a service alley at the club's rear. Dropping a gear, Tranh leaned the bike over and plunged between two oncoming cars into the inky blackness of the laneway, the headlight barely penetrating the obstacle course of old fruit boxes, dumpsters and rotting garbage.

'Slow it, mate,' said Mac into Tranh's ear as they neared the fenced compound behind the Mekong Saloon. Moving into the spill of the floodlights, Mac saw the open gate in the fence and three men standing on the concrete parking area. The European among them pointed at Mac, holding his jaw as he did so. Beside him, a solid Chinese man in a blue Mambo T-shirt reached for the small of his back.

'Go!' said Mac, and the motorbike surged down the alley. 'Kill the lights.'

Plunging them into blackness, Tranh kept the bike in second as slugs slammed into a dumpster and bounced off the bricks.

Two red tail-lights flashed at the end of the alley as a vehicle braked. Next thing they were accelerating right, revealing a dark SUV shape.

'That's the one,' yelled Tranh as he wound the power on, almost making Mac fall off the back of the bike as it picked up.

Hitting the headlights again, they narrowly missed a cat and ploughed through a puddle of sewage as they reached the end of the alley. Putting his left arm around Tranh's waist, Mac leaned into the turn as they inserted themselves into Cholon's traffic and leapt like a salmon into a Saturday night in Chinatown.

'That them?' yelled Mac, pointing the SIG at a dark green LandCruiser Prado two cars in front of them in the inside lane.

'That's them,' yelled Tranh, finding fourth and swerving in front of a van as he kept the momentum building straight down the double yellows, South-East Asia's 'third lane'.

Worrying about how many shooters might be in the LandCruiser, Mac motioned for Tranh to get alongside the vehicle. Moving over a lane, they got behind a small car which was going too slow. Stepping down a gear, Tranh swerved into the inside lane and poured on the power, accelerating past the small car and swerving in front of it, allowing them to ease adjacent to the LandCruiser.

Keeping the SIG behind his back, Mac waited until the bike was alongside the 4x4 before slowly turning to look at the driver. Through the open window Mac saw a Mediterranean heavy – Italian or Croatian – with a mo and earring.

Thinking they might have the wrong vehicle, Mac looked away momentarily and then looked back. The driver's lips had been moving, meaning someone was in there with him. The driver sneaked a quick look at the motorbike and then the passenger was leaning forwards and Mac was suddenly locking gazes with those dark eyes.

'Fuck,' said Mac, as Red Shirt's handgun came up in front of the driver's face and the bike surged ahead with such a blast that Mac's knees lifted up under Tranh's armpits.

'Sorry, boss,' said Tranh, who'd obviously seen the gun too.

The tail-light of the car in front of them exploded with a burst of red plastic and someone on the footpath screamed as Tranh screwed on the revs. It was almost nine o'clock and Cholon's entertainment district was just getting busy.

Now they were in front of the LandCruiser and another shot sounded as the bike careened down the crowded boulevard, its big engine thumping. Mac tightened his left arm around Tranh as they swerved out of their pursuers' headlights and into the third lane. The back-lit speedometer read ninety-five kph and Mac looked over his shoulder, saw the LandCruiser falling back in the traffic.

Ahead, a major set of lights had turned red and Mac realised they must be travelling eastbound, about to cross the major intersection which signalled the end of Cholon.

'Duck down there,' said Mac, pointing to the right side of the intersection.

Riding slowly in first gear, they moved with the pedestrians into the cross street, where they stopped and waited for the main boulevard traffic to go again.

'You can leave if you want,' said Mac, dismounting and checking the borrowed SIG. 'But I'll need the bike.'

'I'm driving,' said Tranh, no emotion.

'Shit,' said Mac, finding an empty clip and one round left in the spout.

'You want to follow them?' said Tranh, oblivious to their lack of firepower.

'Yeah, mate,' said Mac. 'Wait there.'

Pushing the SIG under his sweaty trop shirt, Mac walked to the corner. Peeking around the brick building, he saw the green LandCruiser in the middle lane of the boulevard.

'They're moving straight through,' said Mac, breathless as he got back on the bike. 'Let's see where they're going. I'm betting they'll change that vehicle.'

After one more block in the mainstream traffic, the LandCruiser turned right and moved into the dark colonial streets that led to the river. Intermittently killing the headlight to disguise their whereabouts, and drawing on a local's knowledge of which parallel streets would meet up, Tranh managed to stand off while also keeping contact with the 4x4.

Mac's mind raced. Who were this crew? What was Quirk involved in? What was familiar about Red Shirt? What *was* it about that guy?

Stopping behind a parked minivan, Tranh killed the engine and they watched the LandCruiser pull into an old-fashioned parking garage.

'Parking,' said Tranh, pointing. 'If they want new car, maybe from here.'

'Are there any other exits?' asked Mac, looking up the four levels of the building's glass and concrete sides.

'Don't know,' shrugged Tranh. 'Usually come in, go out the same way.'

Lights shone through the frosted-wire glass on level two as a large engine revved.

Mac readied himself. 'Think we're in business, mate.'

Twenty seconds later a white Ford Explorer bounced out of the garage, turned away from Mac and Tranh's position and accelerated, its V8 engine screaming in the quiet street.

'Gotta be them,' said Mac, making a mental note of the whereabouts of the garage.

Losing the Explorer as it disappeared down a secondary street, Tranh accelerated to the point where they'd last seen it. As they leaned into the corner to follow the Explorer, a set of full-beam headlights were switched on directly in their path, blinding them. As Tranh straightened to go around the obstacle, the driver's door of the white vehicle flung open, knocking Tranh and Mac to the tarmac.

Bouncing on his right shoulder, feeling his shirt tear loose, Mac gained his feet as the bike slid along the street on its foot pegs.

Pulling the stolen SIG from the small of his back, Mac stood, his left knee almost giving way as he straightened.

The driver raised his handgun and Mac fired instinctively. The shot missed, but the driver reflexively looked away, allowing Mac to race in with a kick to the bloke's groin, which the driver easily deflected and countered with an open-handed strike to Mac's face.

Finding himself stunned and sitting on his arse, Mac looked up in time to see Tranh throw a perfectly balanced roundhouse kick to the driver's gun hand, and as the weapon landed on the hood of the still-ticking SUV, Tranh threw a kick to the bloke's kidneys followed by a brutal kick to the face off the same leg.

Looking for Red Shirt, Mac realised he'd been tricked. The driver was the only person in the Explorer.

Standing, Mac watched the driver launch a flying headbutt at Tranh, who ducked slightly and took the shot above his left ear. Limping over to the driver's handgun, which had slid across the hood and landed in front of the Explorer, Mac picked it up and turned to use it as Tranh threw a fast elbow into the driver's teeth and followed it with a whippy left hook.

'Okay, that's it, champ,' said Mac, levelling the handgun at the driver as he fell to the asphalt.

'No, this is it,' came a voice, and Mac saw the gleam of those dark eyes in the back seat of the Explorer. Throwing himself to his right, Mac hit the road as the glass of the driver's side rear window exploded.

'Get the bike!' said Mac as Tranh crouched in panic, wondering where the shot had come from.

Duck-walking across the street, Tranh picked up the fallen bike as Mac slowly stood, holding the pistol in a cup-and-saucer grip. He peered over the level of the shot-out window, but the back seat was empty, as was the load space in the rear. There was movement from the front and Mac swung the borrowed handgun and aimed past the windscreen pillars and front seats to where Red Shirt stood on the other side of the hood. They eyeballed one another as a siren sounded, the red lights of the Cong An flashing behind the grille of an approaching car, about a block away.

Tranh kicked the motorbike into life and revved it impatiently. Looking from Red Shirt to the Cong An and back again, Mac considered a shootout, but decided to live another day. Swapping a final look of mutual loathing with Quirk's killer, Mac jogged for the bike. Hopping on, they blasted away, into the path of the approaching cop car.

Looking over his right shoulder as they swerved into an alley with no lights on, Mac saw the Explorer accelerating in the opposite direction, the rear tyre bouncing over the former driver's head.

The last thing Mac saw before they plunged into the alley was the cop car flashing past. A totally focused face stared over the wheel of the white Camry: a focused female face.

# CHAPTER 17

Tranh pulled over at the public park, beside where the canal cut westward from the Saigon River into the southern interior of the city.

'How you shaping up, mate?' said Mac, sitting at a park bench and checking his knee.

A freighter slid downriver, its lights making it look like a Christmas tree lying on its side. The humidity pressed in on them, crickets noisy in the night air.

'Bleeding on my thigh,' said Tranh, pulling back the torn flap of his wrecked chinos and exposing his grazed leg, the white pocket liner stuck to the drying blood.

'That's nasty. I'm going to need an ice bag,' said Mac, only just managing to straighten his left knee to a full extension. 'In a couple of hours I won't be able to walk.'

Holding his leg, Mac felt a shape in one of the pockets. Pulling it out, he examined the memory card he'd retrieved at the Mekong Saloon — the card that had fallen off the computer table as the man in the red shirt had taken off. The card was a standard SD, but white. Trousering it again as Tranh lit a cigarette, Mac pulled the recovered handgun from his waistband. Unlike the flat, seven-shot SIG, this was a bulky fifteen-shot Ruger 9mm. It looked the same as the one Tranh had secured for him at the boat.

'Rugers popular in Saigon?' asked Mac, checking it for load and safety before placing it on the seat between them.

'For Cong An and army,' said Tranh. 'So lots around – easy for fixing.'

Thinking it through, Mac decided he had to go on alone. If things got really bad, he had a consulate, he had a government and he had the financial capacity to buy his way out of Vietnam. Tranh lived here. And it wasn't just the Cong An. Whoever'd executed Jim Quirk was serious. What he initially thought was familiar about Red Shirt was not his face, Mac had decided, but his style: the man was an intelligence professional and if Red Shirt continued the killing Mac didn't want Tranh on his conscience.

Mac's watch said it was 9.56 pm.

'I'm going to cut you loose, mate,' he said, watching the freighter. 'You were just the driver and the cut-out, remember?'

Looking away, Tranh said nothing.

'I mean it, Tranh – you're proving too useful to me. I can't draw you any further into this.'

'I am in this,' said Tranh, drawing on his cigarette.

Mac smiled at the enthusiasm. 'No, mate. You drive me, you handle messages, you give me a local's lay of the land. You're not paid to do what you did tonight.'

'I drove you,' said Tranh.

'Sure, but –'

'I gave you message when Apricot was coming.'

Mac wanted to head this off. 'Nice work.'

'And I do lay of land with that ape,' he said, with no hint of machismo.

Looking away, Mac felt strangely emotional. All his life, he'd been the one looked to for the rough stuff, the one to escalate a situation and get in the blue. He was feeling quite touched that a skinny contractor he'd only known for twenty-four hours was prepared to walk up to a bigger man and start kicking him in the teeth. And that was only the physical side of it – Mac hated riding pillion on a motorbike, thanks largely to his mother being a senior nurse at Rockie Base Hospital who'd seen too many young men brought into the emergency ward in meat buckets. But he liked Tranh's driving. And when he'd dropped the comment about collaborating with Captain Loan, Tranh's instant response had been openness. Mac trusted this guy.

'Yep,' said Mac, trying to stand. 'You gave that ape a decent slap. So I have one last job for the night, then it's beddy-byes, all right?'

'What it is?' said Tranh, confused, as Mac limped back to the motorbike. 'You want better bike?'

'No,' said Mac. 'Beddy-byes — you know, a kip?'

'Umm,' said Tranh as he flipped up the bike stand, not getting it. 'So we going to find Mr Apricot?'

Looking at Tranh, Mac realised the local didn't know about the murder.

'No, mate,' said Mac. 'We're gonna find the pricks who did.'


Seventeen minutes later, dressed in new clothes from a market by the river, they glided with the light traffic past the garage where Red Shirt had dumped the LandCruiser. Mac was in pain and he was scared. He had no idea how he was going to tell Scotty about Jim Quirk, but he wasn't going to walk away from a search of that LandCruiser.

Walking into a side entrance of the garage building, they jogged up four flights of dimly lit stairs until they stood in front of the door with the 'hai' sign on it. Pushing through into level two, they waited for signs of security and looked at the ceiling for cameras. It looked clean.

The LandCruiser was parked in the area where Mac thought the Explorer had been started — pointing over the street. After waiting for a Tamil family to get in their car and leave, Tranh got to work on the LandCruiser and found an entry through the rear hatch, then unlocked the doors. They sat in the vehicle; Mac in the front, Tranh in the back.

'What am I looking for?' asked Tranh.

'Anything,' said Mac, his hopes fading as he said it. The interior had been cleaned out.

The glove box was empty — not even a manual or a map. The door pockets were wiped, as was the centre console and the clips behind the sunshades. There was a faint smell of tobacco, and pulling out the ashtray Mac found a single butt, scrunched up against the end of the tray, a cardboard match jammed beneath it.

Peering closer, Mac saw why he'd smelled strong tobacco: the butt was a Camel.

Pushing the tray back just as he'd found it, he released the driver's door and stepped onto the concrete, leaning back into the vehicle to search under the seats.

'How you going back there?' he asked.

'Nothing, Mr Richard.'

Running his hand across black nylon carpet under the driver's seat, Mac came up with a small plastic envelope.

'Know what that is?' said Mac, passing it to Tranh.

Pulling his hand from under the driver's seat, Mac's hand hit something else. Undoing a wire twist tie, he pulled out the spare Toyota LandCruiser keys – by the look of them, they'd never been touched.

'Well, well,' said Mac.

The red plastic tag had the rego and the colour written in ballpoint on a card slipped into a clear window on one side; flipping it over, the red tag advertised in silver letters: *Cameron Toyota – Kuala Lumpur.*

'That's a sheath for an SD memory card,' said Tranh, returning the plastic envelope.

'For a computer?' said Mac, losing interest as he walked around and lifted the bonnet to record the VIN on the engine bulkhead.

'Yep,' said Tranh. 'You have something?'

'At the very least,' said Mac, jiggling the keys, 'we now have a backup car.'


Having sent his second update on Operation Dragon, Mac checked that Tranh was focused on the satellite TV service in the next office: a Fox News reporter screaming a piece-to-camera as his helo flew over the Japan Sea, telling viewers how this storied sea lane that separated Japan, Korea and China was about to become the most tracked and satellite-surveilled patch on Earth as North Korea announced its missile-testing schedule for next week.

Mac snorted; the news media had to do its location reporting early for the missile tests because for the seventy-two hours while

North Korea fired its Taepodong rockets over Japan, the most powerful electronic eavesdropping devices attempted to vacuum every piece of telemetry out of the sky and out of North Korea's computers and comms links. The wall of electronic measures and counter-measures – some coming from US satellites in space and others from Chinese listening posts mounted on the sea floor – were so intense that shipping and commercial airlines stayed out of the area during the tests as communications became virtually impossible in the wall of white noise.

Easing his office door shut, Mac dialled Canberra. After establishing his bona fides, he was patched through to Scotty on a secure line. By Mac's estimation, it was about one-thirty in the morning in Australia's capital.

'Macca,' said Scotty, croaking himself awake. 'How we doing?'

'I filed one minute ago,' said Mac. 'It's in the system.'

Like a lot of military and intel people, Scotty could become alert in a hurry. 'You okay?'

'Look,' said Mac, grabbing a water bottle, his hand unsteady. 'Umm . . . Jim Quirk's dead.'

'What?!'

'Yeah – haven't told Chester yet. Looks like the Cong An's working on it as we speak.'

'*Dead?*' said Scotty. 'What did you . . . ? I mean, how?'

'It wasn't me,' said Mac.

'So, suicide? Run over by a bus? What the hell's going on?'

Stress was settling in Mac's clenched jaw. 'He was shot.'

The trademark sound of Scotty's cigarette lighter flashed in the background. 'Where?'

'At the nightclub,' said Mac.

'The Saloon?' said Scotty.

'Quirk was being roughed up by these thugs, Eastern European, I think . . .'

'You were there? This was a surveillance gig, mate.'

'We already knew about the Mekong Saloon,' said Mac. 'I needed to see what was in there. I was having a quick look around, and suddenly Quirk's there, being forced into a computer room by these standover blokes.'

'And?'

'And I followed them in, saw Quirk at this computer terminal, being made to do something.'

'Yeah?' said Scotty, sucking on the cigarette.

'Yeah – looked like a bunch of code.'

Scotty paused. 'But Jim died?'

'I tried to help and this bloke shot Jim in the head.'

'Like that?'

'Five metres from where I was standing,' said Mac. 'I couldn't do anything.'

'Fuck, mate,' said Scotty. 'I told you – passive surveillance, get me a report and then we'll decide. Remember?'

'Yeah. Sorry, Scotty,' said Mac.

'Well, are you okay?'

'Yeah, mate,' said Mac, looking at his leg.

'Don't lie to me, Macca – are you okay?'

'We had a small bingle, but we're good.'

'Bingle?' said Scotty. 'Sorry, can I have the non-Queensland translation for that?'

'Well . . .'

'Did you beat up anyone?'

'Yep,' said Mac.

'Get in a gunfight?'

'Ah, yeah.'

'A car chase?'

'We were on a bike.'

There was a new tone in Scotty's voice. 'Shit, Macca!'

'Everything okay down there?'

'Nothing I can't handle,' said Scotty.

'Look, I want to work on this.'

Scotty's voice rose in intensity. 'No, mate – you're not working on anything.'

'You sure everything's okay?'

'I'm sure you're a fucking headache,' said Scotty. 'Here's my direct order: no more operations. You pick up the new recruit tomorrow and then we talk again after I read your report. Fuck's sake.'

'Okay, Scotty.'

'Stay out of trouble – that's an order,' said Scotty and the line went dead.

Getting Tranh to drop him around the corner from the Grand Hotel, Mac hobbled the half-block to the double doors.

As he limped through the tiled lobby, the night manager called out, 'Mr Richard?'

'Yeah, squire,' said Mac, his left knee not wanting to bear weight.

The bloke handed over an envelope. 'Message for you, sir.'

'Thanks. Can you send up a bucket of ice, *cam on?*'

Pushing off his shoes in the living area of his suite, Mac cracked the tab on a can of 333 from his fridge and looked at the envelope. The porter came in with an old-fashioned ice bucket and Mac tipped him with dong.

Pouring the ice into a plastic laundry bag, he fashioned it into an ice pack and eased it onto his knee, which was stretched out on the coffee table.

Opening the envelope, he saw Captain Loan's business card. On the reverse side it said, *Please call asap.*

'Jesus wept,' he said, shutting his eyes and slumping back into the sofa as the ice took some of the pain out of his knee.

Regardless of how spies were portrayed in books and movies, the central factor in their success was the ability to move within and between countries without attracting the attention of the local gendarmes. It was one of those boring requirements of the job and Mac should have been able to operate in a foreign city for thirty-six hours without a police captain – a detective, for Christ's sake – asking him to call.

He felt stupid, amateurish. And he felt exposed: the death of Jim Quirk was just sinking in. He couldn't get the eyes of the killer out of his head and at the same time he knew the shooting was going to make him a person of interest to Captain Loan. She had him where she wanted him; so long as he was in Saigon, she was going to watch him like a rat in a maze . . .

Keying his phone, Mac waited for Tranh to answer.

'Tranh,' said Mac, 'sorry to bother you, but I was thinking about our chat about Captain Loan.'

'Yes, Mr Richard,' he said. 'I thought I tell her we were in Vung Tau tonight.'

Mac smiled. 'Great minds, mate.'

'It will be easy for her, and for you.'

'Okay,' said Mac, liking this guy. 'Where did we stay?'

'Didn't, Mr Richard. We drove back, arrived few minute ago.'

'Who saw us in Vung Tau?'

'My cousin, he has noodle bar – he serve us at quarter past nine, right? No way we can be in Vung Tau and at Mekong Saloon.'

'Thanks, Tranh,' said Mac. 'And you're picking up Lance tomorrow morning at the airport. He's staying at the Rex, okay?'

'I'll call you when I get him,' said Tranh.

Tapping the phone on his teeth, Mac thought about it. He needed to call Canberra, have a quick chat.

Dialling the number for the Saigon consulate-general, Mac was put through to the duty guy, who called himself Justin.

'I need a secure patch to the Casey building, thanks, Justin,' said Mac, meaning the Aussie SIS headquarters in Canberra. Most Asian intelligence services monitored phone calls out of their country, so Mac liked a secure line for offshore chats.

'Um,' said the bloke, flipping through his manual, 'I haven't done this . . . I . . .'

'Just give me the connection,' said Mac, friendly. 'If they think I'm a fruitcake, they'll cut me off, trust me on that.'

'Okay,' Justin said.

The line went blank for five seconds, and then it was ringing.

A person called Samantha picked up in the secure-comms section of RG Casey and Mac identified himself as Albion, giving the code to say he wasn't sitting there having his fingernails torn out.

'What can I do for you, Albion?' said Samantha, when she'd cleared him.

'Can you run a VIN for me, please?' said Mac, reading out the VIN sequences from the green LandCruiser.

Ninety seconds later, Samantha announced she had the data.

'Okay,' said Mac. 'I need you to query the JPJ database in Malaysia and see if you can match that VIN to either a first owner, or the buyer of the vehicle through Cameron Toyota in KL, okay?'

'Cameron Toyota,' said Samantha. 'This a stolen vehicle?'

'I don't know,' said Mac. 'If Cameron Toyota doesn't come up on the JPJ, you'll have to do a company search to find the entity behind Cameron, and then do an ownership match from there. Can do?'

'Can do, Albion,' said Samantha.

'Then we need to match that VIN against new registrations in Ho Chi Minh City – I think we query the Traffic Police Department.'

'Sure, Albion – what are we looking for?'

'Ownership, I think, perhaps compliance paperwork for an imported vehicle,' said Mac, kicking himself for not knowing if the rego was Malaysian or Vietnamese.

Having a fast, hot shower, Mac plundered his toilet bag for painkillers and came up with his last two Panadeine Fortes. Washing them down with the beer, he gasped as he got his leg into position under the bedcovers and adjusted the ice pack on his left knee.

Drifting off, he tried to get the image of Jim Quirk out of his head and attempted to fit Geraldine McHugh into Captain Loan's thinking. Why was a cop asking about Quirk's wife?

As sleep took him the phone rang, waking Mac with a start. Picking up, he croaked his hello to Samantha and fossicked for a pad and pen on the bedside table.

'Yeah?' said Mac, sitting up.

'The VIN was registered to a company in Kuala Lumpur in August 2006,' said Samantha.

'Name?' said Mac, his head swimming.

'Highland Surveying. It's listed as a provider of surveying services to the logging and mining industries.'

'Okay.'

She continued, 'Ho Chi Minh Traffic Police has no record of the VIN or rego.'

'Okay, what about Hanoi?' said Mac.

'Vehicle rego is national in Vietnam,' said Samantha.

Thinking about it, Mac wondered if he had the wrong VIN – but it couldn't be that because the VIN had already been paired with Cameron Toyota's spare key under the seat.

'Can we try Cambodia?' said Mac, knowing how much traffic flowed between the two countries.

'Can you give me five minutes?'

'I'll wait,' said Mac, limping into the bathroom on the hunt for more painkillers.

As Mac wondered if this call counted as staying out of trouble by Scotty's definition, Samantha came back on the line.

'Royal Government of Cambodia registered that VIN in February of this year.'

'To whom?' said Mac.

'A company called Bright Star Consulting,' said Samantha. 'Listed as infrastructure consultants for inbound foreign investors, specialising in forestry, mining and resources processing.'

Mac recognised the kind of front company he'd spent most of his working life hiding behind. 'Got an address?'

'Sure,' said Samantha, reeling off a Phnom Penh street and number.

'Can we reverse-search?' said Mac, already fairly confident that the address would be a law or accounting firm.

'That address has two tenants,' said Samantha. 'Law firm on levels one and two, a partnership of accountants on two and three –'

Mac was fading, irritable with pain.

'You want more?' she asked.

'No,' said Mac. 'I get the picture.'

# CHAPTER 18

The sound of the phone woke Mac from his sleep. Rolling to grab it, his knee caught and pain surged up his leg.

'Faaarrrk,' he moaned as he looked at the phone screen – it was a text. He didn't know the alert sounds yet.

Clicking, he saw the message: *Call me. Ben.*

Rolling gingerly onto his back, Mac realised he was lying in a puddle of water from the melted ice. He decided to walk around the suite and get the leg working. He had things to do and a new arrival to get rid of. With Quirk now dead, Lance Kendrick wasn't needed and he didn't want some new-guard 'whiz-kid' adding to his headaches.

As he put weight on the knee, the pain sang like a concert-hall organ, echoing in his brain as he opened his mouth to scream. Shaking in that spot beside the bed for ten seconds, Mac breathed it out with some deep diaphragm actions, making himself take the pain, forcing his brain to accept the signals and then get on with the day.

He managed to get through his shower and have a shave. Then, as he turned to grab a face towel, his leg gave way beneath him.

The consulate doctor arrived thirty-four minutes later.

'It's not broken,' she said, poking his balloon-like knee with a wooden spatula. 'But there's ligament trauma.'

'Yeah. Just like in footy, right?' said Mac, trying to get the conversation around to him walking, not convalescing.

'You've had injuries like this before?' she said, wrapping her hands around the puffy joint and squeezing the interior ligament. 'That hurt?'

'No,' said Mac, catching his breath with the pain. 'It's not painful, it just won't support my weight.'

'Oh really?' said the quack, a fifty-something expat Aussie who eyed him suspiciously over her half-glasses. 'Just won't support your weight? Is that all?'

'Yeah, doc − shot of corty should do it. Just to get me going.'

'Hydrocortisone? Oh my God − you are a footy player, aren't you?' she said, moving to her medical bag. 'You're worse than my brothers.'

'Where from?' said Mac, as she opened a steel box.

'Gladstone,' she said, holding a bottle to the light.

'Oh yeah?' Mac rolled his eyes at the mention of a rival town from his childhood. 'Fagstone?'

'And you'd be from . . . let me guess: Frockhampton, right?'

'Yeah, well,' said Mac, eyeing the needle as it plunged into his knee, 'just so long as you're not from Mackay.'


Keying the phone from his seat on the cyclo, Mac looked down at the heavy blue brace that was now strapped around his knee − the trade-off the doctor had demanded to clear him for field duties.

Tranh came on the line and verified that the Air Vietnam flight from Bangkok was on time.

'You speak with Loan yet?' said Mac.

'Yes, Mr Richard,' said Tranh. 'I told her we're in Vung Tau − the name of my cousin's restaurant is South China Dragon. We had barbecue fish and two beers. I say you went to see a school library official but not around.'

'Nice work, Tranh,' said Mac. 'You scrub up okay?'

'What?' said Tranh. 'I have bath.'

'Beaut. See you at eleven o'clock,' said Mac and hung up.

Shoving his hand in his left pocket, he pulled out Captain Loan's business card. He didn't want to call her but he knew she'd come after him anyway, maybe get him down to the cells. So it'd be easier to remain available and fake her out.

Mac listened to the ringing as they slowed for a red light. They were heading for the Southern Scholastic offices, where Mac wanted to make a secure call to Benny in Singapore.

'Xin chao,' came the female voice as Mac's call connected.

'Captain Loan – Richard Davis here. You called?'

'Yes, Mr Richard, thank you for calling back,' she said. 'I'd like to have a chat, if you wouldn't mind.'

'I'm in a meeting right now,' he said. 'Just stepped out for coffee and then I'm in back-to-backs all day. Yeah, so, I'm just looking at my diary –'

'What about now?' asked Loan.

'Well, yeah, okay then, let's see,' said Mac. 'I've got an eleven o'clock at An Phu, and then a one o'clock at the Pharmacy University, down in Cholon – that's always a two-hour affair, you know what academics are like.'

'Okay,' said Loan.

'And I'm looking at my diary, it's right in front of me . . .'

'No, I mean right now.'

'Well, I've just stepped out of this meeting to make this call –'

'Why not talk in the car, rather than ride in that cyclo?'

Mac turned slowly and saw the white Camry parked behind the cyclo.

'Yeah, why not?' said Mac, and hung up.

Sliding into the passenger seat, Mac felt self-conscious. The doctor had given him a bottle of T3 painkillers and he was starting to wish he'd eaten more food on top of them.

Loan didn't greet him. 'What happened to your leg?'

'Spider bite,' said Mac.

'Big spiders in Vung Tau,' said Captain Loan, as she accelerated into the traffic. 'Seen the paper this morning? Aussie killed – at the Mekong Saloon.'

'That's in Cholon, isn't it?' said Mac. 'Famous place.'

'Tourists and expats seem to like it,' she said, nodding slowly. 'You're not interested that an Aussie was killed there?'

'I'm interested, Captain.'

'Don't want to know the deceased's name?'

Mac stayed cheery. 'Haven't even got my seatbelt on yet.'

'Thought you Aussies stuck together?'

'He could be anyone,' said Mac, wanting to be out of that car.

'How you know he's a he?'

'Oh, come on,' said Mac, trying to make light of it.

'It's one of the consulate officers,' she said, and left it there.

They drove in silence for just over three minutes.

'It could have been you,' she said, out of nowhere.

'Really?'

'You were there last night, weren't you?'

'Must have the wrong guy,' said Mac, smiling. 'I was down in Vung Tau.'

'The staff are talking about an Aussie man who was there.'

'What, who looked like Brad Pitt? Moved like Muhammad Ali?'

'No – tallish, blond. Heavily built. Barman thought he was a soldier.'

'Well, that counts me out,' said Mac, his mind racing.

'Does it?'

He took her in: she'd put on make-up, she was chewing gum and – the big giveaway – her nails were bitten down.

'Parents must be proud, eh, Captain?'

'Sorry?' she asked, as if she hadn't heard correctly.

'Your parents – they must be proud to have their girl making captain in the police?'

They stopped at traffic and Loan whipped her sunnies off, looking at him. 'You want to play games, Mr Uc?'

Mac was taken aback. 'Look . . .'

'No, you look, Mr Richard, or whatever your name is. You know very well that any man who sends his daughter to Monash University is going to be disappointed when she comes home and joins the police.'

'Well,' said Mac.

'And I don't chew my nails because I can't find a husband.'

'I'm sorry,' said Mac.

'The dead man is James Kirk.'

'Quirk,' said Mac before he could stop himself.

109

'Ah,' said Captain Loan, smiling as she put her sunnies back on. 'You seem to know more than me.'

'Only because you told me –' said Mac, but she was grinning ear to ear.

'I want to show you something,' said Loan, and threw the Camry across traffic before Mac could reply.

Mac followed Loan and the landlord up the wooden staircase of the colonial apartment building. On the second-floor landing, the landlord – a short elderly man with a cigarette stuck to his bottom lip – searched for a key and opened the door with the number 3 screwed into the wood.

Leading Mac inside, Loan shut the door. 'This is where we tracked Geraldine McHugh,' said Loan, as she walked to the living-room bay window and looked down on the hyperkinetic street activity of Cholon.

'Geraldine McHugh?' said Mac, confused, joining her at the window. 'Quirk's wife?'

'Yes.'

'I don't understand,' said Mac, the T3s clouding his thinking as he looked around at the bare walls and a sparsely furnished apartment.

'I don't understand either,' said Loan. 'Want to tell me about it?'

'I can't,' said Mac, trying to think of where to go with this. 'What do you mean, you *tracked* her here?'

'White woman, blonde, living alone. In *Cholon*?' said Loan, as if it was the moon. 'We got a tip-off – one of the neighbours was worried about her. She didn't seem to know what she was doing and she had unsavoury company.'

'So?' said Mac.

'So we had her under surveillance and one of our guys says he recognises her – that she'd been at an Aussie consulate barbecue two years ago.'

'Really?' said Mac.

'So we went through the diplomatic files and connected Jim Quirk and Geraldine McHugh. Husband and wife, but he's living in the compound at An Phu, while she's living here.'

'Maybe they're separated?'

'Then why's she in Saigon, Mr Richard?' said Loan, whose intellect was starting to grate.

'I don't know, Captain Loan,' said Mac. 'You have a theory?'

'Well, at first I thought she might have been kidnapped – you know, held against her will.'

'How did you rule that out?' asked Mac.

'Women's intuition,' said Loan. 'And a listening device under the coffee table.'

'So what was she doing?'

'Some sex, with a man she called Dodo,' said Loan. 'Nickname, I think. We established she wasn't being held here, if you see what I mean.'

'I think I do, but –'

'By the way, does the phrase "BP" or "Beep" mean anything to you?' asked Loan. 'Is that an Australian saying?'

'One's an oil company,' said Mac.

'Hmm,' she said, losing interest. 'Not what I wanted.'

Rattling the keys in her hand, Loan made to leave the apartment.

'So, what's the theory?' said Mac, wanting the final pieces.

'I think she was pretending to be kidnapped. The few calls she made were to Quirk.'

'Why would she come all the way to Saigon to pretend to be kidnapped?' asked Mac.

'She was getting him to go to the Mekong Saloon each day,' said Loan, her eyes boring into Mac's. 'Before we could get answers, Quirk was dead.'

'Where?' said Mac.

'The compound behind the club – in the alley.' Loan was walking towards the door. 'Single shot to the temple.'

'So where's Geraldine?' said Mac, following her.

'You tell me.'

'What?'

'She left last night,' said the captain, holding the door open for him. 'Neighbours say she was picked up around midnight.'

'Taxi?'

'No,' she said. 'Man in a white Ford Explorer.'

# CHAPTER 19

The steaming-hot taxi ride back to the Southern Scholastic offices took forever. Saigon's traffic congestion was fast approaching that of Jakarta or Manila but motorbikes and cyclos still dominated the roads.

Popping another T3 capsule and washing it down with water, Mac thought about Captain Loan and the case she was pursuing. McHugh was pretending to be kidnapped and getting Quirk to make regular trips to the Mekong Saloon? Well, Mac was one step ahead of that story: he'd seen what Quirk was doing at the club. He'd seen the computer terminal he was being forced to work on and he'd heard a conversation about it. How did it go? Something like, *I don't care about your passwords — we want access.*

Slugging at the water again, Mac glimpsed the Reunification Palace down a cross street on his left as they neared the destination. Relaxing, he tried to replay the conversation between Red Shirt and Quirk. It wasn't just about passwords and access. There was another noun in there that he just couldn't remember.

Paying the cabbie, Mac got out east of the tax department and limped towards the river, stopping like a tourist every few shops to have a look and see who was tailing him. It annoyed him that Loan had played him so well; rather than harass him or bring him down to the Cong An station, she'd gambled that a bit of curiosity would change Mac's attitude. And she was probably going to win that bet: from the second he walked into Geraldine McHugh's apartment, he'd been trying to work out how to stay assigned in Saigon and close to the Quirk murder. He'd technically screwed up by being in that club, but he'd done it and now he was part of it, and his next step was to find Red Shirt and this Dodo character. If they were the same person, Geraldine McHugh was in trouble.

At the top of the stairs, outside the door to Southern Scholastic, Mac heard the satellite TV news – it sounded like the CNN feed out of Honkers. Inputting his security code, Mac knew he was late for the meet and that the Quirk surveillance was technically over. But if this Kendrick was as smart as Scotty claimed, then Operation Dragon might be expanded slightly. He'd have to talk with Scotty and maybe Tobin, see how it developed.

Walking into the conference room area, Mac clocked Tranh leaning against the kitchenette counter, playing with his mobile phone. Standing up straight when he saw Mac, Tranh nodded quickly at the two sofas that faced the TV screen.

Looking over, Mac saw a shaggy-haired bloke in his twenties on one sofa and an older man on the other.

'Hi, darling, I'm home,' said Mac, walking around to the TV area.

Snapping out of his TV torpor, the younger bloke stood, running his palms down his jeans. He wore a loud Hawaiian shirt and an ironic goatee.

'Lance,' he said, offering his hand.

The TV was turned off as Mac shook. 'Richard – Richard Davis,' he said, tightly enough that Lance Kendrick and his guest understood Mac's cover.

Turning, he came face to face with someone he knew well.

'Dave,' said Mac, shaking Dave Urquhart's hand. 'The fuck are you doing here?'

The phone rang in Mac's office and Urquhart kicked at something on the floor. The moment broken, Mac moved away.

Picking up the handset as he swung the door shut, Mac gasped with pain while pushing sideways into his desk chair.

'Yep – Davis.'

'Mate, Paragon,' came the strong Aussie accent. 'The sky is blue?'

'And the clouds are white,' said Mac, confirming he didn't have a gun pointed at him. 'How are you, Scotty?'

'I'm good, mate, but the chaps have shut down Dragon.'

Breathing out, Mac tried to stay calm. Through the glass panel of his office he could see Urquhart shoving his hands into his trouser pockets and rocking back on the balls of his feet as he spoke to Kendrick.

'They've canned it?' said Mac. 'It's just getting going.'

'Dragon was surveillance,' said Scotty, that tone from last night coming through again.

'Yeah, I know, mate – so the surveillance now shifts to the shooters, to the Aussie connections.'

'Aussie connections?' said Scotty. 'Australian *government*?'

'Maybe.'

Scotty sighed, and Mac realised that his old mentor was being used as the reluctant messenger. In Mac's two foreign operations since his return to the fold, three people had been executed. All on Mac's watch, under conditions he'd designed himself. The Firm didn't like coincidences and it didn't like criminal investigations.

One of the reasons that intelligence organisations were so strict about agents declaring their medical consultations – especially for psychological problems – was the danger of personality disorders developing in long-term field officers. The classic symptoms were burnout, from sustained stress, or complacency, when false identities became normalised in the agent's mind. Either disorder was a threat to the whole outfit and Mac could feel the judgment of his peers weighing on him.

'Macca – time to pull up stumps and come home. Word's come down,' said Scotty.

'It's not over.'

'When the deceased is an Aussie consular guy, that means the Feds will turn up,' said Scotty. 'And when the cops turn up, it's over.'

Mac rubbed his temples. 'Shit, Scotty.'

'Let's do it like pros, okay? Put it all in a bag, put a match to it and see if Qantas can't find you a nice single malt in business class.'

'I didn't get Quirk killed,' said Mac. 'I've done a thousand recces like that without one of ours getting his head blown off.'

'I know, I know,' said Scotty. 'We just get on with it, right? Like the wise man says: when it turns to shit, we start wearing brown.'

'Ha!' said Mac, laughing. 'You're a mad bastard, mate.'

'That's what my third wife screamed at me,' said Scotty, 'just before she called in the lawyers.'


Massaging his face with both hands, Mac barely heard the soft knock at the door. When he looked up, Dave Urquhart was easing into the office, a plunger of coffee in one hand and two mugs in the other.

'Knee looks nasty,' said Urquhart, as he took a seat. 'Walk into a door?'

'Wife beat me up,' said Mac, straightening in his chair. 'Sorry about the welcome – didn't expect you here.'

'No,' said Urquhart, pouring the coffee. 'Last minute thing, you know?'

Mac grabbed the coffee. 'Come in from Bangers?'

'Sure,' said Urquhart.

'You with Kendrick?'

'I am now,' said Urquhart with a smile. His suit, his shoes and his side parting were all perfect. It looked like he'd shaved in the cab from the airport and his colourless, plasticised skin refused to flush in the pre-monsoon heat – a quality that had earned him the nickname of 'Madame Tussaud' among certain crowds in Canberra.

'So what can I do for you?' said Mac, sipping the coffee.

'Nothing much. I'll be sharing the office for a couple of weeks.'

'You know I've been recalled,' said Mac, already annoyed by the passive slickness of his old friend. 'So I won't be sharing anything with you.'

'Yes,' said Urquhart. 'Just didn't think it was my place to bowl in here announcing it.'

Turning his mug, Mac decided to play Urquhart for all he was worth. 'It's a pity really,' he said.

'Oh?'

'Yeah. I was going to call you today, bring you in on a few things I found out after our discussion in Canberra.'

Urquhart focused. 'Really? I thought that was a brush-off?'

'Yeah, but things change.'

'They do?' said Urquhart, drawing his mug across the desk but not taking his eyes off Mac.

'That was Canberra,' said Mac, pointing at the phone. 'I'm on a plane tomorrow – Dragon's over, burn the bag, the whole nine yards.'

As Urquhart's eyes burrowed into him, Mac stood and made for the door. 'It's a shame, 'cos we –'

Urquhart's arm went out, touching Mac on the stomach. 'Steady – let's not burn anything just yet.'

Stopping, Mac sat on the desk, looking down at Urquhart.

Urquhart cleared his throat. 'So, what have you got?'

Mac sipped coffee. 'Let's start with what I get.'

'I'm not really in a position –'

'Well, then,' said Mac, standing.

'Shit, McQueen,' Urquhart hissed. 'You're a difficult bastard.'

'Who you working for?' said Mac.

'Executive branch,' said Urquhart. 'So what do you want?'

Mac tried to link what he knew about Urquhart's movements and motives with what might bring him suddenly to Saigon. It was starting to look obvious, and as little as he trusted the man, Urquhart's secret mission might just keep Mac in Saigon.

'I want to be seconded to you, Davo,' said Mac. 'I want an attachment to the McHugh case.'

Looking away, Urquhart lost his composure for a split second before recovering. 'What's the McHugh case?'

'Geraldine McHugh – Quirk's wife. I think that's who you're interested in.'

'Really?' said Urquhart with a fake chuckle. 'Why would you say something like that?'

'Because you're hot for your traitor theory,' said Mac. 'And as soon as you heard about Quirk, you zap in here, have me thrown out, and I'll bet the AFP liaison in Honkers, Manila and Singers have been deemed inadequate for this gig, right?'

'Really?' said Urquhart, a poor liar for one who practised so much.

'Yeah, Davo. The AFP'll have to fly someone in from Sydney or Perth, which gives you a day's head start – those flights don't land till almost four. It also means the visiting fed has no relationship with the Cong An.'

Urquhart recovered his superiority complex. 'That's all a wonderful theory, Macca, but I have no idea what you're talking about.'

'That's a pity, Davo,' said Mac, walking for the door. 'Because when it comes to theories, that's the one the Cong An is going with.'

'What?' said Urquhart, almost throwing himself at the door.

'The Cong An – the cops.'

'I know who the Cong An are – what do they know about Geraldine McHugh?' said Urquhart, wide-eyed.

'Thought you had no idea what I was –'

'Okay, okay.' Urquhart held his hand palm-down like Mac was the one who needed to relax. 'The Cong An and McHugh?'

'They've had her under surveillance,' said Mac, casually.

'How do you know this?' He said it like an accusation.

Mac smiled. 'I was in her apartment this morning, mate.'

'Okay, this has gone far enough. I'm working for the Prime Minister's office under authority of the Attorney-General,' Urquhart said, meaning he had the right to break the law. 'I'm invoking the Official Secrets Act on what you've just told me – the lot, okay?'

'Sure – I was about to burn the bag, remember?'

Nostrils flaring, Dave Urquhart stood his ground in front of the door, his eyes darting downwards to the right – a man trying to put something together.

'So, the Cong An is talking to you?'

'Sure,' said Mac.

'And to the consulate – to Chester?'

'No, just me,' said Mac.

'I think I can find a spot for you on the team,' said Urquhart, chewing his lip. 'But this will be a loop of two, right? You'll be reporting to me, not to Scotty or Tobin.'

'Okay, Davo,' said Mac. 'So long as it's in writing, it's a loop of two.'

'You think you can take orders from me?' said Urquhart.

'As long as you don't put me in danger.'

'Fair enough,' said Urquhart.

'Oh,' said Mac, 'and Tranh comes with the deal.'

'The local bloke?'

'Yeah – he was promised two weeks' work and he shouldn't have to scratch-and-feed with DFAT accounts just to get a cheque.'

'I thought we'd use Lance,' said Urquhart. 'He can do everything whatsisname is doing, and he's TS-PV.'

'No one can do what Tranh does,' said Mac. 'And by the way, Lance probably needs some work on his craft, and that'll be my call.'

'Okay, Macca – that's your call, but you report to me,' said Urquhart, his eyes burning with resentment. 'Got a number?'

Reading out his mobile number, Mac made to go.

'Where will you be?' said Urquhart.

'Don't know,' said Mac. 'But it'll have a big screen, the Wallabies will be playing and they'll serve Bundy without adding too much ice.'

Urquhart stood aside as he brushed past.

'Just tell me, Macca: why were you in her apartment?'

'Simple,' said Mac. 'Cong An have fitted me for the murder.'

# CHAPTER 20

Lance was watching TV again as Mac sauntered out of his office. The corty was killing the pain in his knee but it still felt unstable. On the screen, another Australian mining negotiator was being led into a Chinese courtroom with his wrists cuffed under a jacket, the Asian media going into a frenzy of flash photography and screamed questions as the accused was marched past.

'For such a closed society, the Chinese love a photo opportunity, eh, Lance?' Mac eased himself onto the neighbouring sofa as Lance hit the mute.

'Yeah, it's a circus up there,' said Lance, some rounded vowels creeping through his street pretensions. 'Do they really think they'll control Aussie ore prices by bullying our mining guys?'

'So long as our mining guys have Asian faces and Chinese names, they think they can get away with it,' said Mac.

Lance turned to look at Mac. 'You reckon?'

'Yeah, I reckon,' said Mac, as Urquhart closed the office door. 'So, Lance, you with the Firm?'

'Currently,' said Lance, a glint of an earring sparkling under his rock-star hair. 'I've been on a series of attachments.'

'Attachments, eh?' said Mac.

Aussie intelligence had a mutual-attachments system between

the Firm, federal police, ASIO, the defence intel departments and the executive arms of Prime Minister & Cabinet and Attorney-General's. People were always being attached for what the HR people called 'skills transfer'; it helped agency inter-operability when the pressure went on. But attachés always had a home tribe and Mac wanted to know who Mr Kendrick was gossiping to when he was having a few quiet beers.

'So how's Jase, in Bangers?' said Mac, to see if Lance had been at the Bangkok embassy long enough to know the declared ASIS guy, Jason Tremain.

Lance shrugged. 'It was a fast assignment in Bangers – I've been in Jakarta for a while, working with the Feds.'

'Not the CI training thing?' asked Mac, referring to the AFP's counter-intelligence training program.

'No. Broader issues.'

Mac decided to drop it. 'Well, talking of broader issues, you've probably had some craft training, right? Learned how to make a stranger go into the street and wave a shopping bag around like a goose?'

'Yep,' said Lance.

'But you haven't done any live field work, have you?'

Lance looked away. 'Well . . .'

'Relax, mate – I had a first time too.'

'Okay,' said Kendrick. 'What do I do?'

'See Tranh over there?' said Mac.

'Yeah.'

'What do you notice about Tranh?'

Turning down his mouth, Lance shook his head. 'Nothing really – looks fairly typical for South-East Asia.'

'Good answer,' said Mac, standing and walking over to Tranh, digging out a sheaf of dong. 'Tranh's going to take you down to his favourite market, find you a barber, get you a shave and get you kitted in something a little less Guns N' Roses.'

'Are you kidding me?' said Lance. 'You're not my mother.'

'No, champion,' said Mac, handing the cash to Tranh with a wink. 'But if I were my mother, I'd be reaching for the jug cord you keep talking like that.'

'Okay, okay,' said Lance. 'Let's go shopping.'

'Oh, by the way,' said Mac, as Tranh pulled out his van keys, 'you got a safe in your room, right?'

'Yeah, I think so – why?'

'Somewhere to leave that earring, okay?'


Ordering the ginger duck and rice, Mac sat in the rear of the tiny restaurant and watched the street traffic move along Dam Street in the lee of Sunwah Tower. He wanted to return Benny's call but he needed time to think first.

Opening the esky on the floor beside the counter, the owner pulled out a bottle of Saigon *bia*, tore the top off it and dumped it on the table with a tiny glass. Vietnam's beer was a similar style and temperature to Queensland's: a cold, light drink to have with lunch.

Sipping, Mac felt the heat rolling in waves off the street and thought about what he might salvage from this operation. The only thing that could be done for Quirk's family was catching the shooter and getting him into a courtroom. And that wouldn't happen if Mac sat around in Canberra for a week retelling his story to a bunch of back-seat drivers.

Dave Urquhart's hands-on involvement was strange. His old friend had made a commitment to his corporate ambitions long ago, and in Canberra the only way to the top was by staying in the office and never getting your hands dirty. The idea of Urquhart venturing into the field was about as natural as a politician standing back and letting someone else take the credit.

Urquhart was known as the silent guy sitting at the back of the interagency meetings, jotting in his notebook. When he was assigned to ONA, he seemed to spend most of his time in the PM's office; when he was officially in the PM's office, he was seen lunching with DGs from ASIS and ASIO. He was one of those rare operators who gave both cops and spooks the creeps, while makings politicians feel comfortable and relaxed.

Now Urquhart was in Saigon as soon as Quirk was killed. Mac had made the Quirk connection merely as a last-gasp attempt to stay assigned in Saigon. It was only a guess, but Urquhart hadn't disputed it.

Mac decided he had to be careful: when a snake like Urquhart ventured into the light, someone was going to get hurt, and Mac wondered if he shouldn't demand a consular passport and the legal protection of a declared position under Chester.

The phone rang and Mac hit the green button as his duck arrived. Urquhart, wanting to know where he was.

Seven minutes later, Dave Urquhart staggered into the open front of the restaurant and asked for water.

'Shit, it's hot,' he said, gasping and seating himself at the table, his waxy pallor dripping.

'Yep, and when it breaks it'll be like someone poured a bucket out of the sky,' said Mac.

'You're back in,' said Urquhart, examining Mac's lunch as the owner brought a bottle of European water and two glasses.

Mac paused as he raised his fork. 'Who with?'

'Let's just say PMC,' said Urquhart. The operation was for the Department of Prime Minister and Cabinet.

'Let's just say that's a bit vague,' said Mac.

'It's via the AG's — there's a letter sitting in the safe,' said Urquhart. 'And there's a letter of attachment from Tobin in your secure email.'

If Urquhart was telling the truth, the legal paperwork for this operation was from the Attorney-General's office — the legal enabler of Australia's domestic spy agency, ASIO.

Urquhart eyed him. 'But there's a string attached.'

'That's a shock,' said Mac, sipping his beer.

'We have an asset in Phnom — code-named Calhoun.'

'Yes,' said Mac, checking the other diners.

'He manages a bar called the Taberna. Your first job under me is to meet him, debrief and take the photos he gives you. Bring them back and we'll talk.'

'Debrief on what?'

Urquhart sneered slightly. 'He'll tell you, Macca.'

Mac focused on his lunch. 'I'll leave this arvo.'

'You want to take Lance?' said Urquhart, too casual.

Sensing a snitch being foisted upon him, Mac could think of nine excuses for not taking Lance, but he let it go. He was never going to change Urquhart's infighting instincts and besides, a short road trip with the newcomer might be a chance to gain some insights.

'Sure, he's welcome,' said Mac.

Clicking his fingers at the restaurant manager, Urquhart called her over. 'I'll have what he's having.'


Opening his second bottle of water, Mac tried to stay hydrated as the Toyota van laboured to keep the air-con running against the heat.

'This evening?' said Mac, pointing at the thickening clouds over Cambodia in the distance.

'Think so,' said Tranh, nodding. 'We'll stay at Hawaii, if you want.'

Fiddling with the radio, Mac looked for an English-language station. 'Okay, mate – Hawaii it is. You want to book?'

Picking up his phone, Tranh went to work.

'Hawaii?' said Lance, leaning between the front seats. 'Did he say Hawaii?'

'Yeah, it's a hotel in Phnom,' said Mac. 'It has an elevated lobby, which is what you want when the monsoon strikes in Phnom Penh.'

'Why?'

'Because everything floods,' said Mac.

Tranh rang off. 'We got best rooms.'

'For half the price,' said Mac, knowing that locals never paid the tourist rate.

'Yeah, but maybe extra guests?' said Tranh.

Easing around in his seat, hiding his face behind the head rest, Mac scanned through the rear window. A steady stream of trucks, vans, cars and motorbikes were flowing north along the Trans-Asian Highway to the Cambodian border crossing of Moc Bai.

'Which one?' said Mac.

'Red Patrol,' said Tranh. 'Just went past.'

Turning to face forwards, Mac saw the red Nissan 4x4 slipping in front of them thirty metres ahead. 'Get a look?'

'Two men – Chinese.' Tranh cracked his window two inches and lit a smoke. 'They photographed us.'

'Camera?' said Lance.

'Phone, I think. Held it down here,' said Tranh, putting his forearm on the windowsill.

'Phone, you say?' said Lance. 'Modern one?'

Tranh sucked on his smoke. 'Yes, Mr Lance – a slider.'

'That could be convenient,' said Lance, rummaging in his backpack. He drew out a black box and flipped an aerial on it.

'Hold that,' he said to Mac. Pulling an Apple laptop from the pack, he passed forwards a power lead. 'Can we get some juice?'

Pushing the power plug into the cigarette lighter, Tranh swapped a look with Mac.

'So, technology's your thing?' said Mac, looking back at Lance.

'It's my training,' said Lance. 'They graded me as an intelligence officer, but I specialise in ICT – counter-measures, surveillance, infiltrations.'

'What ICT?' said Tranh.

'It's a wank,' said Lance, connecting the black box to the laptop. 'It just means anything that transmits or receives electronic signals.'

'So what's this?' Mac nodded at the black box.

Lance turned the laptop screen for Mac to see. There was a small graphic box with a listing of two items. The first line said *Saigon Services*, and the second line said *Nokia 6250i*.

'What is it?' asked Mac.

'Watch.' Lance clicked the cursor on *Saigon Services*. 'Let's see the address book.'

The screen showed a bigger box with a listing of about seventy names, mostly in Vietnamese. Glancing down the list, Mac saw 'Richard' and, looking further, he saw something else.

'So, *Chanthe*, is it?' he said to Tranh. 'Pretty cosy, mate.'

'What are you looking at?' said Tranh.

'I think it's your address book,' said Mac.

Going back to the original box, Lance clicked on something else and Tranh's picture files came up.

'What is there?' asked Tranh, trying to twist around.

'Nothing, mate,' said Mac. 'Just those pics of you, the monkey and the Cool Whip. Try that one,' Mac said to Lance.

A picture came up: Lance clicked forwards. It was a series of the same two people on the step-through motorbike who had followed Mac when he first landed in Saigon.

'You knew those Cong An on the bike were following me?' said Mac.

'Yep,' said Tranh.

'And you didn't tell me?'

'Told Captain Loan,' said Tranh. 'Told her if she want to talk with the Uc, just go talk – he won't bite.'

Mac let it drop. 'So what are we doing here, Lance?'

'I'm using the Bluetooth transceivers in your phones to clone them.'

'Clone?'

'It means I stream all the data on your phone with a Bluetooth connection, then re-create your phone's operating system on my laptop. Every file stored in the phone can be accessed here, and if I wanted to, I could make a call, send a text, change the address book, even change your wallpaper.'

Mac thought about it: how much surveillance had Lance and Urquhart already done on Mac and Tranh? He and Tranh swapped a quick look.

Lance tapped his secret device. 'This box tricks Bluetooth into thinking the acceptance and password has been given.'

'So why can't we tap into Mr Nosey-Poke's phone?' said Mac, gesturing to the red Patrol.

'We could be too far away – Bluetooth is optimum to ten metres, then it fades.'

'Okay, then,' said Mac. 'You want to do this?'

'Sure,' said Lance. 'But turn off your phones first. They could have the same technology.'

Moving up alongside the red Patrol, Mac and Tranh kept their eyes straight ahead as Lance tapped away in the back seat, adjusting his black box. After thirty seconds, Lance told Tranh to move on.

Settling into the space in front of the Nissan, Tranh set a course for Moc Bai as Lance fiddled.

'So, what did we get?' asked Mac.

'We got nothing and something,' said Lance.

'Sounds like Marxist economics,' said Mac.

'There're no devices to pick up in that four-wheel drive,' said Lance. 'Yet the phone Tranh saw was the latest – and they all have Bluetooth.'

'Which means?' said Mac.

'It means they've switched their phones off, or, more likely . . .'

'Yeah?'

'They have naked phones – which is not particularly good news.'

'Why not?' asked Tranh, trying to see Lance in his mirror.

'Because naked phones are used by intelligence services,' said Lance.

'Like the MSS?' said Mac, turning slightly to look over his shoulder.

'The MSS invented these boxes,' said Lance. 'They wrote the book.'

# CHAPTER 21

The cold feeling that had been lurking at the bottom of Mac's stomach since Singapore was turning into an iceberg as they closed on the border crossing of Moc Bai. Realising Lance had been quiet since the sighting of the tail, Mac turned back and saw someone who looked very uncomfortable.

'That haircut suits you much better.' Mac pulled a bottle of water from his pack and handed it to the novice. 'Drink that – keep your fluids up.'

As Mac knocked his backpack against the console, a set of keys and the SD memory chip he'd found at the Mekong Saloon fell on the floor in front of Lance. Ignoring the keys, the youngster picked up the memory card. 'What's this?'

'Memory card,' said Mac, gesturing at his keys.

Grabbing the keys and handing them back, Lance held on to the chip. 'What's on it?'

'Don't know,' said Mac. 'Plug it into the laptop.'

'No slots,' said Lance. 'Where did you say you got it?'

Mac caught sight of the Patrol trying to jockey closer to the van as they closed on the border crossing. 'Can't remember.'

Mac took the memory card back and turned to Tranh. 'Our friends in the Patrol – they with us from Saigon?'

Tranh nodded.

The Chinese never left home without a backup crew or some kind of electronic measures, and as the taupe arches of the customs and immigration gates rose in front of them, Mac thought about the choice between playing it safe and pretending not to notice the MSS, or flushing them out and seeing if they declared their intentions.

The manual said to act as if nothing was wrong, to go to fallbacks and then switch to counter-surveillance. Such techniques could be useful but they were usually taught by people who didn't live in the field and whose experience was confined to being a declared intelligence officer at an embassy or consulate.

In Mac's world, where you lived an undeclared corporate cover, never ventured near Australian consular premises, and could be tried as a spy if caught, the rules were different. In Mac's world, to react to surveillance by the book amounted to an admission of espionage. Besides, thought Mac, as they joined the non-truck queue into Cambodia, if these Chinese blokes had held off in Vietnam, who knew what they felt licensed to do in Cambodia?

'Tranh, where would you rather deal with the MSS: here or Cambodia?'

'Cambodia is no good,' said Tranh, turning his mouth down. 'Chinese do what they want over there.'

'Can we lose them in this queue?'

Looking in his mirror, Tranh focused and lit another cigarette. 'Maybe – see who we have on the gate.'

The queue edged forwards, the Vietnamese border guards asking for passports or registration at every fourth or fifth car. The guards nodded Tranh through and they joined the queue across a tarmac courtyard to go through Cambodian customs.

'They behind us?' asked Mac, as the Cambodian customs officer walked towards Tranh's window.

'Yep – one car, then it's them.'

The Cambodian officer counted the occupants, said something to Tranh and put his hand out. Collecting the passports, the guard took his ten-dollar greenback from the top booklet, stamped the passports on his little shaded lectern, and returned them to Tranh.

Joking with the guard, Tranh got him laughing, handed him the rest of his pack of Marlboros and gestured with his thumb over his shoulder. Mac liked Tranh's style: the man was an enlister.

As they eased out of the customs area onto the highway into Phnom Penh, Mac heard the official who'd stamped their passports yelling into the guardhouse and an overweight senior guard staggered out into the heat.

Hitting the gas, they accelerated to full speed and, through the back window, Mac and Lance saw a group of guards descend on the red Nissan Patrol.

'Nice work,' said Mac, as the Nissan's driver was hauled out of the car. 'What did you tell them?'

'I said the cases of Johnnie Walker we taking into Phnom are all in the red Patrol – tell him our friends got a case for the guards.'

'Ha! You hear that, mate?' said Mac.

'Yep – that's pretty cool,' said Lance, wide-eyed and gulping.


Crossing the Mekong at a little after four pm, they followed the famous river north from Banam into Phnom Penh, keeping pace with the trucks that plied National Highway One between the two former jewels of French Indochina. Circling the Hawaii Hotel, they stopped one block away and Mac asked Tranh to check in and pay with cash.

When Tranh re-emerged they headed across town, the clouds weighing heavy in the late afternoon, and booked into the Cambodiana Hotel under Tranh's name and passport. When the MSS bribed a night manager to have a look at the guest manifest, Mac wanted them scanning a whole pile of names native to the Mekong Delta.

Parking around the back, they headed for their rooms with Mac calling for a meeting in fifteen minutes in his suite. As the doors shut, Mac turned immediately to Tranh, who had a room in Mac's suite.

'I've got someone to see tonight,' said Mac, handing over five US ten-dollar notes – a small fortune in Phnom Penh. 'I want you to take Lance out for a drink and a look around.'

'You want me to talk with him?'

'I want you to shut up about anything to do with Captain Loan, the Mekong Saloon or Jim Quirk. I think he's reporting to someone.'

'Okay, Mr Richard.'

'So, just go to all the Aussie bars and be seen, eh?' said Mac. 'I want to get an idea of the Chinese, see how many there are.'

'Okay – but look after Mr Lance?'

'Yeah, mate, let's get him drunk and see what he's about. I'll meet you at the Ozzie Bar at eight.'

Briefing Lance to stay close to Tranh and obey his instructions, Mac gave him the location of what he called Red Fallback: the boat-hire precinct on Sisowath Quay, at the end of Hassakan.

Leaving by the laundry entrance at the rear of the Cambodiana after slipping an American one-dollar note to the duty manager, Mac strolled down the alley behind the hotel and waited at the intersection with the street. Hailing a cyclo, he asked the rider to head across town. Approaching the river, they ducked into a side alley that connected with a rear service lane. Paying him four US dollars, Mac asked him to stay where he was for half an hour. Mac wasn't going to use him again – he just didn't want any surveillance teams to see the cyclo emerge from the lane without the passenger.

Hitting the buzzer at the rear of the Taberna, Mac presented his face to the camera. 'I've got a package to pick up,' he said, looking up and down the alley as the first spits of rain started. Miles up in the atmosphere, a thunder clap shook the air, making Mac flinch.

Cambodian voices ummed and aahed.

'You can bring it out if you want,' Mac shouted at the speaker as the thunder bellowed and the cyclo rider pulled his plastic poncho from under his seat and put it on.

Around them the roar of the monsoon drowned out all other sound as the rain started in earnest and increased its volume to such an intensity that Mac couldn't speak without his mouth filling up with water, raindrops bouncing chest-high off the concrete laneway that until thirty seconds ago had been dusty.

'Let's go around to the front entrance,' he said to the cyclo rider, easing himself back into the seat which was now a pond.

As Mac spilled out of the cyclo and hobbled on his dicky knee for the bar entrance, the rainfall boomed like a naval battle. Walking to the counter, dripping, Mac saw the source of the vagueness – a middle-aged local.

'You the mister on speaker?' the man asked, confused but benign.

'Yep,' said Mac, holding his arms out as a puddle formed around him.

The man gave him a towel. Taking a seat at the bar as he clocked his surrounds, Mac saw someone he recognised – a heavily built man in his fifties, sitting at a table.

'Macca!' said Boo Bray, standing and laughing as he took in Mac's drenched form. This was not Calhoun.

Towelling his hair and easing out of his wet shoes, Mac wondered what Bray was doing in Phnom Penh. Boo Bray was a former RAN military policeman who headed the Australian government's I-team – a group of ex-military and law enforcement people who retrieved official Australian representatives when they went off the rails.

'In Phnom Penh for long, Macca?' said Boo.

'Long enough for a beer,' said Mac, deciding he was going to get dry clothes from the market before returning and doing the pick-up from this bar. He wasn't going to seek out Calhoun in front of Bray.

'I'll join you later – where you boozing?' said Boo, his big red face friendly enough considering Mac had once had to punch it very hard.

'Ozzie Bar,' said Mac. 'So why you up here?'

'I was in Saigon for a retrieval,' said Boo.

'This is Phnom Penh, Boo.' Mac wiped off his arms.

'Yeah, I know,' said Boo, drinking his beer and looking at his watch. 'Arrived in Saigon and this high-flier bird is missing.'

'Missing?' said Mac, wondering where Geraldine McHugh really fitted into the failed Operation Dragon.

'Yeah, she's AWOL, mate,' said Boo Bray. 'They can go bad, even the best of them.'

# CHAPTER 22

Mac brooded on Boo Bray's gossip as he hailed a tuc-tuc and asked for the night markets. Geraldine McHugh – if that was the high-flier in Saigon Boo was talking about – was on the Canberra radar before Quirk was murdered. Why wasn't Mac told about it?

The tuc-tuc surged down Sisowath Quay, the bike ploughing through the monsoon water like a speedboat, before they turned left and stopped at the markets.

Gasping as he got out of the passenger trailer, Mac stood to his mid-shins in water as the driver joined him. 'Mister want the porn? Mister want the pro'tute?'

'No, champ,' said Mac, as the driver opened a large black umbrella and held it over his head. 'Mister want dry shirt and shorts.'

Leading him into the market area, where the traders had erected a shanty town of various tarpaulins and plastic sheets to keep their stalls dry, the driver seemed to know exactly where he was going in the labyrinth.

'Okay, the clothe – for you, mister, best pry,' said the driver as he stopped at a stall and began a machine-gun exchange of haggling with the owner. For five US dollars, Mac got two pairs of shorts, two shirts, a fold-up umbrella and a pair of sandals.

The rain had eased by the time they got back to the Taberna, and Mac asked to be dropped fifty metres past the bar.

Limping up the footpath, Mac assessed the largely empty street before walking into the Taberna and taking a seat at the south end of the bar. The tourists had cleared out with the rain and Boo Bray had also left.

'Yes, mister?' said the barman, a youngster.

As Mac made to answer, an American voice interrupted. 'That's a Bundy and dry – easy on the ice, thanks, Bourey.'

Standing, Mac took in the tanned, white-haired vision of Harley Maggins, owner of the Taberna.

'Hey, Macca,' said the American, shaking hands with genuine affection.

'Maggs,' said Mac. 'Drove all your drinkers away – must have known I was coming.'

'Albion?' said Maggins.

'Calhoun?'

Catching up with the small talk, Mac let the memories come back as he observed Maggins. The American was one of the overstayers from the UNTAC days, when the United Nations was attempting to stabilise Cambodia after its atrocious postcolonial history. There were warlords and remnants of the Khmer Rouge in the north and drug lords, arms dealers and slavers working with impunity in what was a failed state in the early 1990s. Mac had spent some time in Phnom Penh with the Australian delegation to UNAMIC, which ultimately became a wider operation as UNTAC. He'd met Harley back then, when neither of them were declaring who they were or which departments they were really answering to. UNTAC had been a transitional government in a lawless territory and Mac was going on military patrols into places where Thailand, Vietnam and Laos were securing commercial advantages they shouldn't have had. It wasn't helped by the presence of Bulgarian blue helmets in Kampong Speu province who were giving the Khmer Rouge the idea that they could opt out of the peace process.

While posing as a logging consultant, Mac shared a meal with a KR commander called the Duck, so-named because of his horizontal upper lip.

As they'd discussed a ten-thousand-acre forestry concession, Mac had been offered a child for sex. Refusing, Mac had kept the strongman sweet as he got more drunk; Mac eventually learned that the KR in this part of the world was kidnapping children from villages and selling them to Thai slavers.

When a skirmish broke out in a neighbouring valley, the Duck sent his men out to deal with it and kept drinking with Mac. Finally they'd gone for a walk down to a warehouse where about thirty kids were being kept in wire-mesh cages until they could be onsold to paedophiles in Europe and North America.

Mac had opened the cages, rung the UN policing unit and then driven his yellow Toyota HiLux back to town. The Duck was later found lying in a dumpster with a third eye. That was the way the news had travelled to the UNTAC heads of mission in Phnom Penh who – in order to keep the elections on track – had to be seen to do something about the murder.

At about the point when Mac was going to face charges brought by the UN's Indonesian military police, the allegations went away as an eyewitness fingered a rival Khmer Rouge commander as the culprit.

Mac had never officially been told where his alibi came from but unofficially he'd discovered that an American intelligence operator by the name of Harley Maggins had stepped in and provided the right intelligence at the right time.

The two of them had never discussed it, but after Mac came back to Cambodia in the late 1990s and found Maggins running the Taberna, they'd forged a friendship.

'So what's going on, buddy?' said Maggins, clinking drinks.

'Just enjoying the climate of Indochina.'

'Yeah – it's the right time of year.'

'So, Maggs, have the Chinese been around?' said Mac. 'You know, MSS, PLA – that sort of thing.'

'This is Cambodia,' said Maggins with a laugh. 'The Chinese think they own the place, man.'

The street was enjoying an eerie silence, the period of grace that followed a big monsoon downpour. A cricket chirped and birds squawked.

'I think I was followed, from Saigon,' said Mac, enjoying the drink.

'From Vietnam? That's serious,' said Maggins, pale eyes steady.

'We lost 'em,' said Mac. 'But we won't stay lost for long in Phnom Penh.'

Bourey asked for another order and Maggins raised a peace sign. The barman had been rescued from Bangkok ten years earlier, where he'd been kept in a brothel with his two younger sisters. Maggins had agreed to give him a job after he'd been brought back to Cambodia by the Sisters of Mercy. The Sisters weren't nuns – they were an informal network of women working in law enforcement, diplomacy, intelligence, foreign aid, health care and NGOs who tried to unpick the cronyism that allowed sex slavery to thrive in South-East Asia. To do that they shared information they shouldn't share, wrote reports they were not allowed to write and alerted newspapers and politicians to the outrages that they were being asked to whitewash. The Sisters of Mercy were almost an intelligence service unto themselves, and even though Mac was pretty sure Jenny was one of them, he'd never pushed the issue. While it was an all-female affair, Mac knew that Harley Maggins was a trusted operative for the Sisters.

'So nothing on the MSS?' asked Mac.

'I'll ask around,' said Maggins, eyeing a German couple who had crept in from the canal-like Sisowath Quay. 'But the Chinese are business as usual these days. It's the privateers you have to watch, which is what that's all about.'

Mac followed Maggins' nod and saw a manila envelope on the counter beside his right shoulder. The young barman must have put it there.

'Anything I should know about?' said Mac, picking up the package and opening it. There were three colour prints, two showing a green LandCruiser but with no view of the rego plates.

'Intrepid put the word out, and these guys had been drinking here.' Maggins lit a cigarette. 'So getting pics wasn't a hassle.'

'Mercenaries?' said Mac.

'I'm guessing ex-intel guys.'

'Who?'

'They're Israeli,' said Maggins. 'Could be Mossad, IDF, whatever. But definitely Israeli.'

The third picture showed a group of tanned men sitting at one of the Taberna's outside tables. All wore sunglasses, generic shirts and slacks. Hidden slightly by a man leaning forwards in the group was the unmistakable profile of the man who'd killed Jim Quirk.

# CHAPTER 23

The Ozzie Bar was filling with English-speaking tourists in the orange glow of the post-monsoon sunset. As a band sang about a woman who keeps no secrets, Mac held back in the shadows of a tourist T-shirt shop, peering over the clothes rack, trying to determine where the Chinese had their watchers.

His G-Shock said it was eleven minutes before he was due to meet Tranh and Lance for a drink. There were no obvious eyes on the street but, as he watched, a tuc-tuc pulled up outside the bar and Boo Bray eased his bulk out onto the drying tarmac and fished for money.

Wearing a South Grafton Rebels JRLFC polo shirt and pair of white pointy shoes under his jeans, Bray looked like the typical Aussie on the prowl as he ducked through the Ozzie Bar door.

Staying put, Mac let the street unfold, looking for new patterns and eyes. Two minutes went past and Mac was about to move when a young Chinese man stopped two doors from the Ozzie Bar and consulted a tourist map, while at the same time a tuc-tuc stopped almost in front of Mac's position. The athletically built Chinese man sitting in the back of the tuc-tuc made no effort to get out and a flash of recognition crossed between him and the tourist across the street.

'Shit,' said Mac. Boo had been followed from Saigon?

Keeping his eyes averted, Mac slipped out of the T-shirt shop and moved through the gaudily lit street, away from the Ozzie Bar. The crowds were back after the torrential rain and he blended quickly with the tourists and traders.

It didn't take more than thirty seconds of walking before Mac found who he was looking for. The woman sat cross-legged on the seagrass mat, her limp baby draped across her lap like old celery, its head almost inside the begging bowl.

Tearing a US fifty-dollar note in half, Mac showed her one half of the note, making her single good eye light up while the empty socket of the other crinkled with focus.

'Other half – him there,' he said, pointing back to the man waiting in the tuc-tuc. 'You go now – money for you there.'

As the woman grabbed at the half-note and stood, Mac moved to the next beggar – a dark man with opium eyes and no legs.

'You want fif' dollar?' asked Mac, showing the man his remaining half-note. 'Chinee tourit – he got money for you.'

His eyes following the line of Mac's pointing finger, the beggar snatched the note and started swinging his torso through his arms as he headed across the street, his eyes not leaving the watcher with the tourist map.

Giving the two beggars a ten-second start, Mac wandered into the street, casually weaving through the traffic as the woman started haranguing the man in the tuc-tuc. Moving on his rag-covered fists, the legless man covered a lot of ground very quickly and accosted the Chinese 'tourist'. As the man looked around in a panic, not knowing what to do with this beggar demanding money, a trader came out of a shop and joined the argument. The trader poked the Chinese watcher in the chest, at which point the spy raised his hands in surrender, turned and walked away from the Ozzie Bar. As Mac neared the bar entrance, he stole a glance across the road where two portly women were yelping at the guy in the tuc-tuc. Their body language said, *Well, what are you going to do for this poor woman?*

As the watcher turned his back on the Ozzie Bar to face his accusers, Mac slipped into the bar where Boo Bray was throwing back a bottle of Tiger.

'Buying, are ya, Boo?' said Mac as he stood beside the ex-MP, casing the bar over the big feller's shoulder. Lance and Tranh had a table in the corner, in the darkness, giving them a view of the entrance, the bar and the toilet doors – a classic piece of field craft. The bar was filling with Anglos trying to get drunk and find a bedmate.

Boo's pale eyes scanned the crowd over Mac's head. 'What's your poison?'

'Tiger should do it,' said Mac as the band opened with the first notes of 'Friday on My Mind'.

Keeping Boo at the bar, Mac caught up with the gossip: the Foreign Affairs lifer in Hong Kong who'd become a victim of the casinos in Macao and had started raiding the chancery coffers to sustain his habit; the bright up-and-comer in the Los Angeles Trade Commission who'd fallen for the overtures of a foxy Frenchman who was actually a Belgian spy.

'These people are amazing,' said Boo, shaking his head softly as he asked for two more beers. 'She cried all the way home. I said, "What were you thinking, love? The dip-sec told you he was no good." And she says, "Yeah, but I *love* him."'

'Those Frenchies are bloody charming, mate,' said Mac.

'Sure,' said Bray, handing Mac a fresh beer. 'But nothing a slap wouldn't fix.'

Acknowledging Tranh across the bar, Mac tried to keep things social with Boo while fishing for information. Boo and Mac had known each other for a number of years through the Jakarta and Manila embassy colonies, their personality differences always forgiven because of the number of Aussie rugby teams they'd played in together. Boo was pushing fifty but he'd played in the most recent ANZAC Day footy match against the Kiwis and he'd apparently got himself into one of his traditional blues. Mac's last encounter with Boo Bray and I-team had occurred a few years earlier in Makassar, where Boo and his sidekick Marlon had tried to retrieve Mac during the *Golden Serpent* debacle. Mac had busted Boo's wrist and dislocated Marlon's shoulder.

Mac couldn't sense any hard feelings about the incident. 'So, how's Marlon?'

'He's still working,' said Boo, looking around the room as if he'd never stopped being an MP. 'He's on this gig.'

'Not around?'

'Just looking into a matter,' said Boo with a grin, knowing how that would annoy a spy.

Mac made to move to Tranh's table. 'Come and meet my friends.'

'Nah, mate,' said Bray, nodding across the room. 'Thought I might say hello to the sorts.'

Two European women were laughing at a stand-up table and Mac chuckled at Boo's optimism. 'I'll leave you to it, mate.'

Boo tested his breath. 'Just ride shotgun – no follow-through, okay?'

'Nah, mate – I'm sweet,' said Mac.

Ordering a round of beers, Mac heard a phone ring and, turning, watched Boo answer. Bray's head sank into his chest and then he was placing his beer on a table and walking towards the exit beside the kitchen. Standing, Mac felt his pulse rise as he hooked his finger at Tranh.

'Stay in here, get eyes on any watchers,' said Mac as Tranh and Lance moved to him. 'Call me when they arrive – and no heroes tonight, okay, fellas?'

He was talking to Tranh, but he was looking at Lance. As he turned to go Tranh grabbed him by the elbow.

'You armed, Mr Richard?'

'No, mate,' said Mac, wanting to get on Boo Bray's tail.

Turning to hide his body from the patrons, Tranh fished a Ruger handgun from under his trop shirt and pushed it into Mac's hand.

'Where the fuck . . .?' said Mac, before realising it was ridiculous to tell the locals to go unarmed.

'Okay – we'll meet back at the clubhouse,' said Mac, shoving the Ruger into his waistband and covering it with his market shirt as he made for the exit.

The rear door behind the kitchen opened into a service alley that smelled the same as every service alley in South-East Asia – like an open sewer.

Mac stepped carefully into the putrid darkness, encountering two kitchen hands smoking and complaining from their apple-box perches. To his right a silhouette of a man jogged away towards the lights of the cross street and paused at the edge of a building. Crouching beside the kitchen hands as Boo Bray turned to check if he was being followed, Mac kept eyes on him and watched the Aussie look left and right and then move slowly out of the shadow he was hiding in.

Standing, Mac checked his own six o'clock and stealthed towards Bray, staying close to the wall and mountains of boxes, his mind racing. What had drawn Boo out into the night so quickly?

As he closed on Boo, an engine revved and Mac made himself a promise: all he wanted was a look at the set-up and perhaps some insight into Jim Quirk's murder.

Boo Bray's right hand moved with reflexive ease to the small of his back and what Mac assumed was a concealed firearm – the seven-shooter automatics that lay flat under a waistband. Then Boo stalked out of the darkness and crossed the street at the tail-end of a bunch of chatting locals.

Jogging through the darkness, Mac closed on the end of the alley as the engine's revs climbed to a scream.

Making a hide behind a stack of boxes twenty feet before the end of the alley, Mac saw a large 4x4 flash by. Accelerating, the SUV was doing at least seventy kph in second gear as it hit Boo Bray with the front bumper bar, sending the Aussie eight feet into the air. Spinning over the bonnet like a rag doll, Boo slammed into the driver-side windscreen pillar and was flung onto the tarmac like chaff flying out of a combine.

Female screams blended with the shriek of the over-revved motor as it continued to accelerate into the distance. Breaking from his hide, Mac raced to the middle of the street where Boo Bray lay tangled and unconscious. Blood seeped dark and wet on the road as Mac knelt, grabbed Boo's gun and trousered it – there was no need to complicate a road accident with concealed firearms.

'Doctor – ambulance!' yelled Mac at the growing crowd as he gulped for air.

A young man yelled into a mobile phone while giving the

thumbs-up and Mac turned back to Boo: the blood was coming from the head, and the left arm – collarbone too, probably – was broken. Trying to keep his own adrenaline out of the equation, he felt Boo's carotid and identified a pulse but decided against moving him for fear of exacerbating a spinal injury.

A siren wailed in the distance and Mac stood up slowly, panting with fear, his hyper-anxiety shutting out the yelling of the crowd which was openly gawking at the big Anglo lying in a twisted wreck. Beyond the throng, Mac focused on the hit-and-run vehicle, which took a left-hand corner a block north at high speed and disappeared.

Moving away from the crowd before the police arrived, Mac ducked into a store front on the other side of the street and dialled Tranh.

'Mate, there's been an accident.'

'I know, we're on the other side of the road. I'm looking at you now,' said Tranh. 'That's your friend, right?'

'Yeah. Tell Lance to stay with my friend, okay?' said Mac as he glimpsed Tranh and Lance through the rubber-neckers. 'Lance can go to the hospital, practise his cover.'

'Okay,' said Tranh.

'You and I, we're going to find the people who tailed my friend here, okay?'

'Sure,' said Tranh. 'I think that's them in the tuc-tuc, north of you.'

Looking, Mac saw the same tuc-tuc that had pulled up in front of the Ozzie Bar thirty minutes earlier: waiting, but with the driver seated and obviously on the clock, two heads in the back seat.

'Brief Lance and get over here,' said Mac as the tuc-tuc moved into the northbound traffic.

Hailing his own tuc-tuc, Mac got into the back seat and watched the crowd disperse as the ambulance and police arrived. Tranh jogged up, got in and issued instructions to the driver.

Mac had come up to Indochina to tail and report like a mature forty-year-old, but whoever was tailing him had moved to another level. In the Royal Marines, the entire culture was counter-attack: *you hit me – I hit you; you shoot at me – you'd better have your vest on, mate.* The first ten weeks of basic training at Poole had seen endless one-minute rounds of boxing where two candidates with gloves would slam the snot out of one another with no ducking or defensive manoeuvres allowed. You couldn't retreat in these contests – once you toed the line, that's where your toe stayed until the instructor called 'time'. If you retreated you'd be thrown back in until you could no longer be called a 'pea-heart' – the lowest designation on a Royal Marines base.

It was brutal and bloody but it taught Mac a very important lesson: when intellect and guile were no longer options, the only way home was to bludgeon the other bastard harder than he could bludgeon you.

'Tell him to keep eyes but hold back,' said Mac, his face hardening as he touched the Ruger and felt Boo's gun in the small of his back.

'Did you see who ran down your friend?' said Tranh.

'Yeah.'

'You know them?'

'No, but they know us,' said Mac. 'From Saigon.'

'Saigon?' said Tranh, eyes wide.

'Yeah, Tranh – my mate was run down by a green LandCruiser.'

'Not the Prado?' said Tranh.

'Bingo,' said Mac.

# CHAPTER 24

The tail didn't last long. The tuc-tuc carrying the Chinese men stopped at an intersection and then the two men who'd followed Boo Bray to the Ozzie Bar emerged from the cab and walked to a red Toyota Camry parked in front of a fruit store.

Mac got a look at them as his own tuc-tuc paused thirty metres behind the Toyota: one was tallish and slim, the other older – perhaps Mac's age – and stocky but a smooth mover. Probably ex-military, decided Mac; most special forces soldiers eventually walked with their hips so their shoulders remained stable.

'That them,' said Tranh, as the older of the two men looked briefly in their direction before ducking into the passenger seat of the Toyota.

'Them who?' said Mac, abandoning the tuc-tuc to hail a taxi.

'The strong one,' said Tranh as a battered Nissan slowed to pick them up. 'The one taking our picture.'

'In Vietnam?' said Mac, getting into the taxi.

'In the red Patrol that passed us,' said Tranh, frowning.


The tail wound westward through the changing territory of Phnom Penh, the taxi maintaining a hundred-metre distance from the red

Camry. Phnom Penh was still an enigma, all these years after Mac had first explored it: some streets were cosmopolitan and Western — or at least Hong Kong — in outlook, while others looked and smelled like something out of the nineteenth century. Wafts of sewage and rotten cabbage suddenly gave way to miasmas of incense outside trendy restaurants. In some blocks, people slept on the streets, guarded by dead-eyed men in shorts and singlets, while neighbouring blocks were well-lit and seemed as prosperous as Singapore.

Mac's mind was spinning as they moved further away from the river. What was going on? The crew who'd killed Jim Quirk in Saigon now runs over Boo Bray in Phnom Penh? Were the Chinese spies part of the same gig?

There was another problem, thought Mac as he keyed his phone.

'Lance — Mac,' he said, cupping his mouth.

'Shit, McQueen!' said the novice, his breath short. 'I mean — sorry.'

'It's okay, mate. Can you talk?'

'Yep,' said Lance, almost panting.

'You at the hospital?'

'Yep, shit, I —'

'Contact the embassy?'

'Um, yeah — dip-sec's here.'

'Warren or something?' said Mac.

'Warner, Luke Warner,' said Lance. 'But there's —'

'Cops collared you yet?'

'They tried.'

'You weren't there, saw nothing, don't know the bloke, right?'

'Yes,' said Lance. 'Just being the good Aussie Samaritan.'

'Good man,' said Mac, as the taxi took a right and sped down Mao Tse Tung Boulevard after the Camry. 'How's Boo?'

Lance's tone changed. 'He's alive, but there's something else.'

'Like what?' said Mac, not wanting anything else.

'The detective asked me if I was travelling with Barry Bray, and I said no.'

'Yeah?' said Mac.

'Then he asks me if I'm travelling with Marlon T'avai and I said no.'

145

'So?' asked Mac.

'So then he wants my passport and hotel address and I say that I wasn't driving the hit-and-run car, and he says he knows that – he's investigating an attempted homicide!'

'Okay, mate, stay calm,' said Mac, keeping his eyes on the Camry.

Lance sounded close to losing it. 'This was a murder?'

'Not yet, mate,' said Mac. 'Did you give the Hawaii as your address?'

'Yeah,' said Lance.

Mac pushed further. 'You sweet with this cop?'

'Yep, I think so.'

'Good. I want you to walk out of there and go find a tourist bar, have a few beers, sit where you can see all the entries, buy your own drinks and try not to look at surveillance cameras, okay?'

'Yep, sure,' said Lance, sounding anything but.

Mac could only hope that the kid would be okay. 'I'll call when I know the hotel's not blown – and Lance?'

'Yes, boss?'

'If a good-looking bird wants to befriend you, and it seems too good to be true . . .'

'Yeah, yeah – I know,' said Lance, regaining his composure. 'I'll wait for your call.'

'If you haven't heard by midnight, go to Red Fallback.'

'Got it,' said Lance and rang off.


Just west of the Hotel InterContinental the Camry suddenly lurched to the right of the westbound lanes and the scenario finally made sense.

'They tailing someone,' said Tranh.

'Ask the driver to close up – thirty metres,' said Mac, eyes now scanning the lanes ahead of the Camry.

'So, what did Lance try to get out of you?' said Mac as the taxi accelerated.

'Tried to get me talk about myself and then talk about Saigon and then talk about what I'm doing with you.'

'And?' said Mac.

'Two out of three ain't very bad,' said Tranh.

'Well done, Mr Tranh – any clues from Mr Lance?'

'He interested in Apricot,' said Tranh. 'But he referred to him two times as "they".'

'They?' said Mac.

'Yes, like Mr Apricot is with someone else.'

The red Camry slowed and turned right into an area of affluent Western-style serviced apartments of the type that travelling executives and businesspeople rented when they were in Cambodia for more than a few weeks. The Camry pulled to the kerb in front of them and Tranh snapped a command at the cabbie, who pulled in about fifty metres back.

Peering through the darkness, looking for the Chinese agents' quarry, they saw a brief flash of light as a motorised garage door opened and a vehicle moved forwards under the four-storey residential building. They couldn't make out the colour, but the shape of the vehicle was distinct.

'Prado?' said Mac.

Tranh nodded.

Swallowing the stress, Mac and Tranh focused like a couple of hawks as the taxi driver's eyes grew large with fear in the rear mirror.

'He say it the end of his shift,' said Tranh after the driver had whispered something.

Pointing at Tranh's pocket, Mac turned back to his surveillance. The Chinese were staying in the car.

Tranh paid the cabbie but Mac didn't want to break cover. He didn't know if they'd been made but he didn't want to toss a coin on it – he'd rather wait to see what the other players were going to do.

'How we looking at our six?' said Mac.

'What?'

'Behind us – anyone running around in a ninja suit?'

Turning, Tranh confirmed negative.

They sat still as the driver squirmed, wanting to be elsewhere. There was a faint movement at a third-floor window – a curtain closing – and then a faint glow of light from behind it.

Whatever else was happening, the lunatics in that green Prado were pros: always shut the curtain before you switch on the light, and use table lamps if they're available. No need to light up the street-facing room.

The two Chinese men in the Camry emerged onto the footpath, conferring in the darkness of a tree.

Pulling the Ruger from his waistband, Mac handed it back to Tranh. 'That's yours, mate.'

Tranh looked confused. 'We going in?'

'Just for a look,' said Mac as he pulled out Boo Bray's gun. Checking for safety and load in the stainless-steel Colt Defender, he found a full clip and nothing in the spout, giving him seven shots.

The Chinese moved towards the apartment building, one of them pausing beside the Camry and taking what looked like a Heckler & Koch submachine gun from the passenger seat.

'What about the driver?' said Tranh, pointing at the red Camry, where a plume of smoke flew out the driver's window followed by a spent match.

Mac ignored the question. he wasn't planning on being made by the Camry driver. 'Last job of the night for our driver – take us to the service lane.'

The driver sighed and shook his head at Tranh's command. But Tranh produced more US dollars and the driver put the Nissan in gear.

# CHAPTER 25

The service lane was muddy but relatively garbage-free. Numbering off the rear entries they stopped just past a floodlit compound surrounded by cyclone fencing and containing the large black garbage wheelie bins signifying a Western apartment building.

Tranh and Mac had barely hit the pavement when the cabbie accelerated away. Moving to the fence, they cased the area. No obvious security cameras but there was razor wire along the top of an eleven-foot fence. They could see a security door against a cinder-block wall that would lead into a communal area, the elevators and stairwells.

Mac found a length of old carpet rolled beside a garbage bin. Hauling it back to the fence with Tranh, they threw it over the razor wire and Mac clambered up on Tranh's cupped hands, then straddled the wire and reached down for the other man.

As they landed on the concrete pad, Mac pulled the carpet down and hid it behind the bins. They paused, waiting for a burglar alarm or a woman calling for her husband. Walking to the security door, they heard voices on the other side and a shuffling sound. Tranh made to flee but Mac held him by the bicep and gave him the wink as he reached into his pocket and pulled out the hotel key.

'So, I'm saying to this bloke, I'm like, "Who the fuck do you think you're kidding, mate?" and this prick is right up in my face,' said Mac theatrically, pulling Tranh along for the ride.

The security door opened and a well-groomed Anglo woman pushed through with a big bag of rubbish.

'Hi, love,' said Mac with a smile and wink. 'Need a hand with that?'

'I'm okay, but thanks,' said the woman in an American accent.

Turning to Tranh, Mac continued the charade: 'So, I'm sick of this prick by now, right?'

Holding the door open, Mac jabbered away to Tranh while the woman dumped her bag and hurried back to the held door.

'Thank you.' She smiled at Mac as they all moved into the courtyard, a leafy area of about twenty square metres with a central pond and high shrubs and lighting in the undergrowth. Apartment balconies looked down on the garden and Mac moved to the shadows in the lee of the south wall. The glass door slowly moved back towards a locked position as the American woman disappeared into the foyer and around the corner to what was probably the elevators. As she moved out of sight Mac lunged at the slow-motion door and stuck the toe of his sandal in the gap before it could shut.

Pushing into the light of the foyer, Mac looked back to check that Tranh had his Ruger out.

Moving to the stairwell door marked 'G', Mac drew the Colt, clicked off the safety and took a deep breath. He pushed down on the door handle as Tranh leaned in close, the handgun held cup-and-saucer behind Mac's head. Upstairs, a door slammed; moving further in, the light was strong and the stairwell was empty. Mac scoped the stairwell with his Colt by making a box with his aim. Nothing – the stairwell looked clean.

The elevator dinged and light flooded into the foyer as the lift doors opened.

Turning to his left Mac saw only Tranh's widening eyes and watched the pupils flash dark as the Vietnamese pulled the Ruger down and let a shot go, roaring in Mac's ear.

There was movement from the elevator and instantaneously the foyer was filled with the flash of automatic gunfire.

Throwing himself into the stairwell, Mac rolled on the concrete, his ear screaming from Tranh's gunshot at such close range. The bullets flew behind the door and Mac leapt off the ground and smashed the stairwell light bulb with the Colt, plunging the space into blackness.

Opening the door two inches, Mac took shelter around the corner and shot left-handed in the direction of the elevator, using four shots. The foyer floor was covered in glass and Mac couldn't see Tranh through the darkness and gun smoke.

'Tranh!' he yelled, but fell back as rifle fire chewed the doorframe, blasting a cloud of concrete shrapnel into his face.

Pulling back into the darkness of the stairwell, almost dropping his gun in the process, Mac's hands came up to his face. He couldn't see. He was sure he hadn't taken a bullet but the concrete dust had penetrated his eyeballs with such force that he felt like they were on fire.

'Faaaark!' he screamed as the gunfight raged on the other side of the door.

Feeling with his hands Mac climbed the stairs with no vision, in a blind panic. Turning at the first landing, he pushed too hard and slipped on his bad knee, dragged himself to his feet and kept climbing as his eyes burned deeper, creating swirling patterns of red and orange and bursts of pain behind his forehead.

Panting as he crawled and clawed his way up the stairs, Mac worried that the tears flooding down his cheeks was blood – what if the exploding cinder block had taken out his eyes?

The gunfire had stopped by the time Mac had ascended to what he estimated was the fifth-floor landing. He got to his knees and clawed for a door handle, but the stairwell doors required security keys to open them.

Pushing himself back on his arse into the corner of the stairwell landing, Mac coughed a chunk of concrete out of his throat and tried to control his breathing as he checked the Colt by feel.

Listening for approaching boots, he considered his options: they had assault rifles, they'd already killed Jim Quirk and Tranh, and now they were coming for him. Mac had three shots of .45-calibre loads left in the Colt and he was going to wait for them to come, take three random shots and let God decide.

His face ran with tears and his eyes hurt so much that all he could do was whimper as he awaited execution. He was vaguely aware that he was sitting under a light bulb but he still couldn't see.

And then the door at the base of the stairwell opened and he could hear a low whisper – more than one of them. They were coming – the fight he should have settled back in Saigon when he had the chance had come back to haunt him. He thought of those dark, piercing eyes, goading him as Jim Quirk was executed.

Gulping down his panic, Mac held the Colt at a point where he thought they'd come from, blinking as high and hard as he could to regain some sort of vision. He thought about Jenny and he thought of his beautiful girls, Sarah and Rachel. He thought about a life doing others' dirty work and he decided it wasn't too bad – if all he could go out with was one more kill on the bad guys, he'd take it. They could write what they wanted in his obituary; he'd take payback right now.

He heard another whisper and a boot sliding on concrete – still two floors below. A woman screamed. Mac gasped for air and waited, and then suddenly there was a hand on his gun wrist and a steel object pushed against his cheek. The click that accompanied it was unmistakable.

His throat dry, Mac waited for death. But what came was a male American voice.

'Drop it, McQueen, and you might live.'

The waterworks were running out of control down his face as Mac dropped the Colt, which clattered on concrete.

'Stand,' said the voice.

Sliding himself up the wall, Mac was led up the stairs to the top floor. More light flooded into a faint glow behind his marred vision as a door was opened and Mac was pushed along what sounded like a corridor. Then another door opened and he was shoved through it so hard he lost his feet and sprawled onto carpet.

A muttered conversation occurred close by, and then he was being rolled onto his back and his head was placed on a cushion.

'Keep 'em open,' came another American voice, and Mac felt a warm liquid wash across his eyeballs, making his eyelids flutter up and down.

'The fuck's that?' said Mac, croaking as the briny fluid ran down his tear ducts and into his throat.

'Saline solution,' said the voice. 'Just relax and we'll get you cleaned up.'

'Cleaned up?' said Mac, blubbering through the fluid, not knowing if he was laughing or crying. The absurdity of it caught him by surprise and he laughed. 'You're cleaning me up?'

Heaving for air as he giggled like a pot-smoking undergraduate, Mac began to cough concrete dust from his bronchial tubes. The fit got worse and worse until he was dry-retching in agony.

As his sight slowly returned, Mac's wrists were cuffed behind his back and he was seated on a comfortable sofa. He could make out two men in the room; they looked Chinese. The stocky one – Mac realised it was the Chinese agent they'd been tailing – stood in front of him and moved a finger back and forth.

'I see it,' said Mac.

'Good,' said the Chinese agent in his Midwestern accent. 'Let's start with the basics: when did you start working with the Israelis?'

'Israelis?!' said Mac, surprised.

'Drop the games, McQueen,' said the stocky guy. 'Tell us where the girl is and this can end with smiles all round.'

'The girl?' said Mac. 'Which girl?'

'McHugh,' said Stocky. 'Hand her back and you can go home.'

'*Geraldine McHugh?*'

'I need her address, smart-ass,' said Stocky. 'Not her fucking name.'

# CHAPTER 26

The tall Chinese stood at the side of the street-facing window and scoped the action outside. The eerie wash of red and blue lights illuminated the ceiling of the apartment.

In front of Mac's perch on the sofa, the stocky Chinese lifted his cell phone and dialled. The mumbled conversation wasn't pleasing to Stocky: 'Okay, so you lost them – what I want to know is, can you find them?'

Mac assumed the Chinese driver who'd waited out the front had lost the trail of the gunmen.

'Keep looking, keep me informed,' said Stocky, snapping the phone shut.

Voices rose from the street and the flexi-cuffs around Mac's wrists dug in.

'Cops are here,' said Tall, in a Texan accent. 'An ambulance too.'

Stocky sipped on bottled water, not dropping the stare he had on Mac.

'How many cops?'

'Three cars – uniforms and Ds,' said Tall, his back flat to the wall adjacent to the window.

'Time to go,' said Stocky. 'Just have to decide what we do with Mr McQueen.'

'Leave him here,' said the tall one. 'See if he's got problems talking when the local cops drag him into the basement.'

'He's not going to the basement,' said Stocky. 'He's probably consular. Cambodians won't touch him.'

Mac gulped; he knew that whatever or whoever these Chinese-Americans were, they had to interrogate him, kill him or let him go. Either way, they didn't want to spend an evening talking to the police and explaining why their apartment was filled with guns. Mac hoped he represented some value alive – that the same connections Urquhart liked so much might buy his life.

As Stocky mulled it over, a cell phone trilled. Stocky looked down towards the sound coming from the sofa, then stepped forwards and pushed Mac onto his side so he could pull the pre-paid Nokia from Mac's back pocket.

'Number unknown,' said Stocky, reading the screen and inclining his head towards a black briefcase on the kitchen bar. The phone kept ringing as Tall opened the briefcase and extended a thick black aerial out of it. Stocky sat beside Mac on the sofa and held the phone between their ears so they could both hear.

'Be nice, okay, McQueen?'

Mac shrugged and Stocky hit the green button.

'Hello,' said Mac, croaking.

'Hi – perhaps I have the wrong number? Who's this?' came a heavily accented voice. It sounded like the man who'd killed Jim Quirk.

'No, you got precisely the right number,' smiled Mac. 'Why else would I be answering? Who can I say is calling?'

'I was looking for Mr Davis. Richard Davis, of Southern Scholastic Books?'

'He's not here right now, Mr . . .?'

'No, that's okay,' said the man, gentle but in control.

'He has an answering service,' said Mac.

A pause opened and Mac thought he heard a sigh. Then the thick accent started again but with a nasty edge. 'Okay, my friend. Tell Mr Davis that the delivery from Saigon was not to my liking. Tell Mr Davis that he has no involvement with my business interests, but if he wishes to be involved, I will resolve that situation very quickly.'

'Situation?' said Mac. 'What situation?'

'Tell Mr Davis that when we all stick to our own business, we can all prosper – but I will not tolerate interference.'

The connection ended and Stocky looked at the display, where a blinking phone icon informed that 00.58 seconds had elapsed.

'Shit,' said Mac, flopping back on the sofa.

'Get it?' said Stocky, moving to the briefcase.

'Yep,' said Tall. 'MobiTel roaming charge to VinaPhone – made the call from a cell zone called "Royal Palace".'

Stocky made to leave. 'Ring Eagle, let him know.'

Royal Palace was on the Tonle Sap, across town and half a dozen blocks north of the Australian Embassy. The Israelis were moving fast, but to where? Mac thought quickly about what he could do to stay in this game. Two minutes ago his every instinct had been to get away from these two, but now he wasn't so sure.

'Are we locked on?' said Stocky, collecting his phone and gun from the kitchen bar and shoving them into a backpack.

Tall got off the phone to the driver. 'We've got a lock but I doubt they'll use that cell phone again.'

'It's in the ditch as we speak,' said Mac, deciding to involve himself.

'You talkin' all of a sudden?' said Stocky.

'If you're gonna catch these pricks, sure,' said Mac.

'No, tough guy,' said Tall from the other side of the room. He'd closed the briefcase and was stowing his own backpack. 'You'll talk because you want to live.'

'Oh really?' said Mac, smiling now that he'd split their team. 'So how will you explain Captain Loan's investigation into McHugh?'

'Captain?' said Tall as he moved on Mac, fists clenched. 'The fuck you talking about?'

'See, you don't know where the Cong An fits into this story, but I do, and I'm sure Jim here prefers me alive and talking to dead and making the maggots fat.'

Stocky held up a hand to silence his partner as he eyeballed Mac. 'What's your deal? And make it fast, McQueen.'

'Get me out of here. I'm no use to you if the Cambodians get involved.'

'And what do you get?' said Stocky, shouldering his pack.

'I get enough to track down the pricks who just called me,' said Mac, hoping he could see interest in Stocky's eyes.

Stocky looked at Tall quickly. He had a round Chinese face, with slab cheekbones and a nose that had been broken at least once. His hair was groomed to look civvie but it cried out to be military. Mac was hoping he was right and this bloke was ex-military – at least he'd understand why these Israelis had to be hunted down.

'Your partner?' he said, not taking his eyes off Mac. 'He Vietnamese? Slim build, hard-on with a gun?'

Mac smiled. 'Sounds like him. Did he make it?'

'Don't know,' said Stocky. 'I'm Sam – that's Phil.'

'What do you need, Sam?' said Mac.

'You answer one question honestly, and you're out of here. Lie to me and I feed you to the cops, maybe plant a gun on you.'

'Hit me,' said Mac, wanting to speed this up.

'Why were you following us?'

'Actually, it was you who followed a mate of mine to the Ozzie Bar,' said Mac, his eyes feeling like raw meat. 'When he was run down I assumed you guys were involved – the green LandCruiser was gone but I saw you getting out of a tuc-tuc and into a Camry. We followed you to this building, someone shot at us, I got a face full of concrete. That's it.'

Sam swapped a look with Phil.

'Sounds about right,' said Sam as he pulled out a pen knife and turned Mac to get at the flexi-cuffs. 'Think you can act like a normal human long enough to walk out of here?'

'I can shave off a few IQ points, hide the movie-star good looks,' said Mac. 'That what you mean?'

Sam smirked as he headed for the door, but Phil fronted Mac and gave him the look. It was the kind of gesture that if it happened in Rockhampton would have triggered a brawl. But as he slid around Phil to follow Sam into the hallway, Mac gave him a wink.

Phil now hated him, which meant he was just where Mac wanted him.

* * *

157

The Phnom Penh streetscape flashed past, Mac in the front passenger seat wondering how this was going to end. Phil sat in the back of the silver Mazda retrieved from the apartment building, a SIG on his lap aimed at Mac, the cell phone tracking device sitting beside him. The submachine gun was now looped over Phil's shoulder.

The location of the mystery cell phone had frozen on Wat Phnom, a religious landmark on the river about fifteen blocks north of the last lock.

Mac needed more information. 'So, you going to tell me who you are?'

'Sam and Phil.'

'Good American names,' said Mac. 'So tell me about these Israelis.'

'They're up to no good,' said Sam.

'Private?'

'You plug us in to what you know, and maybe we'll talk,' said Sam.

They pulled into the leafy surrounds of Wat Phnom about twenty minutes later. The big roundabout that encircled the seven-hundred-year-old temple-hill was crowded with cyclos, taxis and tuc-tucs – Phnom Penh was still backwards enough for a near-new green LandCruiser to stand out, especially if the occupants were hammering along.

Sam pulled to the inside of the circle and leaned out the window, waving a US one-dollar note. The beggar crouching behind a park bench with his family came forwards and eyed the cash.

Spewing out a stream of Cambodian, Sam kept the money out of the beggar's reach. Mac recognised good field craft – engaging the man, getting him talking but staying in control.

Finally Sam gave the man the dollar and then gave him another, and they were screeching for the road that connected Wat Phnom with the Sisowath Quay road.

'Saw them go past only five minutes ago,' said Sam as they hurtled past the Electricity Cambodia building towards the river. 'Said he saw them go across Sisowath and into the docks area.'

'Think they're there now?' said Phil from the rear.

'Well, they didn't turn north and get out of town,' said Sam, threading through the traffic.

'So they've got a boat?' asked Mac, now caught up in the chase.

'Wouldn't bet against it,' said Sam, as they paused at the Sisowath Quay main road and saw the lane into the river docks area on the other side. Edging across the traffic, the silver Mazda slipped into the courtyard in front of a depot building and Sam paused while he looked left and right.

The darkness created by the overhead trees and the generally deserted nature of the riverfront made Mac nervous. A bat jostled in a tree and screeched, and in the car they all jumped slightly.

'Could be time to hand back that Colt, eh boys?' said Mac as Sam took the right-hand turn and they slipped further into the darkness.

The quay apron opened up on the other side of the trees, partially floodlit. A selection of old vessels were tied up at the quayside and two large floating piers were sitting in the river, connected to the quay by concrete walkways. Sam brought the Mazda to a halt.

'You're not getting the Colt back,' he said. 'But you can make yourself useful and drive.'

Mac got out of the car and walked around it, his stomach grinding with anxiety, while Sam pushed himself across the centre console.

Getting in, Mac thought he saw movement at the end of a building at the rear of the concrete quay. Putting the car in gear, he eased forwards. 'There's something at the end of the building.'

'I saw it,' said Sam and Mac killed the lights. Behind him, the sound of Phil's SIG being cocked broke the tense silence and Sam reached out and touched Mac's arm.

Stopping the car, Mac switched off the engine and they watched the old warehouse on the quay, bathed in dim light.

'You're the driver,' said Sam as he checked his own SIG for load and safety. 'Stay here — be ready for anything. Now hit the trunk.'

Mac pulled the boot release and held his hand over the interior light as the two men eased silently from the car. They moved to the back of the Mazda, rummaged softly in the boot and then moved to the right of the car, towards the tree line that ran behind the warehouse. Mac could make out assault rifles in their hands, M4s by the look of them: the cut-down, souped-up M16s used by US Special Forces.

Disappearing into the shadows of the trees the two men moved towards the warehouse.

Mac reached over to the back seat, searching Sam's backpack for his Colt, but came up empty. 'Shit.'

Beyond the warehouse a light went out and Mac could now see the noses of a line of vehicles. One of them could have been the grille of a LandCruiser, but he couldn't tell in the darkness. The warehouse was the commercial base for the boats that plied the river and activity in the car park on the other side of the building was hardly suspicious.

Mac searched the centre console for a weapon – even a knife would be better than nothing. The ambush at the apartment building and his temporary blindness had produced a mild shock and Mac noticed his right hand was shaking as he pulled it out of the console.

Checking the glove box, Mac found a sheaf of Hertz rental papers. A 'Samuel Chan' had rented the Mazda in Saigon a week ago; the papers contained lots of good stuff, such as a US address and a credit card imprint. As he put the papers back, he realised there was a California driver's licence sitting in the glove box.

Watching the Americans move behind the warehouse, Mac could feel his adrenaline coming up. In the Royal Marines they'd said adrenaline could give you extra speed and strength, or paralyse you. It was always up to the soldier to harness the fear, not be strangled by it.

Beside his left hip, his fidgety fingers touched the boot release lever and he had an idea.

Mac pulled up the lever then eased out of the Mazda and walked to the popped boot. Looking around, he raised it, dipped his head inside to stop too much light escaping. In front of him was a Remington pump-action shotgun of the type used by American police departments, with four belts of replacement shells. That was reassuring, but there were also two grocer's boxes, and from the opened flaps on one of them, they seemed to contain US hundred-dollar notes – perhaps a million dollars' worth in each box. Mac grabbed a handwritten note from the top of a box, but couldn't decipher the writing. He trousered the piece of paper.

As he stared at the cash, light filled the boot. Standing and turning, he watched a vehicle approaching down the same leafy laneway they'd just come down in the Mazda.

Blinded by the headlights, Mac lifted his arm. It wasn't until the vehicle passed by that the passenger in the front seat locked eyes with Mac.

Those dark eyes struck him at the same time as he realised the vehicle was a late-model LandCruiser Prado. Green.

# CHAPTER 27

The LandCruiser's brake lights flared red as the 4x4 hissed to a stop on the concrete.

Reaching into the Mazda's boot, Mac grabbed the Remington – from memory they were five-shooters, and he hoped Sam and Phil weren't the conscientious types who unloaded their shotties before stashing them.

The front passenger door of the LandCruiser opened as Mac primed the Remington with a back-and-forth motion on the pump-grip and brought the shotgun to his shoulder.

Walking around the back of the car, Mac took aim and watched those creepy dark eyes withdraw on seeing the shotgun.

As the LandCruiser lurched away, Mac squeezed the Remington's trigger. The click echoed around the quayside.

The LandCruiser's doors opened as it slid to a stop beside one of the floating piers.

'Fuck,' said Mac, fumbling for the Mazda's boot, realising he'd shut the thing.

Crawling along the car as the Israelis took position fifty metres away behind the LandCruiser, Mac ducked and pulled the boot release lever as the window above him exploded. Running in a crouch to the back of the car, he dived into the lee of the vehicle as five shots slammed into the Mazda, smashing windows and pinging steel.

Pushing the boot lid up, Mac wished his knee was up to this. He could barely straighten it.

Pulling two belts of shells from the boot as the left rear tail-lights exploded in plastic fragments, Mac knelt behind the right rear tyre, his sweaty, panicked fingers fumbling to load the Remington.

'Shit,' he said as he tried to get his fingernails under the brass head of a shell that didn't want to leave its loop.

Getting two shells into the side-loading chamber, Mac stood up behind the Mazda's boot lid, shouldering the shottie as he did so. A coughing burst of automatic fire rang out and Mac instinctively ducked while keeping eyes on the LandCruiser; the shooters were bunched behind the 4x4, but they were no longer shooting at him.

Turning to his right, Mac watched a flare of orange and blue burst out of the darkness on the far side of the warehouse as Sam and Phil unloaded into the LandCruiser, which seemed to drop a foot in height.

One of the Israelis sagged and grabbed at his shin as the rounds flew and Mac could see the man he knew as Red Shirt scrabbling into the 4x4, pulling something out of the rear cargo area.

Pointing towards the river, Red Shirt pushed the injured Israeli towards a moored boat.

The limping gunman tried to jog along the concrete causeway to the floating pier and Mac took two useless shots at him, ducking back as the return fire came in hot.

Looking up, Mac saw Phil running from his hide behind the warehouse to the lee of a flatbed truck parked between the LandCruiser and the warehouse.

Peeking over the lid of the boot, Mac watched Red Shirt pull a dark weapon from the LandCruiser. Assessing the ground, Mac realised that the warehouse was out of range of the Israeli guns, but by running to the truck, Phil had put himself in range.

As Phil laid down fire on the 4x4 – cover for Sam to come forwards – Mac reloaded the pump-action while trying to get Sam's attention.

He screamed as loud as he could, 'Stay there!' Mac didn't know what Red Shirt had pulled out of that vehicle but Phil was looking like an easy target.

Sam's head poked out behind the warehouse corner and Mac became frantic to get his attention and stop him crossing the apron to join Phil. 'Don't move! For fuck's sake – stay put!'

Sam was suddenly into the open and the air was torn apart with the sound of a gunfight jammed on full auto. Mac joined in, loosing four shots at the LandCruiser, but they did no damage except to the paintwork.

Sam was into his fourteenth stride when he took a shot in the thigh. As he sprawled, his rifle clattering free in front of him, a small rocket whooshed through the night air, leaving a blue-grey trail before slamming into the truck's gas tank. The tank contained gasoline rather than diesel, because the orange-red fireball that instantly erupted was caused by nothing else, except perhaps propane.

Flinching away from the shock wave and then the blast of incinerating heat, Mac held up his hand to deflect fire from his eyes and saw Phil under the truck, burning like a monk.

Bile rising in his throat, Mac realised Sam was writhing on the concrete, his chinos on fire.

To his left, two of the Israelis were on the causeway, making for a speedboat that the injured shooter had throttled up and was readying to get underway.

Breaking his cover, Mac sprinted for the warehouse where a red wooden box was bolted to the wall. Smashing the padlock with the Remington's stock, Mac tore the doors open and pulled the red canvas bag off its hooks, racing towards the flaming truck where Sam writhed as the gasoline flames burned through his cotton pants and into his leg.

Throwing the shotgun to the concrete, Mac pulled the fire blanket out as he reached the American, launching himself onto the panicking man with the blanket in front of him. In his military days, they were taught that the point of the exercise was to smother the flame – you couldn't do that by waving the blanket and you couldn't smother a flame when the victim was rolling around. You had to wrap the flame up like you were hugging it to death, which was what Mac did as he landed on Sam's leg: put all of his weight and strength into holding Sam in one place and wrapping the blanket around the American's legs and waist for fifteen seconds.

Sam eventually stopped struggling: he whimpered and heaved for breath as Mac pushed himself off and looked for remaining flame.

The speedboat revved hard and Mac looked to his left, watching the Israeli crew accelerate up the river and into the darkness as more gunfire sounded. Ducking into one another, Mac and Sam waited for the volley of rifle rounds but none came.

Mac peeled back the fire blanket and found the left leg of Sam's chinos was charred and there was a blistered, purple mess up his thigh.

'You'll live,' said Mac, panting.

Sam, grimaced, his lips white in the way that signalled he had about thirty seconds before he passed out from shock and pain.

'Let's get you in the car, trooper,' said Mac, picking up Sam's rifle and groaning as he stood and put full weight on his knee.

'Phil?' said Sam, looking at the truck's gutted chassis.

'Didn't make it,' said Mac, holding out his hand. 'Can you walk?'

Sam reached out his own hand, coughing as the hot gasoline soot started descending. Pulling him to his feet, Mac put an arm under the other man's armpits and wrapped it around the shoulder blades.

As the American put weight on his injured leg, he heaved with the pain. 'Holy Christ!'

Two steps short of the Mazda, Sam slumped unconscious and Mac dragged him to the back door and fireman-lifted him inside, laying him across the back seat.

The ride to Calmette Hospital took four minutes but it felt like an hour as Mac dodged the cyclos and motorbikes on the dark streets, trying to make out their shapes through the cracked windscreen. The soft tropical air flowed through the Mazda, entering via the side windows that no longer existed, and Mac blinked hard, hoping for tears as the gasoline soot worked its way into his eyeballs.

The emergency room took Sam immediately. Awake but groggy, Sam gave Mac an open-palmed shake.

'Thanks, *mate*,' he said, doing a croaking rendition of an Aussie accent.

'No dramas,' said Mac, and the American had a drip spiked into him before being wheeled away on a gurney.

Pulling his Nokia from his pants, Mac realised it was switched off – the damn thing had run out of battery.

At the nurses' station he asked about a recharger, but when none was forthcoming, he wandered outside, got in the Mazda and made for the Cambodiana.

The streets were thinning out as he pulled into the parking lot of the Cambodiana. After a three-minute recce he walked down a service alley that led to the loading bay behind the kitchens and laundry. Taking a right turn into an alcove just before the lobby, he found himself in the security room. A local man in a Cambodiana shirt looked up from his desk, above which the surveillance cameras displayed their black and white shots of hallways, bars and pool-side areas.

'Hi, Richard Davis, with the Tranh party in rooms 303 and 305,' said Mac, smiling and holding out his hand, seeing the name tag identifying the man as 'Poh Khoy – Security Manager'.

Poh rose, took his hand and made a small bow. 'Yes, Mr Richard.'

'Just want to bring you in on something, Poh,' said Mac, lowering his voice and making a show of looking back over his shoulder.

Poh walked past Mac and shut the door.

'Earlier this evening I got a letter under my door. It contained some threats against me and my family.'

'Mr Richard, this hotel is not –'

'I know, I know, mate,' said Mac, showing his palms to the security man. 'This is a great hotel and security is always very good. I just need to see the surveillance tapes for this evening, see who was posting us nasty notes.'

'Rooms 303 and 305, you say, Mr Richard?' said Poh, tapping on his keyboard. A box came up onscreen and he selected 'third floor west' from a drop-down menu then entered a time field, starting at six pm and ending at ten pm.

Mac looked at his watch – 10.06 pm.

'Okay, so here is the hallway,' said the security man. 'Your rooms on right side of hall. Fast-forward now.'

166

Taking a seat, Mac watched the footage rocket along: room-service people pushed trolleys; a manager carried a big bucket of ice to 307; porters collected the spent room-service trays; two Asian children chased each other up and down the hall until their mother leaned out of a door on the left side of the picture and ordered them inside.

Mac had lost interest and was about to head up to the suite when the high-speed tape showed two men walk past the door to 305 – Mac and Tranh's suite – and then walk back to it.

'Here – right here,' said Mac, clicking his fingers at the screen as he sat upright.

It slowed to real time and Mac read the time code: 21.14 – quarter past nine.

The two men wore black baseball caps pulled low and shirt collars flipped up. Mac identified them immediately: one was Red Shirt, and the other the injured speedboat driver. They crowded the door and then they were inside.

'Fuck,' said Mac.

It was brazen – they were either taking the piss or they were desperate for something. In general, if you operated covertly and a gunfight had brought you into the open, you didn't double back into enemy territory such as a hotel room or house. You stayed hidden, surveyed subsequent movements and decided whether you were blown or if you could proceed.

Making himself breathe in and out slowly as he watched the men disappear into the room, Mac watched the time code. At 21.15, they emerged again and headed away from the camera, walked past the elevator and exited through the fire door.

Mac had performed more covert nosey-pokes than most people had had sex. And he knew there was only one way you could make a search in under a minute: you had to know what you were looking for, and exactly where to find it.

# CHAPTER 28

'You know those people?' said Poh, pointing at the screen.

'No,' said Mac.

'I'm coming up with you.' Poh stood and grabbed a cop's flashlight and a ring of master keys. He was out the door before Mac could argue.

They pushed through the fire door marked '3' and walked up the hallway to 305. Poh drew his Beretta 9mm and gave the key to Mac, nodded at it as he took a shooting stance.

This was not turning out the way he wanted it – the last thing he needed was to be storming a room with a rentacop when there could be Mossad-trained professionals inside. Mac didn't like drawing civilians into the world he inhabited, his basic rule being that anyone in civvie shoes got the benefit of the doubt; anyone in boots was a warrior. Poh wore manager's shoes, but Mac also needed to check that room and grab his case. So, turning the key, he pushed the door back with his arm, allowing Poh to walk inside with the gun held in front of him with two hands.

Mac saw why the search had been so fast. His backpack was sitting on the dining table, where he'd left it. Exactly. If someone was ransacking the entire suite, the pack would have been left open, contents on the table.

Carefully unzipping it, Mac went through the layers and the pockets, looking for the trail. The contents – right down to pieces of paper and airline tickets – had been systematically unfolded and searched before being put back where they came from. It was something professionals were trained to do but which professionals like Mac could also pick up very quickly.

Poh went into one of the bedrooms and made a show of searching it.

'This was the room they wanted,' he yelled and Mac padded over to the door of Tranh's room. Someone had made a big production of trashing the room and Tranh's bag, and Mac wasn't even going to look at it. It was a veil for the search of Mac's pack – one of the Israelis would have searched his bag and replaced everything, while the other trashed Tranh's stuff.

If it was supposed to distract Mac, it merely focused him. As he returned to his pack, he wondered what they were looking for, and he assumed from the speed of their search that they'd found it.

Turning the pack on its side and trying some of the pockets, Mac heard Poh go into the kitchen area and then the other bedroom.

Standing the bag upright, Mac noticed something wrong with the outside pocket. He always brought both zips together at the top of that pocket, giving him one-handed access when he needed something in an airport or for a hotel check-in.

Now the pocket had been zipped over so both zippers were jammed together on the far left-hand side. As he slowly opened the pocket he remembered what he'd put in there.

Then there was movement across the living area of the suite and Poh was standing in the doorway of the bathroom.

'Not much to search in here, right, Mr Richard?' said Poh, loving being part of something more important than telling Aussie backpackers to stop having sex in the pool.

Mac opened his mouth to scream 'No!', but just like in the worst dreams, no sound came out.

Poh hit the lights and the bathroom remained dark for one second. Then the room flashed white and bellowed, throwing Poh across the living area and launching him through the curtains. Millions of porcelain chips and a cloud of plasterboard dust surged out of the bathroom, stripping an armchair, buckling the ceiling and pushing the entire window assembly out of the wall and into the night.

Diving behind a sofa, Mac put his hands over his ears and tucked up as the blast of debris waved through the suite and then receded, leaving the fire alarms repeating the honking 'evacuate' sound. The lights had blown out in the explosion, and as Mac raised his head into the cloud of dust he saw the ceiling outside the bathroom hanging by a thread, the wiring sparking and a flood of water spreading into the living area, the faucets obviously sheared by the blast.

Standing, Mac grabbed his bag and moved to the door, thankful for the clean air as he emerged from the maelstrom of dust and debris, his inner ears screaming.

The exit lights flashed as Mac made for the fire stairs, joining the other guests as they chattered about the bang and the shaking of the building. Mac nodded and smiled at a New Zealand couple as they moved down the stairs, only hearing every third word.

Spilling out into the parking lot, Mac could hear sirens and decided to be absent when the police made their appearance. He found the Mazda, removed Sam and Phil's backpacks and pulled out the Hertz rental papers and Samuel Chan's driver's licence. He was going to leave the cell phone tracker, but then decided it could be useful and he grabbed that too.

Finding the van they'd brought from Saigon, Mac threw the bags inside and drove out of the Cambodiana, past the crowd standing around Poh, who lay amid the building debris, looking like a man who'd fallen asleep in a tornado.

His watch said 10.26, which gave him an hour and a half before he made the Red Fallback with Lance and got him to safety. Mac was scared and uncertain of what he'd got himself into but his main worry was what Lance might do. When you went up against a foreign intelligence crew, and they wanted you dead, you only had a very small margin of error to work within, and Mac prayed that Lance didn't get too nervous and make a phone call he shouldn't.

Parking in the guest area of the Holiday International Hotel, just around the corner from Calmette Hospital, Mac changed his clothes and walked to reception. He made the transaction a very simple Indochinese settlement: he booked a room in the name of Sam Chan, put a pile of US dollars on the counter and then put the California licence beside the money. He allowed the night clerk to count the money himself and then took the registration form and filled it out, using the Mazda's rego in the 'vehicle' section. The clerk handed over the room card and didn't even look at the registration.

Standing against the wall of his room in the darkness, Mac looked through the window at the entry driveway. He stood that way for eleven minutes before moving away from the window and sitting in the dark beside a power point.

Plugging his recharger into the wall, he powered up his Nokia and waited for the envelope icon to tell him if there was voicemail. Three came up: two from Urquhart, one from a Singapore number, probably Benny Haskell.

The first call, from 4.43 pm, was just Urquhart wanting a reminder about whether Mac was back in Saigon that evening.

The second was agitated: Urquhart demanding to know what the fuck was going on. What was this about Boo Bray and why was Lance left alone?

Seething, Mac dialled Urquhart's number. One of the hardest things to teach a new field guy was the need to hold radio silence when a gig went bad, and adhere to the fallbacks as agreed. Once you started picking up phones and telling tales to your higher-ups, you put other people at risk, not just yourself. Having that discipline was the big delineator between the naturals for field intelligence and the people who should be writing research at head office.

'Urquhart – Davis,' said Mac as the call was connected. 'You called?'

'Fucking hell, mate,' said Dave Urquhart, losing his oily finish. 'Do you ever check your phone?'

'Why would I do that when your snitch can do all the phone-ins for me?'

Urquhart almost hissed. 'For God's sake, he's a newbie, all right? He's been in for eighteen months and here he is in Cam-fucking-bodia, fending off detectives in the hospital while he watches Boo Bray die. And where the fuck are you?'

'He knew the gig,' said Mac. 'He had his orders – no phone calls. The people tracking us have probably hacked our phones and calling you has not just endangered Lance, it's probably made life more difficult for you and me too.'

Urquhart sighed and took a breath. 'No doubt. But we have one of ours running around out there not knowing what to do.'

Mac could barely believe what he was hearing. 'What? Having a beer and staying out of bed with stray women? That's so hard?'

'Of course not,' said Urquhart. 'But we're not all like you. Not all of us like this stuff.'

'Well, that just shows how little you know about me, mate,' said Mac, more disappointed than angry.

At Nudgee College in Brisbane, Mac had once gone down to Pat Lenihan's cube and tried to get back the fifty-dollar note he'd stolen from a young Dave Urquhart. Pat Lenihan was the dorm bully and his older brother, Jim, was in the cube with him that evening. Mac had to fight them both for the money.

He'd brought the fifty back to Dave with some bark missing, but he'd done it because it was the right thing to do, not because he liked it. Even in adulthood Mac was often surprised at how the back-office guys justified their own lack of activity by labelling anyone who endured hardship as a different class of human. And then they wondered why people like Mac felt more comfortable with their counterparts from rival agencies than they did with the lunchers in Canberra.

'Sorry,' said Urquhart. 'But I want you back at base camp by midday, okay?'

'What about Bray? What about Tranh?'

'Bray's got an embassy girl assigned,' said Urquhart. 'Tranh? You mean that Vietnamese boy? What's he got to do with this?'

'He's thirty-one,' said Mac, massaging his temples to stop the stress driving him mad. 'And he's either dead or they've got him.'

'They? What are you talking about?'

'I can't talk on these lines,' said Mac. 'I'll call tomorrow morning from the embassy.'

'Look, I don't care what's going on with the local kid,' said Urquhart, a whole new tone in his voice. 'Lance is the priority – retrieve him and get back to Saigon.'

The line went dead. Listening to the third message, Mac heard Benny's nasal growl: 'Mate, some more on that matter we'd been negotiating. Something very, very interesting. Call me when secure. Cheers, mate.'

Grabbing a Tiger beer and a bag of nuts, Mac ate and drank seated on the floor, thinking about what had started with the simple tail-and-report of a wayward trade commissioner.

His jaw muscles were setting like concrete and his growing headache was an official splitter; his knee ached and his eyeballs, after the trauma, had settled into a throb of pain which alternated between sandpaper-dry and watery.

Eyeing his backpack, he pulled it towards him. Putting his hand into the outside pocket, there was no sign of the SD memory card that he'd picked up at the Mekong Saloon; the same card that Mac had asked Lance's opinion of as they'd raced eastwards across Vietnam.

Staring into the empty pocket he tried to put the pieces into place. What was on the card? What did it have to do with Jim Quirk and Geraldine McHugh? They'd killed Quirk – done it in front of Mac. They had McHugh, didn't they? What was on the SD card that it warranted so much carnage?

Sipping on the beer and chewing the peanuts, Mac looked for a thread but couldn't see it.

Checking his watch, he rose and resumed his surveillance of the hotel driveway, cursing his knee as he struggled to find a comfortable stance. After ten minutes he decided there were no watchers and, finding Boo Bray's Colt Defender in Sam's bag, shoved it into his waistband and put on a black baseball cap.

The evening was warm and alive with bats and crickets as he walked the street from the Holiday International. He ignored fourteen cyclos until he found one resting and not looking for work. They went south along the riverfront road of Sisowath and stopped a block beyond the boat-hire area.

Mac paid and walked through the trees lining Sisowath and onto the parallel docklands road that – if he kept walking north – would bring him to the burnt-out truck and Phil's charred corpse. Moving through the trees and undergrowth, he found a hide from which he could observe Red Fallback while also getting a line of sight up and down the dock road.

Sitting in silence, Mac smelled the fish curries wafting on the breeze and listened while a monkey spoke to itself above him. There were a few cars parked on the dirt road, but most didn't seem occupied; those that did probably contained horny salarymen with their mistresses, thought Mac.

At 11.58 a white man in casual clothes skipped across Sisowath and walked directly into the meeting area. It was Lance, on time and with a gait far cockier than his apparently anxious state should have allowed. Had Urquhart exaggerated about Lance's nerves, or had Lance talked it up to his mentor?

Deciding to keep the telling-off for the following morning, Mac took a last look down the lane and wandered into the meeting.

'You're early,' said Mac, walking up to the youngster.

Lance stopped. 'So are you.'

Mac saw something in his eyes as he got to him, and then realised Lance was wearing long sleeves despite the heat. It was all wrong but before he could get his hand on the Colt, Mac was looking at a seven-shooter Glock with a suppressor attached – the standard issue to Australian intel operators with an S-2 classification. An S-2 was a licence from the relevant minister to carry firearms.

Raising his hands slowly, Mac stayed calm. 'Didn't know you were armed, Lance.'

'Drop it,' said Lance, nodding at Mac's belt. 'It's in your waistband.'

Behind Lance, a car moved towards them, the lights firing up. Wincing into the high beams, Mac turned side on, removed the Colt and let it drop on the dirt road.

'Wanna talk about it?' he asked, adrenaline pumping.

'Talk about it?' said Lance with a snigger. 'You're not need-to-know, believe me, *champion*.'

'Need to know what?' Mac squinted into the headlights which were now directly behind Lance.

'Shit, you're a dumb-arse, McQueen,' said Lance. 'Haircut – fucking *haircut*! Are you high? Where does some dumb-shit assassin get off telling *me* to cut my hair?'

'Is this a father thing?' said Mac.

The gunshot rang at his feet and Mac did his best not to flinch.

'Where is it?' said Lance.

Mac's reservoirs of concrete dust and gasoline soot were igniting under the strength of the vehicle's headlamps. 'What?'

'The memory card, dumb-shit – what do you think this is about?' said Lance.

'I should ask you,' said Mac as the car doors opened behind Lance and shapes moved up to him.

'I'm asking you, McQueen,' said Lance. 'Last seen in your backpack. I would have grabbed it myself but your room at the Cambodiana no longer exists.'

'The memory card? I don't have it.' Mac's mind was spinning.

'Yes you do.'

'Mind reader as well as anilinguist – I'm impressed.'

Lance breathed out as he sneered, controlling his urge to shoot. 'Let's go to your hotel and discuss it like pros, eh, champ?'

'I'm not going anywhere,' said Mac.

'I think we're way beyond that, don't you, Macca?' came the voice from beside the fullbeams.

A figure stepped forwards, and Mac raised his hand against the glare, deflating slightly as he saw who it was.

'Fuck – *Davo*?'

'Yeah, I know,' said Dave Urquhart, standing beside Lance. 'I hate this field stuff. So let's grab that memory card, mate, and push on like nothing ever happened.'

'Nothing happened?' said Mac. 'You've pulled a gun on a senior guy from the Firm.'

Urquhart smirked. 'Like I said in Canberra, there doesn't need to be any blow-back on this – play it smart and your career might be the winner.'

# CHAPTER 29

The smell of coffee was strong as Mac opened his eyes and took in the surrounds: a high-ceilinged bedroom in a French-colonial house.

Trying to stretch and yawn, Mac was constrained by the chromed handcuffs that held his right arm to the iron bedhead. Wiggling his fingers and toes, he confirmed he was in one piece and, judging by his cognition, he hadn't been drugged – it was old-fashioned fatigue that had triggered the deep sleep. His only worry was his left eye, which seemed to have become glued shut with mucus. He needed another saline wash.

The smell of coffee was joined by grilled bacon and he felt his stomach grumble with anticipation as he sat up and scoped the overgrown back garden evident through the large sash windows beside his bed. He was most interested in finding a feature that could tell him where he was. In the British military they trained recruits to be able to pinpoint their whereabouts at all times. Whether by compass, sun, stars, landmarks, water flow, bird life or simply asking a civilian, your first job was to be able to state your position. The Royal Marines had no use for a commando who didn't know where he was, and candidates who couldn't get the hang of it were called 'tits' by the non-coms – as in 'tits on a bull'.

During Mac's military days in the early 1990s, he'd been team leader on a recon tab across Scotland, one of those exercises where you learned to cover ground by night and keep a proper reconnaissance log of what you'd seen: the height of the rivers, livestock movements, electricity workers, telecom trucks, loggers, surveyors, hunter camps and so on. One of the team tore an ankle ligament and in the kerfuffle Mac forgot to take his trigs and match them with the map; by the time they struck camp and he'd made his six am radio call to the instructors, he couldn't state his team's exact position.

The chief instructor, a legendary warrant officer named Banger Jordan, had told him, 'Then you'd better pull your head out of your arse and take a look around, you fucking tit.'

Mac looked around now, peering beyond the tree line at the back of the garden and trying to catch glimpses of what lay beyond. The early rays of sunlight seemed to be coming from the left of the garden, meaning that was the west and he was facing north. Something glinted behind the trees but he couldn't quite make it out.

The door jangled as the big German deadlock shifted, and a large Samoan-Australian walked through the door with a tray of tucker.

'Marlon,' said Mac, surprised.

'Who'd you expect?' Marlon dragged a stool to the bed with his foot and put the tray on it. 'Elvis Presley?'

'John Rowles would have been a start,' said Mac, eyeing the two bacon and egg sandwiches and the plunger of coffee. Mac had busted Marlon's shoulder a few years ago in Makassar, when the I-team had tried to retrieve him; he wondered if there was any personal enmity between them.

Marlon smiled. 'So, in the shit again, McQueen?'

'Nah, mate,' said Mac, hooking into the sandwich. 'Just laying up.'

'Not what I hear.'

'What'd you hear?' said Mac, always enlisting for information.

'You've got something secret that belongs to the government,' said Marlon. 'And Boo's in hospital because of it.'

'Geez.' Mac shook his head as yolk ran down his chin. 'You believe that, Marlon?'

'Don't know what to believe with you spooks, frankly. You're all bloody liars.'

Mac let that one go. 'How's Boo?'

'He's alive, broken pelvis and collarbone – those hit-and-run boys got him good.'

The door squeaked and Lance shoved his head into the room. His earring had made a conspicuous return.

'Well?' he said to Marlon. 'You gonna chat him up all morning or are you gonna kiss him?'

'Sorry, boss,' said Marlon, sighing.

'I need you, T'avai – now,' Lance said, and disappeared from the door.

Mac could see Marlon wasn't enjoying answering to Lance, but that he wouldn't buck the chain of command.

Pausing at the door, Marlon smiled. 'It's not personal, right, McQueen?'

'I forgive you, my son,' said Mac. 'But before I do anything else I need an eye-bath, okay? A few bottles of saline solution – the good stuff – or I won't be talking to anyone.'

'Okay, I'll sort it,' said Marlon, still not leaving. He cleared his throat. 'Some of the boys said you were in the SBS – that true?'

'Nah, mate,' said Mac, which was technically the truth, since although he'd passed selection for the Special Boat Service, he'd never served in the unit. 'Those guys are pros – I couldn't run with them.'

'But you were with the paras or marines or something?'

'I drove a truck.'

Marlon left the room, muttering to himself.


With a full stomach, Mac now tried to get tears running in his eyes. He couldn't open his left eye without it feeling like a Velcro strip and he wanted that saline. His reasons weren't just medical: Mac knew that Urquhart and Lance wouldn't have prepared the safe house like a field guy would. Experienced operators would always include a comprehensive first-aid kit, given that people had accidents and they preferred to avoid doctors and hospitals. Even toothaches could be salved with a good dentist-strength analgesic gel until the gig was finished. Office guys never thought of such mundane things.

Mac wanted his captors to go out and buy a few bottles of saline solution, which might mean going to a drugstore or an optometrist. But it could just as easily be the public dispensary of a hospital – Mac would be able to look closely at the brand and make an assessment of his position.

Marlon was back with the saline in what Mac estimated was between eleven and twelve minutes, and he hadn't heard a car being started. The three bottles Marlon placed on the tallboy in Mac's room were from a high-quality French medical supplies company, and in the two-litre size dispensed at hospitals.

Allowing for five minutes at the dispensary to select and purchase the correct products, Mac decided there was a walk of four and a half minutes each way, which translated to about two hundred and eighty metres at a casual pace. Allowing for traffic lights, they could be as close as two hundred metres to a hospital – a major hospital, with a public dispensary issuing hospital-grade saline.

Lance sat on a reversed chair beside Mac's bed, Urquhart behind him on another chair.

'Okay,' said Lance. 'Let's start at the beginning.'

'Your daddy forgot to pull out,' said Mac.

'*Macca!*' said Urquhart. 'Let's get this done and we can be on our way, okay?'

'Done? I don't see a tape recorder, I don't see anyone taking notes,' said Mac, 'so I'm not exactly sure what this is.'

'This is an interview, McQueen,' said Lance, who seemed to have some product in his cropped black hair and was now dressed in Levis, cowboy boots and a loose-fitting white shirt that in Rockhampton would have been called a blouse.

'Well, Lance, in an interview we record what is said or we take notes – it's how we do it in the Firm.' Mac tried to stay composed. 'It avoids a small matter of ambitious little shits making political gain from a delicate situation.'

'I don't need to make political gain from you, McQueen,' said Lance, tensing. 'Don't flatter yourself.'

'Thanks – I'll be my guest,' said Mac. 'Why don't we start with you identifying yourself and telling me who you work for?'

'Why don't we start with you fucking yourself?' said Lance, face darkening.

Mac smiled. 'Sure, mate. Uncuff me and I'll show you how that works.'

'Fellers, *fellers!*' Urquhart stood up. 'I don't have all day for this.'

'Then get this silly runt out of my face, Davo, and we'll talk,' said Mac.

'That's not your call!' Lance was standing now. 'This is my gig.'

Mac almost had the situation turned the way he wanted it.

'It may be your gig, Lance, but it's my room. And that gigolo aftershave you're swimming in? It's not working for you, champ.'

Lance bunched his fists and moved towards Mac. 'You're a fucking –'

'*Lance!*' said Urquhart, leaping in front of his protégé, holding him by the arm.

Walking Lance towards the door, Urquhart gave him a small push.

'Get a haircut!' said Mac as Lance left, raising a middle finger.

'Fuck you, McQueen,' came Lance's voice from the corridor.

'I catch you again, I'll put a number two across your head, mate!' said Mac as loud as he could. 'Swear to God, sunshine – I'll hold you down and shear you like a bloody Merino.'

Taking Lance's chair as a door slammed on the far side of the house, Urquhart gave Mac a look. 'All done? Can we talk now?'

'Sure,' said Mac, as somewhere in the neighbourhood the morning prayers started. Another landmark: a mosque. That was the golden glint he'd seen through the trees. Close to a mosque and close to a hospital with a dispensary. That probably meant he was in a leafy enclave of colonial homes on Boeng Kak Lake, over the road from the mosque and alongside the sprawling compound of Calmette Hospital.

'Mate,' said Urquhart, 'I need that memory card and I need it now.'

'I don't have it,' said Mac, pushing a second pillow against the bedhead to get comfortable. 'What's on it?'

'I can't disclose that,' said Urquhart, not looking smug for once. 'I'm not messing with you – I just can't tell you.'

'I could be of more help if I was trying to get it back.' Mac held up his cuffed wrist.

'I know,' said Urquhart. 'But this is eyes-only – PM's office.'

Raising his eyebrows, Mac wondered if he'd ever encountered such a level of secrecy while in the field. 'The air gets thin up there, mate.'

'I know,' said Urquhart. 'As soon as Lance told me you had the card, we had to retrieve it and we had to put you in a security bubble.'

'You hired Lance to do this?'

'You were the first person I thought of, Macca, and the only person who would just get it done. But you told me to fuck off.'

'Where'd you find him?' said Mac, needing more.

'AG's.' That meant ASIO. 'But he's a favourite of the PM – he's done a lot of sensitive burrowing, if you know what I mean.'

Sensitive burrowing for the Prime Minister's office usually meant ferreting the real story out of an ongoing gig and bringing the snippets back to the PM's desk. Sometimes the burrower was also a provocateur, twisting and influencing a report to create a more convenient outcome. Some of the most potentially damaging ASIS and military intelligence reports on Beijing and Jakarta had felt the guiding hand of the burrower over the years – burrowers were a hazard of spooking, but they usually didn't look as out of place as Lance.

'Well, I don't have the memory card now,' said Mac.

'Where did you find it?' said Urquhart, looking a bit like a tortoise sticking his head out of its shell after a long sleep. He was a very different man when out of the snake pits of Canberra.

'It fell off Jim Quirk's computer,' said Mac, thinking back. 'In the Mekong Saloon.'

'How did you get it?'

'You're not cleared for this, Dave,' said Mac. 'I answer to Scotty and Tobin.'

'I've seen the report – you were present at Jim Quirk's murder. I just want to know about the SD card.'

Mac didn't have much more to add. 'The shooter was trying to fiddle with the computer keyboard before he shot Jim. There was a lot of action around that machine before Jim died and I saw this card fall to the floor – I picked it up out of habit as I left.'

'These killers –'

'Probably Israeli.'

Urquhart squinted. 'So you have the memory card and you carry it into Phnom Penh, and then what?'

'Someone steals it from my bag,' said Mac.

'When?'

'Last night, before I went to fallback with Lance.'

'This was at the Cambodiana?' said Urquhart.

'How do you know?' said Mac, alert.

'Made a hell of an exit,' said Urquhart.

'Christ's sake! You were *there*?'

Urquhart shrugged. 'Only once the place was on fire and the ambulance guys were scraping a security guard off the car park.'

'What were you doing there?' said Mac, trying to assess how much Urquhart knew.

'Lance said the memory card was in your backpack – we were going up to the room to grab it.'

Mac thought about the timelines. 'So you were at the hospital together, with Boo?' asked Mac.

'Nope,' said Urquhart, shaking his head. 'Lance called me from a bar after he'd left Calmette – said you were AWOL and the SD card was in a pocket of your backpack. So we met at the Cambodiana.'

'Shit,' said Mac, getting an insight into how the Israelis had intercepted that information.

'What?'

'I think you blokes should stick to your whiteboards and political lunches,' said Mac, trying to control his fury.

'Why?'

'Because there's a young Cambodian who's dead because your buddy Lance doesn't know his craft.'

'What are you talking about?' said Urquhart.

'Lance has changed his clothes, right?'

'Yeah,' said Urquhart. 'He brought them with him.'

'Bring them here, but let's talk about Super 14 for the next three minutes.'

Urquhart came back into the room with two handfuls of clothes and threw them on Mac's lap. 'But anyway, Berrick Barnes seems to be thriving with the Waratahs.'

'Yeah,' said Mac, running his hands over the chinos and the trop shirt. 'flaming traitor.'

'Be great to see the Reds put some form on the field this year,' said Urquhart, peering closer at the clothes.

Mac found what he was looking for and held it up: a metal sphere the size of a ball bearing, with a dozen small wire hooks, that had been hanging from the black cotton under Lance's collar. It was a micro-transmitter of the type that only had enough battery power to transmit for twelve to fourteen hours but which picked up most conversational speech for about five feet around it.

'Yeah, mate,' said Mac, careful not to touch the sphere and let its owner know it had been found. 'I want John Roe back in a Reds jumper. He's hell when he's well.'

Handing the clothes back, Mac pointed to the door. When Urquhart returned, his waxy Canberra pallor was more grey than usual.

'Shit,' he said, sitting and rubbing a hand up over his face and hair. 'That was a microphone? They were listening to everything Lance was saying?'

'Within range, yeah,' said Mac.

'So they heard where the memory card was and beat us to it?'

'Sure,' said Mac. 'That's how it goes in this game.'

'But how did they get close enough to plant this thing on him?' asked Urquhart.

'Pretty girl, alone at a bar, asks a bloke to talk about himself,' said Mac with a wry smile. 'If you think it's too good to be true, you're probably right.'

# CHAPTER 30

Lying on his back, Mac squirted saline into each eyeball, blinking it out again. As his eyes slowly cleaned themselves, he tried to work out what parts of this gig to lie about and what to come clean on.

Lance and Urquhart had obviously tailed him after the Singapore fiasco and it would have been within Urquhart's power in Australian intelligence to have Mac assigned to the Jim Quirk tail. Mac was inclined to believe Urquhart: he'd genuinely wanted Mac to help him weed out the potential traitor who set up Ray Hu. And Mac had genuinely turned him down, at which point Urquhart opted for having Mac assigned to Saigon.

But the routine tail-and-report of Quirk had turned nasty and suddenly Lance was in a van with Mac, seeing the memory card. Lance must have felt the ends coming together quite easily. But then Boo Bray was run over and before Lance could double back to the Cambodiana and grab the memory card, the Israelis had intercepted Lance's ill-advised call and grabbed it, leaving Lance and Urquhart looking like a couple of dilettantes.

Mac could only surmise what was on that card. What worried him was a series of violent attacks from the Israelis, culminating in a light-bulb bomb at the Cambodiana; that is, a light bulb filled with a fuel-oil accelerant such as ammonia nitrate and a small flash-detonator in place of the filament. You didn't need a huge amount of explosive in a small area like a bathroom — there was nowhere for the blast to go except out the door, where the victim should be standing at the light switch.

Someone from Israeli intelligence would know how to make such a bomb. One of the best technical rotations Mac had ever done was with the Shin Bet, Israel's internal spy agency. Most field operators in the Shin Bet became proficient in making IEDs, so they knew a bomb factory when they saw one, and in many cases could smell a bomb-maker if they were standing beside him.

What Mac didn't understand was how Ray Hu came into it.

For now, Mac needed to get out of the safe house before Urquhart or Lance came back with questions about the shootout at the docks the night before. Mac had his own questions about that incident and he had two main priorities that had nothing to do with the memory card: he wanted to find Tranh, and to do that he might need Sam's help. And then he had some payback planned for that Israeli hit man with the mad eyes.

Mac had one thing going for him: Lance had failed to find Mac's backpack or the van. Mac reckoned the backpacks and cell phone tracker were safe in the room registered under the name of Sam Chan until Phnom Penh police reported to the Australian Embassy that they'd found the 'lost' van. Mac had given his vehicle rego as the Mazda's. The van wouldn't be found immediately, but before it was Mac needed to get out of the house.

His black baseball cap was hooked over the back of the chair near the door, and he had an idea.

Eighteen minutes later the deadlock rattled and Marlon brought Mac's lunch into the room, dragged the stool over with his foot and put down the sandwich and a can of Tiger.

'I'm liking your taste in food, Marlon,' said Mac, eyeing the sandwich. 'Ham, cheese and tomato — perfect with a cold beer.'

Smiling, Marlon turned to go. 'By the way, I was at the embassy this morning and I bumped into Alex Beech.'

'How's Sandy?' said Mac.

Marlon's face burst into a big, toothy smile. 'Sandy *Beech* — you cheeky bugger.'

'He loves it,' said Mac. 'Try calling him "Bondi" and watch him come alive. What's he in town for?'

'Didn't say,' said Marlon, taking a seat on the chair and looking mischievous. 'But I got some info on you.'

'From Sandy?'

'Yeah. I asked him why someone from the military would claim to have been a truck driver when they obviously weren't.'

'And he laughed and said the military runs on logistics,' said Mac.

'How'd you know that?' said Marlon.

'Because Sandy shovelled chow – an army marches on its stomach.'

Marlon gave Mac a suspicious look; he'd been a police detective in Brisbane before joining I-team five years earlier and still liked to get to the bottom of people. 'Well, that's as clear as mud.'

'Hey, Marlon,' said Mac, taking a swig of the beer as he swallowed his first bite of the sandwich. 'My eyes are still hurting – can you chuck me that hat to keep the glare off my eyeballs?'

'Sure.' Marlon spun the cap through the air onto Mac's lap.

'So was Sandy with anyone?' said Mac, sure that Beech's appearance was not coincidental.

'He was alone.'

'Who was he meeting with?' said Mac, smiling.

'What you really want to know is if he was asking after you, right, McQueen?'

'The thought did occur.'

'He didn't, but I wouldn't tell him anything – I'm employed by DFAT, not Defence.'

Mac pushed. 'How was he dressed?'

'Relax, cuz,' said Marlon, standing and stretching. 'Your best bet is to tell this Lance fool what he wants to hear so we can all move on. I was due in Honkers yesterday.'


Gnawing at the right side of the cap where the peak met the cap proper, Mac tore a hole in the canvas and exposed the thin steel rim that ran in a semicircle around the edge of the peak.

He drew out the steel rim until he held a flat wire of the type commonly associated with a woman's bra. The wire slipped easily into the keyhole of the cuffs and Mac twisted and needled at the tumbler until he felt it turn. Within ten seconds his wrist was free.

Standing, Mac cat-walked to the door and listened to Lance and Urquhart arguing somewhere in the house. They were classic intelligence dabblers: smart enough to ensure that people got hurt, but not experienced enough to fix their mistakes. If they followed the script used by most of Canberra's whiteboard warriors, they were currently tearing each other apart over the memory card, but by the time they got off the flight into Sydney they'd have shifted culpability onto Mac or maybe even Boo Bray, who had the added attraction of being unable to speak up in his own defence.

Lance and Urquhart would be blameless. Not only would they write the report, but they would be protected by the truism that he who stands closest to the Prime Minister is never hit by the shit.

Moving to the window, Mac checked the latches: they were the old-fashioned horizontal-twist type, but with locked bolts in the sashes.

Slipping the flat wire from the cap into the first bolt lock, Mac worked at it until he felt the wire twisting and losing shape. He gave up on that one and moved to the second, where the wire went in more readily. He had it unlocked in six seconds.

Lifting the window, Mac looked into the garden. He was on the first floor, with a fifteen-foot drop to the vegetable patch. Grabbing his sandals, he walked back to the window and was preparing to throw his leg over when the door opened. Turning, he saw Marlon at the same time Marlon saw him and they locked eyes for a split second, in an exchange of men asking one another, *Are we really going to do this?*

With a stamp kick at Marlon's left kneecap, Mac threw a swinging elbow at the big man's right temple.

Leaning back slightly, Marlon took the blow on his nose and blood spurted across the white door like a Pro Hart stroke. Whipping a right-hand uppercut at that big jaw, Mac instead hit Marlon's thick left forearm coming down with a strong block that threw Mac off balance.

Marlon was about a hundred and fifteen to Mac's hundred and five, but his right hand leapt out like a cobra at Mac's throat, wrapping almost totally around his neck. Mac felt his spine straighten and his feet almost leave the ground as Marlon applied the power with that enormous arm, making Mac feel like a passenger.

Twisting his face away from Marlon's, Mac threw a finger strike at his assailant's eyes. Marlon slackened his grip and smashed the arm off his throat with a right-arm block and lashed a fast low–high left hook combination to Marlon's kidney and then his jaw, sending the bigger man lurching back and sideways into the door.

'Marlon, are you okay?' Urquhart called from downstairs as the door almost came off its hinges.

Marlon's eyes rolled back and he attempted a left-hand punch which glanced across Mac's right cheekbone. Keeping his eyes locked on Marlon's, Mac dropped to his knee and threw a fast groin punch straight into the Samoan's pubic bone.

Air expelled in a whoosh from the bigger man's lungs and Mac was on him as he collapsed to the polished wooden floor. Grabbing the fifteen-shot Glock from Marlon's hip rig, Mac panted for breath and heard someone running up the stairs.

Turning for the window again, Mac looked down on Marlon, whose mouth was open in surprise, still unable to get air in.

'Legs up, under the chin,' said Mac, making for the window and launching himself at the vegetable patch. Throwing himself out so he'd land sideways with his right hip falling first, Mac hoped he could save his left knee. It was a trick he'd learned in the Parachute Regiment's P-company years ago, and the landing worked okay, if getting a face full of cabbage counted as a success.

Standing, he ran for the garden wall and clambered up it, straining at the top of the bricks as Urquhart got to the window.

Urquhart yelled, 'Macca! You're making a mistake!'

But Mac was over the wall and running, the stolen Glock now jammed in his waistband. The humidity was terrible on the street and Mac could feel another monsoonal downpour building. Deciding not to work any fancy patterns or routes, he headed directly towards the Holiday International, keeping his black baseball cap pulled low.

Going in the back way, through the laundry and the trade

entrances, Mac emerged at the lobby and held back by the newspaper racks until he'd surveyed the reception desk. Looking down briefly, something caught his eye and he shook his head to make sure he wasn't seeing things. Breathing out, he dragged his eyes away from the newspaper and got back to the immediate job.

At the reception desk he was queried when his blue eyes didn't match what they expected 'Chan' to look like. Reciting the California address he'd memorised from Sam's licence, he asked for the room key and was given it as he slapped twenty US dollars on the counter.

The 'Do Not Disturb' sign was where he'd left it and he couldn't see any evidence of someone having been in his room. Panting, Mac walked to the wall beside the windows and cased the hotel driveway, looking for overly enthusiastic walking or driving.

Having seen nothing after five minutes, he unscrewed a light bulb from a wall light, entered the bathroom and replaced the main bathroom light bulb. Placing Marlon's Glock on the bathroom counter where he could grab it from the shower cubicle, he stripped and stood under the hot shower, his hands shaking slightly as the muscles in his face spasmed. He was back in the game, but he didn't know if he could do it anymore. Dealing with the violence was not as easy as he remembered – the Israelis' ambush at the apartment building and the rocket attack at the docks, and then the light-bulb bomb at the Cambodiana. Poh being thrown into the night like a piece of garbage, by a bomb intended for Tranh or Mac. He felt vulnerable, exposed and confused – he was in the middle of something he didn't understand and now his own side had turned on him.

Yet that wasn't what had him shaking. It was what he'd seen on the front page of the *Saigon Times* that had thrown him into a spin. The headline read, AUSSIE COPS ARRIVE FOR NIGHTCLUB MURDER, and below he'd seen the photo of a tall brunette in a black trouser suit and white blouse being let into a white Holden Caprice as she spoke into a mobile phone.

He knew that face and knew the way that mouth worked when it was telling some dumb-arse to pull his finger out and get busy. The caption read, *Agent Jennifer Toohey of the Australian Federal Police arrives* at Tan Son Nhat yesterday to assist Saigon detectives with the Jim Quirk homicide investigation in Cholon.

She was coming into an environment where people were trying to kill him. Mac had always promised not to cross into her professional life, but he didn't know if he could hold back in this case. When the bullets started flying, Jenny wasn't a cop – she was his wife.

# CHAPTER 31

The brown contact lenses were the final touch, the exclamation mark that took the black hair, dark moustache, wire-rimmed spectacles and chubby cheeks and altered the entire context.

It was 8.04 am and Mac had enjoyed a deep sleep. He felt recharged.

Peering at himself in the mirror of the hotel bathroom, he saw Brandon Collier. Collier was the non-sanctioned identity Mac had created a decade earlier when he needed an option for those times when people who were supposed to care about his welfare cared more for their upward ambitions. It was against the rules of Aussie SIS – you could only work with identities issued to you, and when the gig was done you had to sign them back in. Mac had a standing riposte to those rules: he who runs the risk of being tortured in a Zamboanga warehouse gets to choose his escape routes.

His baggy chinos and long-sleeved business shirt from Lowes matched the boat shoes into which he put twenty-cent pieces to make his gait more awkward. Amateur disguisers always focused on the hair and face; professionals did that too, but they took particular care with the gait and eyes. Once you'd been in the field for a couple of years, you scanned every room for eyes – their colour and intent became a beacon. As for gait, Mac could tell a soldier or professional sportsperson by the way they carried themselves, and the first thing he tried to do with his Brandon Collier creation was to take away the physically confident gait. Coins in the shoes took the emphasis from the torso and the hips and put the walking effort into the legs. If a spook or a cop or a soldier was on the lookout for Mac, they might find him but it wouldn't be because he looked like trouble.

Peeling back the liner of his wheelie bag, Mac lifted a packet of IDs from their hide and slipped the rubber band off them. There was a Western Australian driver's licence, a WA Health Department inspector's ID and a security card of the type needed to work in restricted areas of airports and docks. The one he pulled out and pocketed was the International Red Cross medical accreditation – this classified him as an Australian with two science/medicine degrees and listed him as 'Medical Doctor – general.'

The only part of the Brandon Collier act that didn't add up was the Colt Defender automatic handgun that was tucked into the waistband at the small of his back.

The walk around the block was pleasant enough except for the growing humidity. Mac estimated the temperature at around thirty-eight degrees which, for someone who had grown up in Queensland, wasn't too oppressive. It was the ninety-eight per cent humidity that sapped the energy.

Phoning the American Embassy, Mac asked for the chargé d'affaires. 'What's his name again? Jim or John . . .'

'No, Clayton de Lisle is our chargé d'affaires. Just putting you through now.'

'I'm losing you,' said Mac, hanging up.

He walked both sides of the street, stopped at a street cart, where he bought a baguette with pâté and cheese, and spent some time looking in shop windows, looking for observers. There were none he could see, and having got his new gait in sync and bought a box of chocolates, he made for his destination.

The Calmette Hospital layout was explained in the lobby by a diagram of wards and Mac inspected them rather than approach the main desk.

Wandering through the corridors, he followed the blue signs that said Intensive Care, taking several doglegs and a flight of stairs to the first floor, and going through a set of heavy plastic curtains with *Intensive Care Ward* stamped on them below the Khmer version.

He headed for the nursing sister's desk and casually pulled his IRC card from his pocket and tabled it.

'Dr Collier – I'm here for Samuel Chan,' said Mac with the condescending yet trustworthy smile of the medical doctor. 'A nine o'clock, I believe?'

The nurse, a friendly local in her early thirties, looked down at a clipboard on her desk and nibbled her lip. Then she looked at her watch: 9.03 am.

'There's no record of a medical visit, Dr . . .'

'Collier – Brandon Collier,' said Mac. 'Perhaps we should get Mr de Lisle on the phone. He's the chargé d'affaires at the American Embassy.'

'Umm, perhaps I should ask –'

'I can get Clayton de Lisle down here right away, but he probably doesn't want to be disturbed; he asked me to handle this with Mr Chan.'

The girl capitulated. 'Okay, I take you.'

Few South-East Asian hospitals wanted to annoy the Americans. The USA gave away as much in humanitarian aid each year as the entire GDP of countries like Lebanon and Sri Lanka. There were hospitals and medical centres all over Asia and Africa that would not exist if it weren't for the US taxpayer, a small point often ignored by the West's Marxists.

Mac followed the nurse and, as directed, walked into the ward with the blue 'D' over the door. Sam Chan was propped up on pillows, the *Economist* open in front of him. He was peering over it at Mac.

'Samuel Chan,' said Mac, approaching and offering his hand. 'The man they couldn't root, shoot or electrocute.'

Chan looked confused and his hand slipped under the sheets.

'Sammy, it's me, McQueen,' said Mac. 'Don't shoot, I only work here.'

Chan smiled and let the tension out of his shoulder. Whatever he'd grabbed beside him, he now let go of and shook hands with the palm grip – an almost total giveaway that his background was military.

'McQueen – glad you showed.'

'Why?' Mac took a seat beside the bed and handed over the chocolates. 'You miss me?'

'Nope. I wanted to thank you for the . . . last night, you know?'

'Yeah, no worries,' said Mac.

'A lot of guys would panic, not even think of the fire blanket.'

'Thank my training,' said Mac, surprised they weren't talking about Phil's demise.

'Royal Marines, right?'

'Originally,' said Mac carefully. 'A long time ago. And you?'

'Army,' said Sam.

'You know John Sawtell – Green Berets?' said Mac.

Sam looked away. Most special forces people neither confirmed nor denied that they knew other soldiers. It was professional courtesy.

'Well, anyway,' said Mac, 'John is a great operator. He was in Mindanao, I worked with him in Sulawesi.'

There was a moment of silence. Mac had just wanted the American to know who to ask should he need a reference.

'Wish we could have saved Phil,' said Mac, looking at the lino floor. 'It just happened so fast, and suddenly that rocket –'

'Nothing we could have done differently, except stand back and let them go,' said Sam. 'And that wasn't the deal.'

Sam showed Mac his burnt leg, which had copped less damage than it had seemed the night before. The rifle shot had passed straight through his right thigh muscle without touching bone.

'I'm having one more test this morning, and then I'm out of here,' said Sam.

Mac looked around at the other patients. 'That's what I wanted to discuss.'

'What's on your mind?'

'You and I are the only ones to have tangled with this Israeli crew and lived to talk about it,' said Mac. 'So we should either buddy up, or you tell me all I need to know about these pricks and I'll hunt 'em down myself.'

Sam laughed softly and looked at Mac. 'Not working with the Australians?'

'There was some internal shit,' said Mac. 'And when it hit the fan, I was standing downwind.'

'Tell me all about it.'

'I can't,' said Mac. 'Get me seconded and we can pool the intel.'

'It may not be that easy,' said Sam.

'Why not?'

'Perhaps we're on different sides.'

'Really?' said Mac.

Sam nodded. 'Australia is part of the problem, not the solution.'

Mac tried to guess what the dispute might be. He realised he'd have to give something before the Americans would trust him. There was only one part of the puzzle that he'd witnessed and it might interest the Americans.

'You and Phil wanted that memory card,' said Mac.

'Sure,' said Sam, eyes shifting.

'If I tell you the story about that card, would you tell me what's on it?'

'I can't make that deal, McQueen,' said Sam. 'What I can do is hear the story and see where you can help. Then, if my bosses like it, we can talk more.'

'That's it?'

'You know how this works,' said Sam.

So Mac told the story of the Singapore gig and the slaying of Ray Hu and the subsequent tailing of Jim Quirk in Saigon. He admitted to carrying the memory card but having no idea of its importance, and then explained how it was stolen from his bag at the Cambodiana by the Israelis.

'You were hauled in by your own people?' said Sam.

'They weren't my people,' said Mac. 'They're answering to a different level of government and they're desperate for that SD card – they think there's a traitor.'

Nodding slowly, Sam looked away, and then back at Mac.

'I'll have a chat – you got a cell phone?'

Grabbing Sam's phone, Mac input his number and called his own.

'I'll call you tonight, regardless of how it goes,' said the American, as a doctor and nurse came to Sam's bed with their clipboards.

'Make it quick,' said Mac.

'Okay – but it's a pity you haven't run across Geraldine McHugh,' said Sam.

'McHugh?' said Mac, his heart quickening as he remembered – McHugh was the central concern of the Americans' interrogation. It was the first thing they'd asked him after they grabbed him in the apartment building.

'I need to talk to her,' said Sam.

'Well, you're in luck,' said Mac, smiling as he stood to leave.

Sam raised his voice at Mac's back. 'You told us you'd never heard of her.'

'I fibbed – I thought I was going to die and I needed a bargaining position,' said Mac.

'Well?' said Sam.

'Well, I have to go,' said Mac.

Sam struggled from the bed as the medicos closed on him. 'No, wait, McQueen.'

'Call me with the good news,' said Mac as he walked away. 'Don't be a stranger.'

# CHAPTER 32

Keeping to the back streets of Phnom Penh, Mac moved south in a cyclo with the sunshade raised. Seeing a line of non-tourist convenience stores three blocks inland from the river, Mac fished eight US ten-dollar notes from his pocket and asked the driver to get him a mobile phone and as much pre-paid credit as he could buy.

Mac watched the rider dismount. 'What company are you with?'

'MobiTel, mister.'

'Good, that's what I want,' said Mac. 'And a ten-dollar calling card.'

The driver was back in ninety seconds and they headed south again.

'You want a new phone?' asked Mac, twisting in his seat and looking up at the rider in his singlet and board shorts.

'Sure, mister,' said the rider, who had a mouth full of snaggled teeth.

'Swap?' said Mac, holding out the still-sealed Samsung box.

Pulling his battered old Nokia from his box on the handlebars, the rider handed it over and Mac switched phones, putting his new SIM into the old Nokia and transferring the rider's SIM to the flash new phone. Happy with the new phone and its internet capability,

197

the rider got wind of more money. 'You need restaurant, mister? Or duty free? I take — I take now.'

'Take me to the Olympic Stadium, and then the Russian Embassy,' said Mac, describing a meandering trail through Phnom Penh. 'But take it slow — I'm sightseeing.'

Loading all of the credit onto his new account via texts, Mac phoned the calling card number in Phnom Penh, selected 'English' and entered the PIN on his card. When the machine asked him to enter the number he wanted, Mac paused and took a few breaths. He'd be taking a risk, but if he could keep his location secret, it might be worth it. Looking at his G-Shock, he saw it was almost ten am local time — two pm on Australia's Pacific coast.

Dialling the number from memory, he waited while the calling card connected to a network and then the number was ringing — the familiar purr-purr of an Australian mobile phone.

'Yep,' came the brusque greeting as the call was answered.

'Scotty — on the tiles yet, you fucking lush?'

'Jesus, mate,' said Rod Scott. 'Hold on, okay?'

Mac could hear a gathering receding as Scotty found a private place.

'Christ's sake, Macca,' said Scotty, louder now. 'You messing with my blood pressure again?'

'You've got five kids to three wives, mate,' said Mac with a smile. 'Don't blame me for the dicky ticker.'

Scotty hissed a long sigh. 'Okay, give me the short answer, Macca — what the fuck is going on?'

'You start,' said Mac. 'I need the full picture.'

'You're asking me?' said his mentor. 'You're having a lend, mate.'

'What?'

'I got dragged out of the golf club yesterday arvo by frigging Greg Tobin.'

'What did the crown prince want?' said Mac.

'He'd been called to a meeting with the DG and the Prime Minister's chief of staff,' said Scotty.

'So what did he need you for?'

'Tobin says he's not going into the PM's office without someone to hang out to dry.'

'It's nice to feel wanted.'

'So Tobin tells me you're running around Cambodia with some state secret, and you maimed Marlon T'avai again.'

Mac had almost forgotten Marlon. 'They had me chained to a bed.'

'So you attacked Marlon?'

'He tried to stop me leaving.'

'He had every right,' said Scotty.

'Yeah, well, an old mentor once told me that when the bad guys catch you, play along and stay calm, then when you see a chance, kill everything in your path,' said Mac, the Olympic Stadium looming on his left.

'But maybe your old mentor had a different technique when the bad guys were from the Prime Minister's office.'

Mac gulped as Lance's claim was confirmed. 'That's official?'

'Yeah, Macca, unless Brendon Pryce is still using the royal "we" purely because he likes it,' said Scotty.

Brendon Pryce was the much-loathed chief of staff for the Prime Minister, a former managing partner at a large law firm who spoke to Commonwealth employees as if he'd scraped them off his shoe.

'Okay,' said Mac as his rider stopped beside the stadium. 'So, they outrank me.'

'Dave Urquhart is saying he didn't second you and the Quirk tail wasn't over.'

'I thought I had a letter sitting in a safe?'

'You sight it?' said Scotty, knowing Mac hadn't.

Mac groaned. 'So it's the Firm's fault, I'm rogue and you're to blame?'

'Hey,' said Scotty, 'you should work in Canberra – you have a feel for this stuff.'

'Sorry, mate,' said Mac.

'No need to be sorry – Dragon never stopped, so I'm running you and my direct order is that you hand over the memory card or whatever the hell it is, to Urquhart, and then we bring you in with no funny business.'

'This whole thing is funny business, Scotty,' said Mac, looking around for a tail. 'If I knew what this was about, I'd be more relaxed.'

'No one knows what this is about,' said Scotty. 'Not even Tobin. We thought you were following Jim Quirk for a week or two. Suddenly, you're seconded by the Prime Minister's office and now they've turned on you.'

'I'll come in, but it has to be you in person, Scotty,' said Mac, motioning to his rider to head across town to the Russian Embassy. 'And I have to find out what's happened to Tranh.'

'The local asset?' said Scotty.

'Yeah – I think he was shot, so he's in a hospital or he's dead,' said Mac. 'There was an ambulance at the building so I'm hoping he was only injured.'

'No promises about Tranh,' said Scotty. 'We'll assess that when I get there.'

'Get *here*?' said Mac. 'Thought we'd meet in Darwin or Perth.'

'I'm sitting in Changi, about to connect for Saigon,' said Scotty.

'Great,' said Mac, his heart sinking. He'd banked on a few days to find Tranh.

'And your number isn't showing up on my phone,' said Scotty. 'You using a call card or Skype?'

'Pay phone,' said Mac.

'Liar,' said Scotty. 'Text it to me – I'll call when I land, okay?'

They said their goodbyes, and as an afterthought Scotty sparked up. 'Hey, Macca, I didn't tell you why Pryce was so angry.'

'His mouthwash still failing?'

'The McHugh family lawyers held a press conference in Sydney yesterday, criticising the Prime Minister and DFAT for losing Geraldine in Vietnam.'

'Not far from the truth.'

'Pryce was going crazy about it – he poked me in the chest, Macca.'

Mac laughed. 'He on solids yet?'

'Just.'

'What was he angry about?'

'The AFP interviewed the lawyer and family. Turns out they've engaged a security firm to find Geraldine.'

'That's not unusual,' said Mac, who knew how many kidnaps were resolved privately in South-East Asia.

'No, but the firm is Western Solutions Inc,' said Scotty, mischief in his voice.

'Remind me,' said Mac, knowing that name somehow.

'Registered in Singapore but operating out of Manila,' said Scotty. 'Managing director is a man by the name of Alphonse Morales.'

Mac rubbed his chin. 'Bongo?'

'The one and only.'

'And Pryce knows about Bongo?'

'He knows that Bongo's a friend of yours,' said Scotty. 'And he wasn't saying it like it was a good thing, either.'

'That was two weeks in Timor, a lifetime ago,' said Mac, feeling cornered. 'I needed protection –'

'Settle, mate, settle,' said Scotty. 'I told Pryce that Bongo had been employed by the Firm for security services – and besides, for an officer's safety we don't divulge details of joint ventures with foreign nationals.'

'How did that go down?'

'Tobin backed me and Pryce didn't push,' said Scotty.

'And the DG?' said Mac, wondering where the head of Aussie SIS stood.

'Our esteemed leader felt it better that he sit that one out,' said Scotty.

'He shafted me?'

'He supported you covertly,' said Scotty. 'Look, whoever briefed Pryce warned him that Bongo is political poison. That's all Pryce had to hear and he was flipping out.'

'Shit,' said Mac. 'Don't tell me what I think you're going to tell me.'

'It wasn't my idea, Macca,' said Scotty, a boarding announcement echoing. 'And it wasn't Tobin's either.'

Disgust rose in Mac's throat. 'We're going to beat Bongo to McHugh?'

'Finding her can't be that hard,' said Scotty.

'Finding Geraldine McHugh is the least of our worries,' said Mac. 'Getting in Bongo's way is the problem.'

\* \* \*

Using the calling card, Mac phoned a business in south Jakarta called the Bavaria Lagerhaus – a bar and restaurant in the consular precinct of Jakarta, owned by a Suharto-era intelligence bigwig named Saba.

Saba had safe-deposit boxes in his storeroom where soldiers, spies and mercenaries kept their spare passports and emergency stashes. He also acted as a general cut-out man for people in Mac's profession; if one operator wanted to contact another but didn't have a number then they'd call Saba. And if Saba liked them or found them useful, he'd put their request on the jungle drum. He didn't charge for what he did – knowing the secrets was a commodity to Indonesian players like Saba.

Mac's call was answered after one ring. 'Who this?'

'Richard Davis, for Saba,' said Mac.

'Wait,' said the man's voice and the line went to generic hold music.

Forty seconds later there was a click and Saba was on the line. 'Mr Mac, such a nice surprise.'

'Hi Saba – how's Jakarta?'

'Hot, dirty – always the traffic jammed,' said the Indonesian. 'Where are you, Mr Macca?'

'Auckland,' said Mac.

'Not Singapore?' said the ex-spy, toying with Mac.

'Maybe – recently,' said Mac.

'Nice view from the Pan Pac, yeah?' said Saba.

'Yes, Saba,' said Mac, admitting defeat. 'I'm looking for Bongo. I just need to talk.'

'Could call him at Manila office,' said Saba, knowing very well that Mac didn't want his calls to that number logged by whoever was spying on Bongo.

'Informal would be better,' said Mac, and read out the number of his new mobile phone.

Mac had always been careful to keep Saba handy but not involved. But Saba was impeccably connected in Indonesia's military and intelligence worlds and Mac needed more from him before he got off the phone.

'Saba, is there much Israeli action around at the moment?'

'Depends what you mean by action,' said Saba.

Israel had no consular presence in Indonesia and people travelling on Israeli passports could not enter Indonesian ports without a sworn affidavit from a foreign Indonesian notary. Yet the world's only Jewish state had vital interests in monitoring the most populous Islamic nation and so the Mossad had used other means to gain intelligence in Indonesia and Malaysia.

Mac prompted him. 'Snatches, infiltrations, assassinations, double agents. All the good stuff.'

'No action,' said Saba. 'In this country the Jews still hide behind their pharmaceutical firms and finance companies.'

'Just thought I'd ask,' said Mac.

'Why?'

'I keep crossing paths with an Israeli crew – could be former IDF or ex-Mossad,' said Mac.

'Nothing down here, Mr Mac,' said Saba. 'But . . . no, that wouldn't be it.'

'What?' said Mac.

'Well, it's probably –'

'Try me.'

'Well, six, seven month ago, Yossi in Bangkok get the tip about the Mossad coming to town; they do the tail and follow the two Mossad across the border into Cambodia, right?'

'Okay.'

'Turn out, these two Mossad are following more Jews, in north Cambodia – right up there at Anlong Kray.'

'More Israelis?'

'Yeah, they Mossad. But Chinese there too,' said Saba. 'Right up in that forest. I try to remember – it was just talking, right?'

'Okay,' said Mac. 'So the Israelis and Chinese, what were they doing up there?'

'I talk with Yossi, and then call you,' said Saba.

'Okay,' said Mac. 'I'd like to know who they are.'

'Were,' said Saba.

'Were who?'

'The Mossad who come through Bangkok?' said Saba. 'The other Mossad kill them.'

A silence buzzed on the phone. The revelation confirmed for Mac that Yossi's Israelis in north Cambodia could also be the ones Mac was looking for.

Saba broke the silence. 'Mr Mac, you there?'

'Yeah, sure, mate,' said Mac. 'Let me get this straight: the Mossad that Yossi followed, they were killed by the other Israelis? In northern Cambodia?'

'Yeah,' said Saba. 'Yossi tells me, "That when I know they not in Mossad no more."'

'Shit.'

'These are the ones?' said Saba.

'I don't know,' said Mac, knowing he'd already given it away. He felt sick.

'You watch it, Mr Mac,' said Saba. 'Jews and Chinese? That bad enough. But when Jew kill Jew – how you say it? Give him the miss?'

# CHAPTER 33

Hanging up, Mac tried to stay calm. Saba might have mangled the Aussie saying, *Give it a miss*, but he'd nailed it in one. It was precisely the smartest option available to Mac: to meet Scotty at the airport, fudge the McHugh search, grab his wife and get the hell out of Indochina before Jenny established a link between Quirk and the Israelis and decided to raise the roof.

He needed a plan for getting where he wanted to go rather than just reacting to events. He needed the information ascendency – the main building block of all intelligence professionals – yet Mac realised he hadn't checked the identities of the Israelis, or even if that was their nationality. He'd been tweaked to their status and background by Maggins and it had conformed with what Mac knew about some of their techniques: the box surveillance around the Mekong Saloon had been pure Mossad, right down to the man with the newspaper waiting beside the entry. The light-bulb bomb at the Cambodiana was also a good indication, as were the clothes: the Mossad had spent decades trying to coach their operators into chameleon wardrobes yet for some reason they couldn't help but dress like someone's great-uncle. The Sansabelt slacks, the Seiko watches, the sensible shoes and the ankle-breezing trouser hems, all worn with an intense confidence which gave it that Mossad smell.

But Mac needed more and he knew who could help. Phoning Indonesia Telekom directory, he asked for *Konstelasi Komputer* in Jakarta and waited while the line buzzed and chirped.

A young male employee answered and Mac asked to be put through to Charlie, the owner.

'He out,' said the lazy kid, a person Mac knew from his last visit to the shop.

'Can you take a message?' asked Mac, and rattled off his number and the beginnings of a long message. 'You're getting this, right?'

The kid issued a snide sigh. 'Okay, okay, I get him.'

Charlie came on the line. 'McQueen – that you?'

'Hey, Charlie,' said Mac.

'What up?' said the man who'd turned cyber counter-measures against the Chinese into an art form.

'I need to access a website without anyone knowing where I am,' said Mac. 'Can do?'

'I can route you through a bot-relay, that what you mean?'

'It has to be secure,' said Mac. 'It's sensitive.'

'This one's used by the MSS,' said Charlie. 'That secure enough?'

Paying off the cyclo rider, Mac descended to the footpath in central Phnom Penh. The streets teemed with locals and Mac felt like the last Anglo left on the planet as he moved among the throng.

Ducking into a street-front cafe, he ordered fish curry and a beer and sat with his back against the side wall, from where he could see most of the street. The clouds were building high and dark and the humidity closed in as if a heavy drape had been dropped on the city. Although his stomach was clenched with stress, he knew from experience that he had to make himself eat. You never knew when the next meal was coming so it paid to force it down when you could.

The curry was excellent and the beer cold, and as he waited for Charlie to call back, Mac pondered the Bongo Morales complication. Bongo was about eight years older than Mac, a former Philippines intel operator who'd also been trained by American outfits such as US Marines force-recon and made a name for himself in Mindanao, chasing and killing terrorists. He didn't just outgun the bad guys – he could out-think them as well. One of the stories that had created the legend of Bongo was the time his cover as a first-class steward on Garuda Airlines had been exaggerated and he'd ended up sitting at the flight deck, flying a 737 to Denpasar. Bongo was the original chameleon spy who could switch from a peroxide-haired gay hustler working out of the Shangri-La to a jungle-stalking hit man – and make the transition faster than most people could tie their laces.

He'd gone freelance in the mid-1990s and become a consultant to the Indonesian Kopassus regiment as they tried to subdue the GAM separatists in Aceh, at the north end of Sumatra. When the Indonesians wanted to test their new American-supplied cluster bombs on civilian villages, Bongo had not reacted well. The result was the Kopassus colonel decided not to push his luck, and Bongo walked away.

Mac had worked with him in East Timor during the independence ballot of 1999. In a very ugly finale to a flawed gig, Mac had been left on an airfield in East Timor to face the Indonesian Army, while Bongo had flown away in a borrowed helo. In the soldier world, Bongo owed Mac – owed him big. On the other hand, Bongo had saved Mac during a shootout in a Dili warehouse. Regardless of what Mac thought of the IOU equation, he knew Bongo would decide for himself. Which was the main problem with Bongo Morales: whether you worked with him, for him or against him, he was never confused about what he was going to do next, and he sure as hell didn't need anyone's input on the matter.

Now, the Prime Minister's chief of staff had decided that in order to save the PM from political embarrassment, Scotty and Mac were going to get to Geraldine McHugh before Bongo Morales. That sort of challenge could only have come from a whiteboard in Canberra. Bongo Morales might enjoy the rivalry or he might not. But if he resented the intrusion, there was a high likelihood that he'd remove the threat. Just like that. You'd be pig food before you had a chance to utter a single *fuck you, Morales*.

Sipping on his beer, Mac remembered the last call he'd wanted to make.

He dialled the number in Singapore and was put through to two intermediaries before a switch clicked over and Benny Haskell was on the line.

'Macca,' he barked. 'You ducking me?'

'No, mate. Changed phones.'

'Secure?'

'Sure,' said Mac. 'What's up?'

'Thought you might like an update, courtesy of my mate at the ministry,' said Benny, who had a friend in Singapore's internal intelligence agency.

'What's he got?'

'The investigation took a strange turn when the Americans turned up,' Benny told him.

'Americans?' said Mac, massaging his temples.

'Yeah, these men in black have been running around, going through all of Ray's books for the funds.'

'The investment business?' said Mac.

'Yeah. So someone asks one of these Yanks what they're looking for. They can't see what it has to do with Chinese spies and ballistic missiles and Ray's execution.'

Mac was lost. 'Yeah?'

'Two hours later, my mate is officially warned off by the Singaporean Prime Minister's office.' Benny laughed. 'Told him to let the Yanks have what they want and back off.'

'Who are the Yanks?' said Mac.

'This is the good part,' said Benny. 'The senior bloke's from US Treasury intel, and the underlings are Secret Service.'

Mac reached for his beer. 'The Secret Service guys guard the President, don't they? What do they want with Ray's fund?'

'Guarding POTUS isn't their only job,' said Benny.

'Remind me,' said Mac.

'They also have a big intel and investigation unit for protecting the US currency.'

'Currency?' said Mac. 'You mean they catch counterfeiters?'

'That's right,' said Benny. 'Look, I have to go now but I'm having a drink with my mate tomorrow – I'll call you if there's anything more.'

'Okay, Benny.'

'And Macca – be careful.'

# CHAPTER 34

Finding a small internet cafe in the locals-only part of Phnom Penh, Mac bought a pot of coffee and took the computer in the far corner. Using the protocols Charlie had given him, he went through a series of pop-up windows until a tag-line in the bottom right-hand corner informed him he was operating from the remote computer network Charlie had stipulated; by the jumble of letters, it looked like a tractor parts distributor based in Wisconsin.

Activating the graphics-free Mozilla browser, Mac found the ASIS website, logged in with his passwords and held his breath, almost expecting Urquhart, Lance and Marlon to burst in the door as soon as he was in the ASIS system.

He searched in the ASIS databases for mentions of Israeli, IDF or Mossad activity in Indochina. There were fifteen files, and Mac opened them one by one. The oldest, from the 1970s, were scanned files in PDF format. He grinned as he scrolled through the old typewritten and telex-printed reports and memos, some sent over the wire from consular communications offices in Hanoi and Bangers, others typed and pouched out of Saigon, Nha Trang and Phnom Penh. One looked like it had started life in Vientiane – an Aussie SIS asset, a coffee importer from Melbourne, had run across a couple of interlopers in the Laotian capital who were talking about big coffee contracts and trying to talk down the Aussie and North American coffee buyers. The report noted that they looked Lebanese but used names like 'John Baker'. One claimed to be from San Francisco, but he hesitated when talking about the view from Russia Hill: a view he should have known. The local asset decided they were Israeli when he saw their appalling driving.

Chuckling, Mac cycled through the files. They were in a report format – there was no desk analysis on Israeli intelligence in Vietnam, Cambodia, Laos, Burma, Peninsular Malaysia or Thailand, and there were no assessments generated in Canberra based on field intelligence of Israeli activity.

The reports rattled off the basics: Mossad and IDF special forces had trained units in the Philippines, Taiwan and Singapore; Israel, according to one report, had paid informers in northern Burma, but that didn't mean much – a paid informer in South-East Asia was someone who'd been shown a stack of greenbacks, and didn't see the harm. Mac didn't take it too seriously because many European intelligence agents in South-East Asia allowed the locals to think they were Mossad, as a way of covering where they really came from. It evened out since Mossad agents liked to intimate that they were from the CIA or British SIS when dealing with informers. There were entire cadres of Mossad agents trained to pass for Syrians, Iraqis and Jordanians.

What he was looking for was mention of a bunch of hairy-chested Mossad operators, not hiding behind a film production company or a photography bureau. The kind of pros who would push Quirk for access to a computer network and then drop him when it suited them; a bunch of tough guys who would put a light-bulb bomb in Mac's hotel room. People like that – no matter how far they'd drifted off as privateers – always gained attention during their official careers.

Pouring his coffee as the traffic outside went about its theatrics, Mac looked at the last file in the ASIS search result. It was stamped April, a year ago. He clicked it open.

It started with a basic intelligence bio card, which was a file containing a passport picture and all the information that defines a person. It was titled *RADOFF, Bernard Levi* and proceeded to list details of Mr (Bernie) Radoff's social persona: a French businessman, former banker, now an import-exporter with textile and printing interests in Thailand, Burma and Cambodia.

The second part of the file told the real story: Bernie Radoff was born Marcel Beyer, French-Israeli, former IDF air force, graduated with a law degree from the University of Haifa in 1991, post-grad economics at the Sorbonne in 1992, trained at Mossad in the early 1990s (while still in Paris), joined Banque Nationale in 1993 as a management trainee in its institutional division and spent the rest of his career drawing two cheques: one from the French bank as a bond writer, and the other from King Saul, the Tel Aviv street where Israel's famous security service was located.

The file noted that Beyer had risen to a senior position with BNP and run the bank's bond desk out of Hong Kong and then Singapore. Australian intelligence estimated that Beyer ceased being an active Mossad agent in 2005.

Mac was about to log out when he realised there were two attachments to the Marcel Beyer file. The first was a story from Associated Press, tagged *Bangkok, Thailand*, from eight months ago.

Reading quickly, Mac grew impatient with the lack of clear information.

The Thai Ministry of Finance has confirmed that French national Mr Bernard Radoff has been handed a suspended sentence in exchange for a guilty plea in a four-month legal action that has been shrouded in secrecy.

The Ministry continued its suppression of proceedings in the Supreme Court today, claiming the charges against Mr Radoff — a French financier with many business interests in South-East Asia — were 'classified' under national security laws and would not be disclosed.

'Mr Radoff has pleaded guilty to the charges brought by the government and the court has passed sentence,' said a brief written statement from the Ministry. 'The Ministry of Finance has no further comment.'

Mr Radoff was arrested five months ago following a series of spectacular raids in Surin province. His suspended sentence means he is free to go — foreign nationals given suspended sentences in Thailand are usually allowed 48 hours in which to leave the country.

Mr Radoff's lawyer, Mr Mati Sutramat, scoffed at questions about his client's possible ties to the Israeli Embassy in Bangkok.

'I can be arrested for talking about the facts of this case,' he said. 'The matter is closed.'

The other attachment was a black and white photograph. It showed Radoff in what looked like the forecourt of the Sheraton Saigon on Dong Du Street, just around the corner from the Grand. He was sleek, tanned and arrogant, and grinning at the camera, which was being wielded by a photographer from the *Saigon Times*. The caption read: *French financier Bernard Radoff has been touring some of Vietnam's pulp and paper operations in the Mekong region as he looks for suitable investments to augment his holdings in Thailand and Cambodia.*

Mac was about to close the photograph when something caught his eye. Radoff was standing in front of a white 4x4. Mac looked closer – it looked like a Ford Explorer SUV, although he couldn't be certain. The photographer had cropped the picture so only the front portion of the Explorer stuck into the picture – it stopped at the windscreen pillar. The window of the vehicle had a faint glare bouncing off it but Mac could see that a driver sat behind the wheel, a baseball cap pulled over his eyes.

His pulse quickening, Mac used the Photoshop software in the ASIS system to draw a box around the driver's face and magnify it.

Saving the magnified image to a notepad, Mac selected the 'repixelate' option in the menu and waited for the processors in Canberra to take the blown-up, blurry pixels of that driver and make their estimations about how it should look as a reconstituted image.

The result stunned Mac as it finally clarified like a fog lifting. Despite the glare of the glass and the shadow-forming peak of the cap, he knew he was looking at the Israeli with the scary eyes – the man in the red shirt who'd killed Quirk.

Cutting and pasting the repixelated image into the 'search' field of the ASIS databases, Mac clicked on the 'match to identity' option and hit search.

The search tumbled for more than six minutes as the digital information was thrown at every facial image in the Australian intel database – a database which had been compiled over eighty years.

Finally, a bio card popped up. The man's name was Joel Dozsa, born 20 March 1970 in – as Mac had surmised – Hungary.

Dozsa had emigrated to Israel as a teenager, and it was suspected he'd been recruited by Mossad in his first months of university at Haifa, Bernie Radoff's alma mater.

Joel Dozsa had done his doctoral work in military history at the Australian National University in Canberra, and had augmented his research with a junior lectureship at the Royal Military College Duntroon, teaching Australian Army officer cadets.

Having finished his thesis, Dozsa was offered a lecturer's position at Duntroon but the offer was suddenly withdrawn after an unfavourable report from the Defence Security Authority, the military's internal intelligence and vetting agency. The reason for the retraction was not in the report, but Mac assumed the Mossad connection had filtered back to DSA.

The last paragraph of the Joel Dozsa bio was both vague and clear:

> Mr Dozsa did not dispute the retraction of the job offer and departed Canberra airport for Melbourne two hours after being informed of the retraction. DSA officers XXX and YYY followed Mr Dozsa to Melbourne, where he disappeared in what appeared to be 'aided' counter-surveillance. Defence Security officers PPP and QQQ attended Mr Dozsa's apartment in the Duntroon residential halls and found a stripped apartment. Fellow residents said two men in grey coveralls had loaded a small van with the contents of Mr Dozsa's apartment. Surveillance tape of RMC Duntroon showed a Toyota HiAce van with false registration plates. Subsequent interagency discussions revealed Australian Federal Police had opened a file on Mr Dozsa following an ANU exchange week in Bangkok, June 1993. Mr Dozsa was observed by an off-duty AFP officer at the Siam City Hotel in Phayathai, Bangkok — a known RV of French national Bernie RADOFF. Radoff is an institutional banker with BNP and a private investor across the Mekong Delta region; he is also understood to be a senior Mossad 'agent-runner' responsible for many deniable operations on behalf of the Israeli government. DSA made a pro forma request to the Israeli Embassy for explanations as to Mr Dozsa's sudden and 'aided' disappearance at Melbourne airport. No explanation was forthcoming.

Mac finally breathed out. He now had a name and bio. Joel Dozsa was smart and organised, and he'd almost embedded himself in Australia's military establishment. RMC Duntroon trained the elite of Australia's and the Pacific's military leaders, and a powerful position

213

such as lecturer would have given Mossad some interesting leverage in the Asia-Pacific region.

Logging out of the ASIS portal, Mac stared at the bare-bones Mozilla screen, still operating off a parts department hard drive in Wisconsin. Bringing up Google, he typed in the words: *light bulb bomb Thailand 1993*.

The first item was an old Associated Press report from July 1993 – Thai criminal investigators were resiling from their initial statement that the Indonesian businessman Ibrahim Sarno had been killed at his golf-resort bungalow at Phuket because of a freak gas explosion. The police investigation had been joined by a team from Thailand's military intelligence agency and the possibility had been raised that Sarno had been blasted to pieces while turning on the bathroom light . . .

Mac looked around, his skin crawling. He'd seen first-hand how the light-bulb bomb worked, and he felt nauseous having to read those words.

Police, according to the AP report, were now accepting the possibility that Sarno had been assassinated by some form of IED triggered by the light switch. The journalist had obviously got wind of foul play once the military spooks had entered the investigation, because the writer concluded with the sentence: *Police refused to confirm that Ibrahim Sarno was a conduit for South-East Asian funding of the PLO, or that his suspicious death was an assassination by Israeli intelligence agents.*

Mac had his man. The light-bulb-in-the-bathroom MO confirmed it. But what now played on his mind was Dozsa's possible success during his time in Canberra.

Mac wanted to believe that the people Dozsa had approached would have told him to rack off, but experience told him otherwise . . .

# CHAPTER 35

The clouds had lowered and darkened by the time Mac paused at the threshold of the internet cafe and pushed out into the street, making for a cyclo rider waiting at the kerb. He wanted to get back to the Holiday International, make a proper search of the Americans' bags, take what he needed and move to another location. Having tapped into the ASIS website and called Benny Haskell, now would be a good time to confuse the trail.

Giving his instructions to the rider, he pulled up the sunshade and checked his phone as they moved with the traffic. Looking up, he noticed they'd turned hard right, and there was now shadow where there should have been oppressive heat.

'Hey!' said Mac, turning, but it was too late.

The steel pressed into the back of his head and as he froze and lifted his hands, the Colt was lifted from his waistband.

'Shit, McQueen,' came an Aussie voice. 'That was easy.'

Turning his head, he saw Lance, who pushed a Glock in his face.

'Lance,' said Mac, as if he'd met an old friend. 'Thought about Tic Tacs?'

'Watch it, McQueen,' said Lance, climbing into the cyclo beside Mac and nodding to the rider. 'And shit – who did the hair and the mo?'

'A lifestyle choice.'

'An atrocity, more like it,' Lance sneered. 'I liked you more as a blond. You look better as a homo than a dickhead.'

They travelled through the streets, heading east towards the river.

'I'm back on the team, Lance,' said Mac, trying to stay calm despite the 9mm handgun jammed in his left kidney. 'I heard from the Firm today. You don't want to do anything stupid.'

'The team?' said Lance. 'What do you know about the team?'

'I was doing my job,' said Mac, trying to spin out the conversation.

'Your job was to tail Quirk and write a report,' said Lance, a waft of body odour suggesting he hadn't slept much or changed his clothes in the past twenty-four hours. 'Next thing we know, you're on some wild-goose chase across Indochina with an item of crucial national security – and then you *lose* it?!'

'I found it by mistake,' said Mac. 'When I asked you about it in the van you could have told me then.'

'Oh, really?' said Lance, revealing mossy teeth. 'You think I was going to brief you in front of a foreign national? And I thought I was supposed to be the novice.'

'You could have waited until the Cambodiana,' said Mac.

'You sent me off to be spied on by Tranh, remember? By the time I got back to the hotel, the place had been bombed. You're a moron, McQueen.'

'Where are we going?' Mac asked.

'To see Urquhart – he's got new orders.'

'I know,' said Mac, as the cyclo stopped at an intersection.

'You know much less than you think,' Lance replied. 'That's why you're chasing the chick and I still have to retrieve that memory card.'

'Send a boy to do a man's job.'

'Shut it, McQueen,' said Lance.

'No, you shut it,' came a harsh American voice along with a slapping sound, and Lance was suddenly sagging into his own lap.

Grabbing Lance's gun, Sammy Chan pushed the groggy Australian back into the cyclo seat and beckoned for Mac to follow him. Jumping from the cyclo, Mac took back the Colt from Lance and followed Sammy to another Mazda sedan, this one red.

'Think I broke his jaw,' said Sammy, shaking out his hand.

'He'd finished talking,' said Mac. 'You weren't interrupting.'

After driving across town for twenty minutes, the American turned the car north and followed the National Highway Five up the Tonle Sap. This was the road to Bangkok. The American's legs were heavily bandaged, a fact he couldn't hide with the military shorts he wore.

'How're the legs, Sammy?' said Mac.

'Looks a darn sight worse than it is,' said Sammy. 'It's infection I worry about, given our location and all.'

'I'm due in Saigon tomorrow,' said Mac as they negotiated the late-afternoon peasant traffic on the highway. 'So I hope we're not going too far.'

'Our conversation this morning got me thinking,' said Sammy.

'So?'

'So there's someone I want you to meet,' said Sammy. 'The two of you hit it off, you can make a deal. You don't wanna dance, I'll take you where you want to go and this meeting never took place. Deal?'

'Deal,' said Mac, watching the lush Mekong countryside rush past.

Seven minutes later, Sammy turned right off the highway and drove under drooping trees until they hit a raised levee of the type common around the Mekong.

As they sped along it, Mac saw thousands of acres of rice paddies extending across the old river flats to a line of trees where the dark brown Mekong River slipped down to the South China Sea. Small hamlets were evident on raised knolls amid the paddies, and Mac could see children and goats, pigs and women going about their business as the menfolk returned from the markets or from day-labourer jobs.

Sammy drove around the corner and stopped in front of a houseboat sitting beneath some trees, on a small canal known as a klong.

A tall black American loomed at the top of the gangplank, his right hand hovering above a handgun on his hip.

'It's okay, Brian,' said Sammy as he started up the gangplank. 'Old man's expecting us.'

Reaching the top of the gangplank, Mac was stopped by Brian and patted down. As he gave up his Colt, Mac wondered if this was the driver they called Eagle.

Ducking his head as he descended from the deck into the houseboat, Mac saw the interior of the boat bore no relation to its rustic facade. Sammy used a swipe card to move through the security doors which closed with a whoosh behind Mac as they moved past another two guards, who patted Mac again and ran an explosives detector over his body.

Mac and Sammy entered a room filled with comms and IT equipment; there were video monitors showing real-time footage of what looked like a UAV circling over Asian jungle; one operator was glued to a monitor, reading out locations to someone over his headset. The monitor seemed to be showing cell zones for a phone connection.

'Nothing here for you, McQueen,' said Sammy, and Mac followed him into a smoky low-ceilinged office. Against the far wall, on the other side of a dark wooden desk, a middle-aged man leaned back in a chair beneath a line of portholes, blowing cigarette smoke at the ceiling.

'I didn't say you were fucking me, Darryl,' said the American in a superior east-coast drawl. 'I said you were trying to fuck me. Let's not get ahead of ourselves.'

Looking up, the man – a tanned, silver-haired sixty-year-old who could pass for late forties – smiled and sucked on his smoke as he turned an expensive lighter end over end on the desk.

'Yeah, yeah, sweetheart,' he purred menacingly into the phone. 'Retract that sentence from your report and we're all buddies, right?'

As he was about to put the phone down, he laughed suddenly. 'You know me better than that, Darryl,' he chuckled. 'I don't threaten people – I bury them.'

Hanging up, the man stubbed out his cigarette and moved around the desk, not taking his eyes off Mac.

'Alan?'

'That's me,' said Mac.

'The name's Charles. How do you do?' Charles held out his hand. 'Hope you don't mind first names – it keeps things simple, okay?'

Mac took the strong, dry hand and looked into pale eyes hooded by a high, intelligent forehead. First names didn't worry Mac and he was accustomed to the way the American intelligence community reverted to them.

'Sun's over the yardarm,' said Charles, moving like a cat towards a large refrigerator. 'Beer, Alan? Bud, Millers, Tiger?'

'Cold and wet is good,' said Mac. 'Thanks.'

Taking a seat in a leather easy chair, Mac sipped at his ice-cold Budweiser as Charles slugged at his beer and lit another smoke. For an older bloke he had a hard stomach and powerful arms.

'I'm sure you have things to do,' said Charles, in a voice that was friendly yet authoritative. 'So I'd like to push this along.'

'Sure,' said Mac.

'Some of our investigations have fallen flat in the past couple of weeks and the problem seems to come back to the Aussies,' said Charles, smiling. 'Sam mentioned the possibility of a joint operation, which might give both of our teams the chance to open up, to share the wealth as it were.'

'That was the idea,' said Mac. 'It seems we have a mutual enemy.'

'It seems so,' said Charles. 'By the way, thank you for your efforts on the docks the other night – Sam owes you his life.'

'No worries,' said Mac. 'I'm just sorry I couldn't have stopped Phil catching one.'

'Rocket-propelled grenade,' said Charles, shaking his head softly. 'What kind of maniac carries *that* around in his car?'

'What I said,' said Mac.

'I suppose it's obvious we are highly motivated about interviewing this woman, Geraldine McHugh?' said Charles, who seemed both old-money and diamond-hard. A strange combination.

'I got that idea,' said Mac. 'There's also the matter of a memory card – I had it until two days ago.'

'I'm interested in that,' said Charles.

'I didn't know what it was.'

'So you weren't briefed on the card?' said Charles, in a way that made Mac realise it was important.

'No,' said Mac. 'Not until it was stolen from my hotel room, and then I was accused of being a traitor.'

Charles squinted. 'I guess there're different Australian organisations working on this, right?'

'I'd rather not comment,' said Mac.

'Just like we had no Aussie comment on the Dr Lao episode?'

Mac stayed silent. It wasn't his place to discuss Lao's treason, but the Americans certainly had a right to know if their testing was compromised.

'Just so we understand one another,' said Charles, keeping it relaxed. 'The ability to stop a Chinese ballistic missile mid-flight is something the Aussie Navy might thank us for one of these days.'

Clearing his throat, Mac maintained steady eye contact.

'Anyway,' said Charles. 'Sammy tells me you have a head start on us with McHugh.'

'I know Captain Loan, from the Cong An in Saigon,' said Mac, watching Charles' eyes for a sign of recognition.

Charles gave nothing. 'And?'

'And she's investigating me for the murder of Jim Quirk at the Mekong Saloon.'

'So?' said Charles.

'So Loan connected the death of Jim Quirk with the disappearance of Geraldine McHugh on the same night, from Cholon.'

'Cholon?' said Charles. 'Who told you Cholon?'

'Loan – she wants to work with me,' said Mac. 'I was going to look her up back in Saigon.'

Charles' left eyebrow rose and he exchanged a look with Sam.

'Well, Alan,' he said, 'that sounds promising.'

'That's where I come in,' said Mac. 'What's your end?'

Leaning back, Charles levelled a look at Mac. They held the stare for several seconds, then Charles looked away.

'My end is this,' said Charles carefully. 'There's a plot by a powerful faction of the People's Liberation Army to hurt the Chinese and American economies and throw the world's financial system into disarray.'

'The PLA?' said Mac, wondering how the world's largest military organisation became involved. 'What happened to the Israelis?'

'Forget all you know – this is about a power struggle in Beijing, using contractors in Cambodia and Vietnam,' said Charles. 'You interested?'

'Shit, yeah,' said Mac.

'Good,' said Charles. 'So let's talk.'

# CHAPTER 36

Growing discomfort made Mac move around in his chair. The story Charles was telling him was a few levels above what he'd prepared for when he arrived in Saigon.

'The Chinese government is nominally communist,' said Charles, starting on his second beer. 'But the communist ideology, as a means, is distinct from the system as an end. History shows us that Chinese ruling systems all come and go but the imposition of authority and order are central to the Chinese experience.'

'Sure,' said Mac, knowing some Chinese history.

'So communism may have been the flavour since 1949, but the reality of Chinese government is different.'

'The reality is power factions, like any system,' said Mac.

'Precisely,' said Charles. 'We've had basically thirty years of economic progressives who have opened up China's economy and allowed the development of an aggressive, wealthy middle class.'

'I see,' said Mac.

Charles lit a cigarette. 'And you know what that means?'

'Economic liberalism usually means social and political liberalism, even if only by degrees,' said Mac, mentally dipping into some of his old history papers. 'So if the Chinese middle classes become wealthy, successful and educated, the next thing that happens is their children want political representation.'

'Australians seem to understand this instinctively,' said Charles. 'Americans are enjoying their cheap consumer goods so much that they don't realise the source of these goodies is at a crossroads – a potentially shattering crossroads.'

'Time to pay the piper.'

'Well, yes,' said Charles. 'Either the middle classes smash the Central Committee's control of Chinese politics, or an existing force arises from the elites and crushes political liberalism before it creates the revolution. Tiananmen Square was an illustration of what kind of forces lurk in the PLA, just waiting for an excuse.'

'The nationalist right wing of the PLA?' asked Mac, remembering the phrase from an intelligence briefing. Chinese elites had traditionally included ultranationalists of the type who gained ascendency in Japan in the 1920s – those who saw China as an expanding hegemony, enforcing its political, economic and even racial superiority.

'That's the one. Have you heard of General Xiang Pao Peng?' said Charles.

'Read about him in the *Economist*,' said Mac. 'What about him?'

'He was marketing himself as the progressive leadership of the future, because of his education at Cambridge and Sandhurst. If you recall the slogan *Peace through Prosperity*, that came straight out of his office.'

'You said "was"?'

'He was sidelined by the Central Committee ten months ago because he was considered too ambitious,' said Charles. 'Among the economic progressives, Pao Peng is known as the face of Chinese chauvinism – a classic totalitarian nationalist with a fantasy about Greater China that makes the Japanese economic cooperation zone look quaint.'

'He was sidelined?' said Mac.

'Yes, and he didn't take it well.'

'Pao Peng is heavily connected, isn't he?' said Mac, wishing he had been more thorough in his reading of circularised research. 'I mean, he's related to the marchers but he's also aligned with bankers and industrialists. How did he get sidelined?'

'He asked for support from the wrong people, is our guess,' said

Charles. 'He apparently had a plan for a reorganisation of Beijing, and the new blueprint didn't include a Central Committee.'

'But it probably included the new Chinese oil provinces of Vietnam and Cambodia, with PLA navy bases at Cam Ranh and Ream?' said Mac.

'Sammy told me you knew your way around here,' said Charles. 'So Pao Peng's in the dog box and his wealthy friends aren't so obvious anymore. But then we uncovered Pao Peng's Plan B – a plot to bring the Chinese economy to its knees and, during the chaos, take political control.'

'How will he do that?' said Mac, the hairs on the back of his neck pricking up.

'We believe he is working with contractors to undermine the US dollar, which in turn will undermine the Chinese economy.'

'That's a drastic way to get the job you want.'

'That's what concerns us in DC,' said Charles. 'It will eventually correct itself, but by then Pao Peng would have seized on the inevitable Chinese economic disaster.'

'How does Australia fit into this?'

'We uncovered some top-secret data taken from the US Treasury,' said Charles. 'It didn't seem like much to begin with, but when we put it all together, we believed it added up to a set of protocols that shouldn't be in the wrong hands.'

'And it's sitting on that memory card?' said Mac.

'We don't know, but we have to cross it off,' said Charles. 'And that's where the Aussies come in.'

'I don't see –' said Mac, but this time Sammy jumped in.

'Remember I told you we weren't necessarily on the same side, McQueen?'

'Yeah, you said the Aussies were the problem not the solution . . . Oh, *shit*,' said Mac as Geraldine McHugh's name leapt to the forefront of his mind.

'Let's not jump to conclusions . . .'

'Not her – she's the thief?' said Mac. 'Geraldine McHugh's a double agent?'

'We can't prove it, Alan,' said Charles. 'But we're hoping you can help us clear it up.'

After three passes, Sammy stopped the Mazda across the road from the Holiday International. Cars and minivans glowed yellow in the car park floodlights.

Mac's old Nokia buzzed and he grabbed at it in a panic, his nerves at the end of their rope. It was a text from Scotty: TNS, 10.55, meaning Tan Son Nhat Airport in Saigon.

'Let's cover your room together,' said Sammy, checking his handgun for load and safety before opening his door. 'Then I want my bags and car keys back, okay?'

'Okay,' said Mac. 'But no one's going into that room.'

Easing out of Sammy's car, Mac lurked in the shadows of the hotel's car park, waiting for eyes. None came and he moved towards the hotel's rear, climbed a cyclone gate and walked through the service area of the hotel and into the laundry.

Handing his room card to a hotel porter named Nhean, Mac slipped a US ten-dollar note into the equation and asked the fellow to pick up his bags and bring them to the Mitsubishi van in the car park. Mac showed Nhean, who was about sixteen years old and friendly, another ten-dollar note but held it back. 'This is for you if you can go into that room and get my stuff without turning on a light. You do it in the dark, okay?'

Nodding, Nhean turned to his task.

'I'm serious,' said Mac, grabbing the boy's arm. 'No lights. Got it?'

Waiting, Mac watched the service gate at the side of the hotel swing open exactly six minutes later and Nhean brought the wheelie cabin bag and backpacks to the van.

It wasn't a bad start: no IEDs under the bags or behind the room's door; no window assemblies flying into the car park. Paying Nhean the bonus, Mac decided to double it to twenty dollars. He'd already contributed to the death of one innocent hotel worker and he felt guilty at having to draw another into the web with the lure of US dollars. It wasn't right and it wasn't fair, but it could also be the difference between Mac living or dying.

Now he waited for signs of Nhean having been followed. After watching the back windows of the hotel and checking for movement, Mac decided it was clear and moved among the other parked vehicles to the Mitsubishi.

Sitting in Sammy's car again, Mac stared at the hotel, looking for pattern breaks. 'I know I asked to work with you guys, but now I know a bit more, I see problems.'

'Shoot,' said Sammy, also looking at the hotel.

'I'm not a Treasury investigator – as soon as the Americans request me in their taskforce, Canberra will want to send a Treasury guy.'

'There're enough of them on this already.'

'So,' said Mac, the comment having confirmed the snippet Benny Haskell had given him, 'Charles is US Treasury, and you're Secret Service?'

'No comment,' said Sammy.

'The other problem is obvious,' said Mac. 'To the Americans, McHugh is a thief; in Canberra, she might be working for someone. Thought about that?'

'Charles is dealing with it – leave the politics to him.'

'You want the other Mazda back?' said Mac.

Pulling into the Cambodiana car park fifteen minutes later, Sammy drove around slowly as they looked for eyes. The Mazda they were looking for sat on its own, with no cars or vans close enough to create an ambush. Driving in a circle they closed on a series of minivans and drove at them with full beams on, verifying their windows were clear and no bodies were diving for the floor.

As they parked beside the Mazda, Mac asked for a flashlight. They got out and Mac walked straight to the boot, examined the latch for signs of tampering and then lay under the rear of the car and looked for explosives or a detonator.

Standing, Mac opened the boot before Sammy could get his hand on it.

'Something interesting I found,' said Mac, smiling.

'Yeah?' said Sammy, frowning as he joined Mac at the open boot.

'Look at this,' said Mac, pulling the lid off one of the cardboard boxes, revealing the stacks of US hundred-dollar notes. 'I found this the other night, and it confused me.'

'It's been a tough few days,' said Sammy.

Mac looked at the American. 'There was a new Remington shottie in there, and in any trunk containing new firearms, the obvious smell would be the gun oil.'

'You'd think,' said Sammy.

'Yeah, but there was this stink of new money,' said Mac.

'You talk too much,' said the American, slamming the boot shut.

# CHAPTER 37

Arriving at the northern outskirts of Phnom Penh, Mac pulled the van off the highway onto a dirt road that ran to a klong. Pulling the old SIM card from the tongue of his boat shoes, Mac placed it in the cyclo rider's Nokia and powered up.

A bird squawked and tested the branch in a tree above the van as he waited. The buzz of the phone came several seconds later, signalling voicemail. Dialling in, Mac listened: one call from Scotty before Mac had told him of his new number; two from Urquhart, apologising for the misunderstanding that resulted in him being chained to a bed, and asking Mac to call him and arrange a meeting; another from Jenny, telling him not to panic if he arrived back to an empty house – she'd been called to Vietnam and Sarah was staying with Frank and Pat. She hoped things were going well in Auckland. Captain Loan had also left a message – yesterday. She reminded Mac of her number and asked that he contact her.

The last message, left three hours earlier, made Mac catch his breath. It was the unmistakable voice of Mr Red Shirt – Joel Dozsa.

*Well, well,* started the message, in that steady Eastern European accent. *Unless the reporters have it very wrong, it seems our intrepid Mr Davis survived where an unfortunate hotel worker failed. Consider yourself lucky, Mr Davis – it's a good* time to return to the paradise of barbecues, beaches and beer before you meet the fate of your Vietnamese friend.

Staring at the battered old Nokia as the voicemail system told him he had no more messages, Mac's head swirled with fatigue and confusion. So Tranh was dead? Or in a hospital? Missing? The message was either deliberately vague or Dozsa assumed Mac knew what had happened to Tranh.

Checking the call log he found 'number unknown', which meant a blocked number or a Skype call.

If Dozsa didn't want to talk – if he didn't want Mac to call back – what was the point of the message? Mossad agents never communicated unless there was an express purpose, even if that purpose was to spread disinformation.

Listening to the call again, Mac realised there were only two pieces of information that Dozsa had volunteered: that his crew planted the light-bulb bomb in the Cambodiana, and that Tranh was probably dead. Dozsa's admission about the bomb was redundant, since Mac would already have worked that out. News of Tranh's 'fate' was not – it was gratuitous, unverified.

Looking at the phone, Mac thought back to the times that he'd hidden a lie in the truth. He'd done it to make sure someone took a right turn when they should've taken a left.

Putting the old SIM back in his shoe and replacing it with his new MobiTel card, Mac turned the van to the south and put his foot down. By the time he was clear of Phnom Penh and motoring at one hundred and twenty k an hour along the west bank of the Mekong, he was sure there were no tails and he reckoned he could be in Saigon by midnight.

Settling between two line-haul trucks, Mac found a collection of Tranh's CDs in the centre console and smiled as he put AC/DC's *Back in Black* into the stereo.

As the bell tolled on the opening song of the CD, Mac resolved himself to the gig. He'd work with the Americans, but his priority was to retrieve Tranh. If Tranh was alive, Mac was going to find him.


The stocky Anglo male with a ruddy complexion emerged from Tan Son Nhat Airport's sliding doors at 11.18 am and looked around.

Mac yelled through the lowered window, 'Mister for Marriott?'

Moving suspiciously, Scotty carefully raised his sunglasses and peered into the van before relaxing his shoulders and shaking his head.

'Shit, Macca, you're a fucking worry,' he said, throwing his bag into the back of the van and climbing into the passenger seat. 'A bloody moustache? You gone rogue again?'

'Nah, mate,' said Mac, pulling away from the apron. 'Just wanted to book into a hotel for one night without someone putting ANFO in the light bulb.'

'I heard about that – you okay?'

'No, but I'm better than Poh.'

'The hotel security guy?' said Scotty, lighting a smoke and searching for the window button.

'That's him.'

Scotty exhaled smoke into Saigon's smog. 'Get me to the Rex – I'll have a shower and meet you in the restaurant, okay? I could eat the crotch out of a low-flying duck.'

'Done,' said Mac, dodging cyclos and other vans and wishing Tranh was still around.

'You at the Rex too?' said Scotty.

'I'd rather not say,' said Mac.

'Shit, mate,' said Scotty, sighing as he examined his phone for messages. 'That bad?'

'A wise old man once told me that paranoid and alive is good when you consider the alternative.'

'He wasn't old,' said Scotty.

'Wasn't wise either,' said Mac. 'Didn't stop him jawing on like Confucius.'

'Fuck's sake,' said Scotty, laughing. 'Get me to a shower, you frigging lunatic. I smell like Artie Beetson's undies after a full eighty minutes.'


Finishing his duck, Scotty slugged at his glass of beer and made the peace sign at the waitress.

'I was pouched something at Changi,' said Scotty, pulling a folded piece of paper from the windbreaker hanging on the back of his chair. 'Hope you enjoy it, since waiting for that was the reason I had to sleep at the airport.'

Mac opened it and read. It was an order from Greg Tobin for Mac to join the American taskforce 'Orion', effective for seven days from date of receipt.

'You've already spoken with them, I gather,' said Scotty, wiping his nicotine-stained moustache with the white linen napkin. 'Just so you know, you're working with the Americans, but you're reporting to me. Tobin's orders.'

'No worries,' said Mac as the beers arrived.

'I'm going to set up here, in the Rex,' said Scotty. 'I'll write the reports, keep Canberra happy, but that means you have to keep me informed, okay?'

'Sure,' said Mac.

'I mean it, Macca – I can only save you from yourself if you let me.'

'Can you save me from Urquhart?' asked Mac, checking out a Chinese businessman as he sat down on the other side of the restaurant.

'I'm not sure they'll be any trouble for us,' said Scotty. 'The PM's office has backed off. So what do we know about Orion?'

'They want to find Geraldine McHugh,' said Mac. 'There's a memory card – it might contain sensitive information from the US Treasury, but they haven't come right out and said so.'

'We know who's chasing you? Who ran over Boo?'

'An ex-Mossad crew run by a bloke named Joel Dozsa – they appear to be contracting for a Chinese faction headed by General Xiang Pao Peng. '

'Pao Peng is that PLA bloke, isn't he?' said Scotty. 'Wants to be an emperor?'

'Yeah – he wants to disable the Chinese economy so he can grab power and reverse the trend towards liberalism in China. Unfortunately, General Pao Peng's plan also hurts the US economy, and our American friends don't see the humour in that.'

'The Americans think you can find McHugh – that true?' said Scotty.

'Correct,' said Mac.

'Tell me about Orion.'

'Run by an American called Charles, his sidekick is Sammy Chan – definitely a military background, but neither are confirming who they work for.'

'This Charles,' said Scotty. 'Tall, silver-haired – about my age?'

'That's him,' said Mac, wondering why Scotty was scowling.

'If it's the same guy, his name is Charles Grimshaw the Third – old North Carolina family,' said Scotty. 'His father was an OSS original, who never officially became CIA but remained one of the Brothers, the true believers.'

'You know this guy?'

'I remember him from a gig in Iraq, in the lead-up to the first Gulf War. He was attempting to unpick the lies and bullshit around all that trade finance being written for rearming Saddam. It was before your time, but the US taxpayer was funding the credit guarantees for Iraq paying its imports – Lockheed or Hughes or Raytheon would fill an order for rockets or landmines, and the American taxpayers were underwriting Saddam's credit risk.'

'What was he like?' said Mac.

'Grimshaw? He conducted his interviews with a tractor battery and a set of crocodile clips,' said Scotty with a chuckle. 'He was hard core.'

'He's Treasury?'

'He does a lot of work for US Treasury but he's more like an intel consultant for the Yanks.'

'So he's not an accountant?'

Scotty smiled. 'Grimshaw was a Green Beret in the Phoenix Program during Vietnam, and then he led CIA black ops teams in Laos, Burma and Cambodia.'

'I see,' said Mac, now understanding what he'd noticed in Charles, lurking beneath the smooth exterior. Agency black ops in those three countries, in the late 1970s, did nothing but assassinate communist leaders.

'What's he doing in a Cambodian houseboat?' said Mac.

'Something involving Oz, which is why we're going to help them find our Aussie girl.'

'Why haven't I heard of him?' said Mac, annoyed.

'Because you might find he works for NSA,' said Scotty, meaning the US National Security Agency. 'He works for the President.'

# CHAPTER 38

Booking into the Rex as Brandon Collier, Mac went to his second-floor suite, removed his moustache and contact lenses and took a quick shower.

Standing in front of the bathroom mirror, he shook his kit onto the marble bench top and selected the men's face scrub. Squirting a palmful, he spread the N10 dye over both hands and massaged the strong-smelling goo into his wet hair for two minutes, and then picked up a wide-tooth comb and ran it through his hair to even the application. After twelve minutes, Mac had another shower to wash out the colourant.

Wandering into the living area of his suite, Mac did thirty push-ups and fifty sit-ups followed by five minutes, and then of shadow-boxing. Dressing himself in new clothes from the menswear store across the road, he returned himself to Richard Davis – textbook salesman – and checked himself in the mirror: now that his short, thin hair had returned to blond he noted a few grazes and scratches along his temples, probably caused by the bits of concrete that hadn't found his eyes.

Dialling the Saigon number for his calling card, Mac worked his way through the prompts then keyed in the number on a tattered white card.

'Captain Loan,' said Mac, when a voice answered. 'Richard Davis here.'

'Where are you?' said the captain.

'In Saigon.'

'You remember the cafe we first spoke in?' asked Loan.

'Sure.'

'Meet me there in half an hour,' said the detective, and hung up.

Walking to his window, which overlooked Nguyen Hue Boulevard, Mac sipped on his bottled water and searched for suspiciously parked vehicles or men reading tourist maps. He especially looked for phone company workers. His gut churned: he was not confident about being in this city or what was being asked of him. He'd only been a couple of years out of the field but it had dulled him slightly. He couldn't put his finger on it exactly, but it came down to his new lack of selfishness: not so long before, Mac would have attacked Marlon without hesitation. But two days before, he'd paused as the big bloke walked in the door. In his profession a pause was as good as death, and he wondered if he had the focus to go up against Joel Dozsa. Saba's story about the real Mossad going into northern Cambodia and being killed by Dozsa's boys was scary. There'd always been factions inside Israel's secret service, but ambushing and killing your former brothers? That was extreme.

The fact that his wife was in Saigon was another distraction. Whenever he looked over his shoulder, the phone taunted him. Was he going to call her, admit he was in Saigon and arrange to meet? Or was he going to revert to his professional habits, never tell anyone in a phone call where he was?

He didn't like lying to Jenny, and not only because she usually caught him out. She'd grown up hard, the daughter of a drunken farmer in Victoria's west who liked to beat his wife and kids. When Jenny was fifteen, she'd hit back at the old man with a crowbar; her father had picked up a rifle and shot at her as she ran through the orchard. So Jenny – as smart and as beautiful as she was – did not trust men easily, and Mac had always done his best to be an honest husband and good friend. It was part of the deal: Mac got the sweet, loving side of his wife's quite flinty personality, and Jenny had her rock and protector.

Picking up the phone, Mac dialled the calling card then input Jenny's mobile number. It rang and Mac hoped that she wouldn't pick up so he could just leave a message and not have to dodge too many questions.

The greeting came immediately. 'Toohey.'

'Darling, it's me,' said Mac, massaging his temples. 'How're things?'

'Tropical, hon,' she said, in a tone that suggested she was trying to get niceties out of the way. 'You get my message?'

'Yep.'

He could hear Jen cover the mouthpiece and say, *In the DFAT file – the blue pages.*

'How long you in Auckland for, Macca?' she said, coming back to him. 'I don't want to rush you but I told Frank and Pat that you were due back on the weekend.'

Looking down at his G-Shock, Mac saw the word *Wed* on the screen above the time.

'Yeah, weekend might do it,' he said, trying to sound convincing. 'Could be Monday, Tuesday.'

'Okay, can you call Pat?' said Jen, as a commotion erupted beside her. 'Hang on, okay?'

'Sure,' said Mac.

He could hear his wife spelling out the record-keeping protocol for this investigation and the fact that she wouldn't be compromising on it today or tomorrow or anytime soon, so they might as well get it right from the start.

'Don't worry,' said Jen, back on the line. 'I'll call Pat and tell her – but can you ring too? Sarah loves getting calls from you.'

'Yeah, sure,' said Mac. 'You in Saigon?'

'Here now,' said Jen. 'Shit – you remember Jim Quirk, from Manila?'

'I *think* so,' said Mac. 'Trade Commission, sportsman of some sort?'

'Cricket,' said Jen. 'He was murdered up here, three days ago.'

Mac hated doing this to her. 'I read about it. At a nightclub?'

'Place called the Mekong Saloon, in Saigon's Chinatown.'

'You investigating?' said Mac.

'Yeah – the AFP teams from Honkers and Manila were held back for some reason.'

'Any leads?'

'Apparently there was a vehicle chase through Cholon after the murder, and the staff at the club say an Australian soldier was acting strangely during the incident.'

'No wonder they called you guys,' said Mac, his heart sinking.

Jen yawned. 'We're only observing – no investigation – but Saigon police are linking the Quirk murder with the disappearance of an Australian woman called Geraldine McHugh.'

'Really?'

'Yes, Macca – and she's Jim's wife.'

'Shit,' said Mac, with no conviction.

'So, I was going to call you anyway,' said Jen, as if he was ninth on her to-do list. 'Remember that creepy friend of yours from Nudgee? Urquhart?'

'Davo,' said Mac. 'Sure.'

'Chester brought him along to our breakfast meeting this morning,' said Jen.

'Did he elaborate on how you could aid his career?'

'He did better than that. He warned me off the McHugh line of inquiry.'

'What did he say?' said Mac.

'National interest, blah blah, regional security, wank wank – said the government would thank me to oversee the murder inquiry and then go home.'

'And you said?'

'I said, "Dave, there is no McHugh line of inquiry, but thanks for the tip-off."'

'Don't stir him, Jen,' said Mac, laughing reluctantly. 'He may look like a wax dummy, but he can hurt you.'

Mac could hear more talking behind Jen. 'I have to go, Macca. And call Sarah, okay?'

'Sure,' said Mac, knowing that he wouldn't.

# CHAPTER 39

Standing in the cool of a fruit shop on Dong Du Street, Mac inspected the oranges while watching the sedan pull up in front of the cafe where he'd first spoken with Captain Loan. She got out of the passenger seat of the car, grabbed her phone and day book and walked to the cafe, flicking back her long black ponytail with a shake of her head.

One man remained in the sedan. Walking towards the car from the rear, Mac blindsided the cop, who was looking up and down the footpath. At the last minute, Mac banged his hand on the bonnet of the car as he walked around it, startling the driver.

Inside the cafe, Mac saw the captain at a table, talking into her cell phone. As he sat down she smiled and quickly finished her conversation.

'Well, Mr Richard,' she said, reaching out for a businesslike handshake. 'Nice to have you back.'

'Back?' said Mac, wondering where this was going.

'You crossed into Cambodia three days ago,' said Loan with a kind smile. 'You crossed back into Vietnam about sixteen hours ago.'

'Yes, of course,' said Mac, as green tea arrived.

'Had a chance to think about Miss Geraldine?' asked Loan, preparing the tea.

'From what the Aussies are saying, I gather she works for Australian Treasury and she was divorcing Jim Quirk,' said Mac.

'What else are they saying?'

'That whoever warned Anglos about Cholon, they weren't kidding.'

'You go down to Cholon, Mr Richard?'

'Sure,' said Mac. 'Some great nightclubs down there.'

'You don't look like a book salesman,' said Loan.

'You don't look like a detective,' said Mac.

'I showed the Mekong barman this picture,' she said, pulling a colour print from her day book. It showed Mac emerging from the Grand Hotel, his face partially obscured by a baseball cap. 'He said this was the Aussie soldier he served the night James Quirk died.'

'I'm not a soldier,' said Mac.

'To Vietnamese people, you look like an Aussie soldier.'

'We all look the same, right?' said Mac.

'I think you were in the Mekong Saloon the night Quirk was murdered.'

'Really?' said Mac, his heart thumping. 'I was pretty hammered that night.'

'What is it, the hammered? You mean you were drunk?'

'Yes,' said Mac. 'I might have been in there for one drink – I couldn't swear to it either way.'

'So it might have been you?'

Mac shrugged. 'I went to five or six bars in Cholon that night, and I could only name one of them. But I think I'd remember if I killed someone.'

'I didn't say you killed Quirk. I think you were there, at the Mekong Saloon.'

'And I'm open to the suggestion that I was,' said Mac, 'but I couldn't identify it by name or show you on a map.'

Captain Loan stared at him for twenty seconds before Mac looked down at his tea.

'Same night, there was an altercation about ten blocks north-east of the Mekong Saloon,' said Loan. 'A fight between men, some shots fired. When we arrived, there was an unconscious man on the street – and he won't talk. A woman saw it all, says a local man and an Aussie soldier were travelling on a motorbike.'

'I see,' said Mac, cold sweat on his brow. 'She get the rego plates on the bike?'

'No.'

'I wish I could help,' said Mac.

'You can,' said the captain. 'I think Tranh was riding that bike – tell me where Tranh is hiding.'

Mac snapped out of his dissembling autopilot. 'I don't know.'

'He didn't cross back into Vietnam with you,' said Loan. 'So where is he?'

'I don't know,' Mac repeated.

She leaned towards him slightly, adding a threat with her body language. 'Where did you last see him?'

'Phnom Penh,' said Mac.

'That's a big city, Mr Richard.'

'At an apartment building, on the west side – over by the Inter-Continental.'

'What happened?'

'Look,' said Mac, gulping at the tea and trying to keep down the anxiety. 'What's this got to do with Jim –'

'I asked you a question,' said Captain Loan, abandoning the charm offensive. 'What happened?'

'We were ambushed in the lobby, lots of gunfire,' said Mac, searching her eyes. Was the other cop about to fly in? Was the conversation being taped? 'I was blinded by a burst of concrete dust, and when I recovered, Tranh was gone.'

He wondered how fast his red consular passport could be pouched into Saigon and whether Tobin would allow its use if Loan threw him in the basement. If he pushed Tobin to invoke the passport it would mark the first time in his eighteen-year intelligence career that he'd reverted to 'declared' while in the field and asked for consular protection.

Loan held his gaze. 'I thought we were going to cooperate, Mr Richard. That was my impression.'

'I am cooperating,' said Mac, his voice croaking slightly.

Her face changed. 'You know Alphonse Morales?'

'No,' said Mac, too fast.

'Really? I saw a photograph of you two together. Our intelligence people showed me a file on Morales, and there was a photo of you and him in – where was it? Dili?'

'Oh, you mean Bongo?' said Mac, forcing a laugh. 'I got confused. Yes, I have hired Mr Morales on occasions, for protection. Dili was not a safe place for an Australian salesman in the late 1990s, as I'm sure you can appreciate.'

'Yes, I can,' she said. 'You know Morales is in Saigon? Asking questions about Geraldine McHugh?'

'I didn't know that,' said Mac, his throat rasping like sandpaper.

'Why didn't you file a missing-persons report in Phnom Penh? And why not inform police in Saigon that your Vietnamese driver is missing?'

'I was scared,' said Mac. 'I thought he might have been mixed up in things I couldn't understand.'

'I think you know what he's mixed up in,' she said. 'Should we go down to the station?'

Mac didn't answer, toying with the idea of declaring himself consular and making a call to Scotty or Tobin; he also toyed with the idea of hitting her and running.

'I don't want you in the cells, I don't even want you in the criminal system,' said Loan, leaning back as she looked around the cafe. 'I can help you with McHugh, but I want Tranh.'

'I'm sorry,' said Mac, his heart fluttering with adrenaline. 'I don't even know his last name – I should have filed a report. I apologise.'

'His last name is Loh,' said the captain. 'But if he were being formally introduced, it would be Loh Han Tranh.'

Breathing deeply through his nose, Mac tried to process the information. Tranh was a Loh Han? The most powerful tong in Cholon? At what level had this gig been compromised?

'Loh Han?' said Mac, very carefully. 'As in Vincent Loh Han – the gangster?'

'Tranh is Vincent's nephew,' said the captain, in a tone that had lost its hardness. 'I want him back.'

'You?'

'I took the Vietnamese version of my name when I went to university in Melbourne,' she said. 'I was born Loh Han.'

'I don't understand,' said Mac, his heart rate hitting one-seventy.

'Look,' she said, 'I know who you are, Mr *Richard*, but I don't want you in the cells and I don't want you claiming consular protections. I will help you find Geraldine McHugh, but –'

'But what?'

'Mr Richard,' she said, eyes full of fear and violence, 'Tranh is my brother.'

# CHAPTER 40

Mac stayed quiet in the back seat of the Cong An car as they pulled up outside the Mekong Saloon. Mac and the driver followed Captain Loan into the nightclub where a few patrons nursed their drinks while a young girl writhed around a pole.

A heavyset manager appeared and walked towards Loan, but backed off when she raised her badge. Ascending the stairs that Mac had climbed just a few nights ago, they reached the mezzanine, the manager chirping beside Loan like a bird.

Mac couldn't understand what they were saying – he didn't need to. It was obvious the manager was nervous and not used to the police being allowed in this building.

Stopping beside the door that led to the sealed computer room, Mac pointed. 'I heard someone yelling, like they were being attacked,' he said, trying for a truthful feel. 'I wandered up the stairs and saw a man – an Anglo man – being dragged through this door.'

'Who was dragging him?'

'There were three men – they looked Eastern European, maybe Middle Eastern. Swarthy and tanned,' said Mac.

'And then?' said Loan.

'I said something like, "Hey – cut that out," and one of them turned and came at me.'

'He attacked you?'

'Yes.'

'And then?'

'I attacked him back and followed the kidnap victim.'

'Into here?' said Loan, pushing at the door and then clicking her fingers at the manager to unlock it.

'Yep,' said Mac.

At the end of the corridor they pushed through another door and Loan's colleague hit the lights. In front of them was the internal glass office, with the exit door on the far side.

No computer.

'The man was screaming, so I kicked through the door and stood right here,' said Mac. 'The man – Jim Quirk – was sitting at a computer terminal.'

'In there?' said Loan.

'Right in front of us. The terminal was the kind where the keyboard is built into the screen and hard drive part of it.'

Putting her hands on her hips, Loan surveyed the room. 'Where did Quirk die?'

'Right here,' said Mac, as they walked to where the computer had been. 'The leader, the Middle Eastern bloke, smiled at me and shot Quirk.'

Mac's throat had dried up; he needed a glass of water.

'Shot him?'

'In the head,' said Mac, still haunted by that night. 'Then he ducked out that door.'

'And?'

'And I left the club, got Tranh to get me as far away as possible.'

Crossing her arms, Captain Loan breathed out and looked at the ceiling and the walls, observing her environment like an interior decorator asked to quote on a job. Turning to her colleague, she rattled off a series of commands in Vietnamese.

Grabbing the car keys from the other cop and drawing Mac out by the arm, Loan walked swiftly down the corridor and then out of the club.

'Thanks for that,' she said as she started the car and made a fast phone call. 'Now I have something to show you.'

Eight minutes later, Mac got out of the car in a rear parking compound and followed Loan in the back door of the criminal investigation centre for the Saigon Cong An – the first precinct building.

Inputting a code at a security door, she pushed through and then hesitated. 'You armed, Mr Richard?'

'No,' he said, and they walked into the police station, took a left and went down two flights of stairs. Yells and demands echoed around the concrete-clad basement as they fronted a desk that looked like a nurses' station and Loan snapped a few words at the young Cong An attendant who wore full greens.

Writing in the day book, the woman in greens stood and led them down to a grey steel door with a small window and the number 8 painted below it in white.

The attendant opened the door with a key from her retractable chain and Mac followed Loan inside. From behind a bolted-down desk, cuffed to a loop on the table, a thin Vietnamese man with bad teeth and big cheekbones looked at them wide-eyed. His left eye puffed closed and below it the prominent cheekbone split horizontally over a shiny skin-egg. Both nostrils were encrusted with blood.

'Have a seat,' said Loan, and Mac took one of the interviewer's chairs, clocking the detainee's blood-covered white shirt, which seemed to have a corporate decal on it.

'His English is okay,' said Loan. 'Want coffee?'

'Sure,' said Mac. 'Name's Richard,' he said to the man across the desk, giving him a wink.

'I am Luc,' he said, nodding.

'What are you doing here?' said Mac.

'I was attacked, and now I arrested,' said Luc. 'I told her this all. Many time, for all morning.'

'Tell me,' said Mac. 'Tell me the whole story.'

'Okay.' Luc indicated the embroidered decal on his shirt. 'So I fly the plane for North Star airline.'

Mac nodded. 'At Tan Son Nhat?'

'Yes,' said Luc.

'KingAir, Dash-8? Something like that?' said Mac.

'Yes!' said Luc, good eye opening. 'KingAir 200 – also Fokker 27.'

'Not the Friendship?' said Mac. 'I love the F-27. Grew up with those planes in Queensland.'

'Yes,' said Luc. 'North Star flying two F-27. They from TAA!'

'Get outta here,' said Mac. 'Those TAA Friendships flew more outback miles than any other plane. Unbelievable.'

'It true,' said Luc, growing animated. 'I tell Captain this, and she not know.'

'Well, I know that those planes were easy to land and impossible to clean,' said Mac. 'So tell me.'

The coffee was delivered and Mac offered his cup to Luc. Taking it, the man – who Mac estimated was in his late thirties – pushed his arms onto the table and eyed Loan before turning back to Mac with a conspiratorial look.

'You must carry some strange passengers,' said Mac.

'Yes, and when I fly Mr Smith and his friends, it start normal.'

'Who is Mr Smith?'

'He the man who hire us two month 'go. We flew him Saigon to Stung Treng province and north from Banlung,' said Luc. These were the wild northern provinces of Cambodia – the final outposts of Pol Pot's Khmer Rouge and all the child slavery and heroin production that was part of the communist utopia.

'What does Mr Smith look like, Luc?'

'He not skinny, but not big neither,' said Luc, looking at the table like he was appraising a wine. 'He got tan, and he the bald.'

'Strong eyes?' said Mac.

'Yes,' said Luc, sitting to attention. 'Very strong eye, very dark eye.'

'You own North Star?' said Mac.

'No, mister,' said Luc. 'But Mr Smith only want deal with me. He pay in cash, but I the one who deal with it.'

'What are you flying to Cambodia?'

'People, bags,' said Luc.

'You look in the bags?' said Mac, winking.

Luc looked embarrassed. 'Only once. It was much, much money – American money.'

'Anything else you carry?'

'Whatever they want.'

'They?'

'Mr Smith have friends – maybe ten.'

'Mr Smith's friends – they businessmen? Engineers? Soldiers?'

Shrugging, Luc looked away. 'Some, like me; some, they are like you, mister.'

'Aussie?'

'No,' said Luc, miming to indicate muscles.

'Okay, okay,' said Mac, aware that Loan was smiling beside him. 'Five days ago, maybe Mr Smith is in a hurry. You remember that night?'

Luc blushed through his facial injuries, averted his eyes.

'It was a crazy night, huh?' said Mac, nodding and smiling. 'Lots going on?'

'Yes,' said Luc.

'What happened?'

'Mr Smith call me on cell phone, tell me he need the plane urgent, right?'

'What time?'

'Three in morning,' said Luc. 'My wife real angry.'

'So you go to the airport?'

'Yes, and pick up engineer on way.'

'And then?'

'Mr Smith and his friends are waiting, and we get plane ready, and they come on board.'

'Were they relaxed?'

'No! They nervous and Mr Smith angry with me.'

'Why?'

' 'Cos when I ask if the woman is okay to fly, he grab me by throat and tell me, "There is no woman – you never saw woman."'

'Tell me about the woman,' said Mac calmly, though his pulse was jumping.

'She tired, or maybe drug.'

'She Vietnamese, Cambodian?'

'No,' said Luc, shaking his head. 'When I close the main hatch, I hear her speak to Mr Smith and she Aussie, mister. She talk like you – she look like you.'

'And then?'

'I fly to airfield in north of Stung Treng, I land and Mr Smith give me cash.'

'Some for North Star, some for you?'

'Yes, mister,' he said, looking at the floor. 'I not racish – I like Aussie. I try help the woman.'

'Sure,' said Mac. 'You remember the airfield?'

'I know how to get there, and it in flight log,' he said. 'But airfield not on map.'

'So what happened, Luc – you get in a fight?' said Mac, thinking he would need to get this man out of the cells.

'No, I going work at airport this morning and then I kidnap,' he said, lip quivering.

Mac averted his eyes. 'By Mr Smith?'

'No. The men, they beat me, want to know where the Uc woman is.'

'This is the woman on your plane? The drugged one?'

'Yes – they say, "Where Geralin? Where Geralin?"'

'Geraldine?' said Mac.

'Yes – that what I say. I tell them the place I take her has no name, but they don't believe me.'

'They?'

'A big ape – I think he police or soldier,' said Luc, eyes moistening.

'And?'

'And very big Aussie,' said Luc, shaking his head at the memory.

'He look like me too?' said Mac.

'No – he dark. Very dark and very big.'

'The other one?' said Mac.

'He same as you – but he Indonesi, Philippine maybe,' said Luc.

'What you tell him?'

'I tell him it all, mister,' said Luc, crying now. 'He . . . he . . .'

'He frighten you, Luc?'

'Yes!' said Luc. 'I put my foot through window when they putting the bag over my head.'

'The bag?'

'Yes, they want me to fly them to Geralin!'

'And then the police came?'

'No – my engineer ask if I okay.'

'Where did this happen?' said Mac, confused.

'In toilet, at work,' said Luc, tears on his cheeks. 'They waiting for me.'

'Tell me about these people,' said Mac. 'How did they speak? Walk?'

'The big ape – he call me "brother" all time, and then he hit me.'

'Did you hear a name?' said Mac.

'Yes – I tell her,' he said, pointing at Loan.

'Tell me.'

'The biggest one, he call the ape *Bongo*.'

'Bongo?' said Mac.

'Yes,' said Luc, nodding too hard. 'Bongo – and he say he coming back.'

# CHAPTER 41

Grabbing the second round of beers from the waiter's tray, Mac put them on the table in front of Scotty.

'So, what have we got?' said Scotty. 'Bongo and this Aussie try to beat a destination out of Luc, but the airfield doesn't have a name – though there're coordinates in the flight logs?'

'Correct.'

'So you ask Captain Loan if she has seized the logs, and she says they were stolen?'

'A clerk at North Star looks up from her desk half an hour after Luc was kidnapped,' said Mac. 'A large Filipino man in a black trop shirt is standing in the operations office – he simply tells her to hand over the logs for the F-27s.'

'Fokker Friendships?'

'Yes – and the clerk hands over the logs.'

'And Bongo walks out?'

'Yes – there's also an unconscious manager on the floor.'

'A manager?'

Mac looked around the roof bar of the Caravelle Hotel. 'A manager tried to stop Bongo's requisition, and suffered a strike to the carotid artery, on the right side of his neck.'

Scotty shook his head. 'Jesus.'

'Anyway, Bongo has the logs . . .'

'So Operation Orion needs Luc?'

Scotty's phone trilled, and he frowned as he saw the ID on the screen and took the call.

'Nah, nah, Davo,' said Scotty into the phone. 'Albion will be working with Orion on the joint venture – no one else.' He rolled his eyes.

Waiters raced to clear tables on the roof terrace. The afternoon monsoon downpour was about to start and a stream of tourists had charged into the bar to escape the impending deluge.

'Listen, Davo,' said Scotty, in the non-carrying voice of the veteran spook, 'it's not my call. Our partners want Albion, not your bloke.'

Scotty raised his eyebrows at Mac – Urquhart obviously wanted Lance inserted into Operation Orion.

'No, Davo,' said Scotty. 'He can't be a lone wolf, because I'm running him, okay? When I know something, you'll know.'

Laughing as he rang off, Scotty sat back in the cane sofa. 'That bloke never stops, does he?'

'Urquhart?' said Mac, taking a drink.

'Says you only remained in Indochina on his say-so, dependent on information from the Saigon cops,' said Scotty. 'That true?'

'It was, but then he claimed to have cut me loose. Anyway, you speak with Yossi?' said Mac.

Scotty knew Saba's mate, Yossi, and he'd promised to put a call in to him and find out about the Mossad shootouts in northern Cambodia.

'He wasn't entirely forthcoming, which means whatever they're working on is probably current.'

'He confirm Joel Dozsa?'

'He didn't correct me when I named him,' said Scotty. 'And he was adamant that Dozsa's team is working with a Chinese cadre in northern Cambodia.'

'What are they working on?'

'Yossi didn't want to talk about it – said the gig was tailing the Mossad hit squad out of Bangers and up into Cambodia. That was their interest.'

'Hit squad?' said Mac.

'They weren't going to a tea party with Dozsa,' said Scotty, stopping as two businessmen sat down at the neighbouring table. A loud woman joined the men, and Scotty relaxed.

'So, how does that work?' said Mac. 'The Mossad tells Dozsa to come in and debrief, and when he refuses, they decide to finish it?'

'Who knows what you have to do to get a death sentence from the Mossad?' said Scotty. 'All I know is that Yossi's no wimp but he was spooked by what happened.'

'The killings?'

'The Mossad hit team travelled as Australian forestry guys and they stayed at a b&b across the river from Stung Treng.'

'Nice area.'

'Yeah, and one evening the Mossad team gets back from surveying the forests, and the bathroom blows up.'

'Fuck,' said Mac, looking around.

'Yeah, thought you'd like that, after your welcome at the Cambodiana.'

Mac controlled his shaky hand as he gulped at his beer. 'Yossi saw all this?'

'Yossi told me the surviving hit man staggers out into the yard, half his face torn off by the blast, and a pick-up truck arrives. Dozsa jumps out and pops this dazed bloke in the head. Two other Israelis clear the remaining body with a black vinyl bag, then they throw all the bodies in the back of the truck.'

'Tidy guys.'

'Yeah – then they torch the place.' Scotty shook his head. 'Whole thing is over in thirty seconds.'

Mac sagged in his chair. 'I feel safer now, thanks, mate.'

'By the way, guess who I saw coming out of the New World Hotel this arvo?'

'No idea, champ,' said Mac, wondering if he could fit in another beer.

'Tall, dark . . .'

'This twenty questions?'

'Gorgeous sheila – fights like a bloke.'

'Watch it,' said Mac, realising who Scotty was talking about.

'Look, Macca, I should have told you this earlier, I just forgot.'

'Told me what?'

'She saw me,' said Scotty.

'Oh, great.'

'Yeah – and she talked to me.'

'Fuck's sake, Scotty.'

'It gets worse – I think she knows you're in town.'

'How?' said Mac.

'I don't know, mate. She asked me how you were going, and I said fine, and she starts talking about Auckland.'

'Shit!'

'Yeah, guess my face gave it away,' said Scotty.

'How did you leave it?'

'You know Jen,' said Scotty. 'Smiling, but staring straight through me.'

Having arranged the meeting for the next morning with Charles, promising to get Luc on the team, Mac eased back on the sofa in the living area of his suite and watched CNN. The headline story was still the North Korean missiles and the Japanese and Chinese response to them. The Japanese military was constitutionally a self-defence shield and Mac noticed that no one from the Japanese government or military would comment on the missile tests. But CNN had found a Japanese academic who taught at UCLA, whose name and number had probably been slipped to the media by Japan's intelligence agencies. She was smart, a good talker with fluent English and her arguments neatly fitted with those of the foreign policy hawks who circled Washington DC: 'Last year's tests of the so-called communications satellites by North Korea revealed no satellites were actually put into orbit,' said the academic. 'Pyongyang does not have a space program – they have a ballistic missile program with nuclear capability and using this program to intimidate Japan is not only provocative but probably illegal.'

The journalist asked if there was a new arms race in North Asia and the academic sidestepped that one. Mac sniggered: Japan had breeder reactors that could produce plutonium and its own 'space program' was essentially ICBMs in disguise.

The next story showed Captain Loan walking into the Cong An building and then file pictures of Jim Quirk and Geraldine McHugh flashed onto the screen. The reporter – standing outside the Cong An's first precinct building in Saigon – said the Australian government was remaining tight-lipped about the circumstances of the murder/disappearance of this Canberra power couple, but that the minister for foreign affairs had warned the McHugh family against employing mercenaries who might interfere with the investigations.

Hitting the mute button, Mac looked at his watch: 7.08 pm.

Dialling Captain Loan's number, Mac waited for the call to be answered.

'Captain,' he said. 'Davis here – you still at work?'

'Here till eight,' said Loan.

'Can I come down?'

'Like I say,' said Loan. 'I finish at eight.'

The red sunset cast a pall on the white concrete and mirror glass of the Cong An building as Mac walked through the swing doors and asked for Captain Loan. Before he could sit in the waiting area, a young woman in Cong An greens arrived and asked him to follow her downstairs to the cells and interview rooms.

Questions, raised voices and answers echoed around the concrete bunker as Mac waited in a chair beside the administration desk. He smelled the muddy dampness and remembered how much of Saigon's history included underground bunkers, tunnels and escape routes. It was a city that seemed as comfortable with its hidden aspects as it was with its official story.

A red light flashed above a door. The attendant walked to it and walked out twenty seconds later with Luc. They turned away from Mac to return to a cell but the pilot caught Mac's eye and gave a smile as he was led down the corridor.

Deciding to have a nosey-poke, Mac stood and sauntered the fifteen paces to the door Luc had come out of. Peering through the small glass window he saw two figures up against the door, their faces framed like a picture.

Reeling to get out of there, Mac couldn't make his feet move before the door swung open and the women moved towards him.

'Mr Richard,' said Captain Loan, her face a mask.

The other woman stepped through, pulling her clipboard to her chest and crossing her arms over it.

'Captain Loan,' said Mac, bowing slightly and trying to stay calm.

Turning to the other woman, Mac introduced himself as Richard Davis, from Southern Scholastic, and extended his hand.

'Jenny Toohey,' said his wife, taking forever to shake his hand. 'Australian Federal Police.'

Loan chaperoned Jenny a couple of strides away from Mac, talking in a detective's tone and swapping pieces of paper.

Saying her farewells, Jenny gave Mac a withering look and walked towards the stairwell, her dark ponytail swishing in a motion that translated to pure rage.

'You wanted to talk?' said Loan, breaking into Mac's thoughts as she returned to him.

'I thought about what you said.'

'Which part?' said Loan, arranging files in her clipboard.

'The part where you're prepared to overlook certain things if I help you find Tranh.'

'I never make deals,' said Loan, looking around for eavesdroppers. 'It's hard enough being a Loh Han and a police detective without pushing for an investigation into my brother's disappearance.'

Mac nodded. 'Why not release Luc?'

'Because he's our only link to the Quirk murders.'

'He's also cooperating,' said Mac. 'And he's done nothing criminal, or he'd be arrested.'

Staring at Mac, Loan took her time responding. 'You're right – he was going to be released tomorrow.'

'Push him out the front door at seven am, I'll keep an eye on him.'

Loan frowned. 'That woman? She's AFP and she's not stupid. If Luc goes missing, I have a big problem with your government and my government.'

'He won't go missing,' said Mac.

'He'd better not,' said Loan.

'No?'

'No,' said Loan with a smile. ''Less you want to sample the Cong An food.'

# CHAPTER 42

Getting the room number for Jenny's suite was simple but finding the courage to knock on the door was not so easy.

Standing in the hallway of the New World as a family of four Indonesians walked past on their way to dinner, Mac thought about what he was going to say.

He raised his fist to the door and knocked.

A female voice sounded from behind the door. 'Yes?'

'Book delivery,' said Mac. 'Southern Scholastic books.'

The door flung open and there was Jenny in a hotel bathrobe, patting at her wet hair with a towel.

'I'm going to make a guess and say you didn't call Sarah, right?' said Jenny.

'Not yet, I've been —'

'Yeah, yeah, yeah,' said Jenny, walking away from him.

Following her into the suite, he noticed the two laptops running on the desk and a collection of maps on the wall, red thumb tacks pushed into various parts of Indochina and Saigon.

'When you're away, she lives for your calls,' said Jenny. 'She's three years old — she knows the difference between you being around and you being away.'

'She told me she misses my snoring,' said Mac, trying to lighten it.

Throwing the towel on a sofa, Jenny crossed her arms and stared at her husband.

'Look, I can't ring up and lie to my daughter about where I am,' said Mac.

'But you can lie to your wife?'

'I can create dissonance with my wife, who knows the basics of what I do and why it's safer for all of us —'

'Dissonance?' said Jenny, eyes like saucers. 'Fuck, Macca — get your hand off it.'

Dry-gulping, Mac tried to get past the sofa for a glass of water, but Jenny stepped in his way.

'Actually, I'm glad you showed,' she said.

'Yeah?'

'I was looking at a circular today, it came into my secure email.'

'Okay,' said Mac.

'Australian nationals missing in foreign countries,' she said, crossing her arms and resting her weight on her left hip. 'Which includes Singapore — you may have heard of it?'

'Sure,' said Mac, ice in his gut.

'And the name on this file was Hu — Liesl. Aussie citizen, Singapore resident. So I had a look, Macca, and she's missing.'

'I see.'

'Since the thirteenth, Macca.'

'Interesting,' said Mac.

'That's what I thought,' said Jenny, her face hardening. 'So I gave Lindsay a call — you know Lindsay Hung? Senior investigator at Singapore Police?'

'Heard of him,' said Mac.

'We go through the file and most of it's got a Singaporean D-notice on it.'

'What's that?' asked Mac.

'It's when their intelligence services classify the details, Macca. They share the basics with other countries, but some things are held back.'

'Like what?' said Mac.

'Like the security footage from Liesl's next-door neighbour,' she said, facetious. 'He's a retired vice-admiral from the Singapore

257

navy. There's footage of the comings and goings at Ray and Liesl's house.'

'I see.'

'Yes, Macca,' she said, inching closer. 'But there's also Liesl's phone logs.'

'Right.'

'So I'm having a general gander and then I'm seeing our phone number, Macca. At Broadbeach.'

Mac nodded at his shoes. 'Okay.'

'Two of them – on the thirteenth.'

'Look,' said Mac, wanting to be out of that room, maybe out of the country.

'And they're within forty minutes of each other; one goes for twelve seconds, and the other for twenty-four seconds. Sounds like she left a couple of voicemails, eh, mate?'

Mac felt like a wombat caught in the high beams.

'But it gets better, Macca, 'cos on the night of the thirteenth you asked me not to call Liesl, remember?'

'Yep.'

'And on the morning you leave for *Auckland* you left me a message about our new phone number.'

'That's a standard operating –'

'Shut up,' said Jenny.

Mac shut his mouth.

'Tell me right now,' said Jen, raising her finger and shaking it at Mac. 'Did my friend try to contact us the day she went missing?'

'I don't know for sure . . .' said Mac feebly.

'Did. She. Leave. A. *Message*?' Jenny's eyes were like hot coals.

'Yeah, she did,' said Mac.

The slap came fast and hard, loud on Mac's left cheek. She was a little punchy because of her violent father, but Mac decided this outburst might be more to do with her cycle.

'I thought we had a deal,' she said, a low cop-tone in her voice. 'I don't mess with your world, and you don't mess with mine.'

Mac nodded. 'We did – sorry, we do.'

'An Australian whose husband has just been murdered, calling us – that's not my job? She goes missing, and you don't tell me there were phone calls from her? Are you high? Liesl's an Australian and I'm a fucking cop, Macca.'

'I know, I'm sorry,' said Mac, the left side of his face on fire.

'Okay, so what were Liesl's messages?' said Jenny.

'She thought there was Aussie involvement in the murder,' said Mac. 'The impression I got was Aussie government.'

'And she wanted you to do something for her?' said Jenny, looking through him.

'Actually . . .' said Mac quietly.

'Yes?'

'She was looking for you,' he said.

Mac barely saw the second slap.


It was just after two in the morning when Mac awoke to a noise. A pillow hit the coffee table beside his sofa bed, knocking over a bottle of water and a pile of loose change.

Mac lifted his head. 'That you?'

'You going to lie there all night sulking?' said Jenny from the bedroom.

'I was sleeping.'

'Sleep here,' said Jenny.

'Thought I was banned?' said Mac.

'Shut up and get in.'

Slipping in beside her, Mac cuddled in and she recoiled. 'I said get in – I didn't say you could touch me.'

Mac lay there in the dark, wanting to sleep but knowing he had to endure a lecture. He'd always known his wife had a temper, and he forgave her for it. Mac didn't speak about her past, but when she lost it at him he was always reminded that in her heart she didn't think highly of men.

'Have you ever thought what it must have been like for Frank?'

'Sorry?' said Mac.

'For your father, a senior cop in the Queensland police, having to introduce you as someone who works in a book company?'

'I might have thought –'

'I'm not asking has it occurred to you briefly; I mean, have you considered what it must have been like for a trusted man in the public eye to know he was telling pork pies about his own son?'

'No, not really,' said Mac.

'What about your wife?'

'I've given that some thought,' said Mac.

'And?'

'And I've tried to do things in a way that doesn't affect what you're doing or embarrass you in –'

'No, Macca,' said Jenny. 'I don't want the Firm's mission statement for wives and other unfortunates. I'm asking you, have you put yourself in my position, asked yourself what it must be like for a federal cop having to tell her friends and colleagues that her husband sells books for a living?'

'It can't be easy,' said Mac.

'And now Sarah's at preschool,' said Jenny. 'You want her standing in front of the class, helping you with your cover?'

'Yeah, look,' said Mac. 'When we first got you pregnant, I decided to quit the Firm for just this reason. I didn't want this burden on you.'

'Okay,' said Jenny.

'But, you know, part-time lecturing wasn't that great, we wanted to move up from that apartment to the house, we needed the money and so I went back,' said Mac.

'What happened to the office job, the nine to five?'

'The Commonwealth has plenty of office guys,' said Mac, not wanting to verbalise where his career was going. 'It's field guys they're short on – people who can work their guts out for a couple of months without a day off.'

'But you've just turned forty, mate,' said Jenny. 'Where're the youngsters who want to be in the field? Don't they watch James Bond movies?'

'The youngsters don't have jobs anymore,' said Mac. 'They have careers – they're encouraged to hang around senior office guys because that's how you get ahead.'

'I thought we could at least drop the salesman act,' said Jenny. 'Back office at Foreign Affairs? Promotions at Austrade?'

'That was Plan B,' said Mac, not wanting to admit that Tobin had offered him that on re-entry. 'Things happened quickly, I was straight into the old game and it seemed easier to resume an old identity.'

'So?'

'So when this is done I might turn into a communications officer at Austrade,' said Mac, meaning it this time. 'It'll be plain Alan McQueen, pumping out press releases from around Asia, writing speeches for the DG and the minister – that shit.'

'That would suit us fine,' said Jenny, snuggling in.

'And by the way,' said Mac, raising his arm so she could move in, 'it's no carousel ride living with a cop, either.'

'Oh really?'

'Yeah. I remember Mum trying to hide the newspaper from Dad on his days off – he'd be reading a story, then jumping on the phone to the detectives' room, carrying on about some important connection, or an incorrect detail that the police prosecutor had laid down in depositions. It never ended.'

'I'm not that bad,' she said.

'No, at least you don't go through the births and deaths, and the auctions – Christ, the bloody *auctions*.'

'Frank did?'

'Oh yeah,' said Mac. 'Dad would go through the auction notices, reading out the lots. If he thought some stolen machinery was coming up for sale, or a consignment had a fishy owner, he'd go take a butcher's. He was a nutcase, and the crims hated him.'

'Just as well you married me, eh, Macca?' she said, bringing her lips closer.

'Yeah, mate,' said Mac. 'And just as well I got that iPod player for the car.'

'Why?' said Jenny.

'No more radio news,' he said, as Jenny took a playful swipe at him. 'So there's no excuse to work the phone on your days off.'

'It hasn't happened *that* often,' she said, getting serious again. 'The Haneef thing doesn't happen every day.'

'Yeah, but when it does . . .'

'Okay, Macca,' she said, pulling his face to hers. 'That would be you in the dog box, remember?'

'How could I forget?' said Mac.

'Watch it.' Jenny kissed him.

'Oh, I watch it all right,' said Mac. 'But your hands are too fast.'

# CHAPTER 43

The van's air-con made the interior either too cold or too warm — there was no middle setting. Messing with the dial while he waited for Luc to have a shower and say goodbye to his wife, Mac's phone sounded.

Mac hit the green button. 'Yep.'

'McQueen — Sammy,' said the American. 'What's this text mean? A plane and a pilot?'

'You guys good for it?' said Mac, observing the early-morning traffic off the main boulevard of Cong Hoa. 'We charter the plane, we get the pilot.'

'Remind me,' said Sammy.

'The North Star pilot — his name's Luc,' said Mac. 'He doesn't have the coordinates but he knows how to fly us to Dozsa's airfield.'

'Okay,' said Sammy, covering the phone and talking with someone before coming back on the line. 'Can do, McQueen.'

'Demand the Fokker Friendship and ask for Luc by name,' said Mac. 'Book it now and with any luck it'll be ready by the time we're out there.'

'This Luc okay?'

'His wife will decide, but I put a sweetener in there for her.'

'Sweetener?' said Sammy.

'Yeah — told him there's five thousand US, over and above.'

'Nice, McQueen. That coming out of your pocket?'

'We receive unto our needs, give according to our ability, right, Sammy?'

'I went to church too, tough guy,' said Sammy. 'Priest said nothing about giving with another man's wallet.'

'Cash works best,' said Mac as Luc emerged from his French-colonial terrace house.


Banking steeply over Phnom Penh, Luc straightened for the runway and eased the red and white F-27 onto the tarmac, its twin Pratt & Whitneys stirring Mac's memory. When he was growing up in regional Queensland the Fokker Friendships had been a staple of travel between small cities and towns: Rockhampton–Townsville, Gladstone–Mackay, Barcaldine–Longreach. If you flew those routes, then you sat in those purring Friendships with the harsh light bending through the egg-shaped fuselage windows. The planes were still used across South-East Asia and India as milk-run planes that could take off and land on short runways and carry a surprisingly large payload.

In the passenger section of Mac's plane were three rows of seats directly behind the cockpit and the rest was a cargo bay, hidden by a dark green canvas quilt hanging off the interior fuselage.

Bringing the F-27 to the hangar with the *Aviation Services Inc.* sign above the open doors, Luc shut down props, hooked his headset on the wall of the cockpit and came through to Mac while the engineer completed the logs and checks.

'Okay, Mr Richard,' said Luc, his face still suffering from Bongo's beating. 'Welcome to Cambodia.'

Opening the forward door, Luc released the folded ladder. Easing himself down the narrow gangplank to the tarmac, Mac squinted and pulled down his sunnies as the tropical sun gained intensity. It was 9.38 am and felt like thirty-five degrees.

Sammy Chan leaned against a black Chevrolet Silverado. 'McQueen — you're early. I like that.'

Sammy greeted Luc and Mac gave some background as they walked to the reception area of the service hangar.

'We need to talk,' said Mac into Sammy's ear as Luc went over to the coffee machine and poured a cup.

'Just have to nip upstairs, okay, Luc?' said Mac, grabbing a coffee.

'Um, yeah, okay, Mr Richard,' said the pilot, averting his eyes.

'Don't worry,' said Mac, moving to the stairs with Sammy. 'I'll get you the money.'

The first-floor area was filled with sofas and coffee tables, which looked out over Phnom Penh International through tinted floor-to-ceiling windows. At one end, Charles spoke in Vietnamese into a phone, a finger jammed in his ear as he spoke too loud. Sammy raised binoculars and scanned the airport. It was the lifelong curse of people from a military intelligence background to obsessively survey whatever ground lay in front of them. In Sammy's case, he seemed to be focusing on the large man in grey overalls and baseball cap who was loading the black canvas duffels from the Silverado into the rear door of the F-27. The luggage man was Brian, the tall American who'd greeted Mac as he'd boarded the houseboat two days earlier.

'Looks like we got some gear,' said Mac, taking a seat. 'I thought we might need some more cavalry.'

'Because?' said Sammy, not dropping the binos.

'Because I had a bird whisper in my ear about this prick Dozsa,' said Mac, sipping on good coffee – Sumatran or Timorese was his guess.

'And?' said Sammy.

'A two-man Mossad hit team passed through Bangers a few months ago, masquerading as Australian forestry guys. Drove up to Stung Treng province – Dozsa's turf.'

'Israelis don't like the jungle, McQueen,' said Sammy, 'and the jungle don't like them. So what was going on?'

'Dozsa's operating up there with a Chinese cadre. They look private but probably PLA.'

'What happened?' said Sammy.

'Dozsa waited, let them get close, then he executed them.'

Letting the field-glasses drop, Sammy sipped the coffee. 'Mossad on Mossad. That's –'

'Scary?' said Mac.

'Your word,' said Sammy, looking away.

Mac saw the look on the American's face. 'It's okay to feel queasy about this guy, but four of us, up there? It might be travelling light.'

'It'll be six,' said Sammy. 'I hired some muscle.'

'Military?' said Mac.

Sammy nodded. 'Uh-huh.'

'Locals?'

'Sort of – between these guys and your pilot, the US government might have change left over for lunch.'

'Speaking of which,' said Mac.

Turning to his backpack, Sammy pulled out a fat envelope and handed it over. 'Tell Luc he can at least serve tea and biscuits for that whack.'

'He might find a few beers for this.'

'So,' said Charles, joining them, 'you two come up with a plan yet?'

'Do some aerial recon with Luc while the rest come in by vehicle,' said Sammy. 'There's a village north of Stung Treng. I've rented the second floor of the local hotel.'

'Cover?' said Charles.

'Forest biodiversity project for the World Bank,' said Sammy. 'Verification audit for the Sam Ang forest region – it's across the river from Stung Treng.'

'We official?' said Charles.

Sammy smiled. 'Got the lanyards in my bag.'

Charles frowned, bit on the arm of his sunnies. 'I don't want to storm this place. The Aussie girl's in there and I don't want this Mossad maniac blowing the whole thing sky-high.'

'It's a stealth assignment, Chuck,' said Sammy. 'I'm not racing out of my trench at these bastards, and neither is McQueen.'

Staring at Sammy and then Mac, Charles nodded slowly.

'Okay, no heroics, no tough-guy scenes,' he said, looking at Mac. 'Remember, we answer to bureaucrats and they would rather we fail than create embarrassment.'

Mac maintained a straight face. 'I turned forty last week, okay, Charles?'

'Maybe it's not just you,' said Charles. 'Sammy, make sure these mercs get the message, okay?'

A smashing sound came from the stairwell and then Luc was in the room, panting and scared.

'What's up?' said Mac, standing and unhitching the Colt from the back of his waistband.

'Down there,' said Luc, trapped between a gulp and a pant.

'Who?' Mac cocked the Colt and moved to the stairwell, Sammy behind him.

'Help me,' said Luc, turning and running towards the end of the long room.

Turning around the edge of the stairwell, Mac looked down the carpeted stairs and saw no one. Moving down one stair at a time, he listened for sounds and heard men's voices.

'Let's go,' Sammy whispered over his SIG.

They got to the door at the foot of the stairwell. Mac's temples were pounding. He didn't know if he was ready for this after the violence he'd seen recently and his hands were swimming and his breath was shallow as Sammy moved beside him.

Looking through the glass panel in the door, Mac couldn't see anyone in the ground-level reception area.

'Shit,' said Mac, hissing it out. The last time he'd burst through a door, Jim Quirk had been murdered in front of him. Now he had the pilot running for his life. Who was down here? The Israelis? The Chinese?

'On three,' said Sammy.

Counting it out, Mac opened the door, put his handgun in a cup-and-saucer grip and strode into the lounge, sweeping the Colt from ten o'clock to two. Sammy joined him as they scanned the empty reception area, wondering what had spooked Luc.

Relaxing slightly, Mac felt his breathing normalise.

'Where's —' Sammy stopped short.

Turning to the American, Mac felt the gun muzzle behind his ear and dropped the Colt, put his hands in the air.

They stood for one second before the man behind them spoke.

'You don't remember too good, McQueen,' said the South-East Asian voice with a faint American twang. 'I told you — you pull on me, you'd better kill me.'

The sweat felt like ice on Mac's forehead as the air-con turned the room into a fridge. That voice came from a decade ago – from East Timor, when Mac was being stalked by Kopassus intel and he'd needed a hired gun to protect him.

'That you, Bongo?' said Mac, trying to sound confident but squeaking slightly.

'When I have the gun,' said Bongo Morales, 'I ask the questions.'

Moving in front of Mac, Sammy had a huge smile on his face.

'Didn't know you two were acquainted,' he said, retrieving Mac's Colt and handing it to him. 'Bongo's coming north with us.'

A large, dark man in military shorts and a T-shirt moved into the room through the front doors. Mac recognised him immediately: a former Aussie special forces soldier named Didge.

Nodding a greeting at Didge, Mac turned to Bongo. 'So you're the muscle?' said Mac, stashing his gun.

'Got brains too, McQueen,' said Bongo, chewing gum. 'You wanna stare at the pipes, that's your problem, brother.'

# CHAPTER 44

The Friendship made good time through the clear skies out of Phnom Penh. Luc turned to Mac and shouted that they were passing over a small town and from here they'd be flying over the Chamkar Leu district of Cambodia, a vast forest wilderness that stretched from north-east Cambodia into Laos and northern Thailand. Under Pol Pot's Khmer Rouge in the late 1970s, Chamkar Leu was part of the infamous 'region 42' of the Central Zone – a part of Kampuchea that even Pol Pot did not entirely control.

Mac craned his head between the pilot and engineer and looked down on the expanse. To his right the glossy brown snake of the Mekong flowed north–south and extended as far as he could see, not crossed by a road until the Pakse Bridge, a hundred miles north in Laos.

It had been to these forests that Pol Pot's cadres had originally fled in the days when they were just a bunch of Maoist revolutionaries who executed anyone who couldn't recite the doctrines. After the Vietnamese Army invasions of 1979–80, it was into the Chamkar Leu that the cadres loyal to Brother No. 1 withdrew, turning the entire area into a KR haven of child prostitution, opium production and slave-trading; it had taken the United Nations more than a decade to bring it under central governance.

269

As they flew over the last vestiges of civilisation, Mac stared into the forest racing past below and remembered the night he'd got drunk at that cadre compound in the forests north of Meanchey with the KR strongman called the Duck: the kids in those cages, some as young as four; the pretty young women; the young mothers with kids; the oddities, such as twins, amputees and dwarves. The smell of warm skin and dry concrete.

He remembered the small details, like the Duck playing Wham's greatest hits on a Sony portable cassette player; like the bar set up along one wall of the main building and the small stage in front of it. The Duck had dragged a fourteen-year-old boy named Ran out of a cage and made him dance sexy, pistol-whipping him until he swivelled his hips. The song was 'Wake Me Up' and the Duck wanted Ran gyrating when the band sang *before you go-go*.

Maggs had alibied him out of the ensuing murder investigation. But Mac's conscience was clear. When the Duck had stepped out the door to take a satellite phone call, Mac had looked that scared, humiliated fourteen-year-old boy in the eye. Something had flashed between them, and – as if in a dream – Mac had walked to the bar, grabbed the Duck's Beretta 9mm automatic, and given it to Ran.

The boy had walked outside and used one shot, before replacing the gun on the bar. Together they'd hauled the Duck into a dumpster where he'd lain with a perfect third eye until discovered by his soldiers.

Mac had been raised Catholic and he'd always used the church's rule for his behaviour in the field. That yardstick said that while you could do good deeds knowing that there might be some bad consequences, you could never do a bad thing, hoping that good would come of it. He'd wrestled with his decision to give Ran the gun – had nightmares and internal debates about it for years. He'd decided, after becoming a father, that his initial argument was correct: that giving a weapon to a slave was a good thing which might have bad consequences; that it wasn't just his ego that was happy when those people had wandered out of their cages, bowing pathetically to Mac like he was a god, holding their kids up to him and touching him on the forehead.

Knowing he was right didn't stop him thinking about it, but he no longer pronounced himself guilty.

A static burst echoed in the cockpit and Luc pointed to a headset hooked to the bulkhead beside Mac's right ear. He put it on and Sammy's voice came through.

'Orion Two, Orion Two, this is Orion One. Copy?'

'I'm here, mate,' said Mac.

'We're an hour away from destination. Any visuals yet, Orion Two?'

'No, mate – we're yet to fly over.'

'Still on ETA?'

'Affirmative, Orion One.'

Signing off, Mac kept his headset on as Luc spoke.

'We twelve, thirteen minutes out,' said Luc, a more confident man when sitting behind the controls of a plane. 'You want fly over or loop around?'

'Loop around,' said Mac, thinking that Dozsa could easily have surface-to-air missiles defending his lair. 'I'd like to plot it and then fly back down the roads, get an idea how we're going to travel in here.'

'Roads?' said Luc, his mouth turning down at the corners.

'Yes,' said Mac.

'Don't know about no road, Mr Richard,' said Luc. 'That why Mr Smith fly here.'

Eleven minutes later the Friendship banked to the west and flattened out at about four thousand feet as it flew across the wide mouth of a valley.

'There,' said Luc, pointing in front of the engineer's face. 'That the airfield where we fly Mr Smith.'

Bringing binoculars to his eyes, Mac scanned the greenery and quickly found the stretch of tawny bare earth on the river flats. It was small and it was immediately evident why it wasn't on any map: it was in the middle of a wilderness, not linked to any towns, not served by any roads that Mac could see.

'What happens when you land there?' said Mac, looking for activity at the airstrip.

'Vehicles come down, they load onto the plane, we fly back to Phnom and Saigon.'

'Where do the vehicles come from?' said Mac.

'Look up the hill from airfield,' said Luc over the roar of the engines. 'There are buildings, but they camouflage.'

Running the binos further up the sides of the valley from the airfield, Mac clocked a large complex of buildings among the trees, shaded by netting and painted in swirling designs of drab olive and lime green.

'What's in the buildings?' said Mac, stunned by the size of the operation.

'I not know,' said Luc, shrugging. 'We never allowed off the plane.'

'Okay, Luc,' said Mac, handing the pilot a USGS topographical map. 'Mark this location and then let's do a wide circle, around the back of the valley, see if there's some kind of track to the river.'

Passing the map to the engineer, Luc banked the aircraft with a turn of the wheel and some rudder and they hooked north again, ducking behind a ridge.

Passing over the top of the river valley, Luc brought the F-27 to the level of the saddle hills, and Mac looked down the valley with the binos. The buildings could now be seen clearly, as could men milling around in the shade of the trees.

'Seen enough,' said Mac. 'Let's find a track.'

After thirty seconds of flying eastwards, away from the Israeli compound, Luc pointed down and Mac saw a narrow track, occasionally becoming clear when the forest was thin or as it forded a river.

'Let's follow it,' said Mac. 'Mark the route on the map.'

His confidence was evaporating by the second. If they were going to successfully infiltrate that compound, they'd need to surprise the occupants, and arriving via that track was not going to create a surprise.

After sixteen minutes of following the track, Mac saw a structure sitting slightly back from it, in the trees. Using the binos, he focused on it, his heart rate rising.

The track became more substantial and Mac could see farmers, carts and motorbikes moving both ways.

Looking up, he saw the Mekong and the town of Stung Treng on the other side – but no bridge.

'Shit,' said Mac, and asked Luc to patch him through to Sammy.

'Mate, we'll meet you in Kratie, okay?' said Mac as the American answered.

'We left there half an hour ago,' said Sammy. 'You okay, Orion Two?'

'Yeah, we're good – need to confab.'

'Copy that, Orion Two,' said Sammy. 'Kratie it is.'


While the gear was secured at a small guest house in a secondary street of Kratie, Sammy grabbed Mac and they crossed a dusty street, through crowds of German backpackers and local hawkers, to a dark bar.

'What's up?' said Sammy, as he returned to their table with a can of 333 in each hand.

'I didn't like Stung Treng for a base,' said Mac.

'Why not?'

'It's the only town near the Israeli compound, and it's the town where the Mossad hit team was killed – Dozsa probably has informants working for him there. It's poor, and the hotel owners and cops like a few US dollars thrown their way.'

'Okay, so we base ourselves in Kratie,' said Sammy. 'Tell me about the compound.'

'It's in the middle of the jungle,' said Mac, sipping at the cold beer.

'Approaches?'

'A track,' said Mac. 'And I mean a bloody goat track.'

'I know what you're thinking, McQueen, and it's out of the question,' said Sammy, watching from the corner of his eye a table of British tourists who were playing back their video footage of freshwater dolphins on the Mekong.

'A small SF insertion, six-man unit, could drop in there with chutes and shut that place down very quickly,' said Mac.

'And it's out of the question,' said Sammy. 'This operation only succeeds if the least number of people know what it's about and even fewer know what's in that compound.'

'What's in that compound?' said Mac.

'The gig is very simple, McQueen.' Sammy ignored Mac's question. 'Get the memory card and retrieve the girl. We call in special forces and we're up to our necks in Pentagon and Agency, and that brings media.'

'Leaky?'

'Like a sieve.' Sammy lowered his voice. 'Remember the hunt for Saddam?'

'How could I forget?' said Mac. 'It was reality TV.'

'Precisely. We let Defense or CIA into this gig and we'll have every back-seat driver in DC appearing on Fox or CNN, surmising what the Chinese are up to and how the world economy is about to go down the toilet. The markets get nervous, the dollar slides and then the whole deal is in the shitter.'

'Didn't know it was that bad.'

'So this compound can't be impossible,' said Sammy. 'You haven't spent your career behind a desk.'

'I don't know what's on my file,' said Mac, 'but the Royal Marines have a very simple rule for this sort of thing.'

'Yes?'

'Don't go in if you can't get out.'

'You'd be pleased to know the US Marines don't train kamikazes either,' said Sammy. 'What did you see?'

'I saw two approaches – a goat track and an airfield – and I saw a ferry crossing from Stung Treng: there's no bridge. I saw a town full of Dozsa informers and on the west bank I saw country so poor that a farmer's loyalty could be bought for what you or I would lose down the back of the sofa.'

Mac took another swig of beer, eavesdropping on the back-packers, who were competing over who was staying in the cheapest guest house.

'Pao Peng's plan is underway,' said Sammy, avoiding Mac's eyes. 'We need to be in that compound asap.'

'How do you know about Pao Peng?'

'I've spent the last seven weeks in Indochina, chasing these pricks – believe me, McQueen: the Pao Peng plan is happening.'

'It would help if I knew the details.'

'Here're the details, McQueen,' said Sammy, anxiety creeping through his growl. 'There's an Australian national – a high-level Commonwealth employee – being held in that compound by an ex-Mossad sociopath. How's that for details?'

Mac eyeballed him. 'I didn't say I wasn't going.'

'I've told you everything I can tell you,' said Sammy. 'A powerful general in the PLA is plotting to bring down the Chinese economy by also attacking the US economy. He's using an Israeli crew – we can stop them once we retrieve that memory card and McHugh.'

The two men drank in silence for thirty seconds.

'So what do we need?' said Sammy.

'We need unobserved aerial reconnaissance,' said Mac. 'And we need motorbikes.'

'I can order up a Hawk,' said Sammy; the US Navy's high-altitude unmanned reconnaissance plane was called the RQ-4 Global Hawk. 'They'd send one in without too many questions.'

'Okay – can we have that in place before we go in?'

'I'll do it this afternoon,' said Sammy. 'What's this about motorbikes?'

'That country is hard on big vehicles,' said Mac. 'Your big Chevs are great on American country roads, but there's no county ploughs in Indochina – no one's dropping gravel and levelling it with a scraper.'

'Okay,' said Sammy.

'Let's have two blokes in the Chev, and two bikes.'

'Why the split?'

'Because the bike team might have to go around a certain point in the track,' said Mac.

'Certain point?' said Sammy.

'There's a checkpoint,' said Mac. 'About ten miles west of the river, there's a shack on the side of the road.'

'Could be a farmer's shed.'

'So those poor farmers have invested every penny they have to run a telephone line to their shack?'

'An Asia Development Bank loan?'

'The line runs inland, Sammy,' said Mac, finishing his beer. 'It runs from the shack to guess where?'

'Okay, okay,' said Sammy. 'I'll get you motorbikes.'

'You do that,' said Mac, banging his empty can on the table.

# CHAPTER 45

The streets of Kratie were crowded with busy locals and backpackers from Europe, and Mac sauntered among them, looking for unwanted attention and eyes that lingered.

Kratie was a favourite for travellers who liked places that were off the beaten track, but only if they'd already been overrun by people just like them.

Regardless of what tourists thought of it, Kratie was an important market town in north-east Cambodia. The peasant farmers loaded their boats and their carts at five in the morning and headed for the town's markets to sell their six chickens, four ducks or three baskets of rice. The fishermen brought their catch into the market and the world of subsistence yeomanry began another day of trying to eke out a living.

'Gets hot in the afternoon, Kratie,' said the man's voice beside him as he looked for a chance to cross the road and walk to the river. 'Faces west.'

Turning, Mac came face to face with Bongo, the big face impassive beneath the dark sunnies and the Elvis haircut.

'You following me, Bongo?' said Mac, a little annoyed that he hadn't picked him up.

'Just wandered out of the post office,' said Bongo, hooking a thumb over his shoulder. 'Thirsty yet, McQueen?'

'It's an afternoon in Kratie,' said Mac. 'I could hit the waterhole like a lizard drinking.'

They sat at a cafe table nursing their beers while Bongo finished a cell phone call.

'Life as a managing director,' said Bongo as he put the phone down. 'Phone never stops.'

'How's that going?' Mac asked.

'Busy, brother,' Bongo replied, emptying his beer glass and gesturing for two more. 'Friend of mine from the old days, we were talking a few years ago and he says to me, "Bongo, you make yourself into a security firm and then the mining company, the law firm, the foreign government, they use your service."'

'So you're not a mercenary anymore,' laughed Mac. 'You're a company director?'

'My accountant says I'm a security consultant; I'm a services provider,' said Bongo, taking his fresh beer and raising it. 'To services.'

'To services,' said Mac, clinking glasses and shaking his head slightly. 'You looking after Didge?'

'Sure – he's a top operator: very hard, very trained and I'm paying him twice what he made in the Aussie army. Talking of money, you get that cash?'

'Cash?'

'Yeah, brother – I dropped it at Saba's, in Jakarta. You forgot about that?'

'Shit,' said Mac. 'The cash. Yeah, it was there – thanks.'

During their gig in East Timor a decade earlier, Mac had retrieved a few bags of cash from a Korean middleman who supplied feed stock for biological weapons. He'd let Bongo have all the dough, but Bongo had insisted that he would put some in Mac's safe-deposit box at Saba's Lager Haus. Following that gig, Mac had checked his box and there were pillows of cash.

'So how we going to do this?' said Mac.

'Do what?' Bongo scanned, the cafe and street like a cyborg.

'You're contracted to the Americans, but you've been hired to retrieve Geraldine McHugh by her family.'

Bongo chewed gum and stared at Mac through his sunglasses.

'What I like about you, McQueen – you always in someone else's business.'

'You can get the girl, collect your fee from the lawyers – I don't care,' said Mac. 'But I can't be competing with you when I'm stealthing into that compound.'

'So don't compete,' said Bongo.

'I'm retrieving McHugh,' said Mac. 'That's the gig.'

Bongo drank. 'We can both do it.'

'I'll deliver her back to Oz, you'll get a big mention in my report.'

'If I find the girl, no one touches her – that's when there's a misunderstanding.'

Mac paused: 'misunderstanding', in Bongo's world, was a euphemism for a dispute ending in at least one homicide.

'I can see your position, mate,' said Mac. 'But if we find McHugh, the Americans must be able to debrief.'

Bongo paused, gave Mac the evil eye. 'You told the Yankees?'

'Told them what?'

'That I'm working for the McHugh lawyers?' said Bongo, stiffening as the cafe owner came from behind the counter and walked to another table.

'No,' said Mac.

'Okay – you keep it that way, and if I find the girl, they can debrief.'

'It's not only that,' said Mac, trying to be delicate. 'The Australian government may not want your name associated with her rescue.'

'That's their problem, brother,' said Bongo. 'You gotta know your friends, McQueen, and they're not in Canberra.'

'What does that mean?'

'Means I was late for the airport this morning 'cos I got eyes on something.'

'What?'

'White Toyota, followed us from the hotel.'

'Followed you?'

'Yeah, McQueen. The driver was that one you know, with the funny skin – Eckhart?'

'Urquhart,' said Mac, the beer threatening to reflux.

'Yeah, him.'

'What happened?'

'Stopped at the lights – Didge got out, went back there and asked the passenger if he knows the way to Bangkok.'

'And?' said Mac.

'And this guy's sliding down in his seat – young Aussie, look like Adam Ant with that bad hair.'

'What did they say?'

'Pointed, said, "That way." Just having some fun with them but I wonder why Urquhart and the lady-man following.'

'They know you've been hired to find Geraldine McHugh,' said Mac.

'Of course,' said Bongo, smiling. 'So why they following me when they know you doing the gig?'

'Don't know,' said Mac, looking away from Bongo's taunting eyes.

'Neither do I.' Bongo gulped his beer. 'Anyway, you know the Yank who was killed in Phnom Penh?'

'No,' said Mac.

'He worked with Sammy. His name's Phil Brown – Secret Service guy.'

'Okay, so?' said Mac.

'So I picked up the phone, talked to my guy – see about Phil Brown.'

'And?'

'And he's operating as a currency investigator, with the C-note Squad. You heard of it?'

Mac recalled the US hundred-dollar bills in the back of Sam and Phil's car. 'No.'

'You want to?'

'Yeah, but –'

'Here's the deal, brother,' said Bongo. 'If I find the girl, I'm flying her back to Australia.'

Staring at the Filipino, Mac wondered how he ever put his life in this man's hands. 'Okay – you got it.'

'The Secret Service's C-note Squad is on a sweep through Asia, clearing up any counterfeiting problems with the current US hundred-dollar bills, before they're changed to the new format.'

'Problems?'

Bongo chewed gum. 'There's some illegal protocols in the wrong hands – come from Beep or BP or –'

'BEP,' said Mac. BEP was the US Bureau of Engraving and Printing – the federal agency that created US currency.

'That's it,' said Bongo. 'BEP protocols.'

Mac didn't see the news flash. 'The fact the Yanks protect their currency isn't entirely surprising.'

'No,' said Bongo. 'But my guy's been dealing with the real C-note Squad, and Phil Brown ain't on it.'


Back at the guest house, Mac ran up the outside stairs of the former colonial mansion as Grimshaw arrived in the car park in his green Camry. Letting himself into the second door on the left, he made a quick search of the tiny room and decided he was alone. Putting his wheelie bag on the single bed, Mac tried to remember where he'd left it or if he'd even kept it: the piece of paper he'd grabbed from the top of that box of US dollars in the back of Sammy's car.

Rummaging through the pockets of the bag, he came up empty. Then he took his clothes from the bag and checked under the lining and in the ASIS-issued bag's three secret hides.

He wondered if he'd even grabbed that paper – he'd been under enormous stress that night and he may have confused his desire to take it with having actually done so.

Standing to the side of the sash window, he looked down on the street and thought about what Bongo had said: Phil wasn't from the Secret Service. So what was he doing?

Looking at his clothes on the bed, he saw the cheap market-bought chinos he'd been wearing on the night Phil Brown was killed. They had an inside coin pocket on the right hip and out of it Mac pulled a folded piece of paper.

Unfolding it, he saw a handwritten note in cursive script. *Intercepted Stung Treng Province. October 12, 2009 – P, I, D, SF, SN = genuine.* It still meant nothing to Mac but he decided to hang onto it anyway.

The sound of a revving motorbike sounded and Mac left his room, walked to the rear balcony of the guest house.

Below, in the parking area, Sammy flipped the stand of one Yamaha 250cc trail bike, while a local dismounted from another and put his hand out for the money.

Descending, Mac had a look.

'Not bad – about three years old,' said Mac, checking the tyres and chains. 'How does yours ride?'

'Rides okay, but it's not mine,' said Sammy. 'I'm running the radio from the truck.'

'That leaves Didge,' said Mac, looking at the odo.

'Not Bongo?' said Sammy.

'No – Didge spent a lifetime on these things in Aussie special forces,' said Mac. 'Besides, you'll feel safer with Bongo, believe me.'

'I hope so,' said Sammy. 'I met with Charles half an hour ago.'

'Yeah?'

'We can't delay this any longer.'

'We start early enough, we'll have a recce of Dozsa's compound by lunch,' said Mac.

'I mean, no delay,' said Sammy.

'What delay?' said Mac, not getting it.

'Waiting is the delay,' said Sammy. 'We're going this evening.'

# CHAPTER 46

The afternoon rains eased shortly after eight o'clock and the four of them made for the pre-arranged ferry ride across the Mekong.

The ferryman didn't want the Chev on his small wooden ferry, but when Mac offered a further inducement, Sammy reluctantly agreed to pay it and they slipped into the dusk, the red sunset poking through the lifting black clouds as they reached the banks opposite Kratie.

Heading north on the riverside track, Mac rode ahead with Didge, doing not much more than sixty k an hour through the mud and puddles, keeping enough distance that the motorbikes did not look to be connected with the truck. A keen observer would see an M4 carbine over the riders' shoulders and maybe handguns on their hips, but the locals were used to UN and World Bank consultants being accompanied by armed escorts.

It was dark as they reached the ferry head opposite Stung Treng and turned left for the interior and the wilderness of Chamkar.

Riding like that for ten minutes past peasant farms and a small village, Mac slowed to a stop in the beginnings of the forest and walked back to talk with Sammy and Bongo, who sat in the front seat of the idling Silverado.

'Give us thirty minutes exactly,' said Mac, as the other men set the mission clocks on their watches. 'There's a fork up ahead – take the left and you'll come to the checkpoint in three or four minutes. And come in hot. Okay?'

Walking back to Didge with two Kevlar vests from the Silverado, Mac laid it out. They would take the right fork in the road, double around, neutralise the checkpoint, and wait for the others. If they got this part right, it would make the compound infiltration much easier.

'Sure, boss,' said Didge.

'I'd like to avoid gunfire, if we can.'

Didge winked. 'No worries.'

Killing their headlights as they made the fork, Mac slowed and told Didge through the radio headset, 'It's all yours, mate.'

Australia's army special forces – the 4RAR Commandos and the SAS – both trained on bikes and were experts across broken ground at night with no headlamps.

After three minutes of running, the radio crackled in Mac's ear. 'Drop to first, boss,' said Didge. 'Stay close.'

Pulling off the track, Didge rode in first gear through the trees. Following, Mac struggled to stay upright as they dipped into dry creek beds, wove between trees and vines, and ducked swinging branches. Mac had no idea how Didge could see his way across the ground – there was only a half-moon and the knots of roots and collapsed tree trunks loomed up at Mac as they picked their way through the forest, the bikes purring at low revs. Mac concentrated on Didge's bulk as it swayed rhythmically until the brake light in front of him glowed red and Mac stopped behind it. Killing their engines, Didge dismounted and crouched beside the bike. Duck-walking up to the big Cape Yorker, Mac looked over his shoulder.

'Our eleven o'clock,' Didge said. 'Lights.'

Bringing up his rubber-coated Leicas, Mac stared through the trees and found two windows in a shack, glowing yellow. As the bikes pinged, Didge put up his finger, sniffed.

'Frying fish,' he said, nodding. 'Raised voices – two males, maybe three.'

Mac couldn't smell or hear a thing.

'You want to cut the lines, boss?' said Didge, unhitching his M4 and checking the breech.

'No,' said Mac. 'If there's a junction box, I'd rather unplug it and then replace it.'

'Okay, boss,' said Didge, looking at his watch. 'We got four minutes thirty till the truck comes through. You mind if I lead?'

'You lead,' said Mac, glad the soldier had offered.

Checking their rifles and magazines, Didge put his left arm through the strap and flipped his elbow over it, pulling the rifle to his shoulder. It was a special forces trick to create what they called a 'good shoulder'. If you had a good shoulder on your weapon, then you forced your shoulders and face to point where the rifle was pointed, so there needn't be a delay between seeing the target and shooting the target. Mac hadn't been in the Royal Marines long enough to perfect the stance, but the professionals could keep a good shoulder all day in the field and many of them swore that the habit had been the difference between a shallow grave and living to enjoy a cold beer.

Following Didge through the high-canopy forest, Mac stayed close. Didge was easily six-three but he moved like a cat, ducking smoothly under branches, fluidly stepping over logs without losing his shoulder on the weapon and avoiding the forest debris that would make a sound if stepped on.

When the shack loomed twenty metres away, Didge found a hide behind a short tree and called up Mac, pointing. Looking along the finger, Mac saw the grey plastic telecom box, about one metre up the side of the wooden shack.

Didge pointed at Mac and made the shape of a gun, and Mac nodded; yes, he would cover Didge.

Slipping out of the shadows into the dull glow from the high windows, Didge paused like a deer, listening and scenting. Moving quickly in a crouch to the telecom box, Didge had the door flap open in two seconds, his hand went in and then the door was shut. The phone line was now disconnected.

Leaning against the wooden wall of the shack, Didge looked at Mac and put his finger to his lips, indicating they had company. Lifting his rifle, feeling the sweat run under his palms, Mac waited as plastic-sandal footsteps crushed gravel and then a figure moved from the light of the shack's front and into the semi-darkness of the well head.

Casting a bead on the figure, Mac put his finger on the M4's trigger — one turn in the wrong direction, and Didge's cover would be blown. Mac would then shoot.

A loud beeping sound came from the checkpoint quarters, triggering male voices. As Mac tensed to make his shot, the figure turned, revealing a pretty woman's face. Mac hesitated and he noticed a hunchback, but the hump moved.

'Shit,' said Mac. He had a woman and child in his sights.

The woman dropped her water bucket as boots clattered inside the shack, the beeping still loud.

'What's the beeping?' said Didge's voice in a whisper over the radio. 'What's happening?'

The woman ran for the shack as Mac burst from his hide and went after her.

Didge beat Mac to the corner and accelerated around the side of the checkpoint quarters to the road, the woman running into the night as Didge kicked the main door open.

'Get her,' said Didge as the door came off its hinges and the air tore open with the sound of automatic rifle fire.

Setting off after the woman, Mac wondered what he was going to do — she was within range, but he couldn't shoot her, not with a baby on her back. The scream of a large diesel engine sounded and the Silverado arrived, its lights killed.

'Stop,' said Mac at the woman's back. 'Stop or I shoot.'

Turning as she stopped almost in front of the approaching Chev, she showed her face and Mac lowered his rifle. Heaving for breath, he turned back to help Didge and a shot sounded. Mac left his feet and headed for the dirt, feeling like a horse had kicked him in the ribs under his right armpit.

Gunfire roared and men's voices raged, and then there was silence except for the ticking of an idling diesel.

Staggering to his knees, Mac heard boots on dirt and then he was being hauled to his feet.

'You okay, McQueen?' said Bongo, as Mac found his balance.

'Don't know,' said Mac, barely able to breathe and reeling with confusion. 'Was I hit?'

Lifting Mac's arm slightly, Bongo licked his fingertips and pulled a flattened slug from the Kevlar vest, flicking it away as the heat proved too much.

'Girl shot you, McQueen,' said Bongo, emotionless. 'Handgun under her shawl.'

'The girl?' said Mac, bending to pick up his rifle and seeing Sammy standing over a prone form on the road. 'Where's her baby?'

Bongo shook his head. 'No baby.'

'On her back – there was a baby on her back,' said Mac, the smell of cordite and blood making him nauseous.

'This your baby?' asked Sammy, an AK-47 in his hand as he approached them. 'It was slung under her shawl.'

'Clear?' said Bongo, as Didge emerged from the shack and scanned the road.

'Clear,' said Didge. 'Maybe one got away.'

Embarrassed, Mac shook his head. A mistake like that could get your buddies killed, and once you'd made the mistake, it altered the power dynamic in the group.

'You Anglos are funny.' Bongo flipped a cigarette into his mouth and offered one to Sammy. 'You think 'cos she the woman, she can't use no gun?'

Bongo was laughing about it – Sammy and Didge joined in.

'Sorry, guys,' said Mac, realising he was the odd man out in a spectrum that included a Filipino, Chinese-American and Cape York Aboriginal.

'I know you are, brother,' said Bongo, exhaling smoke as his eyes made long arcs over Mac's shoulders. 'But now you in my world, right? And in my world, ain't no damsel in the tower and no knight on the white horse neither, okay?'

'Look, I thought she had a baby on her back,' said Mac.

'I know what you were thinking, McQueen,' said Bongo. 'But just 'cos they pretty, don't mean they won't kill you.'


While Didge and Sammy removed the three bodies and hid them in the bush, Mac ratted the checkpoint building for anything useful. It was a bunkhouse with a small stove and sink in the corner. A desk built into the rough wooden wall housed a plastic electronics box with a list of red lights and beside each one a scrawl of Khmer: the top light was still flashing.

'Bongo,' said Mac, 'can you translate this?'

Bongo ran his finger down the red lights and looked at the Khmer designations.

'They're locations,' said Bongo. 'The flashing one says something like *Guard house approach*, and the others say, like, *Camp 25, Camp 20* and so on.'

'I heard a beeping before we stormed this place,' said Mac. 'I guess that would be the flashing light – the guard house approach?'

'They've got the road on optical trips,' said Bongo, meaning light beams that triggered when people or vehicles passed certain points. 'Wonder what else they got?'

'I don't want to wonder,' said Mac.

A scuffle sounded outside, a loud screaming and male grunts. Bursting out of the cabin, Mac and Bongo ran into Didge, who was holding a young girl by the scruff of the neck.

'Found her beside the long-drop,' said Didge. 'Trying to get on a bicycle.'

Rattling off some Khmer at her, Bongo nodded and turned to Mac. 'She lives with her family, between here and the river. She rides down once a day on her bike to deliver eggs and vegetables, sometimes fish.'

Talking with her again, Bongo translated. 'She had a cup of tea with the guards and then the guns started. She escaped out the back window.'

'The one I missed,' said Didge, spitting.

'Does she want to make fifty US dollars?' said Mac.

'Hang on, McQueen,' said Sammy. 'What's this about?'

'We can't get to the camp by road without Dozsa picking up the optical trip wires – we'll need a local to take us the other way,' said Mac.

'How do we know there's another way?' said Sammy.

'This is South-East Asia,' said Bongo, lighting a smoke. 'There's always another way.'

# CHAPTER 47

They ran west through the forest, the half-moon dappling the footpad with enough light to see ten feet in front. Didge and the girl – Tani – went ahead, setting a pace that Bongo, Sammy and Mac struggled to maintain as they slid across mud and ducked low-hanging branches. Carrying backpacks filled with food and ammo, they wore Kevlar vests and carried their M4s across their chests. It was a cross-country tab of the kind that Mac had been forced to endure in the Royal Marines, and for some reason always in Scotland. But this was different: the humidity of the forest made their skin wet beneath their vests and the monkeys were much louder in the Cambodian forest than the deer ever were in the glens.

'That Didge,' said Sammy, panting as they forded a creek. 'He ever slow down?'

'No,' said Mac. 'But if there's any trouble in this bush, he'll kill it long before it comes near us.'

After almost two hours of jogging along the jungle footpad, Mac followed Bongo up an incline and found Didge and the girl waiting and eating.

Falling to the long grass of the clearing, they caught their breath as the moon passed in and out of cloud. Finding a banana and a muesli bar in his pack, Mac ate up and then finished a bottle of water. It was almost 10.45 and he wanted to tab until midnight and then lay up, let everyone have a nap before the fun part started.

'Another hour, then we kip for two hours,' he said.

'Camp's just over the hill,' said Bongo, who'd been talking with Tani.

Looking around for Sammy, Mac saw him crouched twenty metres away, whispering into a satellite phone. Moving towards him, Mac ate an apple and waited.

'Charles,' said Sammy, ringing off. 'Says the Hawk feeds are already coming through in the infrared range.'

'Yeah?' said Mac.

'There's several aircraft on the airfield,' said Sammy. 'Navy analysts are saying they're Dash-8s and extended Fokker F-27s.'

'There were none there this morning,' said Mac. 'What are they doing?'

'The imagery is consistent with the aircraft being loaded and dispatched in fast rotations.'

'Rotations plural?' said Mac. 'How many have taken off?'

'Navy got the Hawk up there at twenty-one thirty and they've already logged three – there's two being loaded and another just came in to land.'

'Christ,' said Mac. 'What are they loading?'

'Can we just get down there?' said Sammy.


The knoll looked down on Joel Dozsa's illuminated compound, the lights making it clear which building was being unloaded and revealing the road that led to the airfield.

Through his binos, Mac could make out a series of trucks backing into the loading bay of the long building that dominated the compound. Large white packages the size of wool bales were slid across rollers by the Chinese workers, from the loading bay into the trucks. The trucks were driven to the airfield, reversed up to the rear cargo doors of the planes – which now waited in a line – and the decks of the trucks were hydraulically raised to the height of the doors and the planes loaded.

Adjusting his field-glasses, Mac could see each plane taking between seven and ten of the bales, depending on the configuration of the plane. Waiting to be loaded was a North Star plane that looked like the one Mac had flown in with Luc.

The noise from the turbo-props echoed in a din around the valley, which suited Mac. Moving the Leicas back to the compound, Mac saw what looked like a barracks and, beside it, a large house. Further out, facing a large parade ground, was a machinery shed.

'That house, between the factory and the barracks,' said Mac, as Sammy raised his own field-glasses.

'Yep?' said Sammy.

'I'll bet that's Dozsa's house – and McHugh's current address.'

'Looks like the whole party is happening at the factory and airfield,' said Sammy. 'We should come around the back, past the barracks, and storm the house.'

'Storm it?' said Mac, dropping the Leicas. 'I thought we were retrieving McHugh?'

Sammy hesitated. 'Sure.'

'We won't be retrieving anyone, Sammy, if we start kicking down doors, making it like the movies.'

'Yeah,' said Bongo, joining them. 'Let's isolate the Israelis, and when we know where they are, find the captive.'

'Okay,' said Sammy.

'Our lead,' said Bongo, moving away with Didge.

Returning to his backpack, Mac knelt and pulled out the Colt and a webbing containing four mags for the M4.

'So, where my money?' said Tani, giving Mac a start. He'd forgotten she was with the party.

'Sammy?' said Mac, looking for the American, but he'd disappeared.

'You promise,' she said, and Mac realised she wasn't a kid – she was at least eighteen.

'Yeah, you're right,' said Mac, slapping his pockets. 'I did promise.'

Looking at what he had on him, Mac found one-dollar notes and fives, but no tens. The only note he could give her was a US hundred-dollar bill. Reluctantly, Mac handed it over, reminding himself to get it back from Sammy.

'This one no good,' said Tani, doing the theatrical frown of South-East Asia.

'Hundred dollar,' said Mac. 'I only promise fifty.'

'Not this,' she said, handing back the money, shaking her head.

Holding it to the moonlight, Mac wondered what her problem was.

'Bongo,' he said, gesturing for the Filipino to leave his intense chat with Didge and join him. 'Tani doesn't like the hundred-dollar bill. What's the problem?'

Bongo and the girl spoke for thirty seconds and then Bongo grabbed the greenback.

'Tani says they make these down at the camp,' said Bongo. 'Make more of these than birds in the jungle.'

'How –' began Mac.

'She been down there when her dad delivers food supplies,' said Bongo. 'Says there's a factory in that long building – factory that makes money.'

'What is this place? And where's Sammy?'

Standing, they walked to Didge, who was checking his rifle. 'Seen Sammy?' said Bongo.

'Went that way.' Didge hooked his thumb in the direction of the camp. 'In a hurry.'

'No kidding,' said Mac, turning to look at Tani. 'You know your way around that camp?'

'Yes, mister.'

'You lead.'


Panting behind the tall machinery shed, Mac regained his composure as they surveyed the ground and Bongo chatted to Tani. The growl of propellers and groaning hydraulics filled the valley.

'She says the last time she came here, a few days ago, there were guards at the rear entrance of the barracks.'

Following Bongo's gaze, Mac saw the rear steps of the barracks building, with no guards.

'What's that?' said Didge, pointing. 'Behind the house.'

Didge's eyesight was acute: there was a small movement through the trees, about sixty metres away, in the shadows of the main residence.

'That Sammy?' said Bongo.

They craned to see, but the movement didn't repeat itself.

'Leave her here,' said Mac. 'Let's look at the barracks.'

Moving along the wall of the machinery shed, Mac stopped at the entrance to it and realised the entire front section was missing.

'Look at this,' whispered Bongo.

One half of the shed was a hangar, containing a silver-grey MH-6 helicopter, its size and bubble-covered cockpit making it readily identifiable as the Little Bird reconnaissance helo used by the US military.

At the other end of the shed was a fleet of Toyota LandCruisers and a Mercedes-Benz Unimog truck.

Jogging across the dirt towards the barracks, Mac joined the other two at the rear steps. Hiding in shadow, they listened for movement but all they could hear was the commotion from the factory and airfield.

'Didge, you on point; McQueen and I will cover.'

'Copy,' said Didge, sticking his face out beyond their hide. 'On my three.'

Counting it out, Didge slipped around the corner and up the six or seven stairs to the back door of the barracks as Bongo and Mac covered the approaches.

'Door's unlocked,' said Bongo, and Mac skipped up the stairs. As Bongo passed through, a crashing sound came from the direction of the house through the trees.

Pausing, Bongo and Mac stared at one another in the dark. Then the shooting started, from a single source – no responding fire. Voices screamed and bursts lit up the house, the windows looking like a TV was flashing on and off inside. It sounded wrong.

'Let's move,' said Bongo.

Pushing into the dark of the barracks, Mac realised they were in a vestibule, an area deliberately separated from the dormitory. Tani had been right – there had been guards stationed here, because this was the stockade. Every military barracks had one.

Slipping slightly, Mac felt his bad knee give way again, the pain erupting in the joint. A hand held him up and he realised he'd slipped into Bongo. Beneath them, on a chair, was a Chinese soldier with a dark grin across his throat. Mac had slipped in the blood resulting from Didge's handiwork.

His pulse going haywire, Mac found his feet again and followed Bongo towards a door that now swung open. Stopping behind Bongo, he looked over the Filipino's shoulder and saw a cell. Didge was kneeling on the floor, whispering encouragement to a blonde woman as he used the guard's keys to undo her manacles.

She sobbed, her crying getting louder, and Bongo stepped further into the room.

'Name's Bongo,' he said, voice low but friendly as he held her by the biceps. 'John and Margaret sent us – your childhood cat was called Sadie, a silver chinchilla whose favourite meal was the eels you caught in the creek.'

The woman blubbered and launched herself into Bongo's arms.

'That would make you Geraldine McHugh,' said Bongo. 'I'm here to take you home.'

Nodding for Didge to hold her, Bongo whipped off his back-pack. Mac had wondered at the overstuffed pack and now he saw the reason for it as Bongo pulled out a spare Kevlar vest and eased McHugh into it.

Turning for the door, Mac tried to block Bongo. He wanted to stay close to McHugh: there was a debriefing to go through yet, a detail Bongo didn't have to concern himself with.

'Where to now?' said Mac, still panting slightly.

'Phnom Penh,' said Bongo.

'Saigon suits me better,' said Mac, regretting it immediately.

Bongo's SIG was not pushed in Mac's face like it would be in a gangster movie, but it was pointing at Mac's throat and it had Bongo Morales on the other end of it.

'Out of here, right now, with my client – that suits me, brother,' said Bongo. 'So you either swim with this, or you swim against.'

Gulping, Mac nodded and stood aside. 'Remember our deal – I get to debrief with the Americans.'

'The Americans?' said McHugh, coming alive. Her voice was raised and Bongo swapped a quick look with Mac.

'It's okay, you're safe,' said Bongo, staring at Mac and gesturing for Didge to follow with McHugh.

The way Bongo had said *okay* was a veiled warning to Mac and he decided not to push the American angle. As they moved to the back stairs of the barracks, sliding in the blood and trying to stop McHugh reacting badly to the corpse, they paused. Across the dirt, people ran from the house, one limping, a little girl running for her life. Two bodies lay dead on the ground.

'What?' said Mac, seeing a hit, not a rescue.

People shouted and ran up from the factory while a man walked among the bodies, checking them with the toe of his boot. The man looked up and stared at the four of them.

'It's Sammy,' said Bongo as they saw his face illuminated by the house lights.

Sammy started jogging towards them, M4 held across his body. His boy scout demeanour was long gone – now he ran like a trained killer.

'What's the problem?' said Mac, trying to understand.

But the conversation was over. The first shots from Sammy's rifle had slammed into the door above McHugh's head.

# CHAPTER 48

Sammy Chan leapt sideways behind a tree as Didge fired back at the American. Getting in behind Bongo and McHugh, Mac slipped off the porch, using Didge's covering fire to escape along the lee side of the barracks building.

Stopping at the corner of the barracks, Mac aimed at the tree and let off three-shot bursts at the trunk as Sammy tried for a sighting around it.

'Didge, your turn,' said Mac, pausing from firing as soldiers ran towards them from the long factory building a hundred metres away.

As Didge ran around the corner, Sammy reappeared from his hide and let go a long burst from the M4 carbine, dropping Mac flat to the ground as the building's corner exploded in splinters of wood.

Finding his feet as Didge grabbed him by the collar, Mac accelerated towards Bongo and McHugh, who were inside the machinery shed. Sprinting after them, still struggling to comprehend what was happening, Mac watched the greenish lights come on in the Little Bird's cockpit — Bongo was going to fly out.

'No,' said Mac, knowing where this was going to end.

Didge stopped and turned back the way they'd come, knelt and fired several three-shot bursts as Mac continued running.

The whine of a helo starter motor began, its beeping alarm

piercing the night, and Mac heard the slow whoosh of a rotor turning as he stopped and covered Didge. Through the partially lit stand of trees that separated the barracks from the machinery shed, Mac could see the compact form of Sammy Chan tucked in behind a tree trunk; a magazine dropped on the ground and the click of a new one being rammed home sounded.

'Go,' said Mac, turning and running up behind Didge as Sammy's full-auto assault ripped through the trees in a right-to-left scything of foliage. Grunting, Didge twisted in the upper body and dropped his rifle as a bullet whipped through the top of his outer bicep, one of the areas not covered by the Kevlar vest.

'Okay?' asked Mac, dropping to his knees to reclaim the rifle as Didge backed up behind a tree, his left hand clutching the wound.

'I'll live,' said Didge, bloody hand outstretched for the rifle.

Handing it over as he crawled behind the tree, Mac found Sammy's muzzle flashes and shot back at them. From the machinery shed, the whooshing of helo rotors intensified as the aircraft prepared to launch.

'You go,' said Mac, barely believing what had happened to this mission yet also feeling responsible for Sammy. 'I'll cover.'

'We both stay,' said Didge.

'No, I'll deal with this prick,' said Mac. 'He's my problem, not yours.'

Turning to look back, Didge shot at Sammy as the American broke cover. Taking at least two shots in the bulletproof vest, Sammy was knocked off his feet to land on his side, winded.

'Like I said,' said Didge, grabbing Mac by the scruff of the neck and throwing him towards the helo with a huge paw.

As they approached the shed, the Little Bird was at full revs and Mac could see Bongo's illuminated face, the same face he wore whether making a difficult shot on the pool table or escaping from a rogue PLA camp in the middle of the Cambodian wilderness. Shots pinged and thudded around them and one put a star high in the cockpit glass of the helo.

Looking back, Mac could see Sammy had dragged himself behind an old bulldozer and the PLA cadres were now closing on Sammy's position and the shed.

The pitch of the Little Bird's turbine changed and Bongo gestured for Mac and Didge to get out of the way as the deadly helo hovered off the dirt and eased forwards in a storm of dust and debris.

'Shit,' said Mac, as the six barrels of the Gatling gun hanging off the helo's skids spun silently in their warm-up revolutions. Throwing himself sideways to the ground in sync with Didge, he watched as the darkness was lit up by the full force of the Gatling gun – known as a Minigun – cycling at three thousand rounds per minute. The air filled with lead as branches fell and trees collapsed; arms and legs wheeled in crazy arcs as the approaching Chinese soldiers were mowed down.

His hands over his head as the helo downwash hit him with incredible force, Mac watched the Little Bird skew slightly and then the Gatling gun was trained on the bulldozer, opening up with five rounds of 7.62 ammo per second – a rate of fire so high that the predominant sound was a demonic whistling amid a thousand hammer strikes. The yellow Kohmatsu looked grey within six seconds and Mac could smell the blast of lead on steel. Even when the Minigun was shooting the bad guys, it was a terrifying weapon that made a man's heart stop.

Standing, Didge waved for Mac to follow and ran to the side door of the Little Bird, throwing his rifle in ahead of his leap. Following the big Aussie, Mac ran to the hovering helo, the blast of noise and wind overwhelming his senses.

As he made to jump on, he saw her from the right side of his vision: crouched behind the tree, hands over her ears and looking like a scared child. It was Tani.

'Fuck,' said Mac, pausing. His mind roared with the choices as Didge's hand reached out of the helo and Bongo yelled from behind his glass bubble. The girl turned to look at him and he saw she was crying – frozen with fear, and Mac didn't blame her.

'Jesus wept,' he said, wanting to turn and jump in that helo, but knowing he wasn't going to.

As he reached the Cambodian girl, a new sound started – the unmistakable thump of a .50-cal machine gun. Looking over his shoulder as he crouched beside the girl and tried to get her on her feet, Mac saw the muzzle flash of the .50 cal through the trees, coming from the back of an approaching Nissan Patrol.

'Come on,' said Mac, grabbing Tani by the upper arm and judging his run to the helo. As he started out, one of the incoming bullets pinged off the rotors and another went straight through the cockpit, causing a flash of sparks and smoke somewhere under the spinning blades.

The Little Bird lifted into the air as Mac dragged the girl across the open ground. He was within twenty paces of a fast ride home when Didge yelled at him and pointed. Turning, Mac saw Sammy appear from behind Tani's hide. He'd dropped his rifle and was using a handgun.

'McQueen,' yelled the American. 'Just let me have –'

But his voice was lost in the din.

Didge laid covering fire from the helo door, forcing Sammy behind a stump from where he shot at the aircraft.

It was too hot for Bongo – he had to get the aircraft moving or it'd be shot down.

As Mac watched the Little Bird rise into the night sky, close enough to see Geraldine McHugh staring at him with saucers for eyes, he felt a knock in his left calf muscle, as if someone had kicked a hot poker into his flesh, right down to the bone. At first there was nothing but the pain and Mac thought he could make it to the machinery shed, grab one of those LandCruisers and blow town.

But the pain turned numb, as if he had no left leg. Tani darted from his grip as his leg folded, and then the ground rushed up to meet his face.

# CHAPTER 49

Birdsong filled the room as Mac opened his eyes. Morning sunlight came through the raised louvre windows into a large factory building.

To his left was a line of interior windows around office space and to his right was the aluminium mezzanine railing to which he was manacled.

Groaning with pain as he tried to sit up, Mac noticed his chinos had been cut at his left knee and the bullet wound bandaged. It ached, but the bleeding had stopped and someone had taken some care.

Using the manacle to get upright, he looked down from the mezzanine onto the long factory floor where a series of high-tech machines were linked before turning into a long printing press. At the end of the building were more high-tech machines and then a loading bay with its large roller door raised.

Stacks of paper held together with mustard-coloured straps fluttered in the morning breeze and pieces of the paper broken loose from the bale-like stacks sitting on pallets had floated down to Mac's end of the building. Looking down, he saw US hundred-dollar notes moving around in the draft like litter after a party. The mustard straps denoted hundred-thousand-dollar bundles and there were thousands of them in each bale.

'Christ,' he said. He was only looking at the leftovers.

'Nice, huh?' came the American voice from behind him.

Jumping a little, Mac turned and saw a face that had been thoroughly bashed.

'Sammy Chan,' said Mac as if he was meeting someone at the pub. 'Since you're sitting behind me, why not give me another stab in the back?'

'Screw you, McQueen,' said Sammy, who had both his wrists handcuffed to the aluminium uprights. 'You've already said enough to last me a lifetime.'

'Screw me?' Mac eyeballed the American. 'You already did that, remember?'

'I wasn't after you, okay, McQueen?'

'Oh really? I guess my leg doesn't count.'

'I was trying to stop Bongo taking the girl – honest.'

'You hired Bongo,' said Mac.

'No, McQueen, that was Grimshaw – Bongo's company is on the pre-approved list for NSA managers.'

'Grimshaw didn't check who Bongo was really working for?'

'He needed someone fast, and Bongo was in town with that big Aussie.'

'So how was it supposed to work?' asked Mac, needing a glass of water. 'The dumb Aussie and a couple of mercs lead you to Geraldine McHugh, and then you snatch her, drop whoever gets in your way. That it?'

Shaking his head slowly, Sammy looked away. 'I tried to get to her first, then I turn around and see Bongo's already got her. After that, I was just reacting – sorry about the leg.'

'You're not Secret Service, are you?' said Mac, watching the American's eyes flinch slightly. 'Not exactly an accountant who's done his proficiency on the shooting range.'

'Don't give me the Pollyanna,' said Sammy, his puffy eyes screwing up with pain. 'I've read your file – the full NSA file – and as an intelligence officer you make a great undertaker.'

Mac pretended not to hear. 'Why is McHugh so important?'

'Mind your own business.'

'Read the file again,' said Mac. 'My business is minding your business.'

'Shut up, McQueen,' said Sammy with a wince, a big split evident in his bottom lip. 'I need a handful of Percodans just to survive that frigging awful accent right now.'

'You going to tell me what this is all about?' said Mac, wanting to keep him talking. 'What is this place? A counterfeiting operation?'

'It's a bit beyond that, buddy.'

'So?'

'You didn't read between the lines when Charles was briefing you? Christ, he went way too far in my opinion.'

'He said General Pao Peng was funding an economic destabilisation strategy, but I don't –' Mac stopped; the question had answered itself as he spoke.

He remembered his first gig after the Royal Marines, in 1991, when the Firm sent him to the tail end of Desert Storm to learn his trade from Rod Scott. He'd patched through Ramstein Air Base on his way from the UK to Basrah and spent a night in Kaiserslautern on the booze with a bunch of US Air Force intel blokes. Mac remembered the bars and oompah of K-town, but mostly he remembered the fact that the locals had stopped taking American fifty- and twenty-dollar bills. A cell of economic agents from the soon-to-be defunct KGB had gambled some massive currency trades hedged in US dollars and had released container loads of bad US currency into Germany, in the hope of creating large profits when they closed their currency positions.

Mac couldn't remember if the Communists had got away with it but he certainly recalled how quickly the local merchants reduced a symbol of economic strength to worthless pieces of paper. Currency, so they said, wasn't money – it was an idea. And as soon as householders and small business owners no longer accepted the idea created by governments and banks, the currency became worthless.

'They're diluting the greenback?' said Mac. 'That's what those boxes of notes were doing in your car?'

'Gee, you're a regular Einstein, McQueen.'

'Is it possible?' said Mac, thinking about the scale. 'Can the Chinese do that?'

Sammy tried to get comfortable. 'You're not cleared for this stuff.'

'I'd bet each of these bales holds – what – a billion dollars, US?'

'So?' said Sammy.

'So they were shipping the bales out all night and this was only one shipment – I'm thinking this has been a huge effort.'

'Okay,' said Sammy, 'this is how it works. There's about eight hundred and fifty billion US dollars in circulation but about four hundred and fifty billion of that is outside the US.'

'More than half is in foreign use?' said Mac, surprised.

'Yeah – and that's important. Because, of the greenbacks in foreign circulation, Asia has about seventy per cent.'

'So almost half the US currency in existence is being used somewhere between Pakistan and Japan?'

'Sure,' said Sammy. 'Asia not only has this massive circulation of US currency but it uses that money at a street level – hand-to-hand commerce.'

'Which means when the streets are flooded with new currency, the Asian economies notice it?'

'Sure do,' said Sammy. 'After last night's effort, I'd say this facility has produced about two hundred of those bales,' said Sammy.

'Well, that's half of –'

Sammy snickered.

'That's serious,' said Mac.

'An extra fifty per cent of the circulating currency is suddenly dumped into the market? That's more than serious, McQueen – that's a currency four billion Asians are about to stop using.'

'And the US dollar devalues? Is that it?' said Mac.

'That's it.'

'But the US Treasury has stop-loss tactics for these situations, doesn't it?' said Mac, trying to remember some of his old briefings.

'Yes, there're programs but they focus on correcting the capital markets.'

'But they can't stop street sentiment in Asia?' said Mac.

'You're smart for a man who drinks rum when he doesn't have to.'

'Shit,' said Mac.

Sammy paused before deciding to go on. 'The big problem is the Chinese economy – Beijing holds about a trillion dollars of US government debt and their currency is pegged to the US dollar.'

'And if the US dollar takes a dive,' said Mac, 'that hurts the Chinese, the leadership gets shaky and Pao Peng gets his shot. Is that it?'

'That's it,' said Sammy, turning away.

Thinking back to that night in Phnom Penh, Mac remembered how struck he was by the smell in the boot of Sammy's car – the smell of all that new money. He was smelling it now, in this printing factory.

Burying his free hand in his pocket, Mac pulled out the slip of paper that he'd found in Sammy's box of cash.

'What's that?' said Sammy, craning his neck as Mac flattened the note.

'I found it in your car. It seemed cryptic, but now I'm not so sure.'

'Give me that,' said Sammy, jerking forwards but restrained by the cuffs.

'I'm betting that P means paper and I translates as ink, right? All genuine?'

'No comment, McQueen.'

'But what's this?' said Mac, concentrating. 'SN and SF?'

'Yes, Sammy,' said a heavy Hungarian accent, 'what's this SN and SF?'

Turning, Mac found himself looking up at Joel Dozsa, dressed in a dark trop shirt and grey slacks.

'You're making a big mistake, Dozsa,' said Sammy, sounding both desperate and angry, which was probably a mistake. 'You don't mess with the US government like this and live to talk about it.'

'Don't you love Americans, Mr McQueen?' said Dozsa, his dark eyes mocking and dangerous. 'Always threatening.'

'Nice place you have here, Dozsa,' said Mac. 'But I've seen enough – you can send up the porter now.'

'Hmmm,' said the ex-Mossad man, eyeing Mac like a specimen. 'You were on the right track with the ink and paper.'

'Genuine?' said Mac.

'I'm proud of that,' said Dozsa, glancing at his watch. 'Now Mr Chan is going to tell us what those other initials stand for.'

'Fuck you, Dozsa,' said Sammy.

Dozsa drew a handgun from his waistband and shot Sammy in the right calf muscle. The screams of agony bounced around the high roof, competing with the echo of the gunshot. Replacing his gun, Dozsa leaned against the office windows, fishing out a cigarette and lighter.

Grabbing at the railings, Sammy gasped for breath, saliva dripping off his lip.

'That's fair, right, McQueen?' said Dozsa, taking a deep drag on the Camel. 'Now you both have holes in your legs.'

'Seems only right that you get one too,' said Mac as blood poured across the concrete floor. 'Lend us the piece for a sec, Dozsa, and I'll get you sorted.'

Dozsa smiled. 'Always the joker – it's a pity we never worked together.'

'I prefer to work against criminals,' said Mac. 'Not with them.'

'You may have seen the worst of me lately,' said the Israeli, his voice losing the mocking edge. 'But when it came down to it, I showed you the courtesy due to a professional.'

'What? Shooting at me and my driver, trying to run me over in Saigon?'

'If I wanted you dead, McQueen, it would have happened long before Saigon.'

'What's that?' said Mac.

'I could have shot you in that hotel corridor, but I hit you over the head instead – remember?'

Mac's ears screamed with the shock of it. 'You?'

'Professional courtesy,' said Dozsa, standing straight as he checked his watch. 'Old-fashioned, perhaps, but never out of style.'

A shot sounded and Dozsa ducked his head into his shoulders as the window beside him splintered.

# CHAPTER 50

Forcing himself to the concrete as gunshots rang out, Mac looked up and saw the source of the incoming fire. Two men crouched on the mezzanine gantry that encircled the printing works, shooting at Joel Dozsa with assault rifles.

Leaping backwards through a shattered glass door, Dozsa disappeared into the office area.

'Oh, no,' said Mac, his hopes falling as he caught a better look at the shooters. Out of the shadows the grim faces of Lance Kendrick and David Urquhart loomed as they ran along the gantry.

'No,' said Mac, trying to project his voice at Lance.

He'd give the lad nine out of ten for balls but he hated the way he carried the rifle like an extra from *Scarface*. Urquhart looked even worse – he wielded his M16 with as much authority as Frank McQueen handled a vacuum cleaner.

Mac waved them away with his free hand. 'Get out.'

'The fuck?' said Sammy, covered in broken glass and surrounded by his own blood. 'These are your guys?'

Continuing to fire into the office area, Lance and Urquhart moved forwards at a fast walk but were thrown to their knees as Dozsa found a rifle and hammered out eight or nine seconds of fire on full auto.

'No!' said Mac over the cacophony, as the remaining glass in the windows shattered and holes appeared in the iron roof. 'Get back!'

His putative rescuers hadn't properly thought out their ground and had trapped Sammy and Mac under a dangerous hail of crossfire. They held their weapons at hip height and waved them, but the cycling rates of modern assault rifles were so great that if you didn't have a proper shoulder on your weapon, you were simply spray-painting.

'You okay, McQueen?' said Lance, as he got off the wall-mounted gantry and duck-walked to Mac.

Mac was incredulous. 'You going to stand there?'

'Umm . . .' said Lance, looking for Dozsa over the windowsill.

'He means you're drawing fire,' said Sammy. 'We're not armed.'

'Oh, yeah,' said Lance, scurrying down the mezzanine landing where he stood up and fired a burst into the office area.

'Think we're clear,' said Lance.

'Get these off,' said Sammy. 'Got more guns? Ammo?'

'Got a plan?' said Mac. 'An exit?'

'Not really,' said Urquhart, moving to Sammy. 'Chan, can you walk?'

'Yeah, sure,' said the American. 'Get these off.'

Holding out his cuffed wrists, Sammy winced as Urquhart shot away the cuff chains with four rounds more than he should have used.

Turning to Mac, Lance raised his rifle at the cuffs.

'One shot should –' said Mac, but he was interrupted as the door at the end of the mezzanine landing flew open and Chinese soldiers poured in.

Grabbing the M16 off Urquhart, Sammy fired at the doorway, forcing the soldiers back.

'Mag,' said Sammy, clicking his fingers at Urquhart as he released the spent mag from the rifle.

'Can someone –' Mac pointed at his manacled wrist.

Sammy took a quick look at Mac then turned back to Urquhart who'd pulled out his handgun.

They were going to leave him, thought Mac.

The mezzanine door opened again and Sammy was ready, dropping one of the Chinese soldiers with a three-shot burst before swinging his stance into the office area where Lance was shooting again.

The sound of jabbering Chinese voices echoed around them as the shots ceased into a quiet lull, gun smoke hanging in the air.

'Sammy, for Christ's sake,' said Mac, trying to stay flat as he braced for the inevitable full assault by the Chinese. 'Unlock me.'

'Sorry, McQueen – gotta ride.'

Straddling the railing, Sammy made a perfect paratrooper leap to the concrete floor below as the doors on either end of the walkway opened and the Chinese poured through.

'Davo, drop the fucking thing,' said Mac.

Realising it was over, Urquhart froze and dropped his weapon, his hands raised as if he'd get burned if he lifted them too high.

Lance swung at the door to his right and the muzzles opened up in a roar of sound as Mac clung to the concrete, pushing his face as flat as it could go. Lance's body hit the railing with a thudding bounce, the M16 clattered and the young Aussie's confused eyes were staring at Mac's chin, his blood running along the floor, feeling warm under Mac's cheek.

'Lance?' said Mac, as the shooting stopped. The kid had been hit in the neck and the shoulder area.

'Dozsa?' said Mac as loud as he could, his ears feeling tinny from all the gunshots. 'Dozsa – man down, man down. Get a medic for Christ's sake.'

Looking away, Mac tried to stay calm. He'd never liked the kid, but Lance had done his best where a lot of careerists would have packed their bags and headed back to Canberra. He'd had a go.

'Don't touch that,' said Mac, as he saw Urquhart eyeing the discarded M16. 'Don't even look at it.'

The Chinese ran up, yelling their commands as the lead soldier slapped Urquhart with his rifle stock, dropping him to the floor. The shattered door into the office swung open and Joel Dozsa clicked his fingers, directing the soldier with the medic's kit towards Lance.

'Well, well,' said the Israeli, a small smile appearing. 'A real little Aussie reunion, eh, McQueen?'

'It's over, Dozsa,' said Urquhart, his voice slurring through his busted lip. 'You know it.'

Dozsa's cigarette was still smouldering and he sucked on it. 'What I know is that you should wear a pad before you go into a gunfight.'

One of the Chinese translated for the others and they laughed as Urquhart sat upright and looked down at the wet patch around his groin.

'Pissed myself,' he said, and passed out.


'What were you thinking, Davo?' said Mac, hissing slightly as they watched a Chinese medic working on Lance. 'You run into a building, shooting at everyone? That was the plan?'

Urquhart patted the mouse-sized lump under his left eye. 'I agree – but Lance felt he couldn't just walk away.'

'How'd you get here?' said Mac, keeping his voice low in front of the Chinese. At the other side of the destroyed office quarters, Dozsa spoke into a radio headset.

'Came in on Luc's plane,' said Urquhart. 'Followed Bongo and Didge to the North Air offices and decided to wait for Luc to return and see if we couldn't pay for a ride.'

'So?'

'So we've been here most of the night, trying to work out how to do something useful, especially after Bongo took off with McHugh,' said Urquhart. 'We were waiting for the soldiers to go and we thought they'd all been flown out – then we came in through the roof, saw Dozsa shoot Sammy, and decided we'd better do something before he shot you.'

'Thanks,' said Mac. 'I don't think he's going to kill me.'

'No?'

'No, mate,' said Mac. 'I don't know what's going on, but I don't think the currency is the end of it.'

'Look, I –' started Urquhart.

'Don't tell me another lie, Davo,' said Mac, staring him in the eye. 'You know where all these US dollars are going?'

'We're trying to track them, but –'

'But you're not going to tell me?' said Mac. 'Jesus, you people are amazing – are you seeing this shit? Are you seeing where these little secrets end up?'

'Don't take it personally, Macca,' said Urquhart, looking sincere. 'Most of Canberra is out of the loop on this.'

'Don't tell me,' Mac spat. 'We don't know if China's going to democracy or military dictatorship, so the Prime Minister's office just makes sure we're buddies with all of them?'

'What can I say?' Urquhart smirked. 'I'm just a poor Queensland boy who loves his cheap plasma screens.'

'What was the point of withholding this from *me*?'

'It wasn't supposed to be you,' said Urquhart. 'I came up here on instruction from the Prime Minister – no one from the intel community was to be indoctrinated.'

'So how did I end up here?'

'You mentioned working with the Cong An . . . on the McHugh issue.'

'What's so secret about that?'

'Because it's about currency – vast amounts of US currency in our neighbourhood – and the less people who know about it the better,' said Urquhart. 'Currency responds to sentiment, you know that.'

'I could have been more use if I'd been brought into it.'

'Perhaps,' said Urquhart. 'But there was an embarrassment factor . . .'

'Embarrassment?' asked Mac.

'Catching up, I see,' said Dozsa, approaching the two Australians as he peeled an orange. 'But we might have to cut it short – we have a plane to catch.'

'To where?' said Mac.

'Not so fast,' said Dozsa, popping a piece of the fruit in his mouth.

Two Chinese soldiers uncuffed Mac and Urquhart and lifted them to their feet. Tottering slightly on his shot leg, Mac was steadied by the soldier's grip on his shirt.

'I think we might talk alone,' said Dozsa, guiding Mac by the arm.

'I want to check on Lance first,' said Mac. 'Let me give him something to eat at least?'

Dozsa paused for two seconds. Mac's request was cheeky, but Dozsa knew it was a professional courtesy to allow a bleeding man to get some sustenance.

Handing over the peeled orange to Mac, Dozsa turned to Urquhart. 'The only reason you're alive is that you followed his instructions, you know that?'

Gulping, Urquhart nodded. 'Yep – I know that.'

'Good, because I'll kill you if you disappoint me. Understand?'

Urquhart stammered as Dozsa turned away.

The medic had a drip into Lance, who'd been stripped to his waist. Bandaged dressings seemed to hold his arm to his body and there was a thick pad bandaged to his neck, the dried blood caked on the scalp beneath his dark hair.

'You know, Dozsa,' said Mac, as Lance's eyes opened, 'the thing to do would be to get him out of here, fly him into Phnom or even Saigon.'

'That's not going to happen, McQueen. I'll keep him alive, that's my best offer.'

Mac looked at Lance. 'Bad news is that you lost a lot of blood, mate. Good news? There's nothing left to bleed out.'

A small smile creased Lance's pale face and he nodded very slightly.

'I want you to have something to eat, mate. You're going on a plane ride and in your state you need something in your belly, okay? Your body needs all the help it can get right now to replenish the blood.'

Mac offered a segment of orange to the young Aussie. 'Your mind will play tricks on you, telling you you're not hungry, but that's just the metabolism wanting to shut down. Instead, you must eat and the easiest thing to digest is fruit, okay?'

Nodding again, Lance opened his white lips as Mac put the segment in his mouth.

'Don't waste your strength chewing – just swallow it,' said Mac.

Lance swallowed it down.

Responding to another radio call, Dozsa squeezed the button on his headset and wandered to the other end of the office.

'So?' said Mac, feeding Lance the orange but looking at Urquhart, who had wandered over. 'Embarrassment?'

'Yeah,' said Urquhart, squirming.

'McHugh's a spy, so the Yanks decide to drop her?'

'Perhaps,' said Urquhart, returning to his slippery Canberra persona.

'You want me to issue a CX saying David Urquhart pissed himself when the bullets flew?'

'Fuck off, McQueen.'

'Then talk.'

Looking at a place on the nylon-carpeted floor, Urquhart took a breath. 'McHugh was part of a sting – a joint operation between US Treasury and the Australian Prime Minister's office.'

'Sting? Who was being lured?'

'The Chinese. The Yanks had logged a number of highly sophisticated firewall and VPN attacks on their Treasury servers. The attacks were coming out of Xinjiang Uygur Autonomous Region where the MSS have their cyber teams.'

An attack from Xinjiang Uygur Autonomous Region was bad news – those MSS teams rarely failed.

Mac thought about it. 'Are the US Treasury's servers linked to any other system?'

'No, but the Chinks didn't need to enter through a connection to the outside world,' said Urquhart. 'They were trying to listen to signatures created by data going through the Treasury's internal routers.'

Mac had more questions but Urquhart glanced over his shoulder then continued.

'McHugh was supposed to masquerade as a visiting Aussie Treasury wonk with vaguely left-wing views . . . a full US Treasury visiting fellowship, access to the US Eyes Only stuff. You know – the Yanks letting the junior partner into the liquor cabinet. Grimshaw called it a honey pot.'

'Grimshaw designed this?'

'Yes,' said Urquhart. 'He called McHugh the "bait".'

'Hoping the MSS would try to turn her?'

'That was the plan,' said Urquhart. 'Then we'd be inside their camp and, right when we can do most political damage, we brief the *Journal*, the FT and the *Shimbun* in Tokyo, and expose the Chinks for the rogues they are.'

'But?'

'But,' said Urquhart, lightly fingering his split face, 'Joel Dozsa turned up in Washington.'

'And?'

'And turned her for real,' said Urquhart, avoiding Mac's eyes.

Blood roared through Mac's temples; if he'd previously been equivocal about Bongo retrieving McHugh, he was now entirely focused on getting her to Canberra and doing a very long debriefing. Once someone had crossed the line, you either had to forcibly retrieve them, or drop them. The Aussie intel community was small – small enough that when one person went bad, the effect on many covers, assets and networks could be fatal.

'That's not good,' said Mac, grinding it out like he was chewing rocks. Urquhart recoiled slightly.

'Look, it was supposed to be run by Grimshaw and –'

'I know, I know,' said Mac, holding his hand parallel to the floor to indicate he'd like less volume. 'So why Dozsa – why did he turn up?'

'Oh, sorry,' said Urquhart, his eyes refocusing. 'You don't know, of course.'

'Know what?' said Mac.

'Dozsa was refused a tenured position at Duntroon, almost twenty years ago.'

'Actually, I did know that,' said Mac, glad he knew at least one part of the McHugh screw-up. 'Just don't know why.'

'Not why,' said Urquhart, happy to have the information upper hand again. 'But who.'

'Who what?' said Mac.

'Who he was grooming.'

'Who?'

'Officer candidate GB McHugh,' said Urquhart, enjoying himself now.

'Fuck me,' said Mac, his mind spinning.

'Oh, there was that too,' said Urquhart. 'Lots and lots of that.'

# CHAPTER 51

Mac squinted in the mid-morning sun, limping behind the soldier through the compound. There were no signs of the Chinese mown down by Bongo's firing practice in the Little Bird and the place had a feeling of calm. It was being shut down.

The soldiers carried standard Chinese AK-47 rifles and no side arms. Thinking about the chances of taking one soldier, disarming him and turning on the other, Mac decided to wait for a better opportunity. With Dozsa now possessing two Aussie hostages, the dynamic had changed, and Mac was not moving easily on his shot calf.

Dozsa waited for him, sitting on the hood of a white LandCruiser in the machinery shed, peeling another orange.

'I have given this some thought,' said the Israeli as Mac got out of the sun. 'I don't want to kill you, McQueen.'

'No?'

'No,' said Dozsa, popping a segment of the fruit in his mouth. 'I think you can be of some use.'

'Really?' said Mac. He was exhausted, but he still had enough energy to kill this person.

'You'll deliver a message to Grimshaw.'

'Why would I do that?' said Mac.

'Because you're going to tell him to get out of Indochina, or these Aussies will die.'

'You think I'm a messenger?'

'I think you're an Australian spy, Mr McQueen, and you would not want it being said in Canberra that you could have saved your countrymen but chose not to.'

Smiling, Dozsa lifted a mobile phone from the pack and Mac could see from its red light that their conversation was being recorded. Dozsa was an intel lifer, and he knew this was one interaction Mac did not want emailed to the ASIS brass.

'If it's about saving Australians,' said Mac, 'give me the keys and I'll take the lads now.'

'No, I'd prefer they keep me company on the next stage of our adventure.'

Breathing out, Mac eyed the orange; Dozsa split off a chunk and threw it to him.

'I deliver a message – that's it?' said Mac, wolfing down the juicy morsel. 'Why wouldn't I grab a crew of hard boys and come back at you?'

'Who says I'd be here?'

'Why not just call Grimshaw?' said Mac.

'An annoying unmanned aircraft has been circling us all night, Mr McQueen, and I don't feel like pinpointing myself just yet,' said Dozsa, observing Mac with eyes that seemed to have no pupils. 'Unless you'd like to use my phone, provide some target practice for the US Navy?'

'I'll pass,' said Mac. 'So Grimshaw leaves Cambodia, and you release Lance and Urquhart – that's the deal?'

'Not quite,' said Dozsa. 'Grimshaw has some property of mine and I want it back.'

'Find a FedEx office.'

'No, McQueen – you will put it in my hand, and with no funny business, no conversations with people I don't like.'

'This property involved with your counterfeiting?'

'You should stop this word, *counterfeit*,' said Dozsa. 'I produce currency with real paper and ink; real printing techniques and the crowning glory . . .'

'Yes?'

'Actual serial numbers and security features.'

'That's the SN and SF,' said Mac, almost to himself. 'Shit, Dozsa – you're producing US hundred-dollar notes with authentic *serial numbers*?'

'That's the US Treasury's nightmare,' said Dozsa, laughing. 'When a glut of notes hits the street and their own people can't tell the good from the bad.'

'You're a lunatic, Dozsa,' said Mac. 'You trigger a currency collapse that hurts China and you have no idea where that leads.'

'I guess a strong man has to step in and stabilise the situation?'

'General Pao Peng? He'll destabilise this region with his Greater China fantasies,' said Mac. 'A hundred years of war is the price China will pay for grabbing its cheap coal and oil.'

'You'd be surprised how many American corporations would love to deal with a China that doesn't have to negotiate for its fuel.'

'Spare me the conspiracies, Dozsa,' said Mac, annoyed.

Lighting a cigarette, Dozsa feigned boredom. 'I'm busy, McQueen – will you do it?'

Mac's calf ached. 'What's this property I'm retrieving?'

'A memory chip,' said Dozsa. 'It's white.'

Mac was confused. 'I thought you guys had that?'

'We did,' said Dozsa. 'But the Americans took it.'

'If they took it, wouldn't Grimshaw have sent it to DC by now?'

'If he knew he had it, he'd have sent it on.' A smile creased the side of Dozsa's mouth.

'What does that mean? How do I retrieve a memory chip from Charles Grimshaw when he doesn't know he has it?'

'You steal it from him, McQueen,' said Dozsa, exhaling a plume. 'You're good at that, I hear.'

'From where?'

'It was on Tranh,' said Dozsa, eyes boring into Mac's. 'I believe Grimshaw now has it.'

'Tranh?' said Mac, blindsided. 'Tranh Loh Han?'

'Your driver. He's an assassin.'

'An assassin?' said Mac.

'For the Loh Han Tong,' said Dozsa.

'He had this chip?' said Mac, reeling.

'We think he stole the chip from your hotel room.'

Rubbing his temples, Mac tried to rewind the last few days and be clear about the events. It didn't add up.

'But you killed Tranh,' said Mac. 'Why didn't you take the memory chip?'

'Who said I killed Tranh?'

'Well . . .'

'I think it was your American friends,' said Dozsa. 'We were in the basement car park when the shooting started.'

'What are you saying?' said Mac. 'The Americans killed Tranh and grabbed the chip from him, but they don't know they have it?'

Dozsa smiled. 'In the shootout Tranh dropped his mobile phone and the Americans retrieved it.'

'You know this?'

'The property manager played me the security tape from the lobby.'

'Tranh dropped his phone. So what?' said Mac, irritated.

'So, the chip is an SD,' said Dozsa. 'It fits into Nokias. I have good reason to believe that Tranh stole the chip from your room and was carrying it in his Nokia – it's how a lot of Asian criminals courier information from one place to another.'

'You had good reason?'

'If Tranh had given that chip to his real employers, McQueen, I'd have been contacted very quickly and we'd be negotiating a price,' said Dozsa. 'The chip isn't in Tranh's luggage and it's not with his employers. So it's in that phone.'

Mac's head was spinning. 'If you'd lost track of it, how did you know the chip was in the hotel room?'

'That piss-ant of yours – his name's Lars?'

'Something like that,' said Mac.

'Our pretty operative put a little device on his shirt, and –'

'Yeah, yeah,' said Mac, knowing about the micro-transmitter. 'So how did you print all this currency without the protocols on that chip?'

'Without?' said the Israeli, confused.

'The chip – the BEP protocols,' said Mac. 'That's the memory card, right?'

'Oh, you don't know?' said Dozsa, his eyes losing their hardness and warming to laughter. 'Ha — those Americans are funny, aren't they?'

'What are you —?'

'They didn't tell you about the girl?'

'McHugh?'

'Yes, her,' said Dozsa, covering his mouth as his laughter triggered a smoker's cough. 'I like you, McQueen, but you sure missed that one.'

'What one?'

'Geraldine McHugh,' said Dozsa. 'She *was* the currency protocols.'


Climbing to the bushy saddle that led out of the valley, Mac stopped the LandCruiser, looked back and saw a white Falcon corporate jet flattening out and preparing to land on the compound's airstrip. The place was clearing out and the currency had already flown — Mac felt exhausted and beaten. He'd spent the past week chasing Geraldine McHugh only to learn that she was a spy rather than a hostage.

Which left the memory chip and Jim Quirk. If the memory card didn't have the currency protocols, what was on the chip and what was Quirk working on?

And where were the hundreds of billions in US currency?

The drive took almost as long as the footpad they'd followed Tani across the night before. It was barely wide enough to allow a vehicle through and was punctuated by boggy creek crossings and deep wash-outs. A two-wheel-drive vehicle would not have made it.

Mac listened to a rural Cambodian radio service that played cover versions of Debbie Boone and Anne Murray and he tried to come up with a plan. He felt snookered in one sense — Aussie hostages always changed the approach. But there were other ways forwards, perhaps. The memory chip was a plus, if he could find it without Grimshaw knowing. Also, McHugh was alive and she could be debriefed, as could Sammy Chan; he didn't know how he was going to make use of Sammy, but the American knew more than he was telling and he'd have to be questioned. If he turned up.

After two hours of driving, Mac had left the highlands and come down to the warmer, monkey-infested climbs of the Mekong river flats. Easing through the dappled light of the jungle, he found the thick bush area near where they'd stowed the Silverado and motorbikes.

Turning up the radio, Mac eased quietly from the idling LandCruiser and limped downhill to the creek bed where they'd left the vehicles.

Eyeing the Silverado through the foliage, Mac cased the area and walked slowly around it for ten minutes, looking for people, smelling for cigarettes and aftershave, and keeping his eyes open for trip wires and other nasties.

Moving forwards, wincing at every cracking twig and annoyed at the constant hubbub of monkeys talking to birds, Mac finally got to the Yamaha he'd been riding the night before. Kneeling, he looked for IEDs, opened sumps, drained gas tanks – all the standard sabotages designed to either kill or frustrate the enemy. It looked clean and the keys were still in the ignition, where he'd left them. Pulling the seat up on its sideways hinge, Mac found the Nokia, also where he'd left it.

Approaching the Silverado's king cab he looked in the tinted windows. It was unoccupied. Lying under the cab, Mac checked for unwanted wires and packages, and checked the brake lines. The light-bulb bomb was still fresh in his mind and he was hypersensitive to the idea of an IED exploding in his face.

The new-car smell wafted as Mac sat in the driver's seat and rummaged in the centre console and the glove box, and had an extended look around the ignition assembly and under the steering column, looking for tampering. The keys were on the sunshade and there was a stash of US twenty-dollar notes in the console, which he trousered. But Mac couldn't find what he was looking for: Tranh's red phone and a first-aid kit.

The rear seats of the king cab were clean too, except for several discarded water bottles. Reaching back he pulled down the rear seat's centre console and found the green nylon bag with a white cross on the cover. Riffling through it he found the T3s and popped two of the painkillers in his mouth, noting the saline vials and the iodine wash that would come in handy when he re-dressed his bullet wound.

There was also a plastic bag on the floor of the crew cab containing a change of clothes. Pulling them out and checking the sizes, Mac stripped out of his possibly bugged clothing and changed into the new fatigues.

Grabbing the keys, Mac headed for the rear of the pick-up truck.

He needn't have bothered with the keys – the closed-in rear section of the Chev was open and as he pushed up the tinted window door, he noticed two things at once: Sammy had packed enough ordnance to take down a mid-sized military base; and the handgun aimed at his nose was cocked before his eyes could widen in surprise.

'Halt,' said the girl, her grip steady and eyes levelled.

'Tani?' said Mac, his heart bouncing as he raised his arms.

'That you, mister?' said the girl. 'Where my fifty dollar?'

# CHAPTER 52

Mac checked the bags for useful weapons as Tani pulled up beside the Silverado in the LandCruiser. One thing he liked about country girls, they could drive anything.

'So, the police,' said Mac, who'd been thinking about Tani's observation that the area around the checkpoint was crawling with cops – that was why she'd been hiding out in the Chev. 'They uniforms – town police – or political?'

'Some town police, some intel,' she said, looking into the gear bag as he rummaged through it on the lowered tailgate.

'But there's another way, right?' said Mac, loading and chambering a 9mm SIG handgun. 'To the river and Kratie, I mean?'

'Sure,' said Tani, grabbing a SIG of her own from the canvas bag and inspecting it.

'You can point me the way,' said Mac.

'I show,' said Tani, slamming a clip up into the SIG's handle.

'No, you don't have to come – this is where you belong,' said Mac, placing his SIG on the tailgate beside the four clips of ammo.

'I show,' said Tani, as if she hadn't heard him.

Mac pulled another bag towards him and extracted an M4 carbine – a shortened, modern version of the classic M16, with a grenade-launcher attached under the barrel.

'I'd rather go alone,' said Mac, holding up his Nokia, annoyed that he still had no cell coverage.

'That work at the river,' said Tani, pointing at the phone. 'Come on – I take you.'

Shaking his head at her stubbornness, Mac stowed the M4.

'I like this one,' said Tani, holding up the SIG Sauer.

The footpad to the Mekong was easier than the one into the hills they'd taken the night before and Mac managed to keep up with Tani's motorbike as they puttered through the jungle.

Yellow light filtered through the high-canopy forest creating a distinct atmosphere that existed nowhere except South-East Asia. It smelled of old smoke, wet dirt and monkey shit. As they motored past a meeting of canoe-bound peasants trading goods on a Mekong tributary, the footpad widened. After two minutes it turned into a jungle highway, populated with carts pulled by cattle and elderly forest people pushing handcarts and carrying poles of catfish across their shoulders. Whenever he heard an Australian complaining of how hard he worked, Mac always reminded himself of Indochina and what most eighty-year-olds did just to fill their bellies.

Emerging on the road that followed the western side of the Mekong, Mac stopped behind Tani's bike and they cut their engines.

As Mac dismounted, a small group of farmers wandered off the road onto the jungle footpad. The one at the back knew Tani and stopped for a chat.

'Police and intel, they gone,' said Tani, as her friend rejoined the group.

'Good,' said Mac, relieved. 'Probably best you don't talk about me.' Flicking Tani three US twenties, Mac asked for the SIG to be returned. 'Trust me, you don't want this to be the talk of the village when the intel comes back.'

'I not tell about you, mister,' said Tani, big eyes and serious mouth.

'Great,' said Mac. 'But I need that gun.'

A tinker moved past them, a whole pile of junk on a cart pulled by a mini horse. Holding up a plastic bag containing his discarded clothes, Mac offered it and the tinker grabbed the bag with a toothless smile, looking through it before tossing it in with the rest of his stuff. It wasn't a high-tech tactic, but it might get Dozsa confused for a few hours about where his messenger had gone.

'Okay, keep it,' said Mac, as Tani made to go. 'But someone asks you about me or the weapon, tell them the truth. No heroes, okay?'

Watching Tani park her bike and walk north with a wave, Mac pulled his Nokia from his breast pocket and fossicked a bottle of water from the canvas bag on the bike's carrier. Dialling, he waited and recognised the Aussie voice that answered.

'Scotty – Mac,' he said, gulping at the water.

'The fuck are you?' said Scotty. 'What happened to the regular updates?'

'Sorry – been out in the forest.'

'Where?' said Scotty.

'Chamkar,' said Mac. 'I need to meet.'

'I'm in Phnom,' said Scotty. 'Setting up a forward base in case you get into trouble.'

'Yeah, well, I'm in trouble,' said Mac. 'Meet me in Kratie at the Sunset guest house. It's three miles south of town, on the highway.'


After a shower in the bathroom at the end of the upstairs hall, Mac secured his room and washed the bullet hole in his calf with saline and then with the iodine solution. Dabbing it dry with a towel, gasping at the sting of the iodine, Mac restrapped himself with bandages from the American first-aid kit and grabbed a cold beer from the fridge.

Moving to the side of the window, he peeked out from behind the curtains to scour the bare dirt courtyard at the entrance to the Sunset, looking for signs of Mossad or maybe even Cambodian intel. He'd hated that story of the Dozsa crew executing the Mossad team at the guest house and he worried it might be a habit of theirs.

The entrance seemed clear. Now Mac wanted some sleep before Scotty arrived.

Picking up the discarded bandages, Mac chucked them at the rubbish bin as he walked to the bed.

Pausing as he lay on the primrose-coloured cotton blanket, he tried to filter his senses for what was wrong. Sitting in complete silence, frozen in that spot, he breathed shallowly and wondered what was out of place.

The pinging, he thought as he rose and walked to the steel rubbish bin. Why would a handful of crepe make that sound on steel? He'd reused the elastic claws on his new dressing – there was nothing hard to bounce off the steel.

Pulling the tangle of dirty bandages out of the bin, he held them up, examining them closely. Sitting in a row along the still-white inside fold of the crepe were three small black dots, each the size of a plastic pin-head. Flicking one with his forefinger, the dot stayed attached to the bandage, held in place with the tiny Velcro-like hooks that surrounded its sphere.

'The bastards,' thought Mac.

Dozsa's crew had patched him up okay, but they'd planted a bunch of micro-dots in his dressings. Sometimes those things picked up conversations, but mostly they were highly effective location and tracking devices, totally hidden from all but the most paranoid victims.

Dressing in ninety seconds, Mac grabbed his backpack and left.


The red Nissan Maxima pulled up in front of the roadside soda shack just under an hour later, Scotty giving a small wave over the steering wheel as the tyres crunched on the pebbles. Mac stayed at his table out of the sun and sipped at his orangeade while he waited to get a proper look at who was occupying the passenger seat. Hand slipping into his backpack, Mac gripped the SIG and waited for the mystery man to show himself.

Walking around the Nissan, Scotty stretched and shook out a smoke.

'Macca,' he said, eyeing the orange drink. 'And two of those, thanks, champ,' he said to the owner.

The passenger door opened as Scotty lit his smoke and sat opposite Mac. Out of the car stepped a powerful man of medium height who scoped every sniper's vantage point in a single instant.

'Fuck,' said Mac, relaxing and taking his hand out of the backpack. 'I asked for assistance and they sent the cavalry.'

'Hey, Macca,' said Sandy Beech, eyes scanning the surrounds like a radar as he walked from the Nissan. 'On the sugar water, mate – doctor's orders?'

'Yardarm's cooling off,' said Mac, standing and shaking hands with the ex-SAS soldier and spook.

Sandy Beech was a surprise. Military intelligence working with Aussie SIS? Not unheard of, but usually an arrangement fully declared from the outset. Sitting, they hooked into their orangeades. Mac smiled and went with the jokes, but Beech's appearance was irritating. Sandy Beech didn't go into the field to resolve issues – his job was to escalate them.

'First thing we have to get organised,' said Mac, 'the US currency coming out of that place – it's real. Real security features, real paper, real serial numbers.'

'Didn't the Yanks have a UAV on it?' said Scotty.

'US Navy had a Hawk,' said Mac. 'Can we get word to the American side that there's between a hundred and two hundred billion worth of bad hundred-dollar notes that got flown out of there last night?'

Standing, Scotty walked into the car park and keyed his phone.

As Scotty spoke, Mac explained to Beech the night at the camp and, with a slight stammer of embarrassment, admitted that Dozsa now had two Australian hostages where he previously only had one.

'The Yanks are on it,' said Scotty, sitting again. 'That Grimshaw's a strange fish, isn't he?'

'What's up?' said Mac.

'I don't know.' Scotty shrugged. 'They're tracking all this US currency so they can seize it, but Grimshaw doesn't seem that interested.'

'It's been a long week?' said Mac.

'Maybe,' said Scotty, not convinced. 'So where's the McHugh bird?'

'Bongo retrieved her,' said Mac, the words choking in his throat.

'Morales has McHugh?' said Scotty.

'When I arrived to work with the Americans, they'd hired a couple of mercenaries, to even it up with Dozsa's guys.'

'Bongo, and . . . ?' said Beech.

'An Aussie soldier called Didge,' said Mac. 'I've worked with him before – 4RAR Commandos.'

'I know him,' said Beech. 'Name's Yorantji – Adam Yorantji. Good soldier, top operator.'

'The Yanks didn't know that Bongo had been hired by the McHugh family.'

'And you didn't tell them?' said Scotty, ticked off.

'I wanted to do the gig and get out of there,' said Mac. 'Bongo and Didge are experts at this stuff, especially in the jungle, and we had a deal.'

'A deal?' Scotty lit another smoke. 'Shit, mate – you had a deal with the Commonwealth.'

'We were going to retrieve McHugh jointly but then Sammy Chan tried to kill her and my leg stopped one of his bullets.'

Scotty and Beech both looked away.

'What's this about, Scotty?' said Mac. 'You knew what Sammy was up to?'

'I knew the Americans were very serious about this,' said Scotty, clearing his throat. 'I knew they didn't want us debriefing her – that was our deal.'

'You had a deal with the Commonwealth, boss.'

'Fair call,' said Scotty. 'All I can think is that when Sammy realised that you and Bongo would end up with McHugh, he tried to drop her. They're in damage-control mode.'

'Macca, we're out of time,' said Sandy Beech, impatient. 'What was the errand for Dozsa?'

'He wants a swap – he hands over Lance and Urquhart, and I give him a memory chip.'

'A memory chip?' Beech sat up and folded his fingers through each other on the table.

'That's what he said – he reckons Tranh was carrying it in his Nokia, but Grimshaw doesn't know that.'

Scotty swapped a quick glance with Beech.

'So, you're supposed to do what?' said Beech.

'Steal it and exchange it for the hostages,' said Mac.

'You know what to look for?' said Beech, his voice now intense.

'Of course,' said Mac, shrugging. 'It was in my backpack for a couple of days.'

Beech looked stunned. 'Macca, you were in *possession* of this chip?'

'Sure,' said Mac. 'It's a white SD.'

'A white SD,' said Beech, looking away in disgust.

'I've said enough,' said Mac. 'Someone tell me what the hell's going on.'

'Mate, we have to find it,' said Scotty. 'But there's no way it can get to Dozsa.'

'Or Pao Peng,' said Beech.

'What's it got to do with the counterfeiting scam?' Mac asked.

'Nothing,' said Beech, gulping at the orange drink. 'The currency just gives Pao Peng the keys to the kingdom. This chip allows him to start a war.'

'What – against the Yanks?' said Mac.

'Forget the Americans,' said Beech. 'This is much closer to home and it's a nightmare.'

# CHAPTER 53

The late afternoon showers were finished by seven o'clock, leaving the trees dripping with water and the crickets rubbing their legs.

Dressing in the civvie clothes Scotty had bought at the riverside market in Kratie, Mac shoved the SIG into his waistband at the small of his back and pulled on a black baseball cap. They'd eaten in a restaurant to the north of the town and were now cruising back through the busy streets towards the Palace Guest House, a few blocks east of downtown.

'That's it,' said Mac as they slid past the two-storey French-colonial mansion they'd based themselves in twenty-four hours ago and which Grimshaw still used as a base.

Mac wasn't sure they had a plan to retrieve Lance and Urquhart, but if they could get the memory card they'd at least be able to bargain.

'Here, thanks,' said Mac, opening the rear door before the car stopped.

'Take it easy, Macca,' said Beech. 'Don't mess with this guy.'

Easing into the darkness of the roadside banyans, Mac stayed still as the Nissan slipped away.

'Red Rover to Blue Dog – copy this?' came Scotty's voice on the earpiece.

'Gotcha, Red Rover,' said Mac. 'Call you when I need a ride.'

Walking back towards the guest house, Mac wanted to be in and out, and no heroes.

There were four cars in the dirt forecourt and Mac saw Grimshaw's dark green Toyota, one back from the manager's office at the entrance. Removing the keyring of jiggers, wafers and bump keys from his pocket, Mac walked to the rear of the Toyota and released the boot lid on the second try. Letting it ride up a few inches, Mac pulled off his cap, bounced up the front steps and pushed into the yellow glow of the office, which consisted of a counter looking over a chess-board marble parquetry floor in what had been in the 1870s the grand foyer of a mansion.

A man sat at a desk behind the counter, watching a Thai game show where money was poured from the ceiling onto hysterical contestants.

'Hey, champ,' said Mac, smiling at the manager. 'Davis, from room four – remember?'

'Sure,' said the manager, nodding his head.

'You seen those thieves out there?'

'What, mister?' said the fellow, putting on his glasses and hitting mute on the TV. 'What is it, the thief?'

'Yeah, two of them, hanging around that American's car. Green Toyota?'

Following Mac into the forecourt, the manager turned on his flashlight – a black Maglite that could be used as a truncheon.

'They were messing around with the door handles,' said Mac, cupping his hands and peering through the driver's window like a concerned citizen.

The manager circled behind Mac, shining the flashlight into the interior of the car.

'Here, mister,' said the manager, raising the boot lid.

'Better tell the American, eh, boss?' said Mac.

Standing in the darkness of the baggage room adjacent to the foyer, Mac waited as Grimshaw stalked downstairs, his voice suspicious.

As the voices trailed into the forecourt, Mac opened the door, checked for eyes and sprinted up the mahogany stairs three at a time. Rounding the first-floor landing, he walked past a hall desk with a Lalique vase, along the runners of Thai silk carpets, and found room 3.

The management had installed new German deadlocks in the old doors and, casing the hallway, he pulled out his keyring and sorted through the Schlage section until he found one that looked the money – a Schlage five-pin.

Inserting it, Mac held his breath and listened for any movement from the other side of the door, his temples pounding. Hearing nothing, he pulled back slowly on the bump key until he felt the slight vibration of the key allowing the last pin to slip back into place. The next part would tell him if he'd used the right bump key. He jiggled the key side to side in a quick but light action, the lock made a sound like a mouse scuttling and the key turned.

Pushing into the fully lit suite, Mac let the door close behind him.

'Red Rover, I'm in,' said Mac into the radio mouthpiece dangling in front of his throat.

'Copy that, Blue Dog,' said Scotty. 'Target's taking his time with the car – doing a total inspection.'

Through the open window at the front of the living area, the voices of Grimshaw and the manager could be heard.

Mac moved quickly around the suite, looking for bags and backpacks. The credenza along the wall of the living area held a briefcase, a satellite phone and two cell phones – none of them Tranh's red Nokia.

Opening the briefcase, Mac found a Harris military radio, laid flat in the bottom of the case and covered with documents. No cell phone.

Searching quickly through drawers and along surfaces, Mac moved around the corner and into the kitchen, where he found a laptop computer, open and running. Looking at it, Mac saw the NSA corporate logo and the security email system embedded within it. Under normal circumstances, he'd stay and have a read, but he was in a hurry.

The kitchen featured a bowl of bananas, the fridge contained half a six-pack of 333 cans and the bathroom – a tiled wonder of the colonial era – held only a toothbrush, shaving cream and a razor.

Taking the SIG from his waistband, Mac moved into the first bedroom where he saw a perfectly made double bed and a carry-on wheelie bag sitting on the luggage rack. Fossicking through it as carefully as he could, the crackles of Scotty's voice erupted in his right ear.

'Blue Dog – target's locked the vehicle and is talking with the manager.'

'Yeah, yeah, Red Rover – copy that,' said Mac, adrenaline rising the longer his search came up empty.

'Blue Dog, Blue Dog – target re-entering the building. Repeat – he's on his way up,' said Scotty.

'Gotcha, Red Rover,' said Mac, panting slightly as he turned from the wheelie bag and looked under the bed. Nothing. The wardrobe held one Oxford shirt and a pair of slate-grey chinos. No phone.

'Shit,' said Mac, entering the hallway, SIG in cup-and-saucer as he moved through the gloom. Pushing on the second bedroom door, the wooden four-panel swung open with a squeak as the radio earpiece came to life again.

'Blue Dog, Blue Dog – target speaking with manager in foyer. Time to ride, Blue Dog.'

'Okay, Red Rover,' he said with a breathless snap. 'I'm outta here.'

Sammy's black Samsonite wheelie bag sat on the spare bed. Moving to it, Mac sorted through the clothes.

'Blue Dog, hope you're out of there,' came Scotty's voice.

'Okay,' said Mac, plunging into a yellow plastic bag and coming up with a house key, a small black wallet and a red Nokia.

Grabbing the plastic bag as he moved back to the hallway, Mac tried the first sash window above the sink but could only get it to rise six inches before it was stopped by a set of locked security bolts.

'Christ,' said Mac, seeing the rest of windows had the same bolts.

Mac heard the door to the suite open as Scotty's voice came over the earpiece, repeating, 'Move, Blue Dog.'

Retreating from the kitchen as slowly as he could, SIG raised, Mac glanced over the NSA email system and saw the subject field of the email Grimshaw had been reading. It said *Op Lampoon – Critical*.

The email featured the word HARPAC.

Moving carefully back to the hallway fronting the bathroom and two bedrooms, Mac listened to footfalls clipping on the other side of the internal wall: Grimshaw striding to the kitchen.

Wondering how he was going to do this without shooting his way out, Mac listened as the footfalls reversed and strode back to the suite's door, which then opened and closed.

Putting his head around the corner into the living area, Mac found the place deserted. The footfalls echoed down the main hallway, and then stopped; a door was opened, the door was shut and Mac could hear two men talking. Moving back to Sammy's room, Mac put his ear to the thin wall and heard the conversation; muffled, but urgent. One of the voices was Grimshaw.

'Blue Dog, Blue Dog – where the fuck are you?' came Scotty's voice over the radio.

'Standing by, Red Rover,' mumbled Mac, straining to hear Grimshaw.

'Get out now!'

Mac made for the kitchen to have another look: what was Operation Lampoon? The laptop was gone, and Mac walked to the door and eased into the hallway.

'Red Rover – time for a ride,' said Mac into his radio as he waved to the manager and skipped down the front steps.

The car pulled up and Mac got in, barely shutting the door as Scotty accelerated away.

'Stop here,' said Mac when they were fifty metres away. 'I want to check something. Anyone got binos?'

'You got the chip?' said Scotty.

Pulling out the red Nokia, Mac peeled off the back cover, removed the battery and saw the white SD card gleaming right where Dozsa had said it would be.

Handing it to Sandy Beech, Mac received in exchange a battered set of folding Swarovskis. Opening the door, he pulled on his black cap and slipped out of the car.

'Give me five, boys.'

Walking through the shadows back to the guest house, Mac smiled as a bunch of teenagers went past on their pushbikes, chattering at each other. It didn't matter the language, you could always tell when teenagers were cracking on to one another.

Pausing by the entrance to the guest house, Mac looked up to the first floor where Grimshaw's and the neighbouring room faced the parking lot. The shutters over Grimshaw's room had been closed, but the hook for the shutters over the neighbouring windows wasn't fully closed and Mac reckoned if he got the right angle he'd be able to have a nosey-poke into that room, see who Grimshaw was speaking to.

Tucking the binos in the back pocket of his chinos, he noticed a car parked on the other side of a large banyan tree. Climbing onto the roof of the car, Mac reached up and hauled himself up onto a branch, staying close to the trunk.

A monkey mumbled in its sleep and put its arm back over its forehead as Mac found a vantage point level with the room. Peering through the Swarovskis, he adjusted for range and focus and could see movement through the shutter opening. It looked like a slashing movement and as Mac got the field-glasses on a better depth of focus, he could see an arm swinging, and then a man walking. Holding the binos on the best angle, Mac watched the man go back and forth across the narrow window of view, before he finally stopped and turned into the light: Charles Grimshaw, bending over, snarling at someone.

Why couldn't he see the other person? Above him, the foliage was thicker – not a good vantage point for a recce, but Mac wanted to see the person in the chair.

Scrabbling and slipping to another level, his calf muscle burning with pain, he disturbed two fruit bats that whacked their wings against the tropical night air, leaving the top of the tree shaking. Holding his breath, Mac waited to see if the noise brought Grimshaw to the window, but he looked to be making too much noise of his own and Mac could hear the odd word drifting into the still night air.

Clearing a bunch of twigs in front of his face, Mac raised the field-glasses and found his field of focus, the magnification of the keyhole scene a strange effect that threatened to make him lose balance.

Grimshaw slapped the object of his wrath and Mac could see there was a black pistol in his hand.

'Get out of the way, Charles,' said Mac to himself.

Grimshaw's bulk swayed back and forth menacingly. Then the American moved out of the line of vision and Mac gasped slightly.

'Holy crap,' he said, breath rasping in his throat.

Charles Grimshaw was interrogating Sammy Chan, and there was blood everywhere.


'There's two hundred billion dollars worth of bad currency sitting somewhere in the Mekong Delta tonight,' said Mac, brooding in the back seat of the Nissan. 'And Grimshaw is in Kratie, interrogating his senior operator. What's that about?'

'Sammy's gone rogue, I guess,' said Scotty, sucking on a smoke and looking over Sandy Beech's shoulder at the mini notebook that was running the SD memory card.

'I don't understand.' Mac opened a water bottle. 'These guys were total believers – you should have seen their set-up outside Phnom Penh, the way they approached this gig. Something's wrong with what I saw back there – something's wrong with Grimshaw being in Kratie when so much US currency is about to be dumped around this region.'

'Shit,' said Beech as his screen opened hundreds of lines of code.

'I'm serious,' said Mac.

'So am I, Macca,' said Beech, turning to face him. 'There's no way we can give this to Dozsa.'

# CHAPTER 54

The Nokia buzzed in Mac's breast pocket as he maintained eye contact with Sandy Beech.

'Wanna get that?' said the military spook.

'I want the card back,' said Mac. 'It's buying two Aussies.'

Turning to Scotty, Beech gave him a look that Mac didn't like.

'Yep,' said Mac, answering the phone before looking at Scotty and mouthing, 'Dozsa.'

'Listen, my Aussie friend,' came the monotone straight out of Budapest via Tel Aviv. 'You be at the main wharf in Stung Treng, at midnight.'

'I haven't got it yet,' said Mac.

'That's why you have till midnight,' said Dozsa. 'And no eyes in the sky.'

The line went dead and Mac looked up from the phone. 'Stung Treng – main wharf, midnight. No UAVs.'

The discomfort was obvious and Scotty cleared his throat.

'What?' said Mac.

'Mate, we're standing down on this one, okay?' said Mac's mentor.

'This one?' said Mac.

'It's not ours anymore,' said Scotty. 'It's with Defence now.'

Mac couldn't grasp it. 'Hang on, Scotty – what's now with Defence? The card? The wellbeing of Lance and Dave?'

Scotty's throat bobbed. 'Whole bit.'

'Fuck that,' said Mac, reaching for his waistband as Scotty's hand slapped down on his wrist. Pulling back from Scotty, Mac heard the tapping of steel on the window beside his head. Freezing, he raised his hands – he knew that sound. Turning, he saw a set of eyes looking down the barrel of a Browning Hi-Power pistol. On the other side of the car, a blond soldier was also aiming at Mac.

'I didn't want it to be like this,' said Beech, eyes flicking to the soldiers who simultaneously opened the rear doors of the Nissan and relieved Mac of the SIG Sauer. 'I wish there was another way of doing this.'

Emerging from the car, Mac looked around and saw four soldiers dressed in the kind of civvies CIA paramilitaries wore: fatigue pants tailored like chinos, military shirts that passed for adventure travel wear and military boots made to look like yuppie hikers' shoes.

'You okay, Macca?' said the soldier closest to him.

'Couldn't get any better if you paid me in beer,' said Mac. 'How you been, Maddo?'

Doug Madden was a team leader in a unit called CDT 4, a navy commando unit based out of Perth. Looking around the car, Mac saw faces he knew and greeted them.

'Macca,' they all mumbled, giving him a nod. During some of Mac's assignments over the years, the boys from Team Four had inserted and extracted him, protected him from bad guys and made him look good. Now they were following orders – it wasn't personal.

'Thanks, guys,' said Beech, closing the mini notebook as he stood beside the car.

'You're calling this wrong, Sandy,' said Mac.

'I'm following orders, Macca.' Beech nodded at Maddo, who stripped the clip out of Mac's handgun and threw it in the dirt.

'Whose orders?' said Mac, stowing the emptied SIG.

'Ask Scotty,' said Beech. 'We got the same message.'

Beech moved with the commandos to a metallic blue Nissan Patrol parked behind Scotty's car, touching his eyebrow briefly as they accelerated away.

Making it around to Scotty's side of the car in three strides, Mac tore open the door where his mentor had his hands up in a gesture of surrender.

'You're a fucking wanker, Scott,' said Mac, nostrils flaring in anger. 'Know that? You're un-fucking-believable.'

'Sit down,' said Scotty, calm.

'Why, so you can shaft me again?' said Mac, knowing he was losing it.

After three seconds glaring at each other, the two men broke from the intensity and started laughing. Slowly at first and then uncontrollably, until Scotty's eyes ran with tears.

'Wanker?' said Scotty as he recovered. 'You cheeky bastard.'

'Yeah, well,' said Mac, sitting on the car's bonnet, wiping his eyes. 'Working without notes.'

'By the way . . .' said Scotty, getting out of the car and offering Mac a water bottle.

'Yeah?' said Mac, closing his eyes and trying to relax.

'I said we were standing down,' said Scotty, lighting a smoke. 'I didn't say it was over.'


Grabbing the water bottle from Scotty, Mac gulped at it as they watched the window of Grimshaw's room.

'So, explanation time.'

'Don't know how much help I'll be,' said Scotty.

Mac was sick of being fobbed off. 'What's Operation Lampoon?'

'I don't know. Defence spooks have been keeping an eye on this Joel Dozsa for a while, and when I let slip that you were on the trail of an ex-Mossad guy, the next day Sandy turns up.'

'And wants what?'

'I think tonight about sums it up. That memory card is the last piece in a puzzle that Pao Peng's people have been building for three years.'

'What's on it?'

Scotty looked around the backpacker bar. 'You know much about routers?'

'Puts a groove in wood?' said Mac.

'No, mate,' said Scotty. 'The other one – the junction box that digital signals go through, decides where the signal is going.'

'Okay,' said Mac.

'Apparently General Pao Peng employed Joel Dozsa to find a way to read the Americans' global traffic in emails, phone calls and signals.'

'What? *All* of it?' asked Mac.

'Pao Peng provides the technology gurus from the PLA; Dozsa has been the deniable contractor, putting it together. This was his thing in the Mossad – putting together managed funds that bought intellectual property the IDF may have wanted. He was under the wing of a Mossad banker called Bernie Radoff.'

'Has Dozsa done it?' said Mac.

'I don't know,' said Scotty. 'What Sandy was looking at tonight – from what I've overheard – is the hardest part.'

'Which is?'

'A list of specifications from a company called Ormond Technik, a Dutch firm.'

'Yeah?'

'Ormond supplies a tiny component used in the routers that run the Milstar program – the Pentagon's military satellite network.'

'How did Dozsa get the specs?'

'A system of front companies, held in a managed fund, bought Ormond Technik,' said Scotty.

'So?' said Mac.

'So, with those specs, the Chinese can listen in to everything going through the Milstar system – everything from a general's warning order, to a Christmas Day call from a marines private to his child.'

'Listen in?' said Mac. 'What, like hacking?'

'No,' said Scotty, moustache dipping in his beer. 'The way it was explained to me is this: the tiny transceiver in the router is like the reed in a clarinet. It creates a signal. If you have good listening posts, and you have the algorithms for the transceiver, then you can monitor every piece of data and you can do it either by compromising the system or you can listen to the frequencies, pick them up like a radio tuner.'

'If this is just the crowning glory, what else have they been assembling?'

'It's hush-hush and the guys at Defence are paranoid about it.'

'Why?'

'Too many questions, Macca.'

'Tell me,' said Mac.

'I'm not supposed to know this,' said Scotty, 'but the Ormond sale was okayed by us.'

'Us?'

'A section of Aussie intel called the BLU – the Business Liaison Unit.'

'Sure,' said Mac, who had done surveillance and written reports in the past for the BLU. 'What's it got to do with us?'

'Because it's an Aussie-managed fund that bought Ormond Technik,' said Scotty. 'It's called Highland Pacific and all the intellectual property transferred across a week ago, a day after our guy signed off on it.'

'Signed off?'

'Yeah, there were suspicions that Highland Pacific is controlled by the Loh Han Tong, in Saigon,' said Scotty. 'But he cleared it.'

'Who?'

'James Quirk,' said Scotty.

Mac's face froze: he thought of a computer terminal in the Mekong Saloon, the fear in Quirk's eyes and the execution by Dozsa. And then a memory card falling off the table.

The implications were terrible. 'This was about Quirk all along?'

'Looks like it,' said Scotty.

'Why didn't I know?'

'Why didn't I know?' said Scotty. 'I thought Jim was off the rails; there was talk about his marriage problems and I wanted you to spend a couple of weeks and clear him. I had no idea – I thought he was drinking, maybe hitting the brothels.'

'So first we have Lance and Urquhart up here, claiming to work for the PM?'

'I think they do,' said Scotty. 'McHugh's involvement in that counterfeiting was really embarrassing and they wanted it hushed up – certainly didn't want Washington catching wind of it via our leaky intel guys in Canberra.'

'And then we get Sandy?'

'There was nothing to be done about that, sorry, mate,' said Scotty. 'Tobin called and stood us down.'

'So you're sitting in the car and he tells you that if I come back with the SD card, he's taking over?'

'Almost word for word.' Scotty chuckled. 'Except he asked to be backed up if you wanted to fight.'

Looking into his drink, Mac pondered his options: there were two Aussies being held hostage, Jim Quirk was dead and Tranh Loh Han was missing, presumed dead.

He had several ways forwards, but he needed to get Scotty onside.

'I have a confession,' said Mac.

'You're not walking away from Lance or Urquhart?'

Mac nodded. 'Can you look the other way? Let me stay here on holiday?'

'I can do better than that,' said Scotty. 'Tobin was very clear – he said we were being stood down, not recalled.'

'So we're in business?'

'What did you have in mind?' said Scotty.

'Talk to Sammy and follow up on a technology question of my own.'

'Count me in,' said Scotty. 'Just go easy on the violent stuff, okay?'

Keying the phone, Mac got himself in character. The call was answered on the second ring and Grimshaw snapped his greeting, a man under pressure.

'Charles – nice night.'

'What's up?' said the American. 'Dozsa shifted all that currency from his compound.'

'Not much I could do about it,' said Mac. 'We need to talk.'

Grimshaw paused. 'You're back with the Aussies, aren't you?'

'I was,' said Mac. 'That's what I have to talk about.'

# CHAPTER 55

Leaving Scotty in the hallway with his gun drawn, Mac walked through Grimshaw's door as it was opened.

'Charles,' said Mac.

'Who's the goon?' said the American, making a quick scan of the corridor, but keeping his gun hand inside.

'My friend,' said Mac, taking a seat in one of the cane armchairs.

Moving across the living area to the kitchen, Grimshaw returned with two cans of beer and gave one to Mac.

Mac noted the drawn face and blank eyes, the look of a man getting no sleep but plenty to worry about. 'I need your help, Charles — I have a deal.'

'No promises,' said Grimshaw. 'But I can listen.'

'I can point you to the SD card — the one with the Ormond Technik code on it.'

'Really?' said Grimshaw, his eyes focusing.

'It's not on me but I can tell you where it is.'

'And?' said the American.

'And I get your help with Joel Dozsa. He has two Aussie hostages and I want them back.'

Silence made the room seem small. No doubt Grimshaw had already found out about the Aussie hostages from Sammy, but he wasn't going to admit that to Mac.

'I may not want Joel Dozsa dead – have you thought about that?' said Grimshaw.

It stood to reason. If you had the chance to keep a Joel Dozsa in a military prison for a couple of years, get him talking about who else had been turned and how far the damage spread, then that's what you did.

'I thought about it,' said Mac. 'And I'm prepared to let Dozsa live if I can get your cooperation right now.'

'That depends on the cooperation,' said Grimshaw, the beer now abandoned on the coffee table between them.

Mac nodded. 'I don't expect a blank cheque.'

'What do you expect?'

What he was about to propose went against his professional habits. 'I can give you the location of that memory card and you'll help me locate the Aussie hostages.'

'If you know where the chip is, why don't you have it?' said Grimshaw, eyes darting to Mac's.

'Because it's being carried by an agent of the Australian government,' said Mac, exhaling.

Issuing a low whistle, Grimshaw rubbed his bottom lip and turned sideways to look out the kitchen windows. 'If you're suggesting what I think you're suggesting, then I guess some people in Canberra don't care too much for those hostages?'

'That's not your fight,' said Mac. 'I can give you a lock on a mobile phone that takes you to the SD card.'

'Right now?' said Grimshaw, sitting on the edge of the seat. 'We're talking about immediate?'

'Sure,' said Mac.

'And what do you need?'

Surprised that the conversation had come so far so quickly, Mac simply came out with it. 'The Israelis put a micro-transmitter on my shirt. I pulled it off and put it in a piece of orange I was feeding to Lance – an Aussie operator.'

'That guy who looks like a drummer?'

'He'd prefer lead singer, but that's him. It's a long shot, but if we can get your signals people to find that transmitter, I get a chance at a rescue.'

Grimshaw managed a quick smile. 'You didn't need to trade for that, Alan. I'd have given you that if I wasn't busy.'

'I know,' said Mac, sitting back. 'Which is why I need a different kind of favour before I give you the chip.'

'Such as?'

'Such as telling me what's going on.'

Looking away, the American shook his head. 'Don't ask for much, do you?'

'What's Operation Lampoon? What's HARPAC? And why is Sammy tied up in a chair next door?'

Reaching for his beer, Grimshaw eyeballed Mac with a look that blended casual interest with homicidal intent. 'Classified, classified, and . . . it's not your fight.'

'I'm serious,' said Mac. 'I joined your team in good faith and I've been played for a patsy all along. If we do this together maybe we both end up with what we want.'

'What can you tell me about the transmitter?' said Grimshaw, reaching behind the back of his chair and grabbing a satellite phone.

'Small, black – size of a silver ball you find on a cake, with Velcro hooks,' said Mac.

'Is it a TWR?' said Grimshaw, dialling.

'Don't know the brand but they're the ones used by the Agency.'

Holding up a finger, Grimshaw changed tone. 'Mike – long time, huh?'

He made small talk then got to the point. 'Mike, wondering if we have any AWACs in the air, west Pacific, South China Sea? . . . That's handy,' said Grimshaw, giving Mac the thumbs-up. 'I have a long shot that you guys might enjoy as a challenge.'

The response was obviously not positive.

'Come on, man,' said Grimshaw. 'That Taiwanese cryptogram made you look like a fucking genius, as I recall . . . Okay, okay,' he chuckled. 'We're looking for a signal from a TWR micro-transmitter – probably US-issue, but not sure . . . Yeah,' said Grimshaw. 'Private use.'

Putting his hand over the mouthpiece, Grimshaw looked at Mac. 'They're coming up with hundreds – they need a name. These transmitters are all allocated frequency, and private ones have to be registered before being allocated.'

Mac shrugged, fatigue and the effects of painkillers starting to mess with him. 'Try Dozsa? Or Radoff, or Beyer or . . . Shit, I don't know, mate.'

Grimshaw gave the names to the person on the other end and, after some waiting, looked at Mac and shook his head. 'They need a company name – what was Radoff's company?'

'He has hundreds,' said Mac. 'His investment fund buys companies.'

'What's the fund called?' said Grimshaw.

Mac rubbed his temples, his mind blank.

'What about Dozsa?' said Grimshaw. 'He have a company?'

'No,' said Mac, deciding he should avoid consuming painkillers and beer at the same time. 'I . . . actually, wait a minute.'

Thinking back, Mac remembered doing a vehicle ownership search on the green Toyota Prado that Dozsa had used in Saigon the night Quirk was killed. As he clicked his fingers for inspiration, his mind went in and out of focus like the shape of a trout swimming in a river.

'Shit,' he said, shaking his head.

'Okay, Mike, thanks for the try,' said Grimshaw, about to sign off.

'Highland.' Mac blurted it out. 'Try Highland Surveying – registered Kuala Lumpur.'

Grimshaw relayed the company name and as they waited, Mac could feel his eyelids drooping.

'It is?' said Grimshaw, sitting up and reaching for a pencil and pad. 'Go ahead.' He wrote quickly. 'Okay, thanks, Mike – I owe ya.'

Picking up his pad, Grimshaw read out the information. Micro-transmitters registered to Highland Surveying were transmitting signals from Kratie, Stung Treng and Prek Chamlak – a village on the Mekong, about thirty miles south of Kratie.

'On the river?' said Mac, surprised.

'He'll get back to me in ten minutes and tell us if they're moving.'

'Thanks,' said Mac. 'So tell me what's going on.'

'You tell me where the card is,' said Grimshaw, smiling.

Reaching for the sat phone, Mac wandered into the kitchen area and gave his security and safety codes to the night person at SIS in Canberra.

'Mate, I've lost track of an agent I'm working with. Name's Sandy Beech, working with Defence Intelligence.'

'Can't you call him?' said the clerk, a softly spoken man called Jonathan.

'I have reason to believe he's under electronic surveillance – he answers a call from me and he'll be pinpointed or we'll be eavesdropped. Either way, it's dangerous.'

'What do you want?' said Jonathan, suspicious.

'Give me a location of his phone,' said Mac. 'It's a Commonwealth device, it should have a beacon on it.'

'Um,' said Jonathan, 'I don't know if –'

'It's a time-critical request,' said Mac. 'You can log this call and I take all responsibility.'

'I'd have to put you through to DIO.'

'We could keep it simpler – I can call Karl Berquist during his family meal, tell him I'm in danger because a person who's supposed to be helping me is giving me the run-around,' said Mac. 'What's your surname?'

'Okay,' said Jonathan, obviously keen to avoid a fight with the deputy DG of the Firm. 'Just give me a sec.'

Turning, Mac smiled at Grimshaw in the other room.

Jonathan came back on the air. 'That phone is thirty-two kilometres south of Kratie, in Cambodia – on Highway Seven.'

'Wait one minute and then tell me where they are,' said Mac, knowing that the beacon was located every sixty seconds in a tiny blip of a signature.

Jonathan broke the silence again. 'Thirty-three kilometres south of Kratie, sir,' he said. 'They're heading south on Highway Seven.'

Reciting the coordinates as Jonathan read them out, Mac watched Grimshaw write them on his pad.

'Thanks, Jonathan,' said Mac, disconnecting and walking back to the American. 'You've got it – so, time for an explanation.'

'I have to go – can we make it fast?' said Grimshaw, checking his G-Shock.

'Be your guest,' said Mac.

'This whole currency scam has been a bit of a red herring,' said Grimshaw. 'It was an opportunity that Dozsa saw because of McHugh's position.'

'Position?'

'She was inside the US Treasury, so she could be useful for money-making schemes. But Dozsa didn't want her for the counterfeiting.'

'No?'

'No – Dozsa knew McHugh was married to Jim Quirk, who had access and security override rights on the Australian security computers.'

'He was signing off on a purchase of Ormond Technik, by an Aussie firm.'

'Yes, Alan,' said Grimshaw. 'But I don't think that Ormond Technik was the only thing downloaded by Jim Quirk onto the chip that night.'

'What does that mean?' said Mac.

'It means Ormond only made two components for the Milstar system – and besides, we've been keeping an eye on the Chinese satellite listening posts for a number of years. It isn't the main issue.'

'So what's on the memory card?' said Mac.

'Been watching TV lately?' said Grimshaw.

'Sometimes.'

'North Korea's missile tests are beginning at five am tomorrow,' said Grimshaw. 'They traditionally fly over – but don't land on – Japan.'

'Yeah, but the Japs are on a hair trigger,' said Mac. 'They see it as a military provocation.'

'Right – all of that chest-beating we love so much between the Japs and the Koreans,' said Grimshaw. 'But what would happen in North Asia if those rockets didn't fall harmlessly into the Pacific, but landed in Okinawa or Tokyo?'

Mac shifted in his seat. 'I guess we'd find out pretty quickly if Japan's space program is really a front for a ballistic missile capability.'

'I think you're right,' said the American. 'And within a few hours we'd also find out if their reactors have been making plutonium all along.'

'That wouldn't suit anyone.'

'No,' said Grimshaw. 'What would China do if the Japs started firing?'

'They'd have an excuse to attack Japan,' said Mac, barely crediting the words as they came out of his mouth. 'And then the Russians and Americans would have to take sides.'

'You've been reading your circulars,' said Grimshaw.

'So what are you saying? Where does Quirk fit into this?'

Grimshaw looked at his watch again. 'You asked about HARPAC and Lampoon?'

'Sure,' said Mac.

'Lampoon is an NSA operation, authorised by the President,' said Grimshaw. 'My job is to find out what exactly a fund called Harbour Pacific – HARPAC – has been buying in the past six months, and who has ultimate control of those assets.'

'And?'

'It's a very large buy-up of router and switching assets – technology used in the North Korean command-and-control systems.'

'What's it got to do with Quirk?'

'He was vetting the Harbour Pacific fund along with its sister fund, Highland Pacific.'

'So where's the report?' said Mac.

'I've read it – he's fudged a lot of the connections, downplayed the kind of things that you and I would be suspicious about.'

'Like what?'

'Like the fact that if you added a clone computer to the assets that Harbour Pacific controls, you wouldn't just listen to what the North Koreans were doing, you'd be inside the Korean defence infrastructure – you'd be able to operate their C and C systems . . .'

'Which control the missile launches.'

'Exactly,' said Grimshaw.

They stared at one another.

'Quirk signed off on Harbour Pacific too?' said Mac.

'Sure did – I think he was being blackmailed by Dozsa.'

'Over what?'

'Outing his wife as a spy for Israel,' said Grimshaw, in a tone that assumed everyone knew this information.

'She was the bait?'

'We think Dozsa had evidence from his time in Australia – he and McHugh had a love affair and it seems he got her to tell him things. McHugh and Quirk were ambitious people who couldn't stand the thought of being accused of espionage – Dozsa played them perfectly.'

'So when the rest of the Central Committee hesitates about attacking Japan, we have General Pao Peng assuming command?'

'Sure, having softened up a billion Chinese with his ultranationalist propaganda.'

'Propaganda?' said Mac. 'You're saying all that stuff about Chinese honour in Nanching and Manchuria is produced by Pao Peng's people?'

'Of course,' said Grimshaw. 'That material is never organic – some of Pao Peng's biggest supporters are newspaper and radio moguls.'

'Smart,' said Mac.

'Yeah, I've been following Pao Peng since they made him a general in '97,' said Grimshaw. 'When his fellow students at Staff College were reading Sun Tzu and Clausewitz, Pao Peng was reading Goebbels and MacArthur.'

'Douglas MacArthur?' said Mac.

'MacArthur was the US Army's first public relations officer,' said Grimshaw. 'He popularised "hearts and minds" – the idea that books and newspapers are as powerful as bombs and bullets. Pao Peng's links to the media are no accident.'

'So what now?' said Mac.

'You rescue your Aussies – I need to see that SD card.'

'But eventually it all leads back to these Pacific funds, right?'

'Yeah,' said Grimshaw, grabbing his backpack. 'It's always the money men.'

# CHAPTER 56

Outboard motors gurgled in the still, tropical air as Mac loaded his kit into the hired boat – two hundred US for a night on the fifty-foot double-hull. On the Kratie wharf, Scotty spoke into a phone, making final arrangements with Canberra.

'Ready, mister?' said the boat owner, a tallish local named Li.

'One call, then we go,' said Mac, pointing at his Nokia.

'No worry,' said Li, twirling the radio in the cockpit and coming up with a Thai rock star's version of 'Like a Virgin'.

Leaping into the boat, Scotty puffed from the effort of jumping.

'Gotta knock off the booze,' he said, poking at the two black kit bags. 'This is it? Thought the Yanks would travel with more than that.'

'Couple of assault rifles and some flash-bangs,' said Mac. 'And Grimshaw didn't want to give up that much, either.'

'It's just us, mate,' said Scotty, reaching for his smokes but catching a look from Li. 'Sandy's operation is totally Defence and we can't even look at those Team Four boys, let alone bring them along for support.'

'Tobin said this?'

'Tobin, quoting Karl Berquist,' said Scotty. 'Defence is a loop with the PM all of a sudden.'

'Tobin tell you to leave Urquhart and Lance?' said Mac.

'You kidding?' said Scotty. 'Firm doesn't need to know about this – I just told him we might need Team Four for a spot of bother and he warned me off like I was asking his daughter to go on a P&O cruise.'

'So we're it?' said Mac, as the stinking river slapped against the hull. 'You feeling fit, old man?'

'Not bad for a desk jockey.' Scotty lit the smoke and held it over the edge.

Mac's Nokia trilled and he answered. Clicking his fingers at Scotty, he repeated the coordinates from the latest fix on the micro-transmitter sitting in Lance's stomach. Scotty scribbled on a map.

'Thanks, Charles – owe ya,' said Mac, signing off.

Mac looked down at the plots, illuminated by the wharf floodlights: the three fixes on that transmitter had Lance moving down the Mekong, about ten miles south of Kratie.

'Know this?' said Mac to Li, pointing to the plots on the map.

'Sure, mister – 'bout fif' minute.'

'Fifteen?'

'Sure, mister,' said Li. 'Go now?'

'Yep, let's go,' said Mac, watching Li's offsider – a boy of about sixteen called Johnny – cast off the lines and jump into the boat.

Mac's adrenaline surged as Li eased on the power from the twin Evinrudes and the bow lifted into the Mekong. The dank smell and the darkness enveloped him as they slipped into the downstream of one of the oldest commercial highways in the world.

Getting the boat onto a plane, Li sat in the skipper's stool and navigated with a small headlight mounted on the right bow while Mac searched in the gear bag. Pulling out a tub of eye-black, he dabbed three fingertips of his right hand into the greasy dark goo, and smoothed it across his face and forehead in streaks.

Scotty lit another smoke. 'Look like one of them Maoris.'

'Your turn,' said Mac, dipping his fingers into the pot and streaking Scotty's face with black greasepaint.

Pulling two hats from the bag, Mac offered one to Scotty.

'These cricket hats?' said Scotty, who'd gone straight from basic training to military intelligence back in the seventies.

'Break up the shape of the head,' said Mac. 'We recognise humans from their gait, and the shape of the head. There's a few tricks we can play with the gait, but hiding the melon is much easier.'

'It works?' said Scotty, turning the American boonie hat in his hands.

'If it gives you half a second, it's working,' said Mac, smiling at his repetition of what Banger Jordan had told them in the Royal Marines: 'A good soldier takes two seconds to aim and take an accurate shot; if you buy yourself half a second, you win and the other cunt's dead.'

Banger had fought in the Falklands, and had been out of uniform for six years when Mac was under him at Poole. The rumour was he'd been doing assignments for British SIS during his absence, a rumour the Geordie had laughed off with jokes about how James Bond never took a crap and called it shite.

Mac remembered getting the feeling from Jordan that the more a man had committed the ultimate sin, the less he wanted people to know that about him. Pulling a box of condoms from the bag, Mac watched the lights of the fishing villages slip by, and realised the circle he'd taken hadn't started and finished in the Firm. His circle was a soldier's journey: he was becoming Banger Jordan.

'The fuck are they for?' asked Scotty, pointing at the condoms. 'You stopping off for a root?'

Planting the M4 carbine between his knees, Mac tore the Durex packet open with his teeth and rolled the rubber down over the muzzle, tying it off against the barrel.

'It's what the British military calls waterproofing,' said Mac as he handed it to Scotty. 'They don't care if you march all day through a swamp, in the rain – your weapon must work when it has to work.'

'Okay,' said Scotty as they scythed through the dark waters of the Nine Dragons. 'What's the plan?'


The lights of the river cruiser blinked through the haze on the Mekong, four hundred metres downstream. It was an eighty-foot diesel-powered Mekong bus of the kind that plied the river between small towns and villages – this was not a tourist vessel.

Mac watched it from the cockpit, using the captain's binos and issuing hushed commands.

'Okay, boss,' said Mac, not taking his eyes off the river cruiser. 'Cut power.'

Mac had just finished his final call to Grimshaw – the micro-transmitter was emitting from right beneath them. There couldn't be any other target than the craft in front of them, the number K 4217 just visible on the bow.

'Know this ship?' said Mac, as Li cut the engines to a burbling idle.

Taking his field-glasses from Mac, Li peered into the darkness, the double-decked wooden cruiser becoming more obvious as it chugged past the floodlights of a general store which had a 1960s Elf bowser sticking out of its decking.

'I not know this one, mister,' said Li, shrugging. 'Much like this. Many.'

'Okay – cut the lights.'

'No, mister,' said Captain Li, shaking his head. 'Water police – no good.'

Placing two US fifty-dollar bills on the cockpit dashboard, Mac saw them hoovered up and the lights go down on the boat.

'Captain Li, that's for you if you stick around, do as I say,' said Mac, pulling four more of the bills out of his plastic Ziploc bag. 'Two hundred US – all you have to do is motor alongside, and ask the other captain if he saw the flares.'

'And when he say "no", I say I saw the red flares – are you in distress?'

'That's it,' said Mac. 'From the first word you speak, to the point you stand off, I must have one hundred and twenty seconds. I need two minutes, okay?'

'Sure, mister,' said Li, gulping.

'And then stand off and wait until we're finished, okay?'

'Okay, mister.' Li avoided Mac's eyes.

'And Li?' said Mac, grabbing the field-glasses and having another look.

'Yes, mister?'

'Keep the kid out of it, okay?'

Sitting in the aft-decks with Scotty, Mac made a final run-through as he fished the SCUBA face mask from the bag.

'So, no heroes, okay, Scotty?' said Mac, stripping to his underwear and wiping the eye-black over his thighs, arms and chest. 'You only show your head with that carbine if the goons on this cruiser don't give me two minutes.'

'Gotcha,' said Scotty, his moustache twitching from his blacked-out face.

Handing the pot of black paint to Scotty, Mac asked him to do his back.

'Look,' said Scotty as he smeared the grease on Mac's shoulder blades, 'I don't know if –'

'It won't come to that,' said Mac, buckling a webbing belt over his hips and slipping a condom over the barrel of the SIG before holstering it.

'Yeah, well,' said Scotty, his hands shaking as he finished the eye-black. 'It's okay for you.'

'Why's that?' said Mac, doing his diaphragm breathing exercises as he reverse-slung the M4 over his shoulders so the muzzle pointed at his left ankle.

'Well, you know . . .' said Scotty, averting his eyes.

Calling Li to the back of the boat, Mac synchronised their watches and gave himself a ten-minute mission clock: after ten minutes, Mac would wait until Li started talking and would take his one hundred and twenty seconds from then.

Holding his G-Shock up to the other two, Mac counted three and they clicked their countdowns at the same time. He felt cold and focused, his mind empty of emotion, his skin a mountain range of goose bumps even as the humidity sat on him like warm dew. He felt fear but not the way he felt it as a teenager asking a girl for a dance at the surf club ball. This fear was a bottled, contained sensation that he used as fuel, and his trepidation was about completing the steps he'd created in his mind, not about pain or failure.

'See you soon,' said Mac, leaning backwards into the water on the starboard side and sliding into the ancient shallows of the Mekong.

Mac swam underwater for seventy seconds, emerging slowly into filthy flotsam about fifty metres downriver from Li's boat.

Taking gulps of air as he trod water, assessing the ground, he ducked under again and swam a line that would take him to the starboard side of the cruiser, the side closest to the riverbank. When Li arrived, Mac wanted all the talk to be on the opposite side of the boat.

After two more underwater swims, Mac tore off his face mask and let it drop to the bottom of the river. The cruiser was about fifty metres away and had lights burning on board. Expanding his diaphragm, getting as much oxygen as possible, Mac watched a figure on the upper decks of the cruiser smoking a cigarette just behind the port side of the wheelhouse.

Looking at his G-Shock, Mac saw the countdown had reached 4.11 – he had some time to play with.

Something hit him on the left shoulder blade and he spun around in time to see a grey-bellied rat float by – a welcome change from the more common floaters in the Mekong.

Another flame flared on the starboard top decks of the cruiser. Then the two goons were laughing and joking across the life-raft boxes. They looked like the PLA cadres from the Dozsa compound, their rifles not evident. The countdown hit 3.46 and the goon on the starboard side – the side Mac had decided to target – unzipped himself and pissed into the river.

Slipping under the water, Mac moved closer, using the blind spot directly behind the stern-mounted rudder to bring him into the craft. As he closed on the thick steel-plated rudder he felt the screw churning the water below the heavy steerage planks.

Reaching for the rudder, Mac mentally ticked off the approach stage from his to-do list and thought about boarding the craft without being seen and without slipping onto the prop; the screws on the older boats were under the stern's hull, and generally weren't a danger, but total fiasco was always just a slip away.

As his fingers searched for a hold, the air whooshed through his nostrils and he gasped as he was lifted out of the water and thumped head-first into the curved stern boards beside the rudder.

Stunned and disoriented as he sank through the murky waters, Mac coughed up a lungful of polluted water and felt his body go into panic.

Spluttering, his arms thrashing, Mac popped to the surface like a child out of a dream and grabbed for a hold on the hull of the craft. He'd been knocked down the starboard side of the ship, and as he fought for breath he heard the Chinese soldiers yelling and laughing. Digging himself into the slippery, lichen-covered hull as he vomited the river swill, Mac trod water with an egg-beater action, reaching for the SIG as the voices came to the rail twenty feet above.

Pulling the SIG up to his face as his left hand lost traction on the mossy hull, he slipped down again, his feet reaching too close to the spinning screw. With all of his strength, Mac pulled himself back to the surface with handfuls of slimy green river moss. Raising the handgun – comical with its condom over the muzzle – Mac saw the Chinese soldiers pointing at something moving in the water near the riverbank.

Following their gaze and praying they didn't look down, he saw a pale-coloured Irrawaddy dolphin flip over and playfully swim backwards. The world's rarest dolphin, trained now to play with European tourists, had tried to give him a ride, not knowing about the crown jewels.

Panting in agony against the hull of the ship, Mac struggled to control his breathing as he watched to see if the beast would come back for another Nutcracker dance. His G-Shock said 1.18 on the countdown as he cursed every Danish backpacker who'd ever encouraged these animals to commune with humans.

The dolphin did its squeaky little bark as it came back for another swim and the peaceful night was rent by automatic rifle fire.

Pressing himself hard against the slippery hull, Mac dug his fingernails into a gap between the planks and waited to die. As the gunfire abated, Mac allowed himself to look over his shoulder, the smell of blood and cordite floating over the oily river making him feel sick.

The dark stain of mammal blood slicked the water twenty feet from Mac's perch and he could see pieces of shredded dolphin floating away on the current.

The Chinese soldiers laughed and a ciggie butt flew end over end, its glow extinguishing in the blood slick.

Breathing deep for composure and trying to ignore the pain in his groin, Mac moved back to the rudder and looked at his G-Shock. It showed 1.04 minutes until Go.

# CHAPTER 57

Pulling on the boonie hat, Mac holstered the SIG handgun and climbed the rudder – a job made easy by the bands of iron wrapped horizontally around it. Lifting his eyes carefully over the transom he cased a dimly lit lower deck which would house a galley, the captain's state room and probably a guest state room. He'd had this chat with Li: the crew's cabins would be below decks and the holds and cargo decks were always forward of the wheelhouse. When locals travelled between towns on these ships, they sat cross-legged on the top decks and on the poop deck at the stern.

The soldiers talked on the upper decks, hidden from Mac's view. He simply wanted to search the cabins and state rooms. If he was discovered, he'd remove the threat.

Climbing over the railing, Mac eased himself to the warm wooden decking and froze, listening for sounds as the water dripped off him. Tearing the condom off the SIG, he reached to a pocket on the back of the webbing belt and extracted a suppressor.

Moving along the port side of the covered deck, he stepped through an open hatch into a passage that led from one side of the ship to the other with a companionway dropping to the below decks.

Two doors faced the corridor. The state rooms, guessed Mac. Opening the first, he pushed his face in and saw the captain's suite.

A low-watt bulb cast a yellow glow over a functional cabin with a single cot, a wardrobe and a desk.

Shutting it quietly, Mac checked his watch. Forty-one seconds until Li pulled alongside.

Opening the second door, Mac eased into a similar cabin, no lights this time. In the darkness he saw a movement and heard some noises. From the cot in the corner, a man's voice expressed confusion and then Mac saw him as he turned his face. Pulling the Ka-bar knife from his webbing, Mac jammed his right knee into the man's chest, slapped his left hand across his mouth and nose and brought the Ka-bar across his throat. Feeling the air leave the dying man, Mac whipped around as he noticed there was someone else in the bed. Aiming his blade at the other face, just inches away, Mac stopped his attack as he looked into big, dark eyes. Adjusting to the darkness, he saw a naked child in the sheets on the other side of the corpse, and as he stood back, realised there was another in the bed – neither of them more than seven or eight years old.

Placing his finger on his lips, Mac made the international sign for silence as he backed towards the door, the white sheets turning black. Pulling the key from the inside lock, he locked the door from the outside, gasping for air as he looked at his watch: eighteen seconds.

Sliding down the companionway to the below decks, he moved through a smaller passageway which opened into a large aft cabin with a central table and double bunks built around it: a stinking rat-hole with white T-shirts and undies hanging from the ceiling, also known as the crew's wardroom.

A bulb glowed in the upper bunk to Mac's right, and pushing the laundry out of the way with the SIG's suppressor, he found himself looking at a young Chinese man lying on his back, reading a PlayStation magazine. Mac shot him once in the forehead and followed with a shot to the temple. The suppressor reduced the noise to not much more than the sound of a Coke can being opened.

Sound came from the other side of the wardroom, and Mac moved carefully through the hanging underwear and around the central table, finding a Chinese man who'd rolled over to get some sleep.

Kneeling softly on the cot behind him, Mac withdrew his Ka-bar and sliced quickly through the carotid artery, clasping a hand over the man's mouth and nose as he did so. The man's head jerked slightly and a muffled yelp came from his lungs before he went slack in Mac's hands.

Above decks, the conversation had started with Li, and Mac could hear the throb of the two Evinrudes against the hull. He reset his G-Shock to a one-hundred-and-twenty-second mission clock and left the room.

Outside the wardroom, another hatch led down a shorter companionway to the engine room – a dark, cramped space stinking of diesel and bilge and containing an old engine that had been cut to idle: Li's story was working.

Pulling the hatch shut, realising he still had the rest of the ship to search, Mac paused. Was there someone behind that condenser? Pushing back into the engine room, he pulled the SIG to a cup-and-saucer stance and, peering into the darkness, he saw it again: between the old engine and the equally ancient condenser there was a foot.

'Hello,' he said, weaving the SIG through a jungle of pipes, analogue dials and jerry-rigged wiring.

'What?' came a confused male voice. In Aussie English.

Moving forwards Mac saw bilge slopping beneath the rotting duckboards, and as he eased around the engine block between the condenser, a face peered at him out of the gloom.

'That you, McQueen?' said Lance Kendrick, ankles bound and hands tied behind his back, Dave Urquhart sleeping against him.

'No, it's the tooth fairy,' said Mac, kneeling and using the Ka-bar to snip the plastic ties.

Murmuring something, Urquhart woke with a start and yelped on seeing Mac's tiger-striped face. They had seventy-six seconds before Li stood off and this ship returned to normal.

Freeing the two men, Mac shrugged off the M4, ripped the condom off the muzzle and gave it to Lance, whose injuries were obvious but not maiming. 'You two okay to walk?'

'Just,' said Lance.

'What about a swim?' said Mac, checking the SIG for load and safety. He had fifteen shots.

'Not if I have to dress like that,' said Lance, nodding at Mac's wet undies, and then examining the M4.

'It's just an M16,' said Mac. 'All you do is point and fire. Okay?'

'Okay,' said Lance, looking scared but resolved.

'And get a good shoulder on this thing,' said Mac, punching Lance in the right collarbone. 'We want dead Chinamen, not holes in the ceiling.'

They moved slowly up the companionways to the first deck. Voices came from the port side so Mac led Urquhart and Lance across the first deck hallway to the starboard side.

Crouching in the shadows beside the railings, Mac looked at his G-Shock. They had under a minute to get to safety.

'It's very simple,' said Mac. 'You slip over the side, make no noise, and breaststroke or swim underwater to the banks. No flailing, no talking, no looking back.'

Looking through the steel railings, Urquhart was hyperventilating. ''Bout fifty metres?'

'Less,' said Mac. 'You keep swimming, keep your head down and when you hit land you keep going – don't stop and look around, especially if these pricks are shooting at you. Okay?'

The two men nodded but Urquhart had a thousand-yard stare.

'Keep walking till you hit the highway,' said Mac. 'Wait beside the road – that's the RV.'

Looking around, Mac felt something change – the engines were revving and then the screw churned the water behind the rudder. Taking the M4 from Lance, Mac offered his forearm and lowered the youngster over the side until they were both stretched out. Lance looked up and let go, disappearing into the slow-moving river.

Mac turned for Urquhart, who was frozen.

'Remember the swimming carnivals?' said his old dorm mate as he stole a scared look at the water. 'Remember how I wasn't in them?'

'You needed a lawyer's letter,' said Mac, not wanting to hear this. Nudgee College had a very simple policy: everyone competed in the athletics carnival; everyone swam at least one event in the swimming carnival. The only exemption was Len Cromie, the pupil with cerebral palsy who defied his parents' instructions one year and swam the fifty metres freestyle. He took five minutes to do it and half the school was in the pool with him by the end, urging him on and making sure he didn't drown. The only other exemption in Mac's memory was Dave Urquhart, who with a High Court judge for a grandfather and a father on the board of trustees somehow managed to get himself excused from the swimming.

'We're grown-ups now, mate,' said Mac, watching Lance's head bob up for air and then duck down and head for the river bank.

'I can't, Macca, I can't —'

Mac stared at him. 'Can't?'

'I never learned — I-I'm phobic,' said Urquhart, with the same nervous stammer he had when the Lenihan brothers came around to see what was in his lock-box. 'It's a medical condition.'

'No,' said Mac, annoyed. 'Len Cromie had a medical condition.'

'That's not fair,' said Urquhart. 'Don't use Cromie against me.'

'You know what Len would say to you?' said Mac, growling. 'He'd say, "You wanna be a piker — go to fucking Churchie."'

'You're a wanker, McQueen,' said Urquhart, straddling the railing and holding his nostrils shut.

'And you're a Nudgee boy,' said Mac, lowering him. 'So get in the fucking river.'

Watching Urquhart panic and strike out for the river bank, Mac hesitated as he swung his legs over to follow him. There were fifteen seconds on his mission clock, more than enough time to drop into the water and escape.

Pulling his legs back over and onto the wooden planks of the deck, Mac cursed himself for what he was about to do. Checking the M4 for load and safety, he padded across the open space to the passageway that would take him back to the state room he'd locked the kids in. He felt foolish — he could hear the shouted conversation between Li and the ship's captain coming to an end, and he knew the next step was going to be soldiers wandering around, finding their comrades dead and sounding the alarm.

Turning the key in the lock, fumbling in haste, Mac pushed in the door and beckoned to the kids. They huddled in the corner, behind the dead paedophile, refusing to move. Crossing the room, he held out his hand and realised that they were both naked – and modest.

Reaching for the girl – who looked the older of the two – Mac grabbed at her arm as she pulled it back. She was protective, pulling the sheet over both of the kids, and hiding the boy behind her.

'In the *sap*,' said Mac, using the Khmer word for river. 'We swim in the *sap*.'

The girl shook her head – she was scared but brave and Mac had a flash of a choice: he could do the Harold, not tell anyone he'd left the kids on Dozsa's boat and leave them out of the report entirely. But he let the weak man's mind take over and started thinking like a father – wouldn't want someone to walk away from his own daughters if they were in danger.

Boots thumped on the upper deck. Grabbing the girl by the arm, Mac pulled back, dragging her over the bloody sheets and the corpse, till she flopped onto the floor. She stood and opened her arms to the boy, who scrabbled over the dead rock spider to the safety of what Mac assumed was his sister.

The door almost hit Mac in the forehead as it flung open, and then Mac was looking into a soldier's eyes.

# CHAPTER 58

The soldier's hand went to his side arm and Mac drove his open hand at a point just below the man's nostrils.

Head snapping back like Howdy Doody, the soldier's knees buckled under him and Mac pounced, slashing his Ka-bar knife as the adversary went down. Raising his arm instinctively the soldier took the knife blow across the forearm, which opened up and spurted blood like a cherub pissing.

Rolling away the soldier swept a low kick and hit Mac in the back of the right leg, making him fall forwards and lose the knife as he hit the wall. Transferring his weight onto his right shoulder, the soldier lashed out with a left foot at Mac's face, which he deflected by shrugging his shoulder and tucking his chin behind it.

Jumping on the soldier, Mac hit him in the heart and followed through with a dropping headbutt, but the soldier turned his face at the last second and Mac's forehead bounced off the boards. Stunned momentarily, Mac watched an elbow fly into his mouth and then the soldier's fingers were in his hair and a knee was pumping into his face, smashing his nose and splitting his cheek before Mac punched the Chinaman in the nuts and rose to his feet with a left uppercut and a jab to the bloke's throat.

Falling backwards onto his arse, the soldier saw a chance to grab his pistol and Mac tried to retrieve the M4 from its position on his shoulder blades. As the muzzles came around at each other, another soldier walked into the passageway, reaching for his own gun. In the confusion and the darkness, Mac took his chance and put bursts of three-shot into each man. A bullet sailed past his left ear and he ducked reflexively, too slow to have avoided it.

Blood splattered the walls and cordite filled the confined space as Mac gasped for breath. Blood ran off his face, and his right leg – already injured from a gunshot wound – quivered beneath him. It wouldn't hold after the adrenaline wore off.

The noise had been deafening and Mac heard the sound of boots clattering and voices raised in panic. Turning, he couldn't find the kids. Peering into the cabin, he saw them sitting in the corner.

'Come on,' he said, gesturing with his hand. The girl shook her head but the boy shrugged free and ran to Mac.

Looking over his shoulder, he saw a shadow moving around the corner and into the passageway. Given the layout of the vessel Mac reckoned that since he'd killed four of the ship's complement, there wouldn't be more than six left: if you took away the captain and engineer, whom he assumed were non-combatants, Mac should have four soldiers to deal with.

As the shadow shortened and a small scrape sounded around the corner, Mac opened up with the M4, tearing out chunks of the woodwork and putting holes in the far wall. A yelp sounded and Mac knew he'd either hit someone or they'd got a face full of splinters.

'Now,' said Mac, snapping at the girl, and she jumped up with hands over her ears and ran to Mac.

Moving with the kids onto the poop deck, Mac kept to the cover of the veranda, suspecting one of those soldiers would've stayed on the top deck and would have a gun trained on the open area below.

Standing in the shadows, Mac looked out over the railing: forty metres to the river bank, at least three soldiers with assault rifles and Mac having to haul two kids through the water. He didn't like his chances, even if they could get into the water without taking a bullet. The choice was between running and dying, or fighting and dying.

Voices yelled down the companionways and a board squeaked above them. Holding his breath, Mac waited. The squeak came again, this time right above his head and Mac pointed the M4 at the source of the noise, pushed the selector to full auto and pulled the trigger. After four seconds, he slung the rifle over his shoulders and looked at the kids, who had their hands cupped over their ears.

'Let's go,' he said, running forwards with a hand holding each child's bicep. As they got to the railing, he leapt over the top rail and the kids jumped with him, the boy hitting his knees on the top as they flew through the air.

The river sucked them down as they hit, a swifter current created between the ship and the river bank. Mac held onto each bicep, trading off their panic at being held with the larger problem of losing them in the Mekong River at night.

Surfacing, they gasped for breath and kicked for buoyancy as they looked around. The current had taken them beyond the ship, which seemed to have slowed. Looking along the starboard side they'd jumped off, Mac saw a soldier limping along the top deck, trying to get a sight on Mac and the kids. Another soldier trotted around the forward cargo hatches with a Chinese AK-47 and took a standing marksman stance on the fo'c'sle railing over the prow.

'Under again,' said Mac, making a theatrical display of taking a deep breath.

They dived again as the bullets plopped in the water. Kicking sideways towards the bank, Mac counted twenty seconds before he felt the boy struggling, and they surfaced again.

Looking around, using all his energy to keep the three of them afloat, Mac saw the ship pointing at them. The Chinese were trying to run them down.

Looking to the bank, Mac saw another thirty metres of swimming — twenty-five if they were lucky. The ship wouldn't want to go too shallow, but the river vessels had flat bottoms and didn't worry too much about grounding.

'Go,' said Mac to the two kids. 'Swim.' He pointed to the river bank.

Dog-paddling ineffectually, the children took off at a pace that would see them run down in twenty seconds. Reaching for his M4,

Mac shrugged it off his back and into his hands as the bullets hit the river again. Lifting the rifle, he took aim as he trod water and shot at the soldier on the fo'c'sle. He missed but the slap of a bullet under the soldier's feet made him lurch backwards and abandon his post for a few seconds.

'Go – swim!' Mac yelled at the kids over the sound of the approaching ship and the clatter of assault-rifle fire.

The limping soldier joined his buddy on the fo'c'sle rail and Mac aimed a shot at his heart, pulling the trigger. The gun jammed and Mac ducked under the water as the two shooters opened up on him.

Dropping the M4, Mac unholstered the SIG and unscrewed the suppressor. He estimated the ship was five seconds from running over the top of him.

Rising to the surface, SIG in cup-and-saucer grip, Mac let off three shots at the fo'c'sle rail but the shooters were gone. He fired another volley at the window of the wheelhouse.

Gunfire echoed from the vessel and an almighty blast of light and sound emanated from the far side of the ship.

Turning for the kids, Mac struck out. If they could aim high enough into the current the ship might miss them. Closing on the children, he saw them standing; they'd reached the muddy shallows but Mac wanted them to keep swimming – a person moves twice as fast across water as they do through mud.

As they clambered through the mud like salamanders, Mac rolled onto his back to take another shot at the soldiers. If they were going to be run down, it would be now.

Looking up, trying to find a shooter, Mac saw the ship had turned away and the shooting was happening inside the vessel.

Clambering up the bank, legs weak, Mac led the kids into the bush as the ship surged back into the navigation channel, its old diesel thumping in time with the gunshots.

They weren't clear yet. If Mac was on that ship, he'd have a boarding vessel over the side by now to chase his prey into the jungle.

'We're going to be okay,' said Mac to the drenched kids as they stopped behind a tree well inside the tree line. The boy's jaw clattered and the girl's wide eyes expressed fear. They swapped names as they caught their breath — the boy was Kai and the girl was Chani, and they weren't siblings: they were neighbours, from the same village in the Chamkar.

They were all naked, he had no food or water to offer them and he had no plan except that he needed to round up Urquhart and Lance. He'd been responsible for the safety of a couple of kids eight years earlier, and he'd screwed it up. Mac didn't want another round of that weighing on him.

Making a check of his webbing belt, he confirmed he had about ten rounds left in the SIG. The knife was gone, as was the M4.

Pulling the boonie hat off his neck, where the drawstring had held it, he gave it to Kai and they fashioned it into a fig-leaf arrangement. Taking off the webbing belt, he helped Chani make it into a modesty garment.

'This way,' said Mac, pulling up his sagging undies and aiming inland for the highway.


By the time they hit Highway Seven — the south–north trucking route from Phnom Penh into Laos — Mac could barely walk. He'd told Lance and Urquhart to get to the road and stay put and he hoped that they'd followed his advice because he was in no mood for finding a couple of office guys in the jungle.

Kai and Chani had found him a branch that Mac tried to use as a crutch but his right leg was creating pain that ignited fire rockets at the periphery of his vision.

In the military they used to say of problems: 'fix it or fuck it'. That is, find a solution or shrug it off. So Mac was manning it out, trying to stay conscious, trying to keep going for the kids.

Looking north and south along the highway, they watched the trucks passing with little chance of flagging one down. In Indochina, hijacking of road, sea and river commerce was a profitable activity among the local gangsters. A Cambodian trucker would as soon stop for an armed man with tiger stripes on his naked body as a media mogul would set up a porn channel on Iranian TV: it simply wouldn't be worth his while.

They walked north, keeping to the footpads that fringed the

major roads in Cambodia – the modern world had arrived but most country folk still walked or rode ancient bicycles.

Mac's small moans of pain had been rising in volume and, after ten minutes of walking, Kai grabbed his left hand. It was functionally useless but as a gesture it meant a lot.

A branch snapped and Mac pushed Kai to the ground and dived into a shallow ditch. Bringing the SIG up to a shooting position, Mac hissed at the kids to come in behind him, staying low to the ground.

They scrambled up behind him and Mac peered into the jungle, the sounds he'd picked up getting drowned out for a few seconds as three trucks went past in convoy.

'Macca – that you?' came a voice from the bush.

'Davo?'

'Yep,' said the voice.

Standing, his heart fluttering, Mac limped to the centre of the footpad as three locals slid past silently on their World War II–era pushbikes.

'You told us to stay put,' said Dave Urquhart, walking into the footpad, Lance behind him. 'What now?'

'Get to Kratie,' said Mac, his head swimming.

'Thanks for the swim,' said Urquhart with a sneer. 'Thought this was a rescue.'

'Come on, Dave,' said Lance, his rock-star image not surviving his dip in the Mekong. 'Be glad we're out of there.'

Mac leaned on the branch, trying to get air into his system. 'You've both got shirts – the kids get one each.'

'Fuck off, McQueen,' said Urquhart, still smarting from the gibes about Len Cromie and Churchie, which was a big Anglican school in Brisbane and Nudgee's bitter rival. 'We've got more serious things to think about – like where the fuck are we?'

'Kids need clothes,' said Mac, his words sounding far away, the pain smothering him.

Lance unbuttoned his expensive adventure-traveller shirt and handed it to Chani.

'Fuck's sake,' said Urquhart, pulling off his wet polo shirt and handing it to the shivering boy.

'I knew a man lived inside you,' said Mac.

'Mister,' said Kai as he slipped into the oversize shirt and pointed to something up the road.

Mac squinted into the darkness while Kai gabbled at Chani.

'He say, there a well up there, mister,' said the girl.

'Water?' said Lance. 'Christ, I'd die for a drink.'

Crossing the highway, they entered the open area with a well and trough in the middle of it – a throwback to the days when Highway Seven was a farmer's donkey track.

They drank and washed themselves, Lance and Urquhart being particularly dehydrated after their incarceration in the engine room.

As Mac scooped water into his parched, sewer-filled mouth, a Toyota 4x4 slowed and then skidded to a halt as it overshot the lay-by. The white reverse lights lit up and then the Toyota was reversing at high speed.

Motioning the team behind the trough, Mac crouched behind the concrete hide and aimed his SIG. Ten shots and a fifty per cent chance of the thing jamming after such a drenching. Against what? A vehicle full of Dozsa's boys? The Chinese cadre? He didn't feel up to it.

Pulse pounding in his temples, Mac cocked the handgun and aimed it at the Toyota's passenger door as the vehicle stopped in the gravel.

Standing slightly for a better stance, Mac counted his shots in advance: two in the passenger door, run to the rear of the vehicle, create visual confusion and then drop the driver as he got out of the 4x4 and hope there wasn't more than one in the back seat.

The door opened and Mac squeezed the trigger. The shot cracked like a stockwhip as the passenger ducked back into the vehicle, the SIG putting a star in the windshield.

Through the haze Mac thought someone was screaming *Macca* but he didn't know why. Then he was falling, fainting, and his face hit the dust and gravel. He was warm now – he could sleep for a thousand years.

# CHAPTER 59

Lying face down on the hospital bed, Mac flinched as the doctor took the hot compress off the bullet wound in his calf and pushed stainless-steel forceps into the hole.

'You get choice,' said the doctor, in clear English. 'Fast and painful, or slow and painful?'

'Just do it,' said Mac, not in the mood for medical humour.

Besides the pain, Mac was dreading having to speak with Jenny. Some husbands' burden was to explain their way out of a game of golf that turned into an all-nighter at the nineteenth, or a business lunch that had ended up at a nightclub. Mac would have to explain how he came to be shooting at his wife in a highway rest stop in central Cambodia.

There was a glugging sound and the nurse leaned in, and then there were strong hands wrapped around his knee and ankle as the doctor grunted and cursed under his breath. After a final sucking sound like a plunger in a blocked lav, the doctor was standing beside Mac's face showing him a small, dark slug in the grip of the bloody forceps.

'That been in you forty-eight hours?' said the doctor, a young man who claimed to have been educated in Perth. 'Amazing that you walking around.'

'I wasn't,' said Mac. 'I was kissing dirt by the side of the road.'

The nurse moved in with a trolley filled with bandages and immediately started on a bed bath for the wounded leg.

'Yeah, well, you should have been to hospital when you are shot, Mr Davis,' said the doctor. 'Can die from the infection – especially you swimming in the river.'

'I'll be using mouthwash the rest of my life,' said Mac, still tasting that foul river-swill in his mouth. 'Where're the kids?'

'Kids are fine,' said Jenny, moving into the curtained area as the nurse dried off the wound.

'Great,' said Mac. 'What are you doing up here, anyway?'

'Dodging bullets from the father of my child,' said Jen, dark ponytail sitting on her right shoulder.

'Sorry,' said Mac, hoping the nurse didn't speak English. 'I had a big night. And you?'

'Captain Loan is following a lead in Stung Treng,' said Jenny, all her weight on her left hip, arms crossed. 'I'm interested. You might be too.'

Pausing to assess the hidden trap, Mac proceeded carefully. 'Really?'

'Yeah – we searched Quirk's apartment in the old BP compound in Saigon and came up with a laundry receipt from a place called the Water Dragon Guest House. It's on the east side of Stung Treng.'

'So it's "we" now?'

'Observing,' said Jenny. 'Chanthe spoke with the owner of the Water Dragon and she said she remembered a regular Australian visitor – called himself John Black but John Black looks just like the photograph we showed her of Jim Quirk.'

'Jim – in Cambodia?'

'He used to stay at the guest house every second weekend. He'd take a suite but would be in and out of the suite rented by what she called Turks.'

'Yeah?'

'Yeah. She later found out the Turks used to stay in a place out of town, across the Srepok, but had stopped going there after a room was blown up and some other Turks were assassinated.'

'So why would I be interested?' said Mac, as the bandages went on his leg.

'Because I called Maggs, asked him about it,' said Jenny.

'Harley?' said Mac.

'I was wondering if he'd seen any Turks through Phnom and he tells me they're probably Israelis – retired Mossad guys.'

'Well, that's interesting.'

'He told me he'd seen you, Macca,' she snapped. 'I can't believe you had a drink with Maggs and didn't talk about the Mossad guys – that's precisely what people like you talk about.'

'Steady, my sweet,' said Mac, trying to work out how many people were listening. The annoying thing about cops was how open they were.

'Well?'

The nurse finished and left the curtained cubicle.

'Yeah, he told me there was a bunch of ex-Mossad hard-ons charging around the place,' said Mac. 'So what?'

'Maggs noted the ex-Mossad vehicle in Phnom – it matches the Turks' LandCruiser at the Water Dragon Guest House,' said Jenny.

'Okay.'

'This Israeli vehicle is a green LandCruiser Prado. A similar vehicle departed the scene of Jim Quirk's murder in Saigon.'

'Common car,' said Mac.

'Patrons at the Mekong Saloon saw a team of Turkish or Israeli men go up the mezzanine stairs that night,' said Jenny. 'They also saw a blond off-duty soldier – Aussie bloke. Know who that might be?'

The curtain was pulled back and Captain Loan walked in. 'Mr Richard, so nice to see you.'

'Thanks for the ride, Captain.'

'I saw what the doctor pulled out of your leg,' said Loan, smirking. 'The bookselling must be tough – anything you'd like to talk about?'

'It's a Cambodian matter,' said Mac, rolling over to sit upright on the edge of the bed. His leg was heavily bandaged, his head spinning with the airless hospital atmosphere and the new round of painkillers.

'Agent Toohey, I really wanted to talk with you,' said Loan.

'Yes?' said Jenny.

'The children – I asked them where their village is and they say it's gone.'

'Gone?' said Jen.

Loan nodded. 'They were rounded up from their village in Chamkar forest two days ago.'

'By who?' said Jenny.

'Slavers,' said Loan. 'Mr Richard got these kids off the ship, but there's a hundred more in the hold.'


Mac's backpack was waiting at the Palace Guest House reception when he wandered in. Picking it up, he saw the clock behind the desk – almost midnight.

Leading the way, Mac showed Lance and Urquhart up to his suite and told them they could share the second bedroom.

'Bathroom's down the hall, boys,' said Mac, ducking out.

He'd seen the lights in Scotty's room, and he knocked gently on the wooden door in case he woke him and gave him a fright.

'Who?' came the slurred question.

'Davis – Southern Scholastic.'

The door swung inwards and Scotty peered out, his Glock along his leg, a cigarette in his mouth.

Taking a seat in the spacious living room, Mac accepted the beer Scotty dug out of the fridge.

'Where the fuck have you been?' said Scotty, cracking a new beer for himself and chaining a new smoke with a trembling hand. 'Christ, I thought we'd lost you.'

'That you with the flash-bang?' said Mac, enjoying the cold beer but not in the mood for drinking.

'Nah, Li threw that,' said Scotty, ciggie hand shaking as he gulped at the bottle of Tiger. 'I was too busy shooting the sky and shitting my pants.'

'Well, I'm glad you did,' said Mac.

'What happened back there?' asked Scotty, sucking too hard on the smoke. 'We could see Urquhart and Lance crawling up the bank – where were you?'

'Found a couple of kids on board,' said Mac. 'Didn't seem right to leave them.'

'They can't have been in more danger than you,' said Scotty, polishing off the beer and standing to get another.

'They were in bed,' said Mac, fatigue pushing down on his eyelids.

'Should have left them,' said Scotty.

'In bed with a grown-up,' said Mac.

Shaking his head slowly, Scotty resumed his seat and gulped the beer. 'What was the first thing I taught you, Macca, when you arrived in Basrah at the end of the war?'

'You told me to make myself priority number one because no other bastard was going to do it for me.'

'Not bad advice, right?'

'It's my eleventh commandment,' said Mac.

'So what the fuck are you doing putting your life at risk for a couple of kids you meet on a ship?' demanded Scotty, stress tightening his lips. 'You don't think you've bitten off enough already?'

'Well,' said Mac, shrugging, 'no other bastard was looking out for them.'

'Don't get old and sloppy, Macca,' said Scotty, pointing with his ciggie hand. 'Priority number one, okay?'

Looking at his G-Shock, Mac saw it had just hit midnight – there was an appointment he wasn't going to make. Taking the Nokia from his backpack, he found a received-call number and pressed it.

'Just a sec, mate,' said Mac.

A satellite phone connection would normally take twenty seconds to start ringing, but Mac's call connected immediately. Then the distinctive Hungarian-Israeli voice came on the line.

'Joel, it's your favourite Australian,' said Mac.

'Ah, Mr McQueen – such a surprise.'

'Where the bloody hell are ya?' said Mac. 'We had a date, remember?'

'Um, yes,' said Dozsa.

Mac noted the hesitation. 'Well?' he said. 'I'm at the Stung Treng wharf and I've got your memory card.'

Dozsa laughed. 'Have you really, Mr McQueen?'

'So where are you?'

'I'm precisely where I need to be, my friend,' said Dozsa. 'I hope you didn't swallow the river water – there's cholera about right now.'

The line went dead, and Mac stared at the phone.

'Dozsa?' said Scotty, exhaling a plume.

'Yeah,' said Mac.

'Knows he's lost the hostages?'

'Yep,' said Mac.

'If we have the hostages and Sandy's got the memory card,' said Scotty, 'I'm ready to fold the tent.'

'What about McHugh?'

'I'm debriefing tomorrow morning. I'll let you know then. It might be a matter for the federal cops.'

'Okay, boss,' said Mac, gasping slightly as he stood and stretched. 'Time to inspect the back of my eyelids.'

'Don't want another beer?'

'Nah, mate,' said Mac as he reached the door. 'You're doing the job of two men.'


The nightmare pushed him up and up, faster and faster, towards the light at the top of the mine shaft and then he was exploding out into the daylight and he yelled slightly as he realised his Nokia's screen was blasting out an orange light, the phone buzzing around on the bedside table.

Feeling his heart thump against his sternum, Mac lay back on the pillows as he grabbed the phone.

'Yep?' he said, throat dry. His G-Shock on the table said 4.12 am.

'Hi, honey, it's me,' said his wife. 'I need your help on that ship.'

'Ah, yeah,' said Mac, rubbing sore eyes. 'I'll talk to you in the morning.'

'What was the name of the ship?' said Jenny.

'No name,' said Mac, disoriented. 'A number.'

'What was it?' said Jenny.

He hated it when she was like this.

'Um, I think it was . . . K 4217, or 4217 K. Something like that.' Mac gently massaged his temples. Being pestered for small details took him back to his military days when special forces people were forced to recall every detail, from a hotel room and cell phone number to a map coordinate and an aircraft rego. Ninety per cent of special ops were for reconnaissance and an operator who couldn't make a detailed report was virtually useless.

'Macca, what was the number?'

'Shit, mate,' said Mac, lured into a fight. 'It's four-thirty in the morning and I'm tanked on Percodan.'

'Sorry, hon,' she said. 'It's important.'

'Right,' said Mac. 'It was K 4217. Where are you?'

'Don't worry – get back to sleep.'

'You're not going after them?' said Mac, sitting up. 'Who's with you?'

'Got given two local cops,' said Jen, voice cracking up.

'What?' asked Mac, the connection dying.

'Local cops,' said Jen through the static.

'There's soldiers on board that ship,' said Mac, but the connection had been lost.

Limping into the kitchen of the suite, Mac grabbed a bottle of Vittel. Drinking it down, he looked out the window over the sink, saw the insects flying around the streetlight. They circled so fast that they ended up chasing themselves.

He didn't think he would ever be able to tame his wife. She got something in her head and she moved like a locomotive. Mac had first met her in the Aussie embassy colony in Manila, where she was the ice queen of the group; good-looking, funny, smart and confident, but aloof and distrusting. She worked in the federal police intelligence taskforces but her specialty was tracking Australian paedophiles into South-East Asia and busting the brothels and trafficking rackets that supported the child-molesting industry. Jenny was relentless and she wasn't scared of men, didn't back down from them, and, being a country girl, was better at blokes' humour and fast retorts than most men.

Certain kinds of men didn't like her lack of respect and she constantly clashed with the police and consular hierarchies, accusing them of being soft on sex slavery. It wasn't helped by the fact that the Indonesian-American-Australian teams chasing the sex slavers were mostly female, which had Jenny and her crew known as the 'Dyke Squad' among men in the embassy colonies.

Mac had fallen in love and then married her. He hadn't taken the easy way by being with Jen, but he had followed his heart.

Letting himself breathe, Mac focused on the swirling insects as he tried to put Jenny out of his mind. He realised what had annoyed him about Dozsa's attitude on the phone. He showed no interest in the card; didn't demand it, didn't try to threaten or renegotiate.

Why not?

The insects chased themselves around and around and he realised that he, Grimshaw and Sandy had been doing the same thing.

Moving out into the hallway, Mac knocked on Scotty's door.

He waited forty seconds before the slurred voice asked what the fuck he wanted.

'Scotty, it's me – open up.' Pushing into the smoky room, Mac shut the door and turned to his old mentor. 'Mate, it's still on – we're not going anywhere.'

'What?' said Scotty, half asleep but fully annoyed.

'It doesn't matter if Sandy or Grimshaw has a card that can gain them access to the North Korean C and C systems,' said Mac. 'Dozsa has a backup copy sitting somewhere.'

'What?' asked Scotty again. 'Then why have we been chasing this fucking thing?'

'Quirk had accessed it through his Top Secret clearance, and downloaded it onto an SD card,' said Mac. 'We assumed there was one copy, one chip.'

'Yeah?'

'But when I rang Dozsa tonight, it didn't worry him that we'd retrieved Lance and Urquhart, that he wasn't going to get the card,' said Mac. 'In fact, the hostages weren't at the Stung Treng wharf – they were nowhere near it.'

'Dozsa never intended to do a swap?'

'No,' said Mac, trying to work it out. 'He did what we'd do – created a diversion and let the good guys chase that.'

'That's a very Mossad trick,' said Scotty.

'By way of deception – one of the craft skills you develop when you want your neighbourhood enemies hating each other, not you.'

Scotty focused. 'You're saying Dozsa wanted you to steal the chip from Grimshaw, and he probably knew Sandy Beech was around?'

'That's it,' said Mac. 'Or he thought Grimshaw would bust me and there'd be a big blue between the Yanks and Aussies.'

'Which there sort of is,' said Scotty.

'While we fight among ourselves for the memory card, Dozsa is somewhere else and getting another copy, or even the original. And if we think it's over, and there's no more UAVs in the air or tracks on mobile phones, Dozsa disappears off the map.'

'So where's Dozsa?' said Scotty, puffing beer fumes.

'That's the other thing about the call,' said Mac. 'Dozsa's on a satellite phone, right?'

'Yeah.'

'When you call a sat phone from a cell phone, it takes about twenty seconds to get a connection.'

'It's going through the satellite system as well as the ground stations,' said Scotty. 'And there's a propagation delay.'

'But when you call a sat phone that's in your local area, what happens?'

'It connects straight through,' said Scotty. 'Sat-phone accounts link to local cell towers and charge back to your account – that's why they're so expensive.'

'Yeah,' said Mac. 'So Dozsa's phone connected immediately.'

'That's interesting,' said Scotty. 'Local call?'

'I think Captain Loan and Jen are on the right track,' said Mac.

'They're heading for Stung Treng aren't they?' said Scotty, smiling in the dark.

'Yep,' said Mac. 'But it'd be a pity to let a couple of cops scare off our mate Joel.'

'Joel deserves better,' said Scotty. 'Let me have a shower.'

# CHAPTER 60

Staggering into the early morning dampness, Mac keyed his phone while Scotty paid the guest house manager.

Jenny's phone was still out of range and he hoped she was avoiding trouble – she tended to pick fights with people who'd rather shoot than argue.

Standing at Scotty's rental car, the pain just starting again in his leg, Mac wondered about firearms.

'Got anything in the boot?' he asked as Scotty reached the car, the hangover making his face fall off him in waves.

'Got a Glock that has to be given back to the dip-sec in Saigon when I leave, and the bags you packed for last night. That's it.'

Popping the boot, Mac inspected the gear bags: two M4 assault rifles, three flash-bang grenades and a single Beretta handgun with one spare clip. In the other bag were three Kevlar vests. It was the kind of cache that would get you locked up for eighteen months in a Western country, but going into Dozsa's territory it looked puny.

'Worth giving Sandy a call?' said Scotty, gulping down bottled water, bloodshot eyes popping out of his head.

Mac thought about it. 'Better if you call.'

'Okay,' said Scotty, pulling his phone out of his pocket. 'But he'll tell me to get fucked.'

Scotty lit a smoke. 'G'day, Sandy – Scotty here, mate.'

Mac chuckled as he saw Scotty try to dodge the obvious: that it was ten to five in the morning.

'Look, we need the navy boys up here for something this morning –'

Scotty was cut short. 'He did? You want me to tell him now?' He covered the mouthpiece. 'Says you set the NSA on them and now they've got one American dead, another injured and Grimshaw as a prisoner – thanks a fucking lot, McQueen.'

Holding his hand out, Mac gestured for the phone.

'Sandy,' said Mac, effusive. 'How are you, darling?'

'Get fucked, McQueen,' said the military spook.

'You helped with the rescue, in spite of yourselves,' said Mac.

Sandy exhaled. 'I'm sure we're all happy for that, mate, but I don't appreciate being dive-bombed by a helo when I'm crossing a border.'

'Charles came at you in a chopper?'

'Sure did – the only thing going for us was you didn't tell him who was in the car with me.'

'You don't need Maddo's boys anymore. Can you release them to Scotty?'

'You been drinking?' said Beech, yelling slightly. 'I'm trying to get out of Indochina with a file stolen from an ex-Mossad mercenary and we're being chased by Chinese cadres and the NSA. You really think I'm about to give you Maddo?'


On the way out of town they passed the Palace Guest House. Seeing it, Mac asked Scotty to circle back.

'What are we doing here?' said Scotty, pulling up behind a tree. 'Thought Grimshaw was down south.'

'Exactly,' said Mac. 'He won't miss all those firearms.'

The dim bulbs of the hallway looked vaguely menacing as Mac worked his bump key into the lock, pulling it back slightly until the pins fell then opening it with one decent left-and-right of the key.

Easing themselves inside, Scotty covered the room with his Glock. They stood still in the darkness as they took in the scene.

'Shit,' said Mac, and turned on the light. The living area had been trashed, but by a professional. Drawers had been opened, sofa cushions unzipped and the rug rolled up.

Moving down through the suite, Scotty checked on the bedrooms.

'Same,' said Scotty as he came back. 'Someone after something.'

'Weapons, for a start,' said Mac. 'The place was crowded with them.'

Leaving the suite as quietly as they'd arrived, Mac had a thought.

'Scotty,' he said in a whisper, pointing at the next-door room where Sammy had been interrogated. 'Might see if Sammy knows what's going on. Might even want a drink of water.'

Mac needn't have bothered lifting his bump key to the door – it was three inches ajar, the light on inside.

Following Scotty inside, Mac saw that the chair Sammy had been strapped to was covered in blood, but it was empty.


The Water Dragon Guest House sat about seven blocks back from the riverfront of Stung Treng, hidden behind a line of established banyans and frangipanis.

It was dark as Mac and Scotty made their first pass, the roads largely deserted except for the odd farmer or fisherman getting an early start.

'See anything?' said Scotty, as they reached the end of the road and stopped.

'Cottages around a central garden,' said Mac. 'Some trees but mostly open ground.'

'Why don't I book in?' said Scotty. 'If Dozsa's in there, he wouldn't know me.'

'Cover?' said Mac, checking his SIG as a nervous tic.

'Barry Hensall, from New Zealand,' said Scotty, saying it Zilland. 'Sales director for Waitemata Irrigation Systems.'

'Had me fooled,' said Mac. 'Must have been the boozy breath and ginger moustache.'

'Works every time,' said Scotty, reaching his hand under the steering column cowling and coming up with a small package held in place with a rubber band. He took his real passport, credit cards and driver's licence from his wallet, exchanged the documents, and put the legitimate collateral in the steering column hiding place.

'Phones okay?' said Scotty, folding down the vanity mirror and looking at himself.

'I'll be waiting,' said Mac, getting out of the car.


The motel across the road from the Water Dragon was filled with backpackers, judging from all the campervans in the forecourt. Getting a street-front room, Mac put a chair on the double bed and found a line of sight through the partly opened curtains, giving him a view with his binos into the Water Dragon's internal garden.

The phone rang at 6.53 am as the sunrise turned from purple to orange.

Scotty. 'I'm in room five – the one with the old park bench outside it, on the lawn.'

'Can't get that angle,' said Mac. 'Dozsa around?'

'No movement – you sure this is it?'

'This is where the Cong An is coming to make inquiries of Joel Dozsa and associates,' said Mac. 'And my call to that sat phone suggests he was in the area.'

'Any ideas?'

'I saw a pet shop in town as we came through.'

'You shitting me?' said Scotty. 'I taught you that one.'

'Yeah, well, let's see you do it, maestro.'

'You're a cheeky bugger. Know that?'


At quarter to nine, Mac watched as Scotty's car arrived back in the guests' drive that wound around the back of the cottages. Through his binos Mac saw Scotty get out of the car, drag a cat box from the back seat, and enter his cottage via the rear door.

The phone rang. 'I'll call every ten minutes,' said Scotty. 'Doors are open, so cover me, okay?'

'Can do,' said Mac.

Scotty chased the kitten across the internal garden. Kittens, puppies and children were one of the best ways of getting close to people and starting conversations – a highly intelligent woman would start a conversation with Nosferatu if he was playing with a kitten. If you couldn't get the person you wanted out of their hide with such diversions, you could revert to knocking on doors and asking if anyone had seen your kitten or child. It wasn't very complex, but the best ploys weren't.

After eleven minutes, Scotty rang to check in. 'Honeymoon couple from Belgium, mining guy from Darwin and the manager's father, who *loves* cats.'

'Any ideas?'

'There's a couple of cottages opposite mine – twelve and thirteen – with closed curtains. So we might shift to the lost kitten.'

'Be careful,' said Mac, scanning the scene with his field-glasses.

'I'll start with twelve,' said Scotty.

Thirty seconds later, the kitten stowed in his room, Scotty moved across the garden and sauntered around the porch of number 12. Mac could make out Scotty's feet and could guess what he was saying: *My kitten was around here somewhere – you seen her?*

Someone moved into the garden behind Scotty – swarthy, muscular. Shifting to take it in, Mac recognised Dozsa's driver.

Mac hurried his view back to Scotty and couldn't find him. 'Come on, come *on*,' said Mac, heart rate building.

The driver disappeared into the other side of the garden and Mac jumped from the bed, gasping with pain as he landed on his wounded leg.

He ran down the external staircase, then waited for traffic and crossed the road in a blast of heat, insects and birds going crazy.

Circling around the rear driveway of the complex, Mac touched the SIG in his waistband as he got to Scotty's cottage. Pushing through into the cool of the room, Mac smelled the cat immediately – Scotty hadn't bought a litter box.

Parting the curtains on the front windows, he scoped cottages 12 and 13. They were painted blue, about forty metres away. An old Khmer man sat on the park bench in front of the window.

Checking his SIG for load and safety, Mac put the weapon in his waistband under the polo shirt and, grabbing the kitten, left the cottage.

Throwing the animal on the grass, Mac tried to herd it across the garden, keeping one eye on cottage number 12, holding his breath as he waited for someone to open that door and start blasting at him.

The cat veered to the left, between cottages 10 and 11, and Mac followed as the black and white beast bounced like a rabbit.

Once behind cottage 11, Mac forgot the cat and drew the handgun. There was no movement, but he heard the low rumble of male voices. Between the cottages was parked a green LandCruiser. Moving behind the cottage, he scoped the gap to cottage 12, and walked swiftly across it, making the back door without being seen.

As he leaned against the doorjamb, Mac's heart banged and his breath rasped. Slowly turning his head against the frosted glass, he squinted and tried to make out what was happening. Where was Scotty?

Standing back, he took a deep breath and ran at the door, raising his right leg and kicking it from its locks, following through into the cottage, sweeping his SIG at the scene in front of him.

A man standing in the porch turned and Mac whacked him in the mouth with the butt of the SIG. He kept moving through, arcing the gun back and forth in a cup-and-saucer sweep, as Scotty became visible at the far end of the room.

'It's okay,' said Scotty. 'I'm fine, Macca.'

Turning back to the man on the ground, Mac held the SIG at his ear.

'Hands where I can see them,' he said.

Turning from his prone position, the man looked up, blood running from his mouth.

'Shit, McQueen,' said the American, looking dazed.

'Sammy,' said Mac, recovering. 'What the hell are you doing here?'


'You sure it's them?' said Scotty, looking through a chink in the bed-room curtains that gave a view across to cottage 13, ten metres away.

'Three Israelis, one of them's Dozsa,' said Sammy, dabbing a wet flannel on his swollen lower lip.

'I saw Dozsa's driver from that night on the docks,' said Mac. 'How long you been here?'

'Since last night. When Grimshaw took off I thought I'd give this place a try.'

'Why?' said Mac.

'Does it matter?' said Sammy.

'I don't know, you haven't answered,' said Mac. 'Look – you shot me first, okay?'

Sammy shook his head. 'Grimshaw took a call back in Kratie – I could hear him through the walls.'

'And?' said Scotty.

'All I heard was Grimshaw saying, "Water Dragon Guest House in Stung Treng – are you sure that's where he is?" I decided to check it out.'

'Three of them?' said Mac.

Sammy nodded. 'I took the gear from Grimshaw's room, but what was I going to do with one on three?'

Mac wondered how to raise the subject of the Grimshaw–Sammy split – he wanted the subject in the open.

'Scotty and I dropped in this morning, make sure you had food and water,' said Mac.

'You're a nosey son of a bitch, know that, McQueen?'

'Lucky I get paid for it. What's the story with you and Grimshaw?'

Sammy kicked at the carpet. 'It's old Washington shit – it's not your battle.'

'Grimshaw's NSA?' said Mac.

'Yeah, and you've guessed where I'm from,' said Sammy.

'The Pentagon and NSA clash sometimes, but duct-taped to a chair?'

Sammy gave Mac a stare. 'Maybe Grimshaw wanted to be taken to the HARPAC codes, but he didn't want a Defense guy touching them.'

'He beat you?' said Mac.

'He thought I'd allowed Bongo to take McHugh, and he thought I'd found the SD card. He decided I was working against him – he's paranoid.'

'The SD chip was in Tranh's phone,' said Mac. 'He was carrying it in the memory slot beside the battery.'

'Tranh?'

'The Vietnamese driver I had in Phnom Penh,' said Mac. 'I think he was killed in the apartment building.'

Sammy nodded. 'We got his phone, but he didn't die.'

'No?'

'No, I winged him after he pulled on me,' said Sammy. 'And he was taken by another crew.'

'Dozsa?'

'No,' said Sammy, 'locals, gangsters – they appeared at the entry doors, grabbed your driver and took off.'

Mac was stunned by the revelation. 'There was an ambulance – didn't someone die?'

'Yeah, it was a woman, an expat. She was waiting for the elevator and got between me and Tranh. It was an accident.'

'Shit,' said Mac, remembering the night and the woman taking her garbage out to the bins. She'd let Mac and Tranh into the building.

'Two o'clock,' said Scotty, pulling Mac to the right angle to see through the curtains.

'Oh no,' said Mac, seeing the figure walking to the door of cottage 13.

'It's that cop from Saigon,' said Scotty. 'Loh Han, isn't it?'

'Loan,' said Mac. 'And yes, it is.'

# CHAPTER 61

Running to the front door, Mac opened it slowly and stuck his head outside.

'Psst,' he said, trying to keep his voice down. 'Captain Loan. *Chanthe.*'

The captain had already turned away from him and was talking to the two local cops who walked across the garden with the manager.

'Here we go,' said Sammy.

An engine roared to life, car doors slammed.

'They're leaving,' said Scotty, and turning back into the cottage Mac saw his mentor grabbing an assault rifle from Sammy's bag. 'Just got into the car.'

Following Scotty to the back door, Mac saw Sammy Chan, in standing marksman pose, about to unleash with his assault rifle.

Mac yelled at him. 'No! Leave it, Sammy!'

Distracted, Sammy turned to Mac, who burst past Scotty and put a hand on the American's weapon, pushing it down. 'Not with the cops at the door, mate.'

'Fuck – *look*,' said Sammy, incredulous.

An engine screamed and the green LandCruiser behind cottage 13 threw gravel as it accelerated out of the guest house campus.

'I had 'em,' said Sammy, his face telling of bad interrogation techniques.

'No, you had twenty years in a Cambodian prison,' said Mac. 'And that's all you had.'

'Might want to put that away,' said Scotty, nodding at Sammy's rifle.

As Sammy walked back into the cottage mumbling about Australian pussies, Captain Loan walked through the gap between the two cottages, looking stylish in her black pant suit.

'Captain,' said Mac, smiling. 'You following me?'

'No,' said Loan, surprised. 'I was going to interview the –'

Turning to her right, she looked through the dust and listened to the LandCruiser's tyres screeching as they hit the tarmac.

'The neighbours?' said Mac. 'They just left – in a hell of a hurry, too.'

'Neighbours?'

'Yeah,' said Mac. 'Israeli boys in a green LandCruiser.'

'Thanks,' said Loan, shouting at the local cops as she ran back to the manager's office.

Loan's white Camry turned left, heading for Highway Seven's southbound exit out of Stung Treng. She drove fast and Scotty did well to keep the car at a casual distance while doing a hundred and forty kilometres per hour as they flashed past the *Stung Treng Ville* sign, a massive circular-saw blade welcoming people to the provincial capital.

'Think they know where they're going?' said Sammy from the back seat, breathing heavily.

'She's been on Dozsa for a week,' said Mac, squinting to see her car through the heat and dust of the highway. 'She's got the Cambodian cops working for her – she should know more than us.'

'Shit,' said Scotty, jumping on the brakes and holding the car in a long sideways skid as they left the road and slid across dirt and gravel into bushes along a levee road.

Sammy's head bounced off the back of Mac's seat. 'What the fuck?'

Gunning the engine, Scotty drove the car through the scraping branches and onto the levee road, where he stopped and waited.

'What are we – ?' asked Sammy, just as the white Camry flashed past, engine screaming as it headed back to Stung Treng.

Pulling back onto the highway, Scotty floored the accelerator and they raced through the morning traffic, taking the third lane down the middle as they flashed past trucks, buses, scooters and donkey carts.

'There she is,' said Mac, seeing the white Camry in the distance, pulling wild overtaking manoeuvres. Losing sight of Loan's car as they approached the town limits, Scotty hunched over the steering wheel looking left and right for a side road.

'Come on,' he said to himself. 'Fucking come on.'

As they went past a dusty road to the right, Mac looked down it and saw a procession of donkey carts and a tractor that looked one model away from the iron-wheeled traction engines. The white Camry was almost hidden in its own dust cloud, between two tractors.

'Back here, Scotty,' said Mac.

Throwing the car into a sliding donut at a hundred and ten kph, Scotty lost the tail in the road-side dirt and hammered the throttle as they were thrown around like a tossed salad. Truck horns sounded and air brakes hissed as Scotty brought the car around to face the opposite direction, tyres squealing.

Scotty floored it as they turned in to the side road.

Realising he'd been holding his breath, Mac made himself breathe out. They hit a crest and saw the Camry about half a mile in front of them. Mac saw something else, just as Sammy saw the same thing.

'Airport,' said the American, pointing between the front seats.

'Should have been the first place we tried,' said Scotty.

Seeing the plane tails in the distance, Mac decided the Israelis would be trying to get on a plane and would turn their guns on Loan and her cops. Mac had seen what Dozsa's firepower looked like and as he gripped his Nokia he tossed up whether he should call Captain Loan. What did he owe her? Anything? A ten-second phone call?

'This cop could be useful to us,' said Mac.

They flew over another crest – all four tyres leaving the ground – and Scotty swerved around a cart as they touched down, leaning on the horn.

'So?' he said.

'I should warn her about Dozsa's people.'

'Warn?' said Sammy, leaning between them. 'Who? The *cop*?'

'Loan's no use to us dead,' said Mac, scrolling down his contacts list.

'No cops, right, Scotty?' said Sammy. 'We're cleanskins.' Undeclared intel operators were supposed to go unnoticed when in-country.

Scotty lost the tail of the car in the right-hand ditch and wrestled the machine back into line with three fishtails.

Scotty finally spoke. 'This Loan – is it personal, Macca?'

'Fuck off,' said Mac.

'I mean, she's a good sort, and she's your type.'

'I don't have a type,' said Mac.

'Sure you do,' said Scotty. 'Tall, sexy, don't like men.'

'Watch it,' said Mac.

Rounding a left-hand bend, Scotty hit the brakes, putting the car into a 360-degree spin and then into the ditch with a bang. Ahead, three figures were out of the white Camry, moving carefully towards the green LandCruiser parked fifty metres down the road.

The heat shimmered through the white dust and Mac tried to open his door, which was jammed against the side of the ditch.

Following Scotty out the driver's door, they stood on the road and watched as the three figures from the Camry split and ran to opposite sides of the road. A wall of automatic gunfire plunged into the Camry, its tyres blowing out and a gas-tank fire starting after five seconds of the onslaught.

Mac saw Loan and her two cops trying to approach the defunct car as the green LandCruiser moved on.

'Let's get this car out,' said Scotty, walking back to the ditch.

Sammy and Mac pushed and then they were back on the road, the transmission now featuring a loud scraping sound.

Swerving past the burning Camry, Mac ducked down in his seat to avoid Loan seeing him. As they cleared the fire, Scotty held his foot to the floor and they sat in stressed silence as the car limped and ground its way towards the airport, not managing more than a hundred and ten kph.

Scotty pulled into the dirt car park of the airport as smoke drifted into the car from the floor. There were two other cars parked, but neither of them was a green LandCruiser.

'Maybe it wasn't the airport,' said Scotty, cruising slowly around the car park and trying to look in the glass front doors. The place looked deserted.

'I'll check,' said Mac, opening his door before the car had stopped.

Limping up the concrete apron to the front doors, he pushed through carefully into the coolness. It looked like an abandoned factory cafeteria, with floor-to-ceiling windows at the far side, looking over the shimmering tarmac.

Taking his gun in hand, Mac entered and realised a middle-aged woman was sitting behind a counter, but with nothing to sell.

Mac smiled, hiding his gun. 'Good morning.'

'Good morning, mister,' she said.

'Any flights this morning?'

'No, mister.'

'No scheduled flights today?'

'Scheduled flight, sometimes,' said the woman, nodding. 'It depend.'

'Thanks,' said Mac, smiling. He'd spent so long getting those sorts of dual responses in South-East Asia that it didn't worry him anymore. If Garvs had been talking to the woman, he'd be arcing up by now, trying to nail her down to a real answer and suspecting her of loyalties to Brother No. 1.

Turning back to the entrance, he saw an old hangar on the other side of the tarmac and some movement around it.

Walking to the windows, he cupped his hands against the glass and peered out. Something was spinning in that hangar. He focused harder, wishing he had his binos. Then he saw it: figures moving away from a green vehicle parked at the side of the hangar, a sign over the entrance saying North Air.

Sprinting for the front doors, Mac got to the car and found Sammy leaning on the bonnet and Scotty on his knees, looking under the car.

'Let's go,' said Mac, opening the boot and pulling out the M4s.

'Car's rooted,' said Scotty, standing.

A puddle grew under the front axle.

'Come on,' said Mac, throwing one of the assault rifles to Scotty. Leading them around the south side of the terminal, through an alley and out onto the tarmac, Mac pointed to where the Friendship was emerging from the hangar, its props spinning with a whining sound.

Sammy ran, but slowed as the Friendship straightened and gained speed with its opened throttles.

Mac rested his hands on his knees as the aircraft flashed past with its signature drone and climbed into the sky.

'He'll keep,' said Scotty, gasping for air.

'Oh really?' said Mac, as he caught a flash of Dozsa's face in a window.

It was an expression he hadn't yet seen in the Israeli: Joel Dozsa was laughing.

# CHAPTER 62

Scotty's face had turned bright purple from the run across the airfield. 'Well, we fucked that up.'

Mac eyed the hangar as his chest heaved. 'Let's check the Cruiser.'

Scotty hit the phone and arranged the rental car people to deliver a new car as Mac walked to the green LandCruiser. Checking the vehicle for wires and bombs, Sammy gave it the okay and they started their search.

Scotty lit a smoke and headed for the control tower to see if the pilot had logged a flight plan.

The LandCruiser was clean and Mac felt very tired. He was now sure Dozsa had an alternative way into the North Korean launch systems for their missile tests, but the only way of stopping it had just flown out of Cambodia.

Slamming the driver's door, he moved away to stand in the shade. As Sammy came around to join him, Mac noticed something on the vehicle. Moving to the Toyota, he kneeled and put his hand out. There was a piece of yellow paper sticking out of the bottom of the driver's door.

Opening the door, Mac peeled off a yellow post-it note with black ballpoint writing on it. It looked like a code: 555M.

'Mean anything to you?' said Mac, passing it over.

Sammy made a face and did a search on his smart phone.

'It's a bus route in Chennai,' he said. 'And it's a golf club.'

Scotty jogged towards them as a green open-topped jeep entered the airfield beside the terminal and motored towards them.

'Air traffic says the log shows Phnom Penh airport,' said Scotty, panting.

'And then where?' said Sammy.

'That's all they have to log,' said Scotty, turning to see the approaching police jeep.

Sammy keyed his phone and walked away, talking into the device.

Captain Loan stepped out of the jeep with a wry smile, staring at Mac through Wayfarer sunnies. 'You following me, Mr Richard?'

'Nah, mate,' he said. 'Just enjoying the fresh air.'

The Cambodian cops searched the LandCruiser and Loan walked around it, stopping and nodding at the assault rifles leaning against the vehicle.

'Don't tell me – it's a Cambodian matter, right?' said Loan.

'Well . . .'

'I can see if the officers would like to take this up as a Cambodian matter.'

'I'd rather not.'

'We need to talk,' said Loan, not looking at Mac.

'Okay,' he said, as she led him by the arm away from the Land-Cruiser and the other men.

'I've given you lots of freedom, Mr Richard,' she said, a harder tone in her voice.

'Yeah, and I gave you an eyewitness account of Quirk's murder,' said Mac, tired and annoyed.

'I released Luc to you,' said Loan. 'I expected some cooperation in return – this *is* an Australian murder I'm investigating.'

'Fair enough,' said Mac, fishing in his pocket. 'Found this falling out the Toyota door as we pulled up.'

'Where's Dozsa?' said Loan, taking the post-it.

'In a North Air Friendship, flight plan says to Phnom Penh.'

Pulling out her phone, Loan issued an order in Vietnamese and signed off as she looked at the note.

'Singapore,' she said. 'Changi Airport.'

'What?' said Mac, grabbing the note from her.

'W-S-S-S is the code for Changi,' said Loan, turning the note the correct way up.

'Thanks,' said Mac, handing back the note.

'We need to talk,' said Loan.

'Give me a couple of hours,' said Mac.

'Make it one – and don't leave town,' she said, heading for the control tower.


They spoke about the post-it note as they shovelled down fish and rice at a Stung Treng restaurant that overlooked the river.

'Dozsa's dropping off something in Changi, or he's meeting someone,' said Mac. 'Either way, Singapore is all we have.'

'He leaves an entire US currency printing press up there in the hills, and fucks off to Singapore?' said Scotty, flushed with the heat. 'Why would he do that?'

'The currency was just one part of the plan with Pao Peng,' said Sammy. 'It may have been opportunistic and it will be very damaging if we can't plug all of it. But the HARPAC operation is the heart of it – Pao Peng needs a nationalistic cause to fire up the Chinese.'

'And what better than a fight with the Japs,' said Scotty.

'So it all comes back to these managed funds?' said Mac.

'But you knew that – that's how come Singapore, right?' said Sammy, drinking his beer and casing the room.

'How come Singapore what?' said Mac.

'Well, you started your involvement in all this through Singapore.'

'I started with Jim Quirk,' said Mac, looking to Scotty for guidance. 'In Saigon.'

'I'm sorry,' said Sammy, waving it away. 'Thought we were talking about something else.'

'What else?'

'You know – the whole Ray Hu thing,' said Sammy, checking for email on his phone.

Freezing mid-mouthful, Mac looked at Scotty and then back at

Sammy. Reaching over, he grabbed the phone out of Sammy's hand and flipped it over his shoulder.

'Hey,' said the American, as the device bounced on the boards behind him.

'Focus for a sec,' said Mac. 'Ray Hu?'

'Well, yeah. That's what you were doing at Ray's house, right?'

A vein bounced in Mac's left temple. 'You were there?'

'Calm down, tough guy,' said Sammy, leaning back. 'Ray was of interest to us and I had him under surveillance – I didn't whack him.'

'So?'

'So HARPAC was buying all these companies that make the transceiver components in routers – we thought it was aimed at the US, but it turned out the *Highland* Pacific fund was the one making inroads into the Milstar satellites. Harbour Pacific was different.'

'Go back two steps,' said Mac. 'Harbour Pacific?'

'Harbour Pacific is a Singapore-based fund,' said Sammy, like it was obvious. 'It was run by Ray Hu.'

The skin was being stretched over Mac's temples like a kettle drum. 'Ray?'

'Don't sound so amazed,' said Sammy. 'What page are you on?'

'You tell me,' said Mac.

'The big Chinese crime families are supporters of Pao Peng,' said Sammy, shrugging.

'So?' said Mac, completely lost.

'So, Ray was probably a proxy for Vincent Loh Han,' said Sammy as if speaking to a child. 'Ray Hu was the money man for the Loh Han Tong.'

Mac sat at a picnic table overlooking the Srepok, the tributary river that met the Mekong at Stung Treng. Irish and Scots backpackers lay around on a blanket getting hammered on beer in the midday heat while the fishermen and boat people cruised up and down the brown river, hiding from the sun under their conical hats.

The phone call with Jen had been quick and unhelpful: the river boat Mac had pulled Lance and Urquhart off had been found downriver, abandoned: no kids, no clues. Jen had hauled in from Jakarta the old FBI/AFP crew, which she was no longer part of. Those women would usually interact with the local cops to rescue the children, and Jen would go to war with some ambassador or police chief about how they were obstructing an investigation, and then the sniggers about the Dyke Squad would start again.

'Your friends come all this way to drink alcohol and be sick?' said the low voice.

Captain Loan walked past him and sat on the other side of the table. She was wearing a sun hat.

'Not my friends,' said Mac. 'When you're Irish, every day out of your country is a cause to celebrate.'

A roar of laughter and swearing went up as a man and a woman attempted to drag an unconscious bloke into the river. His pants were falling down and one of the women yelled, 'My God, John – but you're *huge*.'

Mac got straight to it. 'You wanted to talk?'

'Yes,' said Loan.

'I'll go first,' said Mac. 'How's Tranh?'

'He's good, Mr Richard,' said Loan. 'Got a shot hand.'

'I thought he was dead.'

'So did I,' said Loan. 'But he's okay – he asked after you.'

'He could have called,' said Mac, annoyed.

'He was staying uninvolved. It wasn't his idea.'

Loan opened a water bottle and sipped from it. She was nervous, as if wanting to say something but unable to bring herself to.

'Suppose you want to know what kind of books I sell?' said Mac.

Loan laughed. 'We are past that, I think. I am going to ask you an unconventional favour.'

'Yes?' said Mac.

'I have avoided my family business all my life – my father broke away before I was born and he wanted me to at least have the education so I could be a good citizen of the world.' She said it with no irony.

'You've achieved that, Captain.'

'But the intelligence arm of my organisation has brought some matters to my attention,' she said. 'To do with this Joel Dozsa and his associations with foreign generals.'

Mac stiffened. Was she trying to bring him in? Hand him over to Vietnamese intel? Casually glancing up and down the riverfront park, he looked for white vans and people reading tourist maps.

'I don't mean like that,' said Loan. 'It's not appropriate for me to become involved in this – I can't be a police officer and speak for my family.'

'I see. What can I do?'

'I would like you to speak to someone.'

'Someone?' said Mac.

'Someone who could resolve this Dozsa matter and perhaps help you stop larger political problems.'

As they stared at one another, Mac wondered who would break first. He wasn't about to offer a thing – this woman had stood off for two weeks, because it suited her. She still held enormous power over him.

Mac broke. 'Who is this someone?'

'My uncle,' she said, clearing her throat. 'Vincent Loh Han.'

'He asked you this?' said Mac, shocked.

'Yes, Mr Richard – he has a plane waiting at the airport.'


Screeching tyres woke Mac as they landed at Tan Son Nhat Airport in Saigon. The crisp air-conditioning of the Citation corporate jet gave way to waves of heat and humidity as he descended the stairs and was ushered by two heavies into a silver GMC Yukon.

Sitting in the back, Mac watched CNN on the in-car TV feed, mounted in the back of the seat in front. The headline news from the CNN Asia desk was the flurry of last-minute diplomatic and military talks between Japan and North Korea as the communist nation prepared to do its annual testing.

There were pictures of a Japanese admiral and a North Korean general sitting in armchairs beside one another; there were Asian guys in suits disappearing into ornate rooms; there were Asian men in suits thumping lecterns and pretending to pull out their own hair, which could mean only one thing: Japan's Diet.

Televised maps showed two routes for the ICBMs – missiles that left Earth's atmosphere and plunged down on a predetermined target at mach 10. One route flew over the Sea of Japan and then almost over Tokyo itself, dropping its booster rockets along the way before falling in the North Pacific. The other route flew south-east, over Okinawa, landing in the South Pacific. Either way, they flew over Japanese soil – although the Koreans would probably avoid Okinawa given the fact the US had a large military base on the island.

The tests were deliberate provocations of the Japanese, which the country was tearing itself apart over: ultranationalism was as alive in Japan as it was in China, and Japanese nationalists were waiting for their own excuse to drop the self-defence force and resurrect it into the most powerful military in the Western Pacific.

The report showed the Chinese and Americans trying to broker an agreement, but the Japanese and North Koreans weren't bending. The China–Japan–Korea argument was old and deep, and the onset of the Cold War had merely papered over a significant conflict that pulled together racial, political, economic and territorial claims in one festering boil.

An analyst from a Washington-based institute was interviewed by the anchor: he said one of the worst things that could happen in the Asian region was China and Japan being lured into a military dispute over Korea. The regional disruption, not to mention the economic damage, would hurt the entire Western Pacific, which relied on the super-economies of China, Japan and Korea.

After fifteen minutes of driving through Saturday crowds, the Yukon was ushered into a private space behind an enormous grand-stand. The heavies stood around the door, looking for threats, as Mac was beckoned out of the back seat.

A goon frisked him at a small entry door – even though he'd been thoroughly searched before getting on the plane – and then Mac and the bodyguards walked through a series of hallways, up several flights of stairs, and through a door. The roar of the crowds exploded into Mac's head and he blinked at the sudden blast of light. There were thousands of people around the brown circuit of the Phu Tho race track in western Saigon.

In the middle of the grandstand, roped off from the crowds, sat several people, spaced around a single man in a sand-coloured suit and sky-blue shirt.

Leading Mac into the enclosure, the heavies walked respectfully up to the man and waited for him to stop talking to an aide, who scribbled down the man's bets and then left with bricks of money.

The larger of the heavies leaned into the man's ear and the second heavy gestured for Mac to step forwards and take a seat. Sitting, Mac turned to the round-faced Asian man, who shooed away the heavies and called a waiter.

'Vincent Loh Han,' he said, all smiles and Singapore dental work.

'G'day,' said Mac, shaking hands.

'Would you like a drink, Richard?' said Loh Han in good English. 'Or should I call you Alan?'

# CHAPTER 63

Vincent Loh Han started with the history of the Saigon Racing Club and then explained why he attended the Magic Millions sales on the Gold Coast each year.

'There's only one legal horse-racing track in Vietnam,' said the gangster. 'So the Asian trainer don't concentrate on Saigon – we get the tired or the spelled horse from Thailand, Malaysia, Hong Kong. They either building up, or they on the way down.'

'They look okay to me.'

'Now they look okay, Mr McQueen,' said Loh Han, taking the gin and tonic that was delivered to him, 'because I went to Magic Million for many year buying the good bloodstock and the fast yearling.'

'Expensive hobby,' said Mac, taking his beer from the waiter.

'Yes, and popular,' said Loh Han. 'Vietnamese people love the Aussie horse – maybe not the long bone of Europe and North America, but the big heart.'

'I know people who go to the sales, Mr Loh Han, and they say that it doesn't matter how much you spend, there's no certainties in this sport,' said Mac.

'Ha.' Loh Han shook a playful finger at Mac. 'That the Aussie wisdom – I like that.'

The race finished and while Loh Han's horse came fourth, he had a win on his betting. The aide took fresh orders for the next race and Loh Han doled out cash from a black leather overnight bag.

'Chanthe is one of the favourite people in my whole family,' said Loh Han, as the aide departed. 'She is very honest and well meaning – and I don't have a daughter of my own.'

'Sure,' said Mac, sipping the beer.

'Beautiful and intelligent too,' said Loh Han. 'And as we know, such women can be very insecure, easily exploited by certain men.'

'I guess so,' said Mac, careful.

'I want you to know that Chanthe likes you perhaps more than professionally.'

'Look, I –' said Mac, a little stunned.

Loh Han raised his hand. 'I also know that you have not pressed your advantage in that regard, and that makes you a gentleman.'

'It makes me married, Mr Loh Han,' said Mac. 'It's not as if I haven't seen what she looks like.'

'Ha,' said the gangster. 'Good answer.'

As the fifth race was loading into the starting barrier, Loh Han stopped the small talk, and drew closer to Mac.

'I have embarrassed myself, Mr McQueen,' said Loh Han, lighting a short cigar. 'I allied myself with some people who could now destroy my country, bring war to this region.'

'The general?'

'Pao Peng, yes,' said Loh Han. 'This started because I helped the general acquire certain technologies that would help his ambitions. My family has long ties with his and I allowed myself to help.'

'You started managed funds that bought the assets?'

'Yes,' said Loh Han. 'These are technologies open to sale and purchase on the world markets and I did not see a crime – I had some discussions with my chief money adviser and he set up the fund, started buying selected technology companies.'

'Ray Hu?'

'Correct,' said Loh Han. 'The general felt that if the fund was managed by a man famous for buying defence-related stocks and companies, then we would attract less attention from the various governments.'

'And he's an Australian fund manager, operating from Singapore?' said Mac. 'The Americans and British would ask the Aussies to do the audit?'

'I believe that was the idea,' said Loh Han. 'Ray and I were very close – I spoke with him about many things, not just money. I shall miss his wisdom and humour.'

'So will I,' said Mac.

'You knew Ray well?'

'When I see something funny, I think of Ray laughing,' said Mac, remembering how Ray would get drunk and hold forth on what an idiot some politician was, his cruel imitations reducing people to tears.

'When I see a problem, I see Ray being three moves ahead already,' said Loh Han. 'I see how easily he beat me at chess – I'm his fool's mate.'

'Fool's mate?' said Mac.

'Yes,' said Loh Han. 'It's a chess strategy that creates checkmate in four moves. It's what Ray would say if he was about to beat another bidder to a parcel of shares or make a takeover offer that he knew the directors couldn't block.'

'So, Ray was running this fund?'

'Yes – I make money, the general is happy and Ray is making more money than ever.'

'So what happened?'

'I am introduced to a Jew who I do not like,' said Loh Han, looking at his cigar. 'He has charm and intellect, Mr McQueen, but it is corrupted charm. You know this type of man?'

'I know Joel Dozsa,' said Mac. 'And he's all that.'

'Well, the general says Dozsa has an idea that will allow me to print real American currency – and that gets my attention because he can get all the codes from the US printing service, the . . .'

'The BEP,' said Mac.

'Yes, that. And because I owe Pao Peng for getting the contract to supply new toilet bowls to the PLA's barracks renovations, I go along with the counterfeit idea – we help with logistic and freight, and we provide premises and other things.'

'An office at the Mekong Saloon?'

'Yes, and an airline and –'

'Airline? Is North Air a Loh Han business?'

'Controlling interest,' said Loh Han.

Mac's heart sank. Loh Han pilots probably didn't log genuine flight plans.

The gangster watched the horses jump from the barrier. 'So, this Dozsa starts to change things.'

'Yeah?'

'I have lunch one day with Ray – at this restaurant right here,' he said, pointing over Mac's shoulder at the VIP suites at the back of the grandstand. 'And Ray ask me what the new fund is really for.'

'Harbour Pacific?'

'Yes – and I know nothing about a new fund; it was supposed to be Highland Pacific. So after I argue with the general about Harbour Pacific, it seem Dozsa has overstepped and just forget to tell me about this fund; he thought the general had told me.'

'Okay,' said Mac, smiling.

'Yes. So three weeks ago, I find out that Dozsa has not helped me print some real US dollars for my own amusement – he has built a factory in the forest and is printing the US currency by the billion.'

'That annoy you?'

'Yes, Mr McQueen, it annoyed me,' said Loh Han, finishing his drink. 'I am a businessman. Most of my income is from my banking and lending interests. We have assets in freight, shipping and trucks; we own hotels and we rent more motor scooters to tourists in South-East Asia than any other company.'

'So?'

'So a man printing US notes by the billions is not trying to get rich – he is trying to collapse a currency and, with it, the economy,' said Loh Han. 'People are rude about me because they say I the gangster, right?'

'Sure,' said Mac.

'But I do not want the US currency to collapse in Asia,' said Loh Han, eyes wide. 'That the exchange currency for business – that's our benchmark currency! Why I want to ruin that currency?'

'You don't, I suppose.'

'No. So when I hear that an Aussie spy is coming to Saigon to follow the corrupt Australian, I try to get Tranh to be the driver, right?'

'You did – he's a good man.'

'A good kid,' said Loh Han. 'But he reporting back and I realise you not following Geraldine McHugh, the currency traitor. You following her husband, Jim Quirk.'

'Surprised?'

'Sure,' said Loh Han. 'I ask why. I dig deeper, I follow you and then I follow the Americans.'

'And?'

'And the Americans are following you and their phone calls are talking about HARPAC, and I think this can't be Harbour Pacific, can it? This can't be my fund that I didn't even start?'

'Shit,' said Mac, breath hissing out of him. If the various arms of Aussie intel had worked together – and the Prime Minister's office wasn't so keen to outsmart the spooks – Mac would have known about the Harbour Pacific problems a month ago. He wouldn't have put Ray in that position with Lao at the Pan Pac Hotel.

'So, what happened?' said Mac.

'I made one of the great mistakes of my life,' said Loh Han. 'I rang Ray, said I wanted to come down and go through the Harbour Pacific books, to see what we were really buying. My private jet was being used by my accountants in Honolulu, so I flew Singapore Airlines and stayed with Ray and Liesl.'

Loh Han paused as the aide returned with a heavy chunk of cash in a canvas bank bag. Loh Han took the bag, issued orders for more bets and handed out a wad of cash. Mac laughed to himself: Loh Han kept every bag of winnings along with the betting chit – he probably checked his payouts later to ensure his own people weren't stealing.

'We went through the asset manifests, Mr McQueen, and we made a lot of calls. Ray talks to many people in defence technology so he was calling his friends in the Netherlands, Germany, United States and Japan. And it all added up to one thing.'

'Yes?'

'Harbour Pacific had the asset that allow us to control the launch of North Korean ballistic missile system,' said Loh Han. 'The last piece was a micro-transceiver that sits between the general staff's key and mission controller – only when both are accessed at the same time can the missile be launched and controlled. Harbour Pacific owned the British firm that make the silicon-copper switch for this safety device – we had total control. It didn't make me feel powerful, Mr McQueen, it made me feel sick.'

'What about the vetting?'

'An agent of the Australian Tax Office had visited two weeks earlier, demanding to audit Harbour Pacific because Ray was the Australian citizen.'

'Who was the tax guy?' said Mac.

'Ray assumed he was spy from Aussie intelligence,' said the gangster. 'I took the tape from Ray's office and showed it to my friends.'

'And?'

'The auditor was James Quirk – recruited by ASIO while still a student, then joined trade department of your diplomatic corps, and from time to time was asked to vet sensitive purchases in South-East Asia. When I see his photo in the paper, matters became clear.'

'What did Ray want to do?' said Mac.

'He wiped the asset manifests and all technical specs from his fund hard drives. He said it couldn't be used by someone like Pao Peng.'

'Wiped it? Completely?'

'No, he kept a secret copy for us,' said Loh Han. 'And he said the Aussie intel copy from the vetting was safe in Canberra and would never be accessed by Dozsa or Pao Peng.'

Mac's guts churned: he now knew what he'd been witnessing that night when Dozsa demanded Quirk work on that terminal. And he knew why the SD card was so valuable. Quirk had accessed his audit hard drives in Canberra and downloaded Harbour Pacific's assets and technical specs to the chip. The whole lot was sitting in Mac's pocket for two days, and he'd had no idea what he was carrying.

Loh Han continued. 'Ray said we'd sit on the secret file because the next day he was meeting someone who would know what to do.'

'At the Pan Pac?' said Mac, wincing.

'Yes,' said Loh Han. 'That was you?'

'Shit,' said Mac, rubbing his temples. 'That's all he said?'

'He was confident you'd resolve everything – called it fool's mate.'

Looking out at the race track, Mac fought reflux. He was confused and tired, and his leg would need more painkillers in the next half-hour. Mac had been Ray's solution but Mac had been in the dark. He blamed himself for leaving the Firm for two years and falling behind on the kinds of things he should have known about. He blamed himself for not being more paranoid about those SingTel technicians when he first saw them outside the Pan Pacific Hotel that afternoon.

'I have a proposition, Mr McQueen,' said Loh Han. 'I help you shut down this missile madness.'

'And?'

'And you give me the person who killed my old friend.'

Mac sensed a trick. Loh Han knew Mac would not want to give up Dozsa, not before ASIS had its chance at a long debrief. The gangster was luring him into a lie.

'I can tell you the name, but I can't let you have him,' said Mac, trying to avoid the man's eyes.

'The name,' said Loh Han. 'You were there, Mr McQueen – you know who did this. I need that name.'

'Joel Dozsa,' said Mac.

Loh Han's eyes flashed wide before narrowing again. 'Him!'

'I found out yesterday,' said Mac. 'He also whacked Jim Quirk, at your club in Cholon.'

'What have I done?' said Loh Han, easing back in his seat and lifting his field-glasses as the jockeys took their mounts for a warm-up down the back straight.

'If the situation allows it, you can have him,' said Mac, standing. 'But I need something from you.'

'Haven't I just given you what you want?'

'No,' said Mac. 'You've given yourself a way out of your predicament while staying sweet with a powerful general in the PLA.'

'Ha,' said Loh Han. 'You're a smart man – you need a job? I put you in charge of my hotels, see if you can stop the managers robbing me.'

'I need to know the whereabouts of a shipload of kids last seen on the Mekong south of Kratie.'

'That's a big river.'

'Registration K 4217,' said Mac, gesturing to an aide and getting a pad and pen. 'This was last night.'

'Why would I know about a shipload of children?' said Loh Han, slow and icy.

'Because the vessel was crawling with PLA cadres from the counterfeiting factory,' said Mac, writing Jenny's phone number on the pad. 'They were Dozsa's people. This number is for Agent Toohey, Australian Federal Police – just call anonymously and give her the location, and don't get into an argument with her.'

Loh Han took the paper and crooked a finger at a minder who'd been sitting at the gangster's right. He whispered something to the minder, then watched him leave before turning back to Mac.

'So we're square,' said Loh Han. 'Those two men who flew you here? They're yours for now, Mr McQueen. Leave the Jew to me.'

# CHAPTER 64

Buckling himself into the forward-facing seat in the jet, Mac ran through his list. He'd have Scotty and Sammy waiting for him at Stung Treng, but then what? Where was the Harbour Pacific file kept by Ray? And where was Dozsa?

The engines revved and Jon – the senior minder – went to lift the stairs inside.

Looking up, Mac saw an argument at the hatch and Jon waving. Finally, Jon dropped the stairs and an athletic Vietnamese man bounced into the cabin and took a seat facing Mac.

'Hello, Mr Richard,' said Tranh, smiling despite the heavy bandage on his left hand.

Mac smiled too. 'Well, it's Harry Houdini.'

Jon came over. 'He can't come with us, Mr Richard,' said the minder, a heavily built man who looked like a young version of Bongo.

'Why not?' said Mac.

'Because the boss don't want him being shot no more,' said Jon.

'I'm the boss now,' said Mac.

Jon and Mac stared at one another until the Vietnamese broke.

'Sure, boss,' he said, pulling up the stairs and securing the hatch.

The flight time to Stung Treng was a shade over twenty minutes but it gave Mac a chance to talk with Tranh, who said he'd been ordered to stand down by his uncle after the shootout in Saigon, but he'd kept one step ahead of Vincent's heavies so he could go to Phnom Penh with Mac.

'You defied your uncle?' said Mac.

'I was ashamed,' said Tranh. 'This Dozsa is behaving this way, and working for my family? I wanted to help you.'

'Why'd you steal that memory card from me, Tranh?' said Mac, wanting to trust him again but not so sure.

'I saw the way Lance looked at it in the van,' said Tranh. 'Then, when I take him for a drink, he went to the lavatory and he taking some time. I go into the lavatory to make sure he okay, and I hear him in the booth, talking into a phone.'

'Yeah?' said Mac, laughing.

'Yep – and he telling someone that the memory card's in the pocket of your backpack and he'll grab it when he gets away from me.'

Mac remembered why he liked this bloke.

'So when Lance come out I have a new bourbon and Coke for him, and then I say I have to buy more credit for my phone and for him to stay there.'

'And you go back to the hotel and grab the SD card before Lance can get it?'

'Yes, and hide it in my phone. Then all the hell is breaking loose and I forget to tell you. Then I am shot and I lose my phone, which is where –'

'You hid the chip,' said Mac. 'Where did you go after we were ambushed at the apartment building?'

'I run through the smash window, my hand shot, and I am caught by Jon,' said Tranh, pointing. 'So I am back to Saigon and in hiding and told to forget it, but I cannot forget it.'

'Jon?' said Mac, getting the heavy's attention. 'Luc still working for the boss?'

'Sure,' said Jon.

'Can we get Luc and find out exactly where he's flying today?'

Jon moved to the back of the cramped cabin where a Harris radio was mounted on the toilet bulkhead.

'So,' said Mac, 'you were shot by the Americans?'

'They were Chinese,' said Tranh. 'They shot me.'

'Was it an accident?'

'They shot the lady and when I run away they don't shoot no more.'

'Mr Richard?' said Jon. 'Luc's heading for Singapore.'

'Okay.'

'And he say not to call back no more.'

'He can't talk?'

'He sound scared,' said Jon.

'I bet he did,' said Mac, holding out his hand for Jon's satellite phone. 'How do I call Australia on this thing?'

The heat and dust invaded the Citation's cool atmosphere like a bad smell as Scotty and Sammy clambered into the jet on the tarmac at Stung Treng airport shortly after six pm.

'Just had a call from Urquhart,' said Scotty. 'Wants to know where you are – says he has the PM's authority.'

'Does he?'

'Not until Tobin tells me so,' said Scotty. 'Just warning you that the wheels are turning in Canberra.'

'So where are we going?' said Sammy.

'You'll see when we get there,' said Mac, still not trusting the American. 'In the meantime, I believe you'd like to apologise to my friend Tranh.'

Moving to the rear of the aircraft, Mac asked Scotty to join him.

'What's the kid doing here?' said Scotty, inclining his head at Tranh as the jet roared to life and sped down the runway.

'He's Vincent Loh Han's nephew, and he's with us.'

Scotty frowned. 'So what's the plan?'

'Dozsa's about to land in Singapore,' said Mac. 'I think he'll head for Ray's house.'

'Not Ray's business?'

'No, Dozsa knows that Ray wiped the missile details from the official fund records. So he's looking for the one copy made by Ray and he probably thinks it's in his house.'

'We sure there's only one file besides the one Sandy Beech is travelling with?'

'The only other one is on an ASIO hard drive, from Quirk's audits.'

Scotty checked for eavesdroppers. 'This is embarrassing. You're saying we send a bloke to audit the buy-up of technology used in the North Korean missiles, and our guy just downloads a copy for an ex-Mossad psycho?'

'Under duress,' said Mac. 'This was a Canberra power couple, and Quirk was doing what he had to do to keep his wife out of prison. Here she is in this sting with the US Treasury, and suddenly Joel Dozsa's back in her life.'

'By the way,' said Scotty, 'I found a business centre at the airport and did some research on the computer Quirk was using.'

'Yeah?'

'It was bugging me, the way you described it.'

Scotty pulled a piece of paper folded into four squares from his pocket and handed it to Mac. Unfolding it, Mac saw a colour photograph of the same cream-coloured computer terminal that Jim Quirk died at in the Mekong Saloon.

'Where'd you get this?' said Mac. 'This is it – see how the keyboard is built into the monitor and the hard drive?'

'It's the new TS series of desktops that ASIO had designed for the Australian government.'

A series of companies owned by Chinese intelligence had been buying the firms that made military-grade firewalls and anti-intrusion software. Realising that if the Chinese could control enough routers and firewalls they'd be inside the government's systems, ASIO's protective security people – T4 – commissioned a series of PCs for the Australian government. They were noteworthy because they couldn't be networked and couldn't be 'queried' by incoming or unsolicited pings from cyberspace. They were also 'paired' with designated routers built by the PC manufacturers. The designated routers would only respond to one of the numbered PCs.

'I remember,' said Mac. 'So what was the terminal doing in a nightclub in Saigon?'

'I had a chat to my guy, and it was probably stolen from the Jakarta intelligence section,' said Scotty. 'They're doing that big shift

411

to the new embassy – apparently there's a report in the techie circles that they were short of one Top Secret PC after the move.'

'There's something else, mate,' said Mac, keeping his voice low beneath the hiss of engines as the ascent continued. 'And I don't want you to get upset – we just have to think through some of the events.'

'Okay,' said Scotty.

'Ray Hu and Vincent Loh Han are sitting in Ray's study, making their calls and working out what this HARPAC fund is all about. Ray makes one copy – probably on a USB key or SD – and then uses his override passwords to wipe the information from the Harbour Pacific hard drives.'

Scotty nodded.

'Then, when Loh Han goes off to bed, Ray hides his download and the next day he goes to the Pan Pac, to do a gig with me.'

Scotty's eyes widened. 'So how did Dozsa know to whack Ray? How did he know the deal was blown?'

'That's what I was thinking,' said Mac. 'Ray's house and office were swept by our contractors every week – he wasn't bugged.'

'Well, shit,' said Scotty. 'There were only two people –'

'Three,' said Mac.

'Ray, Loh Han . . .' said Scotty, numbering them on his fingers.

'And Liesl,' said Mac.

Scotty gave Mac the death stare. 'No way.'

'Who else?'

'Liesl?!'

'I'm just trying to work it through.'

'Why would a girl who had everything be spying on her own husband?'

'So where else did Dozsa get the information?'

Scotty looked away. 'Don't do this, Macca.'

'Ray closes down the missile file and the next day he's executed. Ray and Loh Han had no interest in telling anyone.'

'So what was Liesl Hu's interest?'

'Look, I know she's popular – we all love Liesl – but I don't see another link.'

'Well, maybe we should be thinking about something a bit simpler,' said Scotty.

'Like?'

'Like where's Liesl right now? And where's Dozsa? And where's Ray's download?'


A black Escalade was waiting on the apron as the Citation pulled into its port at Singapore's Seletar Airport. Night had fallen and Scotty arranged customs clearance.

'Drop me here,' said Sammy, as they drove past the Epiphany Church and made to hit the Tampines Expressway.

'You sure?' said Mac.

'Check-in time,' said Sammy, getting out of the SUV. 'You know how it is.'

'Is he cool?' said Scotty, lighting a smoke and dropping his window as they accelerated away.

'I have no idea,' said Mac.

Turning right off Central into Holland Road twenty minutes later, Mac readied his SIG between his legs, stripping it and cleaning out the Mekong dirt before rebuilding it and checking for load and safety. The worst water damage to an automatic handgun was usually the loads and Mac had used a new clip and cartridges.

Mac could hear Tranh and Scotty in the back seat readying their weapons as they swung into Ray's street, sweet frangipani drifting on the evening breeze.

'Just here, thanks, Jon,' said Mac, selecting a park that had a sight line to Ray Hu's driveway while also sitting in the darkness of a large banyan.

Breathing out and in, Mac turned to Scotty. 'Ready for this?'

'Let's make it fast,' said Scotty.

Digging a radio set out of the gear bag, Mac gave the base handset to Tranh and plugged the other one into his ear, where it dangled, creating a mouthpiece.

Mac pushed the gun into his waistband. 'If we're not out in thirty minutes, come in – number sixty.'

Walking to the gate, Mac felt grimy. He hadn't showered since his dip in the river and he had stubble growing on his jaw. Moving carefully down the drive he kept an eye out for traps and unwanted interlopers.

'She's gone,' came a voice from through the trees, and Scotty cowered to a crouch.

'Sorry,' said the voice. 'It's just me – over here.'

Taking his hand away from the small of his back, Mac followed the voice and saw the outline of a man through the hedge that divided the Hus' house from the retired vice-admiral's.

Mac peered into the darkness. 'Who's gone?'

'Liesl. I'm feeding her dog.'

'I'm just here to pick up some things.'

'They've already been, twenty minutes ago,' said the neighbour. 'Said they came for Liesl's things.'

Mac tensed. 'Did they take anything?'

'No.'

'Well, that's why we're here,' said Mac, his face hurting as he smiled. 'You know how women are.'

Waving Mac away, the neighbour returned to his house.

'Shit,' said Mac, as they got to the front door. 'Is he still looking?'

'He's in the kitchen, having a stickybeak,' said Scotty as Mac jiggled at the lock with a bump key.

The lock popped on the second go and Mac let it swing inwards.

'Well, Christ,' said Scotty. 'Someone *was* here.'

# CHAPTER 65

The house was a wreck. Chairs dismantled, sofas slashed, ceilings pulled down and drawers scattered on the ground. They walked amid the rubble, checking on the dismantled electrical goods, the plasterboard pulled back from around light switches and the skirting boards torn off walls.

The computer in the study had been stripped down, the hard drives were missing and the phone had been smashed: a sign that the vandals had listened to the voicemails and not wanted anyone else to.

Scotty sighed. 'Looks professional. Let's call the cops.'

Scotty phoned the AFP's Singapore office as Mac wandered back to the living room. Among the cushion stuffing and smashed vases lay a large slab of marble and wood that Mac and Ray had sat at many times. Ray had called it his 'Dominican' chess board because he claimed it had been used in a Spanish Dominican monastery some time in the fourteenth century. Mac had said he wasn't sure Dominican monks were allowed to play any games, and Ray had argued that the Dominicans – the founders of universities and the champions of deductive reasoning – didn't see chess as a game, but as an intellectual exercise.

Ray thought it hardly mattered because he'd been offered more than a million US dollars for the set and he was happy to let it sit on display because thieves would always take the DVD player and stereo, and leave the Dominican chess set. It was his insurance, he said: his *hidden* insurance.

Staring at it, Mac wondered.

'Scotty, gimme a hand?' he said, kneeling beside the monstrous thing which had been knocked off its heavy wooden base, crushing everything under it.

Straining under its weight, it took them three goes and some backyard engineering to get the square board section onto its base.

Panting, Mac knelt again and looked around its edges as Scotty collapsed against the sofa, exhausted.

'What's that?' he gasped. 'Hundred kilos? Hundred and ten?'

'This is how Ray used to make a fool of me,' said Mac, looking along the sides of the leviathan chess board. 'He called it his hidden insurance because he was sure no thief would know its worth.'

Running his fingers along the wooden casement, Mac couldn't find anything. He tried the other side; still nothing. Putting his hand on the corner, he pushed to stand up and something moved. Looking back, Mac knelt again and wrapped his fingers under the wooden frame – there was a small trigger. As he pulled it, the casement clicked and something released. Doing the same on the other side Mac played with the two corners until the entire underside of the board was detached from the marble. Pulling it as if sliding out a drawer, Mac looked down at the contents. Papers, a Beretta 9mm pistol and a USB key.

Picking up the key, Mac examined it: the word HARPAC was written along the white insert on the black plastic handle.

'What is it?' said Scotty, sucking on his smoke.

'Insurance,' said Mac. 'Hidden insurance.'


Walking back to the car, Scotty shuffled the papers as Mac thought aloud.

'I think we should get into Loh Han's plane and get to Canberra; what do you say, boss?'

'I think you should look at these,' said Scotty as they approached the Escalade.

'What are they?' said Mac.

'Details of Ray's safe house,' said Scotty. 'It's all there.'

Mac looked at the documents as he took his seat. The safe house was owned and serviced by company fronts. Ray had given himself a place to hide out, but would he have told Liesl and would she be hiding there?

Scotty gave Jon the address and they moved away, the USB key burning in Mac's pocket. He wanted to be in Australia, have this thing wrapped up.

It was past nine o'clock when they drove up to the intersection with the Asian Golf Academy and stopped for traffic.

'Left,' said Scotty, winding down his window for a smoke.

Something flew through the air. Tranh noticed it first and then Jon shouted before flopping against his window, hands over his face. A yellowish smoke gushed from the floor in thick clouds, and Mac coughed. A gas mask was looking in the window as he passed out on Scotty's back.


The sound of car horns woke Mac.

Lifting his head from a big wet patch on Scotty's shirt, he was stunned by the severity of his headache and the amount of fluid dripping out of him. Gingerly, he straightened to an upright position. In the front seat, Jon pushed his door open and vomited.

The car horn sounded again, buzzing around Mac's head like a wasp. Opening the door he lost his balance, falling to the tarmac.

'Get off the goddamned road, you drunk,' came the American voice from the car behind. More horns sounded behind the American's car and a cop siren wailed.

Staggering around the Escalade, Mac just made it to the grass verge, where he fell to his knees and surrendered to vomiting of a type he hadn't experienced since he first tried gin as a teenager. Jon lay on his back with his forearm across his eyes and then Scotty burst into the open, collapsing to the grass as he retched.

As the four of them recovered, Mac patted his pockets out of hope more than anything. Empty. The USB key, and access to the North Korean missile launch, was gone.

Looking in Scotty's window, he saw two dark yellow canisters, each the size of a soup tin. He already knew what they were, but in case he was confused the black lettering on the aerosols said *Fentanyl* – a psychoactive agent that messed with the brain's function. An overuse of Fentanyl canisters had killed scores of hostages during the cinema standoff with Chechnyan terrorists in Moscow.

Holding on to the vehicle for balance, Mac gulped at a water bottle as the Singapore police pulled up.


The safe house was a large bungalow, with a frontage to the road and its backyard facing the Island Golf Course. They drove fifty metres past it and parked.

There were three of them now, with Scotty having volunteered the car, the guns and even the Fentanyl canisters as being his. The cops took Scotty, leaving the other three with the Escalade.

'Circle round the back,' said Mac to Jon. 'Through the golf club. Give us three minutes exactly.'

They synchronised their G-Shocks and Mac and Tranh checked their guns and stowed them under their shirts as they made the walk down Island Club Road.

Turning left, Mac walked straight up the well-lit driveway which contained two cars – a Toyota Corolla and Nissan Maxima from Hertz – and walked up the stairs to the front door.

Light flashed through the gap in the curtains at the living room window and Mac kicked the door off its locks, storming in with the SIG held cup-and-saucer.

Turning left into the living room, Mac swept the area and saw a middle-aged man and woman sitting on the couch in front of the TV, and two women in their thirties at the dining table.

They stared at him and Mac froze momentarily: he was looking at Liesl Hu, which was expected. Sitting across the table from her was Geraldine McHugh.

'Liesl,' said Mac.

'McQueen,' came the Filipino monotone. 'Drop it.'

Dropping the SIG as he felt steel behind his ear, Mac turned and faced Bongo Morales.

Tranh, too, had dropped his weapon and turned, allowing Didge to cuff him with the plastic wrist-ties.

'What's up, McQueen?' said Bongo, pointing the shotgun between his eyes.

'Came to talk to Liesl,' said Mac. 'Making sure she's okay after seeing her house.'

'What happened?' said Liesl, standing and coming to Mac.

'Keep away, please,' said Bongo. 'You don't know him like I know him.'

'The place is trashed, Liesl,' said Mac. 'I knew this was Ray's safe house, so I thought you might be here.'

'It's been a nightmare, Macca,' said Liesl. Her light brown hair had grown lank where usually it was styled every day. 'I called Jen,' she said, tears forming. 'She didn't come.'

'I did, about ten days ago,' said Mac. 'No one was at the house. Benny turned up too – the place was deserted.'

She fell into his arms, the tears pooling in the fabric on his right shoulder. 'Ray,' she said, sobbing. 'They killed Ray.'

'I know,' said Mac.

'They killed him.'

Pushing her back slightly, he looked at Bongo. 'Can we talk?'

Bongo led them into the kitchen and Mac opened the window.

'Jon, come in – no guns, okay, mate?' Mac yelled across the backyard.

Jon came in from the darkness and up to the back door, where Bongo took his handgun and pointed him to Didge.

Mac leaned against the counter. 'Liesl, I have to ask some questions.'

She looked at Mac. 'So, you don't sell books?'

'I work for the government.'

She looked at her hands. 'What do you want to know, Macca?'

'I'm trying to find something,' said Mac. 'Ray tried to hide it, stop it from falling into the wrong hands, but he failed. I need some answers.'

'I'll try.'

'Do you know a man called Joel Dozsa?'

'No, but Ray said his name, and spoke with him on the phone. And I've heard Geraldine mention him in the past couple of days.'

'So you know Geraldine McHugh?'

'Yes,' she said. 'We were at ANU together.'

'Why is she here?'

'She rang me, said she was on the run from Aussie intel and could she hide out with me?'

'Those her parents?'

Liesl nodded.

'So you never met Dozsa?'

'No, but I saw him at Ray's offices once – tanned and bald. Very muscular Jewish man.'

Bongo blinked long – sign language for *I'll tell you later.*

'Liesl, this is important: the night that Vincent Loh Han came to your house, do you remember what Ray said he'd do with a certain manifest of information that one of his funds owned?'

'He told Vincent he'd wipe the whole file – no one would be able to use it.'

'And?'

'And . . . he said he would keep one copy of the file for him and Vincent, but he'd hide it.'

'What did Mr Loh Han say about it?'

'He said, *Good riddance to it – let's hope the Jew drops the whole subject.*'

'Did you tell Dozsa about this conversation?'

'No, Macca,' she said, eyes growing big like a child's.

'You tell one of Dozsa's associates?'

Her voice raised an octave. 'No, I didn't.'

'Who did you tell, Liesl?'

Liesl tried to project dignity. 'I told Dennis.'

Mac looked at Bongo and mouthed the word 'Dennis?!'

'Don't laugh at me, Macca,' said Liesl, tears forming again. 'He was from Aussie intelligence, and I was helping Ray – Ray was out of his depth.'

'Dennis?' said Mac. 'You get a business card?'

'I said don't laugh at me,' said Liesl. 'I was doing my bit.'

Liesl collapsed in tears again, and Bongo grabbed Mac by the arm.

'Let's go see Dennis,' said Bongo.

# CHAPTER 66

At the bottom of the stairs, Mac found himself in an airy basement with a fridge and several sets of skis, removal boxes and a Laser-class sailboat on a trailer.

Flexi-cuffed to the plumbing was a dark-haired Anglo called Dennis, although Mac knew him better as Lance Kendrick.

'Oh, shit,' said Lance.

'Nice place you got here, Lance.'

'It isn't what it looks like, McQueen,' said Lance. 'I swear.'

'What does it look like?' said Mac, opening the fridge and grabbing three bottles of water.

Handing them out, he pulled a dusty deckchair close to Lance and sat down, slurping the water.

Lance stammered slightly. 'I mean, I thought Liesl might be hiding here, so I flew down.'

'Greeted by Bongo and Didge — that must have been nice.'

'Yeah,' he said, indicating the flexi-cuffs.

'You got off that ship, and came directly to where Geraldine McHugh was being kept?'

'I didn't know McHugh would be here,' said Lance. 'I didn't know they knew one another.'

'But you know Liesl?'

'Yes,' said Lance.

'You know what happened to me twenty minutes ago?'

Lance shrugged.

'Joel Dozsa threw a couple of Fentanyl canisters into our car, stole the secret copy of the Harbour Pacific files. Right out of my pocket, while I was vomiting.'

'You had those files?' said Lance. 'Shit – how?'

'What's important is what happens now, Lance. I have to find Dozsa before he uses that information. The Koreans start their missile tests tomorrow morning, usually at about four-thirty.'

'So?'

'So,' said Mac, looking at his G-Shock, 'it's almost eleven at night – that gives us about five hours to grab that file.'

Lance looked at the floor. 'How can I help?'

'What information were you passing to Dozsa?'

'Dozsa?!' said Lance. 'You've gone mad.'

'You were the only leak, Lance,' said Mac. 'I have to find this guy.'

'Listen, McQueen, the operation I conducted with Liesl Hu was authorised and it came from so high up that you'd get a nosebleed just thinking about it.'

'So you debriefed after Ray's execution at the Pan Pac?'

'No.'

'You wrote a report?'

'No, McQueen.'

'You sent an explanatory memo by email to your controller and it's lodged in the system with a time stamp that says you wrote it at least twelve hours after Ray died?'

'No, I don't need –'

'Hear that, Bongo?'

'I heard it, brother,' said Bongo, lighting a cigarette.

'You see, Lance, there is one commandment that all spooks live by in all countries and all regimes,' said Mac. 'And it is this: he who partakes in an operation which results in the death of one of his own guys must immediately explain himself to his fellow spooks. Right, Bongo?'

'Written in blood, my brother.'

'See, Lance, you ran an agent against Ray Hu and, as a result of that operation, Ray was executed. The fact that you haven't debriefed is very fishy. It's the kind of thing that other spies get nervous about.'

'Look —'

'No, Lance, I'm sick of looking,' said Mac, raising his voice. 'I want to listen — so start talking.'

'I was part of an ASIO technology outfit called T4,' said Lance, not meeting Mac's eyes. 'It was basically technology intelligence, of the type the Israelis and Chinese have been so good at.'

'Successful?' said Mac.

'Sure,' said Lance. 'Smoked out some South Koreans in Perth and found an Aussie aerospace engineer selling second-stage rocket booster specs to the Chinese.'

Mac slugged at the water, his brain still fried by the Fentanyl.

'But the DG felt it wasn't worth our little group continuing if we couldn't work offshore,' said Lance.

'So?'

'So the idea was picked up by the PM's office, it was authorised by the attorney-general's, overseen by the PM's chief of staff.'

Mac kept the pressure on. 'And your controller?'

'Isn't it obvious?'

'What was the Liesl op?'

'Get her worried about Ray, worried about who he was dealing with and how much trouble he was in — we were concerned about the Harbour Pacific purchasing and the spooks in Defence and the Firm didn't want to know about it. It was all too geeky.'

'So you get Liesl talking about Ray's conversations, especially with Dozsa and Loh Han?'

'Yes.'

'And what happened when Ray decided to wipe the Harbour Pacific file?'

'Liesl called me the next morning, early, before eight.'

'She panicked?'

'She was scared — she wanted to meet here. We met at half past eight, she told me what she'd heard and I thanked her.'

'Yes?'

'I went back to the hotel and wrote a short report, sent it by secure email to my controller, and then a few hours later the news started breaking about the shooting at the Pan Pac and I got very scared – so did Liesl. I was advised to go to ground but she felt abandoned and I don't blame her.'

'Then?'

'Then, about a week later, I was told to meet my controller in Saigon. Another piece of the Harbour Pacific puzzle – Jim Quirk – had been executed up there, and my controller thought the best way forwards was to piggyback a ride with an experienced field guy who was already in-country and on to Jim Quirk.'

Mac could hear Bongo laughing.

'How was the piggyback, Lance?'

'Scary.'

Mac believed the guy. But there was a leak nonetheless. 'Okay, mate. I'll leave it there. But do yourself a favour – next time you go into the field, and an experienced operator tells you to dress down, just do it.'

'I still don't see why.'

'Because the idea is to blend in. The earrings just broadcast to the world –'

Pausing, Mac eyed Lance as he thought about what he'd just said. 'Mate, how long have you had that earring?'

'Bought it two months ago.'

'In Singers?'

'Yes,' said Lance.

Walking forwards, Mac pulled it out of Lance's ear, twirled it between his thumb and index finger. It was a silver bauble, a large teardrop. He handed it to Bongo who dropped the earring on the ground and tapped it with the shotgun stock. The earring fell apart, a smaller aluminium casing rolling away from the split earring.

'That's our leak,' said Mac, picking up the smaller piece and showing it to Bongo.

Squinting, Bongo held it up to the light bulb. 'Four-month lithium battery, mini-microphone and transmitter, pushing a signal up to five miles in desert, about two miles in the tropics.'

'They gave you top of the line, Lance,' said Mac. 'Would have worked until you dipped it in the Mekong. It's just that the Israelis don't have rivers.'

'Shit, McQueen,' said Lance, face deathly pale. 'I'm so sorry.'



Didge slit the flexi-cuffs off Jon, and Tranh and Mac prepared to leave.

'Geraldine?' said Mac, pausing in the living room.

'Yes?'

'I know you have legal counsel, but without prejudice, it would help me right now if you could give me a clue about where Joel Dozsa might have retreated to.'

McHugh looked at him. She was shorter than her photos suggested and handsome rather than pretty; Mac could see in her the kind of Canberra career-type who felt they were born to be his boss. She looked away and looked back with a more open face. Then she leaned on her knees.

'I saw you in the compound, Mr McQueen,' she said. 'Thank you for risking your life to rescue me – I hope that bullet wound is not too bad.'

'I'll live.'

'But I need another favour before I tell you this.'

'What's the favour?'

'Put a bullet in that wanker for me?'

Mac nodded. 'That bad?'

'He's ruined my life,' she said, sniffing. 'Lured me into something high-spirited as a uni student, and he turns up a quarter-century later to blackmail me for it. Then he kills my husband.'

'No promises,' he said.

She took a deep breath. 'Joel's companies are all called Highland something or other. His compound is supposed to be secret, but one of his sidekicks – Marcus – showed me a picture of Joel's new horse.'

'A horse?'

'Yeah – and in the background of the horse I could clearly see Tanah Rata, a town right up in the Cameron Highlands, off Highway Fifty-nine, I think it is.'

'The picture was looking from the west of Fifty-nine, or the east?' said Mac.

'From the west.'

'How many ridges were between the camera and Rata?' said Mac.

'More than two, no more than four,' said McHugh. 'I remember thinking that their compound must be near a tourist trail called Track Ten – but don't quote me.'

'They ever talk about armaments? Defences?'

'No.'

Mac shook her hand. 'Thanks, Geraldine.'

'Remember – one from me.'

Mac paused in front of Bongo as he left the room. 'Mate, Vincent Loh Han says, *Where's my frigging helo?* Thought you might like to know that.'

'Yeah, well, I was planning on bringing it back today.'

'Yeah, Bongo?'

'Sure, brother – Didge is taking over here.'

# CHAPTER 67

The engineers pulled the Little Bird helicopter out of the hangar at Seletar Airport and had it ready in twenty-five minutes. Sitting in the flight office, they went over the map and narrowed down the possible targets in the hills over Rata. Most were old tea plantations and derelict guest houses from the colonial era, when the Anglos took to the cool hills during the summer heat.

'Dozsa will be here,' said Bongo, planting a big finger on a saddle at the top of a valley. 'He wants a road in and a road out, and he wants some flat land for a helo or plane.'

Looking, Mac saw what he was talking about. An unsealed track passed through the valley and there seemed to be flat areas.

'You know this place?' said Mac.

'It's the old Sanderton Estate,' said Bongo. 'British tea plantation, bought by some foreigner for a lot of money a few years ago.'

'Any easy approaches?' said Mac.

'No easy approaches,' said Bongo. 'This is the Cameron Highlands, brother.'

Mac tried to reach Scotty by phone but it went straight to voicemail. Watching Bongo do his pre-flight tests as Jon packed the gear bags, he keyed the phone again, trying Greg Tobin in Canberra.

'Greg,' said Mac. 'Albion.'

'How are you, old man?' said the director of operations. 'We got that prize yet?'

'No, sir. McHugh is under guard in Singapore.'

'You know where?'

'No,' said Mac. 'Scotty's with the police – we got ambushed by Dozsa in Singers. Fentanyl aerosols.'

Tobin used his tone of genuine concern, knowing that the wrong dose of Fentanyl will kill a man. 'You okay?'

'Yeah, we're in one piece, but Dozsa got the prize and I want clearance to take it back.'

'Where's Scotty?'

'In the cells, I think,' said Mac.

'You have a team? I don't want you chasing Dozsa without a team, Albion.'

'I have the team – I need the authority.'

'For where?' said Tobin.

'Malaysia,' said Mac. 'Can do?'

'Proceed as if it's done,' said Tobin. 'And don't muck around – you wouldn't believe the crowing that Defence is doing because Sandy brought back that file.'

'Well, hurrah for Sandy,' said Mac. 'It's not Defence's file that matters – it's Dozsa's.'


Lifting the gear bags into the Little Bird, the five of them crammed into the tiny aircraft: Mac and Bongo in the front; Tranh, Lance and Jon in the back.

Holding an assault rifle across his legs as they left the twinkling lights of Singapore behind and swept over the causeway into Malaysian airspace, Mac examined the weapon. The guns had been stored in the helo when Bongo had taken off in it from the Dozsa compound, and they weren't conventional US weapons.

'G36,' yelled Bongo over the noise. 'Heckler & Koch – nice weapon.'

Mac noticed its light weight and its NATO 5.56mm ammo.

He worked through the approaches in his mind as they flew through darkness, over the forests, with the occasional burst of yellow lights from villages and small towns. Only one insertion seemed plausible: four blokes on foot would go into the Sanderton Estate, and then call in the Little Bird. Thanks to Bongo, Mac had another piece of firepower in his backpack: two charges of C4 plastique, a box of military detonators and two digital timer fuses. There were many specialty rotations in the Royal Marine Commandos, but the one thing they all learned was how to reduce the bad guys' lair to rubble.

If they could coordinate the attack, it might work. If they walked into a trap, it would be over very quickly.

Bongo broke the silence as they entered the hills, pointing to truck headlights on the road that wound north through the Cameron Highlands forest and then wove his hand left and around in a loop to indicate that he wanted to hook around the back of the Sanderton Estate.

After eight minutes of flying west over darkly forested hill country, they hooked north and slowly descended to a sloping piece of open ground that rolled down to a river.

Depowering, Bongo got out of the helo and joined Mac at the backpacks.

'This is us, right here,' said Bongo, using a map-light and placing a fingertip on a valley west of the Sanderton Estate's main buildings, which he'd marked on the map in pencil. 'The track goes to the top of this saddle,' he said, breaking from the map and pointing to the ridge overlooking their position. 'Then there's a small river, and you climb for a thousand feet to the Sanderton plantation house.'

'An hour to get there?' said Mac.

'Give yourselves two, and then thirty minutes to assess the ground,' said Bongo, holding up his G-Shock. 'You want to do this by radio, or you want to time it?'

'I want radio silence until I give the "go" signal,' said Mac, looking at his watch and seeing it was just past one in the morning. 'Once I know the main defences, I'll want them taken out while we sneak in the back way.'

'Okay, McQueen, but at two hours thirty I'm coming in.'

* * *

They made fast time across the saddle and down to the river, aided by a three-quarter moon. The river wasn't as small as Bongo had promised – a few monsoonal downpours had swollen the watercourse over its banks and they were up to their ankles in water and mud before they reached the main flow.

Pausing, Mac thought he heard an aberrant noise over the rush of water, but couldn't find it. Probably just a monkey breaking a branch. Moving downstream to a fallen tree, Mac led them over the trunk, swinging from a large branch on the end of it and landing knee-deep in marshy water on the other side.

Wading towards higher ground, Mac felt watched. It was an open field with long grass, and even though they enjoyed the cover of darkness, he wanted to be in the trees. When the others had crossed the river, Mac led them to the base of the hill and they drank from their water bottles.

'Shit,' said Lance, gasping for breath. 'This humidity is awful.'

'Mr Dozsa is probably cooking up something slightly worse, but I get your point,' said Mac.

Looking around, Mac still felt uneasy. They were almost on a major footpad and Mac wanted something less obvious.

'Tranh and Jon – fan out and find a secondary trail up the hill,' said Mac, finishing his water. 'I want us off this freeway.'

When the two Vietnamese had stalked into the bush, Mac checked his radio and the G36.

'Thanks for that,' said Lance, his boyish looks now hardened. 'You know, back there.'

'It was Bongo's idea,' said Mac, stripping out the mag and breaking the German weapon down at the breech.

Lance pointed at the G36, which Mac was reassembling. 'How'd you learn all this stuff?'

'Royal Marines,' said Mac. 'And just so you know, I don't think I'm superior because I do the paramilitary gigs, no matter what some of those whiteboard jockeys in Canberra tell you.'

'Okay.' Lance laughed.

'You feel safe out here?' said Mac, letting the trigger box's pushpins click into place as he pushed it into the breech.

Lance shook his head. 'Nope.'

'Good start,' said Mac, slamming home the full mag.

'They say you're difficult,' said Lance.

'Difficult is Joel Dozsa or Bongo Morales – people your buddies are never going to meet.'

Lance nodded in the darkness. 'I'm sorry, about everything. I should have told you about that memory card.'

Mac looked at the younger man and saw someone who had been trained by the wrong people at the wrong time of his life. If Mac had been shoved into a Canberra office clique and rewarded for brown-nosing, he'd have turned out the same as Lance.

'You asked me how I know all of this stuff,' said Mac. 'I learned it because those warrant officers knew more than me, and they didn't let me forget it.'

'Touché,' said Lance.

Tranh arrived back thirty seconds before Jon. 'Smaller footpad this way, boss.'

Halfway up the mountain, Tranh moved back from his position at point.

'Think we have company, boss,' said Tranh.

'How many?' said Mac.

'One, I think,' said Tranh. 'Right flank.'

'Okay.' Mac drew Jon in from the sweep. 'I'll pull back and get on his tail. You guys go slow and be ready, okay?'

The troop moved on and Mac held back, padding quietly to the right of the footpad, hoping to come up behind the shadow. After fifty metres of poking through the dappled blackness of the jungle, Mac found a slight trail only evident from cracked twigs and a boot print in the damp soil. Kneeling, Mac looked at the pattern: American, like the boots he was wearing.

Breathing through his nostrils, Mac eased off the rifle's safety lever and selected full auto. He advanced in a crouch, his injured leg burning with pain, his fatigue playing tricks on his ears: was that a monkey or a man? A rifle being cocked or a bird?

The trail was clear and as he adjusted to the darkness, he sped up, hearing the occasional sound of his troop to his left.

The sweat ran off his face and from under his boonie hat as he paused behind a twist of vines. Across a clearing was a man's shape, in dark fatigues, crouched behind a tree and focusing at where Tranh and Jon would be walking with Lance.

The figure moved into the darkness of the trees and Mac skirted the clearing, quickly closing on the tree the soldier had stood behind. Ducking out for a look, Mac swore under his breath: he'd lost the man.

As he scanned for a trail, Mac's breathing was laboured. He was exhausted and he could feel the first inklings of heat distress as he started mouth-breathing – a rasping pant that meant the brain was not getting enough oxygen.

Forcing himself to breathe through his nose, he calmed the cycles and stopped it turning into hyperventilation. Then, moving forwards, he found another boot pattern in the moonlight and moved to his left, squinting to see through the foliage and the dappled light.

Following the trail through a muddy watercourse, he climbed the other side and lay on the crest, looking over.

As his head raised over the low ridge, Mac's quiet world was smashed by the rattle of automatic gunfire. At his eleven o'clock, cordite puffed and foliage snapped as shots were exchanged.

Running down the small rise, Mac raised his weapon and got a shoulder on it as he came around a larger tree and found the man in the dark fatigues in a hide behind a fallen tree.

'Drop it,' said Mac, aiming at the back of the shooter's head.

The man's weapon was placed on the log but still within reach.

'Cease fire – cease fire,' yelled Mac at his own guys. 'I said drop it, not place it on the log,' he said, panting for air, and the man hesitated.

'I mean it, Sammy,' said Mac, stalking forwards and pressing the G36 barrel to Sammy Chan's head. 'Just drop it.'

The M4 was hurled sideways, and Mac stood back as Sammy got to his feet, hands on his head, and turned to Mac.

'You love to fuck it up for me, don't you, tough guy?' said the American, as Jon and Tranh arrived.

'And the other one,' said Mac, gesturing at the canvas rifle bag between Sammy's shoulder blades.

Dropping the canvas bag, Sammy put his hands down. 'Keep the M4 – but I want that one back.'

'Deer season?' said Mac.

'No, McQueen,' said Sammy, whose face still showed the results of an evening with Grimshaw. 'Not deer.'

A noise erupted above them and they turned. The outline of a helicopter hovered across the forest canopy, a door-gunner peering down into the trees.

Mac dived for the cover of the log as the air filled with bullets. Trees and vines were turned to splinters as Mac dragged Sammy by the scruff of the neck to join him under the fallen tree.

'Red Dog, Red Dog,' said Mac into the radio mouthpiece. 'Red Dog – copy? Over.'

'Blue Boy, this is Red Dog,' came Bongo's voice, as a hail of .50-cal slugs hit the log above Mac.

'Red Dog, we need cover. Repeat, need cover from a bird.'

'Got your six, Blue Boy,' said Bongo calmly. 'Heads down, brother.'

Looking across the clearing, Mac saw Tranh and Lance jammed in behind a tree, but he couldn't see Jon. As Mac used his hand to indicate *head down*, Tranh nodded and grabbed Lance by the shirt, pulling him down.

Another strafe painted across the jungle, felling a mid-size tree and making the log above Mac jump.

Shutting his eyes, feeling stupid for walking into a trap, Mac waited for the bullets to stop.

The sound changed and then the guns were still firing but not at the ground. The *thudda-thudda* of the .50-cal was joined by a whistling, screaming crescendo and the sound of steel being torn apart resounded around the jungle as torrents of brass rained into the canopy. Squeezing out of his hide, Mac looked up and watched the attack helo swirling around like a burning hula hoop, its tail rotor shot off by the smaller helo, which had plumes of white fire bursting from its undercarriage.

The shooting stopped and the attack helo dropped out of the sky, its engines still screaming at high revs as it crashed into the bush fifty metres away and exploded.

'Blue Boy, Blue Boy,' said Bongo over the radio. 'Bandits down – free to proceed.'

'See the house, Red Dog?' said Mac.

'Just over the ridge, Blue Boy,' said Bongo. 'Bandits engaged.'

# CHAPTER 68

The smell of burning kerosene wafted through the jungle as Mac led the team to the ridge and looked down. On the other side of a small valley, three hundred metres away, sat the plantation house of the Sanderton Estate, a few lights winking in the dark.

Lifting his night-glasses, Mac saw a large veranda on the near side of the house, below which was a terrace lawn with a .50-cal machine-gun tripod-mounted behind sandbags. As he watched, a team of seven soldiers ran down the side of the terrace lawn into the gorge between Mac and the house, their bodies leaving faint green trails in the lenses. Two soldiers wandered to the .50-cal, talking.

'Sammy,' said Mac, not taking his eyes from the glasses. 'How about taking out the .50-cal nest with that deer rifle of yours?'

'Got a range?' asked Sammy, unclipping the canvas bag and pulling out the olive-drab rifle with an optical sight the size of a soup can.

'Glasses say two hundred and eighty-three metres,' said Mac, tapping the button to get a range on where he'd focused. 'Can do?'

'Can try,' said Sammy, lying on the carpet of leaves beside Mac and extending the bipod under the barrel.

One of the soldiers at the .50-cal lit a smoke and grabbed the machine-gun's handles.

'Got him, Sammy?' said Mac, as the American twirled a knob on the gun's sights and settled back into a solid shoulder.

'That smoking is a deadly habit,' said Sammy, steadying the DMR – a Designated Marksman's Rifle, usually an M14.

Refocusing on the machine-gun nest, Mac saw the soldier take a drag on his smoke. The DMR clicked and thumped beside Mac and in his glasses, the gunner's body fell backwards without a head and the offsider stood, confused, then threw down his cigarette and grabbed the .50-cal's dual handles.

Sammy's DMR spat again and the offsider's left arm threw back at an unnatural angle. The DMR coughed once more and there was a third eye in the shooter's forehead.

'Nice work, Sammy,' said Mac. 'Can you get any of those glory boys down there?'

Standing, Sammy followed Mac's pointing finger to where the Chinese were running into the forest.

'We can avoid them – much easier,' said Sammy, slinging the DMR into its bag and picking up his M4.

'My sentiments exactly,' said Mac, glad for a kindred spirit who'd rather skirt a fire fight.

Heading right, the five of them descended as the Chinese climbed to their left. It might only give them a five-minute head start, but that was all Mac needed.

Hitting the bottom of the small gorge, Tranh dropped to his knee and fired three bursts before rolling away to hide behind a tree.

Squinting through the darkness, Mac searched for Tranh. Getting a tap on the shoulder from Sammy, Mac found him and Tranh gave the peace sign: two men with rifles.

Standing, Tranh looked around the tree and shot on full auto as Mac and Sammy ran forwards to a tree on the other side of the track.

There seemed to be two Chinese soldiers behind a rock about thirty metres away. Mac watched their beige caps bobbing sideways and he ran at them, rifle jammed in his shoulder, muzzle pointed at those caps. As the soldiers looked over the rock, Mac opened up, putting bursts into both of them without raising his eye from the sight line.

Movement came from the left and a bullet slapped into the rock under his feet. Sammy covered with a heavy burst and the shooter fell sideways from behind his tree.

Regrouping, they panted for breath as they assessed the open ground that now ran from the gorge up to the terrace lawn and then the house.

'They're back,' said Jon, pointing to the house, and they could see two more soldiers at the .50-cal.

Pulling his sniper's rifle off his back, Sammy took a look and then shook his head. 'No angle.'

'The approach is up the side,' said Mac, pointing to the bush to the right that wrapped around the other side of the house.

They ran across the open ground to the trees as the .50-cal belatedly opened up, forcing them to the ground.

Crawling sideways for the shelter of a rocky overhang, Mac dragged them in and counted one short as the big slugs whistled over their heads.

'Who're we missing?' said Mac, looking around.

'Jon,' said Tranh.

In the open ground, Jon lay face down, the .50-cal bullets finding his exposed back several more times as they watched.

'Come on,' said Mac, leading them around the flank of the house as his leg started to throb with pain.

Climbing over the rocky outcrop, Mac noticed silence from the machine-gun nest. Crouching, he heard the hurried whispers of the machine-gunners through the foliage and then heard that signature hiss. The trail of white showed conspicuously against the night sky and then something crashed through the canopy and snaked into a tree, exploding as Mac fell backwards off the overhang to his team below.

Bouncing on his hip as the air turned orange, Mac tucked his head under his hands and prayed into the dirt. In shock, he felt himself being pulled to his feet by the collar.

'RPG,' said Sammy, spitting out leaves. 'Let's finish these bastards.'

He followed Sammy around the far side of the rocky overhang and into the open again, until they faced security doors over a concrete tunnel beneath the house.

'You know about this?' Sammy pointed at the dimly lit tunnel entrance.

'About what?'

'Dozsa's operations centre – built it a couple of years ago when he bought this place.'

'What is it?'

'Lots of satellite and microwave communications, especially two-way traffic with a comms station in Khamti,' said Sammy, meaning a large commercial relay facility in northern Burma that was actually owned by the People's Liberation Army.

'So Dozsa is going to help Pao Peng rule the world from here?'

'At very least, it's where he thinks he'll control a missile launch.'

They were now on the wrong side of the house to be targeted by the .50-cal but Mac was still paranoid. 'We're not storming that tunnel. This isn't a suicide mission.'

'Thought we'd try the emergency exit,' said Sammy.

Looking back, Mac saw the worried faces of Tranh and Lance. 'Where's this exit?'

'On the other side of the house, in a small ravine.'

'Sounds like you know this place,' said Mac.

'Sure,' said Sammy. 'I installed the satellite tracking system with a Singapore contractor.'

'Sneaky bastard,' said Mac.

'I know the layout – we just need a diversion from this end.'

'Ten minutes do it?' said Mac.

'Sure.'

Mac gave Lance and Tranh a ten-minute mission clock and told them to stay hidden until then. Keying the radio, Mac asked Bongo to come in firing on that tunnel door on the stroke of ten minutes.

'Can do,' said Bongo.

They crossed the driveway to the house and got caught in the searchlights of a roofless Humvee accelerating towards them down the driveway, the turret gunner loosing several rounds as Mac and Sammy scrambled over the road and into the trees.

His hands shaking, Mac tried to get control of his breathing. The situation felt hopeless – there were so many soldiers and Dozsa's base was too well defended.

'This way,' said Sammy, grabbing Mac by the arm.

Mac's legs wouldn't move; his lungs were seized.

'Shit – Sammy.'

Stopping, the American looked behind. 'Let's go, McQueen.'

His heart palpitating, Mac heard the Humvee arrive behind him, the excited Chinese voices chattering.

Pushing himself to walk, Mac put one leg in front of another and started jogging towards Sammy, who looked past Mac and sent off a burst of full auto in the direction of the soldiers.

Sammy grabbed Mac and pulled him along. 'You okay?'

'Fine,' said Mac, building speed on a knee that wanted to give up.

Voices and bursts of gunfire sounded through the bush behind them as Sammy turned into a concrete opening that looked like a stormwater culvert. Pulling a keyring from his pocket, he handed Mac a small Maglite and found a large steel key.

'One of the perks of doing my army trade in comms engineering,' said Sammy, jiggling the lock. 'The bad guys let you wander around in their little projects.'

'Nice cover,' said Mac, as the lock yielded and the door swung back to reveal a round tunnel that a man could just stand up in. It was 4.32 am – eighteen minutes until the North Koreans started their launch of the Taepodong-2 rocket.

'You wouldn't believe some of the shit I've seen and the systems I've built,' said Sammy, cocking the M4 and pushing into the small pool of light afforded by the Maglite. 'Last year I helped build a system for an Indian billionaire's super-yacht – it was a control centre for his own satellite.'

Having pulled the door shut, they walked in single file for six minutes before Mac knocked the buttons on his G-Shock and saw they had fifty-five seconds before the ten minutes was up.

'We close?' said Mac as soldiers hammered on the tunnel door and then gave up, convinced their quarry must be elsewhere.

'We're here,' said Sammy, his hand softly slapping another steel door.

They stood in the dark, waiting for the clatter of the diversionary attack on the main entrance as Sammy pushed his key into the lock. Mac's stomach ground like a meat mincer.

The unmistakable sound of the Little Bird's Gatling gun sounded like heavy rain on a tin roof and Sammy turned the key, pushing straight forwards as Mac hovered over his right shoulder with his rifle.

As the door swung back, the noise of the fighting rose and Mac squinted into fluorescent lights in the white passageway. Ducking into an alcove, they watched two of Dozsa's Israelis run out a doorway and down the corridor, handguns at the ready.

Gasping for breath, Mac moved from the alcove and followed Sammy down the hall to a door. The door was locked but they could see behind the security glass a room that looked not unlike the bridge of a modern container ship.

'Ready?' said Sammy

'For what?'

'This is the C and C room for the Taepodong-2,' said Sammy. 'It's a copy of the North Koreans' mission control at Pondong-ni.'

'So . . . ?'

'But destroying this won't do anything,' said Sammy. 'If Dozsa got the whole file that was downloaded from Aussie intel, then he can access the North Korean missile program whenever he wants.'

The sound of gunfire got louder and something blew up.

'Let's take this part slow,' said Sammy.

'I don't see why we don't just blow the whole place,' said Mac, uncomfortable about having the mission seized by a Yank with strange agendas.

'Dozsa might have a copy of the file,' said Sammy, taking his keyring from his pocket again.

'Any file taken from Aussie intel's security system is no-copy,' said Mac. 'That's why Dozsa needed the stolen Top Secret desktop system to get the download. That's what he had Quirk using in the Mekong Saloon.'

'Yeah, well,' said Sammy, opening the door and pushing through, 'that's your story.'

Grabbing Sammy, Mac pulled him around. 'Listen, there is no file copy – we can blow this whole place right now.' He tapped his backpack.

'You brought charges?' said Sammy, nervous.

'Of course I brought charges,' said Mac, sweat running onto his top lip. 'This shuts down the entire Pao Peng power grab.'

'Who do you work for, McQueen?' Sammy sneered. 'The West or the Chinks?'

Mac noticed how people like Sammy could use a racial description that Mac wasn't allowed to use himself. 'Keeping the Chinese out of a war around the South China Sea is good for the West, Sammy, and that means stopping a rogue like Pao Peng before he gets going.'

'You really think my bosses are going to allow that?' said Sammy.

'Allow it?' Mac gripped Sammy's arm. 'This is an Aussie gig, Tonto – I don't need your permission.'

'I'm sorry, McQueen.' Sammy's expression changed as he cocked his handgun. 'Dozsa's room stays live.'

The truth of it dawned on Mac. The Americans didn't want an end to this program: they wanted to own it and run it themselves, probably with deniable contractors, just as Pao Peng had used Dozsa's services.

'You're nuts,' said Mac. 'We have a chance to end Pao Peng's Greater China fantasy right here.'

'Pao Peng will find another way,' said Sammy, pistol coming up to Mac's sternum. 'I'm sorry, buddy – I have my orders. Drop the guns.'

'You're a wanker, Chan,' said Mac, dropping his handgun and rifle as he was ushered into the room by Sammy.

'You don't need to die, McQueen, just stay out of my way.'

Mac saw the banks of screens and four Koreans sitting in front of them. Walking to the main console, Sammy issued commands in Korean as he waved the gun at them.

Standing slowly, one of them argued and Sammy shot him in the heart and then between the eyes before he hit the floor.

The others put their hands in the air and the one Sammy addressed nodded so hard it looked like his head would fall off.

The yes-man jogged to a PC running below the screens and tapped on the keyboard.

'They're already in,' said Sammy, marvelling at the visual displays on the wall. 'Look at those screens – that's the North Korean Army's

C and C systems we're looking at. That's what the technicians are looking at in Pondong-ni, right now. We're going into the ten-minute launch countdown.'

'Can't we stop it?' said Mac.

'Hang on,' said Sammy. 'I want to see how it works.'

After exchanging words with the Korean technician, Sammy turned to Mac. 'Thanks to Ray Hu's excellent buying, this system is cloning and mimicking every router and switch in the North Korean network – this is beautiful.'

'Let's grab the file and get out of here,' said Mac, agitated.

'Just hang on.' Sammy brought his handgun back to Mac's heart.

After another stream of Korean, the technician stared at Sammy wide-eyed, shaking his head. When Sammy pointed the gun at his head, the man continued to protest but used a mouse to change one of the screens.

Looking closer, Mac could see what the technician was altering: the screen showed the North Pacific, featuring a small white cross in the middle of the ocean at which the missile was being aimed. As Mac watched the screen, the white cross moved westwards.

'Sammy, what are you doing?'

The Korean technician, on hearing Mac's tone, turned and yelled at Sammy, tears in his eyes. He wore a third eye before he hit the floor.

'You,' said Sammy, at another technician with his arms raised.

The technician ran to replace his dead colleague, and the cross continued moving, out of the North Pacific to Japan.

'No, Sammy,' said Mac, moving towards the American before facing the barrel of the handgun.

'I like you, McQueen,' said the American. 'But I will shoot you.'

'What the hell are you doing, Sammy?' said Mac, raising his hands further as Sammy's gun steadied between his eyes. 'You can't target Tokyo – who the hell do you work for?'

One of the major themes of the Australian Secret Intelligence Service since Mac had joined was the emphasis on stability in the region. Mac was watching that come undone in front of him.

'I'd never bomb Tokyo,' said Sammy, smiling. 'Watch this, McQueen.'

As the technician shook his head and the first tears rolled down his face, Mac saw why. The small white cross wasn't stopping on the Japanese capital – it continued westwards, across the Sea of Japan and the Korean Peninsula until it came to rest on a thick black circle.

Beijing.

# CHAPTER 69

'No, Sammy,' said Mac, not believing what he was seeing. 'Not this.'

'Why not?' said Sammy. 'There's only one way to deal with North Korea and that's to have the Chinese do it.'

'A missile bearing down on Beijing?' said Mac. 'The Chinese won't deal with North Korea, they'll turn it into a car park.'

'I agree,' said a voice, and looking up, Mac saw Joel Dozsa at a small observation window looking down on the control room. A shot cracked from Dozsa's rifle and as Mac turned to dive under a desk, he saw Sammy collapsing on the floor, a bloody cavity in his chest.

Three more shots thwacked into the lino floor, spraying Mac with blood and concrete dust. It was obvious Dozsa didn't want to put holes in his control room, and looking across the floor Mac saw Sammy was bleeding out over his M4.

Putting his foot out, Mac dragged at Sammy's body, trying to retrieve the rifle, but Dozsa shot at him.

The harsh screech of Korean filled the hallways as Dozsa yelled a command, unable to leave his window to walk around and enter the control room.

One of the technicians walked behind the console, bending to pick up Mac's discarded rifle. Seeing a limited opportunity, Mac accelerated in a running crouch from behind the desk, hitting the

Korean in a ball-and-all tackle as a bullet pinged off the floor from Dozsa's rifle. Taking the Korean in a twisting grapple tackle, Mac hid behind the man's profile as they sailed through the air.

Landing as the Heckler bounced free, Mac realised the Korean was dead, two shots in his chest intended for Mac. Grabbing at the rifle's stock, Mac managed to pull it back without getting one of Dozsa's bullets in his hand.

Checking for load and safety, the lino now slick with blood and stinking of cordite and burnt circuitry, Mac took two deep breaths and turned, firing at the mezzanine window with the Heckler. Panes of glass splintered and the bullets peppered the walls around it. But Dozsa was gone.

Keying the radio, Mac saw it was not responding in the sealed room. Outside, the gunfight raged on, getting closer now.

Looking at his watch, he saw it was 4.42 pm – in eight minutes the real control room in North Korea would lock in its final settings, giving telemetry commands to several hundred different aspects of a ballistic missile launch. At ten minutes before launch, the general in charge of the program would turn his key and the mission controller would turn his, and the final countdown to ignition and firing would begin.

In this case, however, the final countdown wouldn't commence on North Korea's terms – it would prepare to launch according to the override coming from this control room. The systems in the North Korean control room wouldn't register the change; their system would be simply operating in a vacuum while Dozsa's control room gave the real commands. The North Koreans would be unable to change the launch until they looked out the window and saw their T2 missile arcing due west towards China rather than east, into the Pacific.

Standing, Mac looked at the map on the big screen. Waving at it, he tried to tell the Koreans to change the target but the two surviving technicians were hiding, not wanting to come out.

Checking the upstairs window and the door for signs of Dozsa or his soldiers, Mac pulled the C4 charges from his backpack and eyed the framework on which the mainframes and junction boxes were built. Crawling under the frames – essentially heavy-duty Meccano scaffolds – Mac planted a charge on the side of the server stacks and set the timer for five minutes.

Turning, he crawled back to the control room, noticing a hollow clap under his knees as he passed over, and slapped the other charge on a metal upright and set the timer for five minutes. Standing as he picked up the Heckler, he saw a commotion at the door.

Levelling the rifle, he readied to fight it out – whatever happened from here, Mac wanted those charges detonating.

Lance stumbled in, wide-eyed, and Mac lowered his rifle.

'Lance,' said Mac, thinking there was now some hope of finding the file before he blew the control room. He was going to blow it regardless, but he'd like to tell Canberra that he'd retrieved the file.

Lance stumbled forwards, holding his arm awkwardly, and Dozsa slithered in behind him, blood running down from a cut on his tanned bald head.

'McQueen, drop the gun and listen to me,' said Dozsa, pointing his rifle at the back of Lance's head. 'That missile can't land in Beijing.'

'You're telling me,' said Mac, letting his rifle slip to the floor.

'Yes, you, McQueen. You brought that crazy American in here.'

'What are you talking about?' said Mac.

'Chan,' said Dozsa, locking the door behind him. 'You don't know who he is?'

'DIA or Agency,' said Mac. 'Ex-Marines forecon.'

'Emphasis on "ex",' said Dozsa, moving to the Korean technicians while he covered Mac and Lance.

Barking orders in Korean, Dozsa kept his eyes on Mac while the small white cross was changed again, this time to Tokyo.

Dozsa stole a quick look at his watch and Mac looked at the screen: in forty-five seconds the North Koreans would lock the Taepodong-2 into its ten-minute launch sequence, not knowing where it was really heading.

'Why emphasis on ex?' said Mac, noticing blood dripping from Lance's crippled arm.

'Sammy's private,' said Dozsa. 'He's as official as I am, but he's sanctioned.'

'By whom?' said Mac, calculating whether to tell Dozsa about the charges or try an escape.

'Heard of the Syracuse Unit?' said Dozsa. 'Bunch of Pentagon brass, intel parasites and defence contractors who met in Sicily in the late nineties.'

'I've heard conspiracy wackos talk about these guys,' said Mac, glancing at his watch – three minutes till the charges blew.

'It's not a theory,' said Dozsa. 'With the impending election of George W Bush, they met to discuss how the defence and intelligence budgets could be kept at Cold War levels under George W, and they decided that North Asia tearing itself apart was the logical choice.'

'Sounds like Mossad bullshit to me, Joel – no offence,' said Mac. 'Sounds like the kind of thing your secret service keeps telling the politicians so everyone seems worse than the Mossad.'

'We were inside,' said Dozsa, smiling. 'We had eyes.'

'Bullshit,' said Mac. 'Grimshaw is old school – a true believer. He's ex-Phoenix, for Christ's sake.'

Dozsa gestured for Lance to approach. 'Not Grimshaw, he's been stalking me for two years. He wants my head on a plate.'

'So?'

'So, Sammy Chan – planted by the Syracuse Unit – has been courting me while pretending to work for Grimshaw.'

'Bullshit.'

'Why d'you think Sammy went running down that hill and tried to assassinate Geraldine McHugh that night?'

'He said he was stopping her being debriefed by Canberra – blamed it on Grimshaw.'

'And now it is you bullshitting, McQueen,' said Dozsa, dark eyes glinting like a shark's. 'Sammy was cleaning up the mess: Phil, then McHugh – they knew too much, and people knowing too much disturbs the Syracuse gang.'

'What?' asked Mac.

'They tried to turn me, McQueen,' said Dozsa, reaching for a keyboard. 'When I wouldn't, they had to wipe the slate before they took over my little operation.'

'Phil?' said Mac, head roaring. 'What're you talking about?'

'That night on the docks in Phnom Penh, you see where the RPG came from?'

'You,' said Mac.

'Think again, my Aussie friend,' said Dozsa, mouth hardening. 'It came from the river. My guy on the boat was shot and then there's an RPG sailing over our heads into that truck.'

'You're grasping, Dozsa,' said Mac.

'I'm winning, not grasping,' said Dozsa, in that irritating Hungarian accent. 'Phil had been with Sammy when they tried to turn me – he knew too much, so Sammy killed him in a way that was plausible to Grimshaw.'

Shaking his head, Mac watched Lance being lured to the PC below the screen banks.

'Run a test on the HARPAC file,' said Dozsa to Lance, but not taking his eyes off Mac. 'I want to make sure we don't lose comms at the crucial point.'

Lance was stiff with fear, his face white with shock and blood loss. The youngster wasn't going to be much good in the next ninety seconds.

'And don't screw around with it, okay, boy?' Dozsa held the barrel of his rifle to Lance's temple.

A faint beeping sound started in the control room, and looking up at the display monitors Mac could see a red panel blinking in the top right-hand corner of each monitor. 'That's the ignition phase,' said Dozsa. The North Korean missile launch was locked in.

Watching Lance's shaking hand go to the PC, Mac winced. He had only one way to go, and that was to make a run for it – which meant leaving Lance.

The PC screen opened what looked like thousands of lines of code and Lance's fingers danced lightly over the keyboard.

'What?' said Dozsa, distracted by something on the screen. 'What the hell are you doing?!'

The PC screen was scrolling up at a hundred miles an hour, a box flashing over the data. Mac couldn't see what the box said, but it blinked yellow. Shit – was Lance deleting the HARPAC file?

Pushing Lance from the PC, Dozsa moved to the keyboard and Lance lunged at the Israeli, pulling the rifle around in Dozsa's grip and pushing it upwards.

As Mac moved on the two, Dozsa swung the stock of the gun at Lance and crushed his nose, making the Australian stagger backwards in a bloody mess. Mac got to Dozsa as the gun came around and a shot passed his head as he threw a flying elbow at Dozsa's mouth.

Staggering backwards from the blow, Dozsa lost his balance over the back of a chair; the Koreans scattered out of his way, Dozsa's gun firing into the ceiling as he fell on his head.

Retrieving his rifle, Mac let two shots go as Dozsa clambered under the computer monitor desks. Boots kicked at the control room door and faces stared through the security glass – Israeli faces.

'Let's go,' said Mac, grabbing Lance, throwing him under the computer frames as automatic weapons tore into the security door.

Crawling under the load of hard drives and monitors, Mac grabbed Lance by the ankle as they moved over the hollow-sounding floor.

'Here,' said Mac. 'You okay?'

'No.' Lance was hyperventilating. 'But I can move.'

Feeling around the hollow area, Mac found the trapdoor with his fingers. Opening it, he stuck his head under and saw a service tunnel that contained a thick rope of wires and fibre-optic cables, carried six feet above the concrete into the middle distance.

The door caved in and boots tattooed across the room as Mac pushed Lance into the hole and watched him drop to the floor below. Mac followed as automatic gunfire rattled under the frames, causing one to collapse. Looking to his right as he ducked down, Mac saw Joel Dozsa, also under the framework and aiming at Mac's head.

'You're dead, McQueen,' said Dozsa as the gun spat fire.

Mac dropped into the tunnel, his right forearm spewing blood from a bullet nick. 'This way,' he said, limping along the dimly lit tunnel, dragging Lance by the arm.

The tunnel ended in a door. Pushing on it, they descended into a loading bay. Gunfire sounded sporadically, and Mac turned, raising the Heckler. An Israeli head popped down through the trapdoor and Mac opened fire at it until the gun seized – no more loads.

'Red Dog, Red Dog,' said Mac into the radio mouthpiece as he looked around the deserted loading area. 'Red Dog, this is Blue Boy – need a ride.'

Bongo's voice crackled a few seconds later. 'Gotcha, Blue Boy – meet me at the driveway.'

Emerging into the first light of dawn, Mac jumped to the ground from the loading bay and gasped at the pain in his calf. Lance jogged behind him as they skirted the house for the driveway, Mac feeling naked without firearms.

There were dead bodies at the main entrance to the house and it looked as though Bongo had blown a hole in the main entrance. An eerie silence enveloped the area, broken by the thump of helo rotors. Like a giant black beast, the Little Bird rose out of the valley in front of Dozsa's house, Tranh's head lolling unnaturally in the co-pilot seat and Bongo's gum-chewing face expressionless behind the tinted visor on his helmet.

'Let's make this quick, Blue Boy,' said Bongo over the headset. 'The Chinese accounted for – Dozsa and some Israelis still active.'

Staggering to the place where Bongo was landing the helo, Mac felt the nausea of pain blurring inwards from the periphery of his vision. He panted his encouragement to Lance as he limped down the driveway.

A loud noise erupted and the Little Bird's cockpit dome turned to stars. Dropping to the driveway Mac saw Dozsa and the other Israeli emerge at the main entrance, Dozsa holding the .50-cal and the other man shooting an M4.

Trying to bury his head in the gravel as they were caught in the crossfire, Mac heard the helo's Gatling gun spin and then it was spitting death.

The Israeli soldier was torn apart instantly, leaving Dozsa facing the Gatling gun.

It hardly mattered. As Dozsa got a better grip on the heavy belt-fed gun, the house expanded in a fireball of orange and red, the roof blowing off and the main tunnel doors flying fifty feet into the bush as the C4 was detonated. The noise sounded like a massive train crash, forcing hot air out like a hurricane and spewing thousands of pieces of computer, monitor, concrete and steel into the air and across the driveway like high-tech tumbleweeds. A piece of computer flew at Mac's elbow and Lance was hit on the head by a lump of concrete the size of a cricket ball, knocking him out.

Debris rained for another twenty seconds as Mac tried to sit up.

'Watch it, McQueen,' said Bongo, getting out of the helo and pointing.

Turning, Mac saw Dozsa, about thirty feet from where he'd last been standing, his chinos hanging in tatters, flaps of skin hanging off him like bloody gills.

Looking around for his machine-gun, the ex-Mossad man realised it was back on the front veranda and instead he faced Mac and pulled a mini Ka-bar from his ankle sheath.

'I told you to steal the SD chip, McQueen,' said Dozsa, looking drunk with the shock of the explosion. 'Your job was to take the chip and go home to Kangaroo-land, you fucking imbecile.'

'Nice idea, Joel, but why would an Israeli psycho let me go?' said Mac, moving forwards to meet Dozsa. 'And why would he tempt me to take the chip and leave the hostages? It felt like a Mossad deception.'

'You think too much, my Aussie friend,' said Dozsa. 'You could have taken the chip, flown home and got a medal – we could have avoided this.'

As much as he wanted to take Dozsa to the ground and choke him out or break his neck, Mac knew it was impossible with his leg virtually useless.

'We'd never avoid this,' said Mac, getting to within ten feet of Dozsa's battered body. 'You'd fly back to Malta or the Seychelles – wherever you're based – and count the money in your numbered accounts while the people of this region would have China kicking the shit out of anything that moved.'

Dozsa shrugged.

'And why?' said Mac. 'So some passed-over general can dissolve the Central Committee and run China as a military dictatorship?'

'Stability is what he calls it,' said Dozsa, moving the knife to his other hand.

'We don't need that kind of stability in this region, Dozsa.'

Mac heard the crunch of gravel behind him. Turning, he saw Tranh and Bongo.

'Philippines need Pao Peng stirring up the shit?' said Mac to Bongo.

'We got enough fighting, thanks, Dozsa,' said Bongo.

'What about Vietnam?' said Mac.

'Had our war,' said Tranh.

'My heart bleeds,' said Dozsa, lunging at Mac.

Dancing back, Mac tore off his shirt and bundled it in his left hand as Dozsa regained balance and prepared for another strike. Struggling for grip on the gravel, Mac's leg finally gave way and he hopped on his good leg, his eyes rolling back in his head.

Dozsa, seeing his opportunity, leapt at Mac's solar plexus with the knife, slicing through soft skin. Mac hit down on the knife hand with his shirt bundle as the blade passed across his midriff, taking the Israeli off balance. Simultaneously he threw a hard punch with his right hand at the hinge of Dozsa's exposed right jaw and then collapsed on the gravel.

Mac lay on his side, and his mouth sagged open as he tried to move. His body had taken too much punishment and he could no longer stand.

'You fuck,' said Dozsa, looming over him and cradling his broken jaw. 'You moron.'

The Ka-bar's blade glinted in the morning sun and Mac accepted his fate. He couldn't go on – he could barely breathe. A shadow crossed his face and he looked up at Bongo.

'So,' Dozsa spoke from the side of his mouth as he squared off on the Filipino, 'the Aussie hard man needs his big brother?'

'McQueen didn't ask,' said Bongo, circling with the Israeli. 'I offered.'

'Still, it doesn't look good,' said Dozsa, sneering. 'You sure he wants this?'

'Man's got a bullet in his leg, Dozsa,' said Bongo, empty-handed and focused on the ex-Mossad man. 'Not like he's giving up.'

The Israeli crouched like a dancer, his legs and feet light on the gravel as he shifted his weight. Bongo stood upright, mouth slowly chewing on gum. As the two men circled, Mac could feel the bullet hole in his leg running with blood.

'So, how does this work?' said Dozsa, the busted jaw pushing a faint trickle of blood down his bottom lip. 'I come at you, and you pull a gun?'

'Don't need no gun,' said Bongo.

'Get rid of it, Morales,' said Dozsa, 'and let's finish this.'

Bongo's face was implacable behind the dark shades but very slowly he dropped his left hand and raised the bottom hem of his black trop shirt until the grip of a Desert Eagle handgun appeared above his waistband.

'This what you're worried about?' said Bongo, a picture of stillness. 'Drop it.'

'Don't,' said Mac, as his blood ran freely from the bullet wound into the gravel. 'Don't give him the satisfaction.'

Bongo's right hand slowly fell to the Browning. Putting two fingers and a thumb on the butt, Bongo extracted it millimetre by millimetre until he held the weapon in front of him.

The pace of the big man's movements was mesmerising and Mac held his breath. Then Lance sat up and looked around in a daze, catching Dozsa's attention.

Bongo said, 'Catch' and the Browning was arcing through the air at Dozsa, the Israeli hesitating between looking at the gun and focusing on Bongo.

Accelerating like a big cat, Bongo moved across the gap to the Israeli and got a Korean wrist lock on Dozsa's knife hand while the Browning was still in the air.

Realising he was caught, Dozsa lashed out with a finger strike into Bongo's eyes as he lost his balance and fell backwards, his right hand bent forwards onto the inside of his forearm.

Leaning his face away from the digging fingernails, Bongo used his strength to jerk upwards with the two-handed wrist lock, which almost raised Dozsa's feet from the ground. Then, pulling down with all his weight, Bongo drove the Israeli's right elbow towards the ground, destroying the carpal structure of the wrist, snapping the two forearm bones and dislocating the elbow.

In the still morning air it sounded like a child had been smacked and as Dozsa dropped to his knees and fell sideways – right arm now looking like a Picasso painting – his mouth opened in a scream that made the buzzards rise from the treetops.

As the Israeli roared with pain and sobbed in the gravel, Bongo picked up the Ka-bar and offered it to Mac.

'Honours are yours, McQueen,' said Bongo.

Sitting up in the pool of his own blood, Mac took the knife. It felt good in his hand. But trying to crawl to Dozsa, who'd passed out, Mac felt something else overwhelming him and he leaned on his hands, staring at the small dark spots as his tears dropped into the dust.

His back heaved and his face screwed up and before he could control it, Mac was weeping. His face wet, Mac shook his head.

'Shit, Bongo,' he said, trying to get the words out without blubbering. 'I mean, shit – Ray was my friend, you know?'

'I know, brother,' said Bongo. 'Ray was good people.'

'He was,' said Mac, sniffing. 'He was a thousand per cent.'

Dozsa moaned and moved as he regained consciousness.

Looking down at the knife in his hand, Mac discarded it in the gravel.

'Screw this job,' he said, wiping his eyes with the back of his hand. 'I didn't even go to Ray's funeral, know that, Bongo?'

Bongo looked away, probably with his own list of funerals, marriages and christenings not attended because of security concerns – every one of them a source of gnawing regret.

'I'm not going to kill this wanker,' said Mac, suddenly feeling very clear. 'He's going to stand in a courtroom, in fricking Saigon, and he's going to answer for what he did.'

Bongo rubbed his chin. 'This is Malaysia.'

'Then we take the jet to Saigon,' said Tranh, walking to Dozsa and standing over him. 'The pilots are waiting.'

Sitting in the co-pilot's seat of the Little Bird helicopter, Mac felt shivers of shock running through his body as he waited for Bongo and Tranh to secure Dozsa in the rear of the aircraft. Lance was concussed and had lost a lot of blood, but he was alive and talking.

Bongo finally buckled in and started the helo, and Mac realised he couldn't stretch his legs because of a large postal sack in the cockpit's footwell.

'What's this?' he said, putting on the ear cans as the revs built.

'Dozsa's boys were making off with it,' said Bongo as the helo screamed. 'Trying to reach the jungle.'

Mac saw blood on one side of the sack. 'So you relieved them?'

'Lightened their load,' said Bongo, easing the helo skywards.

'They were abandoning Dozsa?'

'They had their reasons,' said Bongo, banking the helo to the south. 'About one point three million of them.'

'This whole story just gets classier.'

'So, we do the same deal, right, brother?' said Bongo.

'Same?'

'Same as Dili. I'll stash your cut,' said Bongo.

Looking out on the lush jungle of the Cameron Highlands, Mac thought about it. He'd never joined the Firm to take money from people, but he could make an exception for Joel Dozsa.

'Nice of you, Bongo,' said Mac. 'I'll give you an address.'

# CHAPTER 70

Mac got his second beer and a shot of Bundy and sat at the end of the bar in Tan Son Nhat's business lounge. The television played a CNN loop out of the Asia centre and he let it wash over him as he prepped for his arrival back into family life – an emotional shock every bit as severe as the disruption of going into the field.

He'd spent a day in hospital and then four days in hotels, waiting for Scotty to pull the plug and order the team back to Canberra. Scotty had finally got the story straight, which was how he liked to run his field people before sitting in front of the brass.

The TV announced the cracking of another Indochinese sex-slavery ring near the Cambodian–Vietnamese border; this time a Chinese–Cambodian gang was responsible rather than the old favourites, the Khmer Rouge. The voiceover repeated the cops' press release —one hundred and twelve captives, seventy-two of them children, bound for places such as Bangkok, Jakarta and Dubai. The footage showed buses being filled with the rescued people and several shots featured Jenny and her long-time FBI colleague, Milinda, talking to local men who had flexi-cuffs on their wrists. CNN showed the ship the human cargo were first transported in and then the warehouse where the rescue had occurred – an address that Mac knew had been provided by Vincent Loh Han.

Mac held his breath until the report was over; he'd never be comfortable with the danger his wife put herself in.

The main story leading the CNN news at the top and bottom of the hour was the North Korean allegation that the Pentagon had infiltrated their recent Taepodong missile tests and attempted to create a diplomatic crisis with Japan. The Secretary of Defense fronted a press conference in Manila, explaining how hard the White House was negotiating for 'workable solutions' in North Asia and denying any US counter-measures against the Korean missile tests.

A British reporter stood up – Mac recognised him as a smart-arse from the *Financial Times'* Hong Kong office. Talking straight over the American TV reporters, he asked if the Department of Defense's intense electronic monitoring of the missile tests could be re-purposed to hack the North Korean control room. The question was delivered in a tone that Americans found rude, and the room went quiet.

The secretary smiled. 'I'd better ask my experts on that one – perhaps I'll use my shoe-phone.'

The press room laughed and the moment was gone, although Mac knew the DIA spooks in that room had their ears pricked up: that journalist was going to spend the rest of his life having his emails filtered and cell phone calls intercepted to find out who he was speaking to.

Mac went in search of a drink and heard the commotion before he saw its source. A man was arguing in a loud Australian voice, claiming that the doctor's orders had no force outside the hospital.

'You can't drink on your medication, Boo,' said Marlon T'avai, pushing a wheelchair into the business lounge.

'Be fucked,' said Boo Bray, who was in a body cast and stretched out in a wheelchair that lay almost flat. 'I'll get enough of that teetotal bullshit from the missus, this is me only chance for a drink.'

Turning away from the argument, Mac hid among the drinkers on the other side of the bar. But as he ordered a beer, Marlon found him.

'Shit,' said Mac, sheepish. 'Sorry about the other day, mate – you going to arrest me?'

'Nuh,' said Marlon, looking down on him with a frown. 'Get me a couple of beers and it's forgotten.'

Taking his beers, Marlon lowered his voice. 'Actually, something else you can give me.'

'Yeah?'

'What was all that shit at Khanh Hoi?' said Marlon. He was talking about the cordoning-off of Saigon Port's largest terminal and the lack of media coverage. 'That was something to do with your gig, right? Wasn't that about US currency?'

'Don't know,' lied Mac. The Americans and Vietnamese had shut down the Khanh Hoi wharves as they secretly disposed of an enormous cargo in one of the warehouses. The media black-out seemed to have worked and Mac mused on what stories would have hit the airwaves had the counterfeit billions been discovered in the West.

'Anyway, thought you'd like to know that an alert hit the wires last night. Dozsa's mounting a defence but he says he can't afford it.'

'Poor Joel,' said Mac, looking around the room.

'Thing is, McQueen, he's saying that he can't pay for his lawyers because he was robbed by Aussie intel.'

Mac nodded.

'He's saying there was more than a million US dollars stolen from his home in Malaysia during a raid by Aussie SIS,' said Marlon. 'I was supposed to be following up but I had to take Boo home.'

'So, it's dropped?'

'No, mate,' said Marlon. 'Media's on to it. Just tell me you don't have that money.'

Mac smiled. 'I can tell you where half of it is.'

'What?' said Marlon, hissing. 'Fuck, McQueen, you got half a million out of Dozsa?'

'More like six hundred and fifty thousand,' said Mac. 'But it's gone now.'

Marlon looked around for nosey-pokes and sighed. 'Okay. Where is it?'

'Try National Road Number One, Sangkat Chbar Ampov.'

'What's that?'

'It's a post office, in Phnom Penh,' said Mac.

Marlon shook his head. 'I don't follow.'

'The person with the money is too poor for a letterbox,' said Mac. 'So her address is care of the local post office.'

'I'm actually trying to help you, McQueen,' said Marlon. 'Who's this woman?'

'Her name's Maly Khoy,' said Mac, slugging at the beer. 'Poh's mum – I hear she bought a headstone.'


By the time the Singapore Airlines wide body was six minutes into the flight south, Mac was quietly drunk. The hostie offered him the choice of four newspapers and he selected the Asian *Journal*. Leading page three was a picture of Vincent Loh Han beneath a headline that said, LOH HAN BANK TO BE LISTED. Reading quickly, Mac got the basics from the first sentences:

> Saigon financier Mr Vincent Loh Han announced his retirement from the banking sector Thursday as he presaged the public listing of his new bank – Harbour Pacific Bank – on the Hong Kong Stock Exchange.
>
> Mr Loh Han, who is well-known to authorities around Indochina but has never been convicted, said he was standing back from the small business-focused bank and that the chairman of the new entity would be his niece, retired police detective Ms Chanthe Loan.

Raising his eyebrows, Mac stared at the story. Vincent Loh Han was going straight and he'd placed his police officer niece in charge of his interests as a way of proving it. It was a stunning story.

A small groan escaped from the man sitting beside him in business class.

'Beer and painkillers,' said Mac to Lance. 'Short of morphine, it's the only cure for bullet wounds.'

Forcing a smile, Lance poured the can of Tiger and sipped. 'Rum work too?'

'Nah,' said Mac. 'That's an old habit from my days in Rockie – like a security blanket.'

'You need a security blanket?' said Lance, his shot arm in a sling and the dressing on his neck stained. 'You're hardly the type.'

Looking around, Mac idly swished the single ice cube in his glass of rum. Flying to or from a gig, intelligence agents were supposed to travel independently of one another. But they'd booked late as Greg Tobin tired of the recuperation excuses extended by Rod Scott, and they'd managed to put Urquhart and Scotty in separate seats, but Mac and Lance were together.

Taking a drag at the rum, Mac thought back to his early days in the field, the mistakes and the sheer stress – the sense that he'd never make it, that everyone knew how incompetent he was. The only thing that had pulled Mac through was his stamina – if, like most intel analysts, you wanted a medal after a few fourteen-hour days, you didn't belong in the field.

'Look,' said Mac, turning to face Lance, 'it's not easy for anyone, okay?'

Lance's bottom lip curled and he dipped his face into his hands and gulped. For ten minutes Mac drank and said nothing as Lance Kendrick wept beside him.

As Mac found a rerun of *Friends* on the in-flight system and looked around for some earphones, Lance blew his nose. 'Sorry about that.'

'Don't be sorry,' said Mac, raising his glass and a peace sign at the stewardess. 'Feel better?'

'I have to admit something,' said Lance, as the hostie came down with two glasses and a bottle of Bundaberg. 'I was relieved when Urquhart wet himself.'

Mac thanked the hostie as she poured two drinks and placed them on airline napkins.

'How bad is that?' said Lance, sniffling. 'I was so scared that the only thing that made me feel better was knowing someone was in a worse way.'

'That's normal,' said Mac, raising his glass and touching it to Lance's. 'Gunfights are primal – they're kill or be killed, so the animal in you takes over.'

Lance shook his head. 'I was so scared when they were shooting at us that I thought my heart would stop. It was beating, like, on the back of my tongue.'

'Ha,' said Mac, recognising the reaction. 'You know how many people would try to take a gun off Joel Dozsa?'

Lance paused, wiped his eyes on the back of his hand. 'I was frozen stiff, actually. Couldn't believe it when my hand was grabbing at that rifle.'

'It happens like that,' said Mac. 'You get in the middle of that stuff and you're just reacting – sometimes you save the day, other times you have some regrets to live with.'

'Umm,' said Lance, before thinking better of asking.

Mac wondered if he'd ever forgive himself for those kids on Sumatra in 2002.

'I was thinking of giving up,' said Lance. 'I mean the field stuff.'

'But then?'

Lance suddenly smiled. The shootings had wiped the smart alec away and left a more mature face, one with a genuine smile rather than a poseur's smirk. 'But then I wondered what would happen if I maybe – I don't know – got my hair cut more conservatively or dropped the earrings.'

'What about respecting your seniors?' said Mac.

'Don't know about that one,' said Lance, and they both laughed. 'Anyway,' Lance drained the rum and washed it down with beer, 'I'm going to stick with it for a while at least.'

'So we haven't scared you off on your first gig?'

'Actually, I learned something,' said Lance.

'What?' said Mac.

'Never, ever give up.'

Mac followed the cackling sounds coming from under Frank and Pat's Rockhampton house. Carrying a bottle of white wine he limped across the lawn past the barbecue and saw Pat and Jen sneaking a fag in the rumpus room where Mac used to play table tennis and listen to Bruce Springsteen records.

'Busted,' he said, pouring wine for his wife and mother.

'That's what wedding anniversaries are for, my dear,' said his mum, tipsy and dragging on her smoke. 'You get to knock off the goody-two-shoes act.'

'Yeah, leave her alone, Macca,' said Jenny, making a face at the paucity of wine he'd just administered. 'And anyway, Pat was just telling me about this missing ribbon.'

Following her finger, Mac saw the display of his old sports trophies and carnival ribbons. The player-of-the-day statues from rugby league were at the front and the swimming trophies were at the back, along with rep jumpers for rugby league and union. Sitting on a cork board on the wall were his blue swimming ribbons, ranging from when he was eight years old until his last year of high school. Pat had pulled them out of their boxes once he went to uni, and put them in order, tacking them up with small pins.

'Nineteen eighty-five,' said Jenny, squinting at the regimented lines of blue. 'Nudgee College swim carnival. One's missing – look, there's a gap and a darker area where it was.'

'Must have fallen off,' said Mac, turning for the door. His brother-in-law had been demonstrating how a slightly tweaked grip could improve his golf and he wanted to get back before Virginia made him change the subject.

'Oh, stop it,' said Pat. 'Tell her.'

'Can't remember,' said Mac, blushing slightly.

'He gave it away.' Pat blinked slowly in the way women do when they're saying, *Can you believe it?*

'Gave it away?' said Jenny, exhaling smoke. 'Why?'

Mac shrugged. 'Another bloke deserved it.'

'He came second?' said Jenny.

'No,' said Mac. 'I really have to get back upstairs.'

'What's the secret?' said Jenny.

'He gave it to the boy who came last,' said Pat.

Mac's face flushed hot. 'Mum!'

Pat grabbed Jenny by the forearm. 'There was an old school friend in the hospital dying, this is about ten years ago. Alan went down to see him and a few days later I realised his ribbon for the fifty metres freestyle was missing.'

'You gave it to someone who'd come last?' said Jen, a little aggressive from the wine. 'Why?'

Mac thought back to that afternoon in 1985, when Len Cromie swam the fifty metres freestyle at the swimming carnival – a mangle of limbs that didn't work properly due to the ravages of cerebral palsy. Standing in his lane, having won the event, Mac waited for a boy who flirted with drowning rather than gave up. It was the

461

end of an era – probably the last time any school allowed someone like Len Cromie to swim in a carnival, lest the school be set upon by lawyers and insurance companies or overprotective parents. Len had conned his way into the heat and was in the water before anyone could eject him. Mac remembered the teachers covering their eyes, unable to look as Len repeatedly slipped under the water only to bob up again for air. He remembered going down to see Len as a twenty-eight-year-old, when he was dying in hospital, and having nothing to give his old classmate but his best wishes and the blue ribbon. He'd left the hospital, embarrassed, when Len started crying.

'I realised there were two kinds of winner,' said Mac finally, staring at the floor. 'The one who comes first . . .'

'And?' said Jen.

'And the one who's never beaten.'

## ALSO FROM ALLEN & UNWIN

### *Double Back*
### Mark Abernethy

**Action-packed and enthralling, *Double Back* confirms Mark Abernethy as a master thriller writer.**

Aussie super-spy Alan McQueen is pulled out of a deep-cover assignment to find an agent who's missing. It sounds like a straightforward operation but, as he digs deeper, the man they call 'Mac' discovers a faction of Indonesia's army plotting against the East Timorese.

From the paranoia of Dili to guerrilla-infested jungles to the machinations of Canberra, Mac finds himself in a world of murder and torture where he must forge alliances with his rivals just to stay alive.

While East Timor is disintegrating into violence and anarchy, Mac finally uncovers a terrifying truth that some of his intelligence masters at ASIS do not want to hear.

As the clock ticks Mac has a life-defining choice: walk away or double back.

'Abernethy conjures echoes of Fleming, Ludlum, Clancy and the Jack Reacher novels of Lee Child.' *Weekend Australian*

**ISBN 978 174175 938 9**

*Second Strike*
**Mark Abernethy**

**This action-packed and gripping sequel to *Golden Serpent* confirms Mark Abernethy as a master thriller writer.**

In the early hours of 13 October 2002, Australian spy Alan McQueen is jolted awake and told to head immediately to Bali, where more than 200 people have been killed in a series of bomb blasts. Assigned to keep an eye on the forensic teams working the bomb sites, McQueen – aka Mac – discovers that, contrary to the official line, a mini-nuclear device probably caused the most destructive of the blasts.

As tensions rise between governments, Mac joins an elite unit of spies and soldiers hunting down the terrorists implicated in the bombings. The pursuit takes them through the wilds of Northern Sumatra, but ends with them watching helplessly as the terrorist ringleaders escape by plane.

Five years later, Mac is back in Indonesia doing some soft espionage. But when bullets start flying and old terrorist foes reappear, Mac is drawn into a deadly game that clearly didn't finish in October 2002. Fighting complacency within his own ranks, Mac keeps track of the terrorists until he can no longer ignore the evidence that they have another, more powerful mini-nuke – and their next target is Australia! Will there be a second strike? And if so, where in Australia will it be?

'Fast-paced and action-packed, *Second Strike* is one of the better post-9/11 thrillers.' *The Age*

**ISBN 978 1 74175 768 2**

Golden Serpent
Mark Abernethy

**Brilliantly written and action-packed, Mark Abernethy's first Alan McQueen thriller, Golden Serpent, will enthral fans of Andy McNab, Tom Clancy, Lee Child and Robert Ludlum. Guaranteed to satisfy even the most seasoned spy-thriller aficionado.**

Alan McQueen, aka Mac, was once a star of the global intelligence community, renowned for being the Aussie spook who shot and killed Abu Sabaya, the world's most dangerous terrorist.

But that was 2002.

Now, during a routine assignment in Indonesia, McQueen discovers that Sabaya is not in fact dead. Instead he's teamed up with rogue CIA veteran Peter Garrison and is armed with a cache of stolen VX nerve agent he's threatening to deploy in a dramatic and deadly manner.

Battling to stay one step ahead of Sabaya's hit-men, CIA double-agents and deep corruption within Australian intelligence, Mac must find the stolen VX before it's too late. His mission will take him on a chase through South-East Asia and test all of his considerable courage and ingenuity.

'Golden Serpent is the most accomplished commercial spy thriller we've seen locally, a discerning read, full of action and a kind of knowing wit.' The Australian

ISBN 978 1 74175 506 0